Hey, Joe !

iUniverse, Inc.
New York Bloomington

Hey, Joe!

iUniverse books may be ordered through booksellers or by contacting:

iUniverse
1663 Liberty Drive
Bloomington, IN 47403
www.iuniverse.com
1-800-Authors (1-800-288-4677)

ISBN: 978-1-4401-2071-8 (pbk)
ISBN: 978-1-4401-2072-5 (ebk)

Printed in the United States of America

iUniverse rev. date: 2/26/2009

Hey, Joe !

by

James Wollrab

In Memory of
Duane Allman, Tommy Bolin, Jerry Garcia,
Lowell George, George Harrison, Jimi Hendrix,
Janis Joplin, John Lennon, Freddie Mercury,
Jim Morrison, Ricky Nelson, Roy Orbison
and the other great musicians
who have left us.

Many thanks to
Fred Bourdin, Maurice Guerin, and our
mysterious friend called Roger
for their suggestions and insights.

1
My Dreams

I keep having this recurring dream.

Hey, Joe, where you goin' with that money in your hand? Hey, Joe, I said, where you goin' with that money in your hand?

I'm goin' downtown to buy a cold steel .44.

Hey, Joe, where you goin' with that gun in your hand?

I'm goin' down to shoot my old lady. You know, I've caught her messin' around with another man. I'm goin' down to shoot my old lady. You know, I've caught her messin' around with another man. And that ain't too cool.

Hey, Joe, I've heard you shot your woman down. Shot her down, now. I said I've heard you shot your old lady down. You shot her down to the ground.

Yes I did. I shot her. You know I caught her messin' round, messin' round town. Yes I did. I shot her. You know, I caught my old lady messin' around town. And I gave her the gun. I SHOT HER!

Hey, Joe, all right. Shoot her one more time, baby.

Hey, Joe, where you gonna run to now? Where you gonna run to? Where you gonna go?

I'm goin' way down south, way down to Mexico way. All right! Way down where I can be free. Ain't no one gonna find me.

Ain't no hangman gonna. He ain't gonna put a rope around me. You better believe it right now. I gotta go now.

Hey, Joe, you better run on down.

Goodbye everybody!

Hey, Joe, run on down.

It's the same and yet different each time. It sits on my mind like pieces of broken glass. When I try to glue the pieces together, the image doesn't last. I need help figuring out what it means…if anything?

All I can do is lay out the pieces as I see and remember them. This won't be easy. But here it is.

Big kid Joey rode away in the sunset covered sky. A lynching mob had strung his girlfriend up right before his eyes. He didn't know what they'd both done. He sure as hell would end up hung. A hot tin notch on the sheriff's gun if he didn't move on, get out of town.

The sheriff followed Joey's trail from New York west. He said he'd put a bullet right through poor old Joey's chest. But Joey wasn't like the rest. He don't like bullet holes in his vest. In fact, he'd do his very best. Don't want any arrest. Don't want to be the guest of the sheriff.

The nights got so damned hot. He couldn't stand the pace. He looked again for the sheriff's men, but couldn't see a trace. Joey found a nice cool place. But then the sheriff solved the case. Poked a gun at Joey's face and said, 'Lookie here…'

Sheriff rode him into town with Joey looking sad. He didn't know about the big six-gun big kid Joey had. Then Joey drew his gun real fast, gave the sheriff one big blast. Now Joey runs the town at last, a legend from the past. Nobody ever messed with the sheriff again!

It's a strange dream, very vague but still makes its point. Was it a warning or a farce? What about the girl? What about the sheriff? What about the gun?

I spoke to the girl in my dream.

"In my dreams I'm dying all the time. As I wake, it's my kaleidoscopic mind. I never meant to hurt you. I never meant to lie. So, this is goodbye. This is goodbye.

"Tell the truth. You never wanted me. Tell me.

"In my dreams I'm jealous all the time. As I wake, I'm going out of my mind. Going out of my mind."

There's a woman in my dreams, but I cannot see her face. She seems kind and generous, yet she still seems out of place. She always has me going with her subtle tease, but when we are together, I feel her heart and soul freeze.

She brings her friends so we won't have to be alone. Fear I might lose my composure without warning. I am a child of fire. I am a lion. I have desires. And I was born inside the sun this morning.

She calls a waitress when it's time for her to go. And I know everyone is eventually leaving. I got a pair of wings for my birthday. I will fall down through the sun to see you.

This dizzy life of mine keeps hanging me up all the time. This dizzy life is just a hanging tree for me.

Whatsoever I've feared has come to life. Whatsoever I fought off became my life. Just when every day seemed to greet me with a smile, sunspots have faded. And now I'm doing time because I fell on black days.

Whomsoever I've cured, I've sickened now. Whomsoever I've cradled, I've put you down. I'm a searchlight soul they say, but I can't see it in the night. I'm only faking when I get it right. Because I fell on black days! How would I know that this could be my fate?

So what you wanted to see become good has made you blind. And what you wanted to be yours has made it mine. So, don't you lock up something that you wanted to see fly. Hands are for shaking, not for tying!

I sure don't mind a change, but I fell on black days. How would I know that this could be my fate? Once I had my heroes. Once I had my dreams. But, all of that is changed now. The truth begins again. The truth is not that comfortable. No. Mother taught me patience, the virtues of restraint. Father taught me boundaries, where not to go. I'm trying to protect my unity. That's when I reach for my revolver! That's when it all gets blown away.

A friend of mine once told me his one and only aim was to build a giant castle and in it sign his name. Sign it with complete community and a taste of trust. Now that the sky is empty, that is nothing new, my dreams have gone bust. Instead they look down upon me when they tell me I am nothing. That's when I reach for my revolver. That's when it all gets blown away and the spirit passes this way.

One part of my dream was particularly strange. A voice from the sky whispered a story into my ears.

"Harmlessly passing your time in the grassland away; only dimly aware of a certain unease in the air. You better watch out! There may be dogs about. I've looked over Jordan, and I have seen that things are not what they seem. What do you get for pretending the danger's not real? Meek and obedient, you follow the leader down well-trodden corridors into the valley of steel. What a surprise! A look of terminal shock in your eyes. Now, things are really what they seem. No, this is no bad dream.

"The Lord is my shepherd, I shall not want. He makes me down to lie through pastures green, He leads me the silent waters by. With bright knives He releases my soul. He makes me to hang on hooks in high places. He converts me to lamb cutlets, for lo, He hath great power and great hunger. When cometh the day we lowly ones, through quiet reflection, and great dedication to master the art of karate, lo, we shall rise up, and then we'll make the bugger's eyes water.

"Bleating and babbling, I fell on His neck with a scream. Wave upon wave of demented avengers march cheerfully out of obscurity into the dream. Have you heard the news? The dogs are dead! You'd better stay home and do as you're told. Get out of the road if you want to grow old!"

If your heart is restless from waiting too long, when you're tired and weary when you can't go on. Well, if a distant dream is calling you, then there's just one thing that you can do. You gotta follow that dream wherever that dream may lead you. You gotta follow that dream to find the love you need.

While in these days of quiet desperation as I wander through the world in which I live, I search everywhere for some new inspiration. But it's more than cold reality can give. If I need a cause for celebration or a comfort I can use to ease my mind, I rely on my imagination, and I dream of an imaginary time.

If I believe in all the words I'm saying, and if a word from you can bring a better day, then all I have are these games that I've been playing to keep my hope from crumbling away. So let me lie and let me go on sleeping, and I will lose myself in palaces of sand. And all the fantasies that I will be keeping will make the empty hours easier to stand.

And I know that everyone has a dream, and this is my dream, my own, just to be at home and to be alone with…my girl.

Here I stand amid the roar of a surf-tormented shore, and I hold within my hand grains of golden sand. How few, yet they creep through my fingers into the deep while I weep, while I weep. Oh, God, can I not grasp one with a tighter clasp? Oh, God, can I not save one from the pitiless wave? Is all that we see or seem but a dream within a dream?

I walk in dreams, and I talk in dreams. I need someone with a love I can trust. And together we'll search for the things that come to us. In dreams, baby, in dreams. And I'm gonna follow that dream wherever that dream may lead me. I'm gonna follow that dream to find the love I need.

Now, every man has the right to live, the right to a chance to give what he has to give, the right to fight for the things he believes, for the things that come to him in dreams. I walk in dreams. I talk in dreams. I live in dreams.

2
Genesis

As I might have said before, my name is Joe, and I was born in New York City. Some people call me Joey, but that's beside the point. We have bigger fish to fry.

I love to play the guitar. I bought a Les Paul model from a friend of mine, and I take it with me everywhere I go. I got a nice travel case with it and several sets of spare strings.

Jimi Hendrix and Jimmy Page are my two all time favorite guitar players. I guess that my parents should have named me James instead of Joseph, but they named me after my Uncle Joe who is a good man. He lives in Chicago so I don't get to see him much, but as I remember, he could play the piano pretty well. He called it 'tickling the ivories'. But he liked jazz, mostly Chicago and New Orleans style. I'm more into rock and roll.

You will never believe my story. I find it hard to believe myself. Although it seems to me that many people have sung and written about it without specifically knowing who I am. As a matter of fact, if you listen to any of the many renditions of the song *Hey, Joe!,* you will get a good idea of what a big part of my life's been like so far. But that's for later. Let me try to begin at the beginning.

Somewhere out on that horizon, out beyond the neon lights, I know there must be something better. But there's nowhere else in sight. It's survival in the city when you live from day to day. City streets don't have much pity. When you're down, that's where you'll stay.

I was born here in the city with my back against the wall. Nothing grows and life ain't very pretty. No one's here to catch you when you fall. Somewhere out on that horizon far away from the neon sky, I know there must be something better, and I can't stay another night.

To start with, I was born under a bad sign, and I've been down ever since I began to crawl. If it wasn't for bad luck, I wouldn't have no luck at all! Bad luck and troubles are my only friends. I've been down ever since I was ten. But, that's not all, as you will soon see. I don't want to make excuses, but I have to tell it like it is.

One of the problems associated with being born in New York is that there are so many people with nothing to do and hundreds of buildings that block out my view. Watched by a tramp with a hole in his shoe, standing alone on the corner. He's thinking that work is all a big joke, while he looks in the gutter for something to smoke. Two hundred kids in one red Mini Moke scream down the street fully loaded.

The tramp came up to me and said, "Have you got a quarter for me? I'll even take a dime, anytime. Standing on a corner, living in the street, I got to make a living from the people that I meet. I'm a tramp, just a tramp."

At least he seemed honest and in touch with reality so I listened.

"Spare change handout, begging all the time. I need a story for a song, some thoughts to put in line. Something good is something gained, like reaching for a star. I'll get a healthy bank account, a suit and a shiny car! I'm a tramp, just a tramp."

He hesitated as if he were doing some serious thinking.

"My older brother was a drifter, moving from town to town. He considered himself an intellectual, which isn't too profound. But, one day without explanation, he found himself in this city's lockup. They took absolutely everything he had in his pocket.

"'Oh, help me in my weakness', they heard the drifter say, as police carried him from the courtroom and were taking him away. 'My trip hasn't been a pleasant one, and my time it isn't long. And, I still do not know what it was that I've done wrong?'

"Well, the judge, he cast his robe aside. A tear came to his eye. 'You fail to understand,' he said, 'Why must you even try?' Outside the crowd was stirring. You could hear it from the door. Inside, the judge was stepping down, while the jury cried for more.

"'Oh, stop that cursed jury,' cried the attendant and the nurse. 'The trial was bad enough, but this is ten times worse.' Just then a bolt of lightning struck the courthouse and put it out of shape. And while everyone knelt to pray, the drifter he did escape."

That little tale brought a smile to my face. As I reached into my pocket to retrieve some change, the tramp went on with his story.

"Well, I feel just like a freight train, baby, running out of steam. I wanna go on down to New York town, but I'm stuck here in between. And I could stay on here at home alone and have myself to thank. But I just made a billion dollars, because I just sold the sky to the sun. So, I could buy for you the moon or put it in the bank.

"Mom, if you could see me now underneath the neon lights. I ought'a keep them on from dusk to dawn and everything's all right. I met a girl with autumn in her eyes and summer in the way. She makes me feel like I was only born today or yesterday. But everyone here hates absolutely everything I say. And the girl…I just don't know if I can last another day.

"So, I guess I'm going back, back to where I belong. Although I ain't got no money, I always have the time for a song. I hope you come along before I get back on that train that takes me…home from New York City to the things I left behind."

I gave the tramp all my change, after all, it was Christmas Eve, and he moved along without another word. I hoped that I would never be in his situation, but you can never tell. Then I went back to my daydreaming in an attempt to remove his spell.

Day in the city. Oh, what a pity. Could be in Berkshire where the poppies are so pretty. I wish that I were there.

People like sardines packed in a can, waiting for Christmas that's made in Japan. And I'm having trouble with my apple flan. Sat in the café on the corner…bored but getting tan.

I walk through the green gates and into the park, where murderers crawl after girls in the dark. Down by the shed I heard a remark. I turned on, but no one could hear me. Then, I thought about Sally. I'll tell you about her later. She was the light of my life, but she wanted to say here.

Hey, baby, gimme your hand. Check out the high spots, the lay of the land. You don't need a rocket or a big limousine. Come on over, baby, and I'll make you obscene. I feel safe in New York City.

All over the city and all of the dives, don't mess with this place, it will eat you alive. Got a lip smacking honey to suck off the jam. I'm on top of the world, Ma, ready to slam. I feel safe in New York City.

Running all over like a jumping bean; take a look at that chick in the tight assed jeans. She's coming your way now. You might be in luck. Don't you fret boys, she's ready to cluck. I feel safe in a cage in New York City.

Down on the street they got toasted bagels, and there's a sale on cream cheese and lox. Nosh on some blintzes and bratwurst to boot. Not in the mood for Jack-in-the-Box. We're gonna schlep on through to Flatbush Avenue...Kielbasa and chopped liver makes my stomach quiver. We're gonna schlep on through to Flatbush Avenue. Or maybe they deliver?

To say it another way, I am just a poor boy though my story is seldom told. I have squandered my existence for a pocket full of promises. Such are promises, all lies and jest mumbled, yet still, a man hears what he wants to hear and disregards the rest.

My grade school and high school years were tough. The mama pajama rolled out of bed, and she ran to the police station. When the papa found out he began to shout, and he started the investigation. What mama saw was against the law.

The mama looked down and spit on the ground every time my name gets mentioned. The papa said, 'Ouy, if I get that boy, I'm gonna stick him in the house of detention'. Well, I'm on my way. I don't know where I'm going. I'm on my way. I'm taking my time. Goodbye to Rosie, the queen of Corona.

In a couple of days they come and take me away. But the press let the story leak and when the radical priest came to get me released, we were all on the cover of Newsweek. See you, me and Julio, down by the school yard.

After high school I went to work for my father at American Cross-Arm and Conduit Company where he was boss at the manufacturing plant over in Jersey. It was strictly physical labor...loading and unloading boxcars, treating cross-arms with nasty chemicals, and feeding the machines that drilled the holes in the cross-arms. College was out of the question for me. No one in my family had ever attended college, and we were dirt poor, relatively speaking, mostly because of my father's drinking and smoking habits. On my first day at the job, my father called me into his office to welcome me to the work gang. It was quite unlike him to be so sociable. So, naturally, I expected the worst.

"Welcome, my son! Welcome to the machine. Where have you been? It's all right, we know where you've been. You've been in the pipeline filling in time, provided with toys and scouting for girls. You bought a guitar to punish me and your ma. And, you didn't like school, and you know you're nobody's fool. So, welcome to the machine.

"Welcome, my son. Welcome to the machine. What did you dream? It's all right; we told you what to dream. You dreamed of a big star. He played a mean guitar. He always ate in the Steak Bar. He loved to drive his Jaguar. So, welcome to the machine."

One of my high school friends, Paul, had some hard times. I remember us talking on the downtown train.

"The world is a vampire, sent to drain. Secret destroyers, hold you up to the flames. And what do I get for my pain? Betrayed desires and a piece of the game. Now I'm naked, nothing but an animal. But can you fake it for just one more show? And what do you want? I want to change. And what have you got when you feel the same? Despite all my rage, I'm still just a rat in a cage.

"I had a job; I had a girl. I had something going, Joey, in this world. I got laid off down at the lumberyard. Our love went bad, times got hard. Now I work down at the car wash where all it ever does is rain. Don't you feel like you're a rider on a down-bound train?

"She said, 'Paul, I gotta go. We had it once. We ain't got it any more. She packed her bags, left me behind. She bought a ticket on the Central Line. Nights, as I sleep, I hear that whistle whining. I feel her kiss in the misty rain. And I feel like I'm a rider on a down-bound train.

"Last night I heard her voice. She was crying. She was so alone. She said her love had never died. She was waiting for me at home. I put on my jacket. I ran through the woods. I ran until I thought my chest would explode. There in the clearing, beyond the highway, in the moonlight our wedding house shone. I rushed through the yard.

I burst through the front door. My head pounding hard, up the stairs I climbed. The room was dark. Our bed was empty. Then I heard that long whistle whine, and I dropped to my knees, hung my head, and cried.

"Now I swing a sledgehammer on a railroad gang. Knocking down them cross-ties, working in the rain. Now, don't it feel like I'm a rider on a down-bound train!"

But my problems on the job were only beginning. Now warning lights are flashing down at Quality Control. Somebody threw a spanner, and they threw him in the hole. There's rumors in the loading bay and anger in the town. Somebody blew the whistle and the walls came down. There's a meeting in the boardroom. They're trying to trace the smell. There's leaking in the washroom. There's sneak in personnel. Somewhere in the corridors someone was heard to sneeze. 'Goodness, me! Could this be Industrial Disease?'

Caretaker was crucified for sleeping at his post. Refusing to be pacified, it's him they blame the most. Watchdog's got rabies. The foreman's got the fleas. Everyone's concerned about Industrial Disease. There's panic on the switchboard. Tongues are tied in knots. Some come out in sympathy. Some come out in spots. Some blame the management, some the employees. And everyone knows it's Industrial Disease.

Now the workforce is disgusted. They down their tools and walk. Innocence is injured. Experience just talks. Everyone seeks damages. Everyone agrees that these are classic symptoms of a monetary squeeze. On Fox and NBC they talk about the curse. Philosophy is useless. Theology is worse. History boils over. There's an economics freeze. Sociologists invent words that mean 'Industrial Disease'.

Doctor Parkinson declared, 'I'm not surprised to see you here. You've got smokers' cough from smoking, brewers' droop from drinking beer. I don't know how you came to get the Bette Davis knees? But, worst of all, young man, you've got Industrial Disease.' He wrote me a prescription. He said, 'You are depressed. But I'm glad you came to see me to get this off your chest. Come back and see me later. Next patient please. Send in another victim of Industrial Disease.'

I go down to Speakers' Corner. I'm thunderstruck. They got free speech, tourists, and police in trucks. Two men say they are Jesus. One of them must be wrong. There's a protest singer. He's singing a protest song. He says, 'They wanna have a war to keep their factories. They wanna have a war to keep us on our knees. They wanna have a war to stop us from buying Japanese. They wanna have a war to stop Industrial Disease.'

They're pointing out the enemy to keep you deaf and blind. They wanna sap your energy and incarcerate your mind. They give you home rule, gassy beer, two weeks in Spain and a Sunday striptease. Meanwhile, the first Jesus says, 'I'll cure it soon. Just abolish Monday mornings and Friday afternoons.' The other one is out on a hunger strike. He's dying by degrees. How come Jesus gets Industrial Disease?

But these weren't my only problems, and I wasn't alone. My schoolyard friend, Anthony, had similar problems. Anthony works in the grocery store saving his pennies for some day. Mama Leone left a note on the door. She said, "Sonny, move out to the country. Working too hard can give you a heart attack. You ought'a know by now. Who needs a house out in Hackensack? Is that what you get for your money?"

It seems such a waste of time, if that's what it's all about. If that's moving up, then I'm moving out.

Nothing much left to say at social gatherings. Nothing much left behind from the time before. Got to learn about losing and pushing your time and trying just a bit too hard. I'm on a one-way road to hell with every step I've been taking now. I'm finding out I just can't turn around.

My dad's friend, Sergeant O'Leary, is walking the beat. At night he becomes a bartender. He works at Mister Cacciatore's down on Sullivan Street across from the medical center. He's trading in his Chevy for a Cadillac, you ought'a know by now. And, if he can't drive with a broken back at least he can polish the fenders.

You should never argue with a crazy mind, you ought'a know by now. You can pay Uncle Sam with overtime. Is that all you get for your money?

I remember that fateful night at the local bar with my friends. My friends called it Alice's Restaurant, but I don't recall that name on the marquee, which read 'Yonkers Bar and Grill'. The place was crowded to say the least.

The only cash I had on me was a small roll of tens. I began to let loose on the city like a flock of geese. I was going to do it with some music, my first original piece. But, as I checked the microphone at the karaoke stand, a drunk ambled up and took it right out of my hand. He was wearing a sailor hat and torn blue jeans and a T-shirt that announced that he was from Queens. He said his name was Woody but that we could call him Arlo.

He had a tale to tell, he announced, and it would be in B flat. It was a story of the very ground we stood on, the very place we were at.

I was glad to let him go first to warm up the crowd. He was staggering somewhat so I offered him a chair. But he declined and began to fill the air.

"I was riding on the Mayflower," he hummed, "when I thought I spied some land. I yelled for Captain Ahab, I'll have you understand, who came running to the deck saying, 'Boys, forget the whale! We're going over yonder, cut the engines, change the sails.' All along the bowline we sang this melody like all tough sailors do when they're far away at sea.

"I think I'll call it 'America' I said as we hit land. I took a deep breath. I fell. I could not stand. Captain Ahab, he started into writing up some deeds. He said, 'Let's put up a fort and start buying the place with beads.'

"Just then this cop comes down the street as crazy as a loon. He throws us all in jail for carrying harpoons.

"Me, I busted out, don't even ask me how. I went to get some help; I walked by a Guernsey cow, who directed me down to the Bowery slums, where people carried signs around saying 'Ban the Bums'. I jumped right in the line saying 'I hope that I'm not too late', when I realized that I hadn't eaten for five days straight.

"I went into a restaurant looking for a cook, told them I was the editor of a famous etiquette book. The waitress, he was handsome. He wore a powder blue cape. I ordered something suzette, could you please make that crepe? Just then the whole kitchen exploded from boiling fat. Food was flying everywhere. I left without my hat.

"Now, I didn't want to be nosey, but I went into a bank to get some bail for Ahab and the boys back in the tank. They asked for some collateral so I pulled down my pants. They threw me in the alley when up comes this girl from France who invited me to her house. I went but she had a friend who kicked me out and robbed my boots, and I was on the street again.

"Well, I rapped upon a house with a U.S. flag on display. I said, 'Could you help me out, I got some friends down the way?' The man said, 'Get out of here, I'll tear you limb from limb.' I said, 'You know they refused Jesus, too.' He said, 'You're not him! Get out of here before I break your bones. I ain't your pop!' I decided to have him arrested, and I went looking for a cop.

"I ran right outside, and I hopped inside a cab. I went out the other door. This Englishman said, 'Fab', as he saw me leap a hot dog stand and a chariot that stood parked across from a building advertising brotherhood. I ran right through the front door like a hobo sailor does, but it was just a funeral parlor, and the man asked me who I was.

"I repeated that my friends were all in jail, with a sigh. He gave me his card. He said, 'Call me if they die.' I shook his hand, said goodbye, and ran out to the street, when a bowling ball came down the road and knocked me off my feet. A pay phone was ringing. It just about blew my mind. When I picked it up and said 'Hello', this foot came through the line.

"Well, by this time I was fed up at trying to make a stab at bringing back any help for my friends and Captain Ahab. I decided to flip a coin. Like either heads or tails would let me know if I should go back to the ship or back to jail. So, I hocked my sailor suit, and I got a coin to flip. It came up tails. It rhymed with sails. So, I made it back to the ship.

"Well, I got back to the ship and took the parking ticket off the mast. I was ripping it to shreds when this coast guard boat went past. They asked me my name, and I said, 'Captain Kidd.' They believed me, but they wanted to know what exactly that I did. I said that for the

Pope of Eureka I was employed. They let me go right away. They were very paranoid!

"Well, the last I heard of Ahab, he was stuck on a whale that was married to the deputy sheriff of the jail. But the funniest thing was, when I was leaving the bay, I saw three ships a-sailing. They were all heading my way. I asked the captain what his name was, and how come he didn't drive a truck? He said his name was Columbus. I just said, 'Good luck!'"

Our drunken performer was a little shaky again as he bowed to the applause, but he had more and the crowd urged him on.

"Better keep your distance from his whale. Better keep your boat from going astray. Find yourself a partner and treat them well. Try to give them shelter night and day. Because here in the blue light far away from the fireside things can get twisted and crazy and crowded. You can't even feel right.

"See how the cormorant swoops and dives. Must be a thrill to go that deep. Down to the basement of this life. Down to where the mermaid gently sleeps. As the tide must ebb and flow, I am dragged down under. I wait the livelong day for an end to my hunger.

"So I dream of Columbus every time the panic starts. I dream of Columbus with your maps and your beautiful charts. I dream of Columbus. There's an ache in a traveling heart.

"Imagine being on one of them boats coming over to discover America, like Columbus or something, standing there at night on watch. Everyone else is either drunk or asleep. And you're watching for America and the boat's going up and down. And you don't like it anyhow. But you gotta stand there and watch, for what? Only Columbus knows, and he ain't watching. You hear the waves lapping against the side of the ship. The moon is going behind the clouds. You hear the pitter-patter of little footprints on the deck. Is that your kids? It ain't! My God, it's this humungus giant clam.

"Imagine those little feet coming on deck. A clam twice the size of the ship. Feet first! You're standing there shivering with fear. You grab one of these, a belaying pin. They used to have these stuck in the holes all around the ship. You'd grab this out of the hole, run on over there, and BAM, BAM on those little feet. Back into the ocean would go a hurt, but not defeated, humungus giant clam ready to strike again when opportunity was better."

A girl in the audience leaped up onto the stage to challenge Arlo. "Clams don't have feet!" she cried.

Arlo held his ground. "Clams was allowed to grow unmolested in the coastal waters of America for millions of years. And they got big, and I ain't talking about clams in general. I'm talking about each clam. I mean each one was a couple of million years old or older. So imagine they could have gotten bigger than this whole room. And when they get that big, God gives them little feet so that they could walk around easier. And when they get feet, they get dangerous! I'm talking about real dangerous. I ain't talking about sitting under the water waiting for you. I'm talking about coming after you."

The woman bowed to Arlo, obviously satisfied with his answer. I was just scratching my head as he continued.

"You know not even the coastal villages were safe from those big clams. You know them big clams had an inland range of fifteen miles. Think of that. I mean our early pioneers and the settlers built little houses all up and down the coast, you know. And they didn't have houses like they got now, with bathrooms and stuff. They built little privies out back. And late at night, maybe a kid would have to go, and he'd go stomping out there in the moonlight. And all they hear for miles around…(loud clap and a belch)…one less kid for America! One more smiling, smirking, humungus giant clam."

Well, after belching, the drunk bowed graciously to the roaring crowd and then passed out cold on the floor. I knew he would be a hard act to follow, but I decided to try because the crowd was chanting for more. But as I tried to revive the unconscious fellow with a glass of soda and gin, a sweet looking little girl picked up the microphone and began a new song; she was thin. To be polite, I didn't intervene. It wasn't the time to cause a scene.

"It's Christmas at ground zero," she exclaimed. "There's music in the air. The sleigh bells are ringing and the carolers are singing while the air raid sirens blare. It's Christmas at ground zero, the button has been pressed. The radio just let us know that this is not a test.

"Everywhere the atom bombs are dropping. It's the end of all humanity. No more time for last minute shopping. It's time to face your final destiny. It's Christmas at ground zero. There's panic in the crowd. We can dodge debris while we trim the tree underneath the mushroom cloud.

"You might hear some reindeer on your rooftop or Jack Frost on your window sill. But, if somebody's climbing down your chimney, you better load your gun and shoot to kill. It's Christmas at ground zero. And, if the radiation level's okay, I'll go out with you and see all the new mutations on New Year's Day.

"It's Christmas at ground zero. Just seconds left to go. I'll duck and cover with my Yuletide lover underneath the mistletoe. It's Christmas at ground zero. Now the missiles are on their way. What a crazy fluke, we're gonna get nuked on this jolly holiday."

She, too, bowed to the wildly cheering crowd and then handed me the microphone. There was one last drunk lunging for the microphone and his chance at glory and stardom. I was now deemed the Master of Ceremonies so I had to give him his chance. He turned out to be pretty good. He played a mean air-guitar.

"If you've ever been to New York City, you know what I'm talking about. Yes, you do. They got such pretty little girls in that big town, make a man want to jump around and shout!

"I met a little girl there. She was about five foot eight. I said, 'I want you to love me.' She said, 'Why man, that'd be great. So, I got my long hair cut, but she took me back, back to see her pad. But the first thing I saw when I arrived there was a big, black, shiny shotgun in the hands of her dad!

"I finally learned my lesson such a long time ago. Next little woman that I date, I've got to know…I've got to know her family, too. But, if you don't want to be filled with shotgun holes, Mister, this is the song for you!"

He staggered a bit, but the audience loved him so he went on by pointing at a nearby TV set..

"Now look at them yo-yos! That's the way you do it. You play the guitar on the MTV. That ain't working! That's the way you do it! Money for nothing, and your chicks for free. Let me tell you. Them guys ain't dumb. Maybe get a blister on your little finger. Maybe get a blister on your thumb.

"We gotta install microwave ovens, custom kitchen deliveries. We gotta move these refrigerators. We gotta move these color TVs. See the little faggot with the earring and the makeup. Yeah, buddy, that's his own hair. That little faggot got his own jet airplane. That little faggot, he's a millionaire!

"I should have learned to play the guitar. I should have learned to play them drums. Look at that momma, she's got it sticking in the camera. Man, we could have some. And, he's up here, what's that? Hawaiian noises? Banging on the bongos like a chimpanzee. That ain't working. That's the way you do it. Get you money for nothing and get your chicks or free. I want my, I want my, I want my MTV!"

The audience was now really fired up so I started my act before my better judgment could kick in. There was no going back or time to moan. It would have been a sin.

"Come out, Virginia, don't let me wait. You Catholic girls start much too late. But, sooner or later it comes down to fate. I might as well be the one.

"Well, they showed you a statute, told you to pray. They built you a temple and locked you away. But they never told you the price that you pay for things that you might have done. You might have heard that I run with a dangerous crowd. We ain't too pretty. We ain't too proud. We might be laughing a bit too loud. But that never hurt no one.

"You got a nice white dress and a party on your confirmation. You got a brand new soul and a cross of gold. But, Virginia, they didn't give you quite enough information. You didn't count on me when you were counting on your rosary.

"They say there's a heaven for those who will wait. Some say it's better. Some say it ain't. I'd rather laugh with the sinners than cry with the saints. The sinners are much more fun! You say your mother told you all that I could give you was a reputation. She never cared for me. Did she ever say a prayer for me?

"So, come on, Virginia, show me a sign. Send up a signal. I'll throw you a line. The stained-glass curtain you're hiding behind never lets in the sun. Darling, only the good die young."

My first number went over well. I pushed on.

"Come you ladies and you gentlemen, a-listen to my song. I sing it to you right, but you might think that it's wrong. Just a little glimpse of a story I'll tell about an East Coast city that you all know well. It's hard times in the city, living down in New York town.

"Old New York City is a friendly old town, from Washington Heights to Harlem on down. There's a mighty many people all milling all around. They'll kick you when your up and knock you when your down. It's a mighty long ways from the Golden Gate to Rockefeller Plaza and the Empire State. Mister Rockefeller sets up as high as a bird, old Mister Empire never says a word.

"Well, it's up in the morning trying to find a job of work. Stand in one place until your feet begin to hurt. If you got a lot of money, you can make yourself merry. If you only got a nickel, it's the Staten Island Ferry. Mister Hudson comes a-sailing down the stream, and old Mister Minuet paid for his dream. Bought your city on a one-way track. If I had my way, I'd sell it right back.

"I'll take all the smog in Cal-I-for-ni-a, and every bit of dust in the Oklahoma plains, and the dirt in the caves of the Rocky Mountain mines. It's all much cleaner than the New York kind."

The place was real quiet, but I decided to continue.

"Shakey Davy's got a twelve gauge in his hand. It's sawed off to the limit. He's got a vague plan. There's this liquor store on Madison. There's another one down on Washington Square. He's pretty sure no one's ever seen him down around there.

"The first one's bird shot. The next four are double aught buck. The last one's a slug just for good luck. He's got his works in his pocket. He wants to score as soon as he's done. He can't wait to get straight to get long gone. He puts on his long coat, scribbles off a short note. Sits himself down and waits for the sun to go down.

"It's right around midnight, and there's still too damn many people on this street. He's walked all the way from Battery Park. He's got sweaty hands and burning feet. He's desperate for a fix. His body's screaming, 'Get me high!' He bursts through the door and lets one fly. "Sunrise in the park and Davey's cold as stone. He got some bad merchandise, and he was all alone. Two more unsolved mysteries. A lot of paper pushed around. Most folks are just waking up in this great big town."

I looked around, and there was some applause so I decided to move on.

"I was walking down the alley when a face I've never seen came from deep in the darkness, and his mouth came on real mean. And I saw that he'd been liquored, and he staggered up…you know…he staggered up to his feet. And he said, 'Boy, you'd better move real slow and gimme your money please.' Wasn't that strange indeed?

"Being born and raised in New York, there ain't nothing you won't see. 'Cause the streets are filled with bad goings-on, and you know that's no place to be. But my car broke down in the evening. You know it was a beater and just stopped stone cold in the street, and a dirty mean man with a shot glass eye, he said, 'Gimme your money please.' Wasn't that strange?

"So to keep a lower profile, I got a bicycle. But my bike broke down in the evening, and a dirty mean man with a shotgun in his hand said, 'Gimme your money please.'

"When the dirty mean man realized I had no money, he smiled and told me to sit down. He just wanted someone to talk to, and I wasn't going to refuse. It seemed like he wanted to be young again and have another chance at life. It was easy to understand so I listened to his story of lost love.

"It was Chrismas Eve, babe, in the drunk tank. An old man said to me, 'I won't see another one', and then he sang a song, The Rare Old Mountain Dew. I turned my face away and dreamed about you.

"Got on a lucky one, came in eighteen to one. I've got a feeling that this year's for me and you. So, happy Christmas, I love you, baby. I can see a better time when all our dreams come true. They've got cars as big as bars; they've got rivers of gold. But the wind goes right through you. It's no place for the old. When you first took my hand on a cold Christmas Eve, you promised me Broadway was waiting for me.

"You were pretty, the queen of New York City. When the band finished playing, they howled out for more. Sinatra was swinging; all the drunks they were singing. We kissed on a corner, then danced through the night. The boys of the NYPD choir were singing 'Galway Bay', and the bells were ringing out for Christmas Day."

I paused for a moment.

"You're a bum! You're a punk! You're an old slut on junk. Lying there almost dead on a drip in that bed. You scumbag! You maggot! You cheap lousy faggot! Happy Christmas your arse! I pray God it's our last.

"I could have been someone. Well, so could anyone. You took my dreams from me when I first found you. I kept them with me, babe. I put them with my own. Can't make it all alone. I've built my dreams around you."

That's when I realized that the dirty mean man was talking not about a woman, but about New York City.

"So you newsy people, spread the news around. You can listen to my story and listen to my song. You can step on my name; you can try to get me beat. When I leave New York, I'll be standing on my feet."

The crowd in the bar was dead quiet. I put the microphone down. Then there was a round of polite applause. That's when I realized that like New York City, they, too, might be glad to see me go. An older guy got up from the first row and picked up the mike, but to my surprise he then shook my hand and gave me a hug. Then he did his best Dean Martin imitation.

"Some folks like to get away, take a holiday from the neighborhood. Hop a flight to Miami Beach or to Hollywood. But, I'm taking a Greyhound on the Hudson River Line. I'm in a New York state of mind."

The audience jumped up and cheered wildly. I felt good because I hadn't left them in a funk.

"I've seen all the movie stars in their fancy cars and their limousines. Been high in the Rockies under the evergreens. But I know what I'm needing, and I don't want to waste more time. I'm in a New York state of mind.

"It was so easy living day by day, out of touch with the rhythm and blues. But now I need a little give and take, the New York Times, the Daily News. It comes down to reality, and it's fine with me because I've let it slide. Don't care if it's Chinatown or on Riverside. I don't have any reasons. I've left them all behind. I'm just taking a Greyhound on the Hudson River Line. I'm in a New York state of mind."

As I walked out the door of the bar with my guitar in tow, I realized that I would probably never return. I began to question whether I should leave or not. My question was directed to my longtime girlfriend, Sally. At least I considered her to be my girlfriend even if the reverse wasn't the case.

"Darling, you got to let me know. Should I stay or should I go? If you say that you are mine, I'll be here until the end of time. So, you go to let me know. Should I stay or should I go?

"Always tease, tease, tease. You're happy when I'm on my knees. One day is fine. Next day is black. So, if you want me off your back, come on and let me know. If I go there will be trouble. And if I stay it will be double. This indecision's buggin' me. If you don't want me, set me free. Exactly who am I supposed to be? Don't you know which clothes even fit me?

"Should I cool it or should I blow?"

After a momentary pause at the steps off the stage, I decided to move on.

3
Leaving New York

My Uncle Jack told me a story about crime in this big city. It was about one of his closest friends. I will never forget it even though I was only twelve at the time. This is how it went.

"Well, the cop made the showdown. He was sure he was right. He had all of the lowdown from the bank heist last night. His best friend was the robber, and his wife was a thief. All the children were killers; they couldn't get no relief. The bungalow was surrounded when a voice loud and clear said, 'Come on out with your hands up, or we'll blow you out of here.' There was a face in the window. The TV cameras rolled. Then they cut to the announcer, and the story was told.

"The artist looked at the producer; the producer sat back. He said, 'What we have got here is a perfect track. But we don't have a vocal, and we don't have a song. If we could get these things accomplished, nothing else could go wrong.' So he balanced the ashtray as he picked up the phone and said, 'Send me a songwriter who's drifted far from home. And make sure that he's hungry. Make sure he's alone. Send me a cheeseburger and a new Rolling Stone. Yeah!'

"'There's still crime in the city,' said the cop on the beat. I don't know if I can stop it. I feel like meat on the street. They paint my car like a target. I take my orders from fools. Meanwhile, some kid blows my head off. Well, I play by their rules. That's why I'm doing it my way. I took the law in my hands.

"'So here I am in the alleyway, a wad of cash in my pants. I get paid by a ten year old. He says he looks up to me. There's still crime in the city. But it's good to be free. Yeah!

"'Now, I come from a family that has a broken home. Sometimes I talk to Daddy on the telephone. When he says that he loves me, I know that he does. But I wish I could see him. I wish I knew where he was.

But that's the way all my friends are except maybe one or two. Wish I could see him this weekend. Wish I could walk in his shoes. But now I'm doing my own thing. Sometimes I'm good, then I'm bad. Although my home has been broken, it's the best home I ever had. Yeah!

"Well, I keep getting younger. My life's been funny that way. Before I ever learned to talk, I forgot what to say. I sassed back my mom. I sassed back my teacher. I got thrown out of Bible school for sassing back at the preacher.

"Then I grew up to be a fireman, put out every fire in town. Put out anything smoking, but when I put the hose down, the judge sent me to prison. He gave me life without parole. Wish I never put the hose down. Wish I never got old."

I never told anyone else what Uncle Jack told me that day. But I was sure he meant the story to be a lesson for me. What the lesson was only became clear over time.

But when I think about it, the key to my survival was never in much doubt. The main question before me was how I could keep sane while trying to find a way out. Things were never easy for me. Peace of mind was hard to find. And, I needed a place where I could hide, somewhere I could call mine. I asked my mother those most important questions.

"Mother, do you think they'll drop the bomb? Mother, do you think they'll like this song. Mother, do you think they'll try to break my balls? Oh, ahhhh, Mother, should I build the wall? Mother, should I run for president? Mother, should I trust the government? Mama, will they put me in the firing line? Oh, ah, is it just a waste of time?"

She tried to make me feel better.

"Hush now, baby, don't you cry. Mamma's gonna make all your nightmares come true. Mamma's gonna put all of her fears into you. Mamma's gonna keep you right here, under her wing. She won't let you fly, but she might let you sing. Mamma's gonna keep baby cozy and warm. Of course, Momma's gonna help build the wall."

I asked her about my girlfriend.

"Mamma, do you think she's good enough for me? Mamma, do you think she's dangerous to me? Mamma, will she tear your little boy apart? Mamma, will she break my heart?"

"Hush now, baby, don't you cry. Mamma's gonna check out all your girlfriends for you. Mamma won't let anyone dirty get through. Mamma's gonna wait up until you get in. Mamma will always find out just where you've been. Mamma's gonna keep baby healthy and clean. You'll always be baby to me!"

"Mother, did it need to be so high?"

My mother was worried about me. So, to please her, I went to see her psychiatrist.

My father didn't have a clue about her visits or the fact that he was the cause. She told me he might help me, too.

So, I went back to the doctor to get another shrink. I sit and tell him about my weekend, but he never betrays what he thinks. I went back to my mother. I said, 'I'm crazy, ma, help me!' She said, 'I know how it feels, son, because it runs in the family.'

The cracks between the paving stones look like rivers of flowing veins. Strange people who know me are peeping from behind every windowpane. The girl I used to love, Sally is her named, lives in this yellow house. Yesterday she passed me by. She doesn't want to know me now.

I ended up with the preacher, full of lies and hate. I seemed to scare him a little so he showed me to the golden gate. Can you see the real me, preacher? Can you see the real me, doctor? Can you see the real me, mother? Can you see the real me?

I went to one of my very favorite places, the Boardwalk, to find the palm reader. Her name was Thelma, at least that's what her marquee said. I had seen her face many times from a distance and through a crowd, but before today I never had the courage to step up and have my palm read. It might have saved me a lot of trouble if I'd done this earlier.

She was there in her booth just waiting for me. At least she gave me that impression when our eyes met. I placed my hand in hers without saying a word, and after a minute or so she gave me these words of mystical advice. How she knew my name is a mystery to this day.

"Little Joe, run for the border. Leave your home. Leave your mother and father. Go to where the reptiles roam on the side of the border that is your home.

"Little Joe, eyes of your lover look back on you as you run for cover. Those sticks and fire won't break your bones. It is a lie. Little Joe, just like your father, your eyes will water, your guts will splatter.

"Little Joe, this town is full of shame. No matter what they say, you are not to blame. In pursuit of love that will not come, the law will beat you like a drum. How high can you jump; how low can you crawl? When they trap your body, can you scale the wall?

"Little Joe, you mean well with all of your heart. But, sometimes you are not very smart. You're capable of thoughts as sharp as a dart, but you always seem to get hung up on some little tart.

"Run away. Run away. Do it now! Remember your trip to the stockyards and what they do to a cow."

I tried to pay her, but instead she told me to follow her advice. Those were words I didn't have to hear twice. It was apparent that she saw danger in my future. I asked her if that danger was nearby, but she could not say for certain.

"It is here and far away at the same time. What your eyes won't believe, your ears will confirm. Danger is cloaked as good. Friends are cloaked as evil. The gun that didn't kill will subdue the devil. The kiss on your cheek will betray. Only you can find the way out."

I went home, but I didn't tell anyone about the palm reader's advice. I asked several acquaintances whether they had ever sat with the palm reader, but they just laughed and called it entertainment. I wasn't so sure. And things started to get worse.

I didn't think much about it until it started happening all the time. Soon, I was living with the fear every day of what might happen that night. I couldn't stand to hear the crying of my mother, and I remember when I swore that, that would be the last they would see of me, and I never went home no more.

So, I laid out my winter clothes while wishing I was gone, going to a new home, where the New York City winters aren't bleeding me, leading me; I'm going to my new home. I kept asking myself that most important question whose answer I must find.

Is this the real life or is this just fantasy? I'm caught in a landslide, no escape from reality. I'm just a poor boy; I need no sympathy, because

I'm easy come, easy go, a little high, a little low. Any way the wind blows doesn't really matter to me.

My childhood memories would fill a good-size book. I charged straight ahead, but I guess I forgot to look at the forces of nature and the obstacles of man that took out my legs and cuffed my hands.

My mother's words came to me again.

"Breathe, breathe in the air. Don't be afraid to care. Leave, but don't leave me. Look around and choose your own ground. For long you live and high you fly. And smiles you'll give, and tears you'll cry. And all you touch and all you see is all your life will ever be. Run, run rabbit, run. Dig that hole. Forget the sun. And when at last the work is done, don't sit down. It's time to start another one.

"For long you live and high you fly, but only if you ride the tide. And balanced on the biggest wave, you race toward an early grave."

One would think that in a city this large, opportunity would lurk over every hill. But there was always a drink for my father as my mother downed another pill. It was all too overwhelming for a single young mind whose identity he was trying to find.

As I looked over my room for one last time, I remembered what my Mother told me about life as I prepared like a young colt to leave the stable. These were words she whispered to me as she rocked me in my very own cradle.

"It's not a place; it's a yearning. It's not a race; it's a journey. It's not an act; it's attraction. It's not a style; it's an action.

"It's a dream for the waking; it's a flower touched by flame. It's a gift for the giving; it's a power with a hundred names.

"Surge of energy, spark of inspiration, the breath of love is electricity. Maybe time is a bird in flight, endlessly mocking. Here we come out of the cradle, endlessly rocking.

"It's a hand that rocks the cradle. It's a motion that swings the sky. It's method on the edge of madness. It's a balance on the edge of a knife. It's a smile on the edge of sadness. It's a dance on the edge of life. Endlessly rocking."

It was my mother who told me what a special place New York City was. She told me to see New York and that special lady standing in the harbor through the eyes of the world.

"Give me your hungry. Give me your tired. Give me your homeless. Give me your wanderers. Statute of Liberty, standing in the harbor. This is America. We try a little harder. We set the standards, and everyone will follow. We've got our own values, but they're built on the dollar.

"Oh, but now it's tumbling, faking, quaking, trembling on its own foundation. There have been so many warnings. Too late, the old lady's falling! The only thing to do is to get out of the way. Anything can happen in the U.S. of A. Ain't no use anymore in trying harder. Statute of Liberty is sinking in the harbor.

"You can be a millionaire by stepping on the needy. Words of equality, but they're written for the greedy. This is America. We try a little harder."

And then I remembered how I lost a dear friend to this maddening city.

Papa hit him. Mama kissed him, made him go to Catechism in their black and white. And all the time those city streets were teaching him another kind of wisdom. When to run and when to fight! Up at the playground after school listening to tales of the prison system and those lawless avenues.

Dawn on a half-darkened street, a child's footsteps repeat. And something there turns them down those lawless avenues.

Silent Joe went down so bad. He was the strongest fighter the avenues had. Stabbed in the chest, he went down swinging. Someone from some other part of town. No one even saw it coming. And you don't hear no church bells ringing. And in the violent night, the police light sweeps across the lots and the yards following those lawless avenues.

Down on a half-darkened street armies advance and retreat and struggle to take control from those lawless avenues.

Manuelito's sister, Rosa, ran away with a surfer from Hermosa. But who could blame her after she saw every boy die who could have gotten close to her. Rosa is young and only wants to see the beauty of the world.

Manuel said, 'You've got to fight for what you want in this life', just before they shipped him overseas to Iraq. Another war without reason. Another war without end, without honor.

And she was fighting to understand when they shipped Manuelito's body home. All she heard was one more shot echoing down lawless avenues. Down on the half-darkened streets, fathers' and sons' lives repeat, and something there turns them down those lawless avenues.

My mother must have known this day would come. I wondered whether every child reaches this point, the point of deciding whether or not to leave the nest but not knowing how to fly. Right then my mother Lena reminded me of the night my high school friend, Terry, was killed. It was as if she was subconsciously trying to get me to leave before the same thing happened to me.

"I was getting you ready for school, Joey, and I told you that on these streets you've got to understand the rules. If an officer stops you, promise you'll always be polite, that you'll never, ever run away. Promise Mama that you'll always keep your hands in sight.

"That same day we took the ride across the bloody river to the other side. 41 shots cut through the night. We were kneeling over Terry's body in the vestibule praying for his life. 41 shots…got our boots caked in this mud. We're baptized in these waters and in each other's blood.

"Is it a gun, is it a knife? Is it a wallet? This is your life! It ain't no secret, my son. You can get killed just for living in your American skin."

Those were the last words my mother said to me that fateful night. She knew I was leaving, and she knew the dangers that awaited me, but she somehow knew it was the best thing for me. At that moment I couldn't have realized how prophetic her words would prove to be.

My father wasn't as loving as my mother. To this day I believe he didn't know what love was. He was born to be a bully. Rather than try to lift himself up, he pushed everyone around him down. He only had two or three people he could call friends.

My father's best friend was named Larry. There were quite a few similarities in their personalities. One night when dad was drunk and feeling unusually melancholy, he told me Larry's sad story.

"Larry loved his rifles almost as much as his hand guns. For shooting defenseless deer and squirrels they were pretty much equal fun. But someone upstairs must have been keeping score. They say that in the end it was a rabid cat or a wild boar.

"Larry got up dressed all in black, went down to the station, and he never came back. They found his clothing scattered somewhere down the track. And he won't be down on Wall Street in the morning.

"He had a home, the love of a girl, but men get lost sometimes as years unfurl. One day he crossed some line, and he was too much in this world. But I guess it doesn't matter any more. In a New York minute, everything can change. Things can get pretty strange."

Lying here in the darkness I hear the sirens wail. Somebody's going to emergency; somebody's going to jail. If you find somebody to love in this world, you'd better hang on tooth and nail. The wolf is always at the door. And in these days when darkness falls early, and people rush home to the ones they love, you'd better take a fool's advice and take care of your own. One day they're here; the next day they're gone.

I pulled my coat around my shoulders and took a walk down through the park. The leaves were falling around me. The groaning city whispered in the gathering dark. On some solitary rock a desperate lover left his mark. 'Baby, I've changed! Please come back.'

It was the cry of a broken heart making one last stand. It could have been up there in the sky or down here on the island. Trembling fingers were carving words of love in solid stone. By touching this rock, one can hear the writer's soul moan.

In the crowded city, I feel like an ant. All I can do for them is work, and all I can do for myself is can't. Why I came to be here, I may never know. But what is certain is that if I fail to leave, I will never grow. And like a tiny ant I will meet my end under a shoe. Or like a horse I will be turned into a jar of glue. And the mystics agree that with every turn of the screw, I will be nothing more than dead, too.

What the head makes cloudy, the heart makes very clear. The days were so much brighter in the time when Sally was here. But I know there's somebody somewhere to make these dark clouds disappear. Until that day, I have to believe that everything can change in a New York minute.

Down on the boulevard they take it hard. They look at life with such disregard. They say it can't be won, the way the game is run. But if you choose to stay, you end up playing anyway. It's okay.

The kid's in shock up and down the block. The folks are home playing beat the clock. Down at the golden cup they set the young ones up, under the neon light, selling day for night. It's all right.

Nobody rides for free. Nobody gets it like they want it to be. Nobody hands you any guarantee. Nobody!

The hearts are hard and the times are tough. Down on the boulevard, the night's enough. And time passes slow between the storefront shadows and the streetlight's glow. Everybody walks right by like they're safe or something. They don't know!

Nobody knows you. Nobody owes you nothing. Nobody shows you what they're thinking. Nobody! Hey! Hey! You've got to watch the street, keep your feet and be on guard. Make it pay; it's only time on the boulevard.

Then I remembered what I heard John Lennon say not too many days before… I loved him and his music so much.

"So long ago. Was it a dream? Was it just a dream? I know. Yes, I know. Seemed so very real. Seemed so very real to me.

"Took a walk down the street, through the heat whispered trees. I thought I could hear someone call out my name as it started to rain. Two spirits dancing so strange. Dream, dream away. Magic in the air, was magic in the air? I believe, yes, I believe. More I cannot say. What more can I say?

"On a river of sound, through the mirror go round, round. I thought I could feel music touching my soul. Something warm, something cold. The spirit dance was about to unfold.

"Standing on the corner, just me and Yoko Ono. We were waiting for Jerry to land. Up came a man with a guitar in his hand, singing, 'Have a marijuana if you can'. He sang, 'The pope smokes dope every day'. Up came a policeman who shoved us up the street singing, 'Power to the people today!'.

"New York City, New York City, que pasa New York?

"Well, we went to Max's Kansas City, and got down the nitty gritty with the Elephant's Memory Band. We laid something down as the news spread around about the Plastic Ono Elephant's Memory Band. Well, we played some funky boogie and laid some tutti fruiti, singing

'Long tall Sally's a man'. Then up come a preacher man, trying to be a teacher, singing 'God's a red herring in drag!'.

"Well, we did the Staten Island Ferry, making movies for the telly, played the Fillmore and Apollo for freedom. Tried to shake our image just cycling through the village, but found that we had left it back in London.

"Well, nobody came to bug us, hustle us or shove us, so we decided to make it our home. If the man wants to shove us out, we're gonna jump and shout 'cause The Statute of Liberty said, 'Come!'

"New York City down in the village, what a bad-ass city! Que pasa New York?"

I'll always miss him.

"New York, to that tall skyline I come, flying in from London to your door. New York, looking down on Central Park where they say you should not wander after dark. New York, like a scene from all those movies, but you're real enough to me. But, there's a heart that lives in New York.

"A heart in New York, a rose on the street. I write my song to that city heartbeat. A heart in New York, love in her eye, an open door and a friend for the night. New York, you got money on your mind. And my word won't make a dime's worth of difference. So, here's to you New York."

When I left my home and my family, I was no more than a boy in the company of strangers, in the quiet of the railway station, running scared and laying low. I sought out the poorer quarters where the ragged people go, looking for the places only they would know.

I came looking for a job asking only workman's wages, but I got no offers. All I got was a come-on from the whores on 7th Avenue. I do declare, there were times when I got so lonesome that I took some comfort there.

As I close my eyes at night and try to sleep, I have a dream…a strange dream. Through the haze and fog I see that in the clearing stands a boxer and a fighter by his trade, and he carries the reminders of every glove that laid him down or cut him until he cried out in his anger and his shame. I am leaving, I am leaving, but the fighter still remains!

It's always something, or it ain't nothing at all. It's feast or famine, too hot or out in the cold. So here I stand, alone together, my back against the wall. If my heart wasn't in it, I wouldn't be here at all. Well, it's blow by blow.

Coming off the ropes and fighting for the hope in us all, is my family in my corner or playing both sides of the wall. So, make a stand, it's now or never because life is much too short, and if your heart isn't in it, you shouldn't be here at all.

I can almost see through the tears, and I've got my pride. The dreams I've hidden for years just won't be denied. So here I stand, alone...together, my back against the wall. If my heart wasn't in it, I wouldn't be here at all.

They say that time is a healer and now my wounds are not the same. If I rang my father's doorbell with my heart in my mouth, I would have to hear what he would say. He would sit me down and talk to me and look me straight in the eyes. He would shout at me in disgust over his shot and beer. 'You're no son of mine, no son of mine! You walked out; you left us behind. And you're no son, no son of mine.'

Oh, those words, how they would hurt me; I would never forget it. And as time slipped by, I would live to regret it. But where should I go, and what should I do? In and out of hiding places, soon I'd have to face the facts. We would have to sit down and talk it over. And that would mean going back...which I would never do!

I remember those evenings as a boy when I sat at the kitchen table. My father would tell me stories that he called parts of an extensive fable. He wanted to be a tough guy, a bully by any measure. That would mean more to him than any other treasure. But to achieve his dream he had to find weak people. And because no one liked him, that left only my mother and I locked in the steeple.

As I sat there absorbing verbal abuse, I stared at the nearby, unlocked door. Because he had just downed a shot and a beer, I had no doubt I could outrun his most vicious roar. But I was a mere child of single digit age, and my common sense whispered, 'Joey, contain your rage.' And so, I kept my powder dry. I made it a point never to cry. And I looked him right in the eye. My day would come, and I would fly!

So, as I packed my suitcase, I began to imagine what it would be like on the road, alone. Hitchhiking, sleeping bags, cold food, cold feet, tired eyes, no home, on the roam, trying to find shelter from the storm. The decision was easy. I had to leave the nest, fly like a bird even if I had no wings.

I'm sitting in the railway station, got a ticket for my destination. I'm on a tour of one-night stands, my suitcase and guitar in hand. And every stop is neatly planned for a poet and a one-man band.

Every day is an endless stream of cigarettes and magazines. And each town looks the same to me. The movies and the factories and every stranger's face I see reminds me that I long to be…homeward bound.

Tonight I'll sing my songs again, play the game and pretend. But all my words come back to me in shades of mediocrity. Like emptiness in harmony, I need someone to comfort me.

But before I could disappear for real, seeing fresh meat the government swooped down, and I was drafted into the army. Soon, I was seeing the world through a porthole and from a ground hole. It wasn't quite what I expected. Saluting was not one of my strong points, but I did learn how to duck bullets real well. It's not that I am not patriotic. But, when I look over Viet Nam and Iraq, it appears to me that someone like my father must be running the show. And all I want to do is cry when I realize how many innocent people died…for what?

Everybody wants to know why I couldn't adjust. Adjust to what, a dream that went bust? I was a clean-cut kid, but they made a killer out of me, that's what they did. They said what's up is down; they said what isn't is. They put ideas in my head I thought were mine. I was on the baseball team; I was in the marching band. When I was ten years old, I had a watermelon stand.

"I went to church on Sunday; I was a Boy Scout. For my friends I would turn my pockets inside out. They said, 'Listen, Boy, you're just a pup.' They sent me to Napalm Health Spa to shape up. They gave me dope to smoke, drinks, and pills, a jeep to drive, blood to spill. They said, 'Congratulations, you got what it takes.' They sent me back into the rat race without any brakes.

"I bought the American dream, but it put me in debt. The only game I could play was Russian Roulette. I drank Coca-Cola, I was eating Wonder Bread, ate Burger Kings, I was well fed. I could've sold insurance, owned a restaurant or bar, could've been an accountant or a tennis star."

Then I remembered the words of my best friend, Ron. He said these words just after we left high school, but he was absolutely correct about the future.

"Well, everybody's asking why I couldn't adjust. All I ever wanted was someone to trust. They took my head and turned it inside out. I never did know what it was all about. I had a steady job; I joined the choir. I never did plan to walk the high wire. They took a clean-cut kid and they made a killer out of me, that's what they did.

"Surrounded by a thousand eyes, the strangers in the night. A city full of broken hearts burning like white light. The streets are made of promises you never get to keep. The streets are full of dreamers walking in their sleep. You come to me for easy living, starlight in your eyes. Don't you know it's all or nothing, so leave before you cry.

"Run away!

"You never liked what daddy said. He never understood the heartaches of a young boy who needs a magic woman. Young hearts chasing images along the boulevards. Young hearts lose their innocence chasing after stars. You come to her for easy lovin', diamonds in your eyes. Don't you see the fall that's comin'? Leave before you cry.

"Run away!"

There's a cockroach in my coffee. There's a needle in my arm. And I feel like New York City. Get me to the farm!

I got terminal uniqueness. I'm an egocentric man. I got caught up in my freakness. But I ain't no Peter Pan. Get me to the farm.

Buckle up my straight-jacket. Insanity is such a drag. Jelly bean thorazene, transcendental jet lag. Sanity? I ain't gonna! Feeling like a piñata. Sucker punch. Blow lunch. Mother load. Pigeon hole. I'm feeling like I'm gonna explode.

Yeah, I wanna shave my head, and I wanna be a Hare Krishna. Tattoo a dot right on my head. Heh. Heh. And the prozac is my fixer. I am the living dead. Take me to the farm! It's not a place you can get to by a boat or by a train. It's far, far away. Follow the yellow brick road.

"Run away!"

The bad thoughts were driving me crazy. I decided to try and think positively about the future.

All the leaves are brown and the sky is gray. I've been for a walk on a winter's day. I'd be safe and warm if I was in L.A. California dreaming on such a winter's day. Stepped into a church I passed along the way. Well, I got down on my knees, and I pretended to pray. You know, the preacher likes the cold. He thinks I'm gonna stay. California dreaming on such a winter's day. If I didn't tell my mother, I could leave today.

"Run away!"

This world is large and small at the same time. I could easily fall as I started to climb. I meant to run, to follow the sun. I just didn't know when I should have begun. The clock is turning like a giant wheel. But my mortal wounds never seem to heal, as the deepening shadows come to steal the life my forebear fought so hard to reveal.

"Run Away!"

Suddenly, my mind grasped at one final straw.

Hey, little sister, what have you done? Hey, little sister, who's the only one? Hey, little sister, who's your superman? Who's the one you want? It's a nice day to start again. It's a nice day for a white wedding! It's a nice day to start again.

Take me back home. There is nothing fair in this world. There is nothing safe in this world. There is nothing sure in this world. There is nothing pure in this world. Look for something left in this world. It's a nice day for a white wedding. It's a nice day to start again.

Before I could run away, I had to make one stop. As I walked down Broadway, I remembered what my Uncle Joe said before he left for Chicago.

"Early morning Manhattan, ocean winds blow on the land. The Movie-Palace is now undone. The all-night watchmen have had their fun, sleeping cheaply on the midnight show. It's the same old ending, time to go. Get out! It seems they cannot leave their dream. There's something moving in the sidewalk steam. And the lamb lies down on Broadway.

"Cousin Billy, he's down by the railroad tracks, sitting low in the back seat of his Cadillac. Diamond Jackie, she's so intact as she falls so softly beneath him. Jackie's heels are stacked. Billy's got cleats on his boots. Together they're gonna boogaloo down Broadway and come back home with the loot.

"It's midnight in Manhattan, this is no time to get cute. It's a mad dog's promenade, so walk tall or, baby, don't walk at all.

"Nighttime flyers feel their pains. Drugstore takes down the chains. Metal motion comes in bursts. But the gas station can quench that thirst. Suspension cracked on unmade road. The truckers' eyes read 'Overload'. And, out on the subway the Rael Imperial Aerosol Kid exits into the daylight, spray-gun hid. And the lamb lies down on Broadway.

"Suzanne tired, her work all done, thinks money-honey-be on-neon. Cabman's velvet glove sounds the horn, and the sawdust king spits out his scorn. Wonder woman, draw your blinds. Don't look at me. I'm not your kind. I'm Rael!

"Something inside me has just begun. Lord knows what I have done. They say the lights are always bright on Broadway. They say there's always magic in the air. And the lamb lies down on Broadway."

4
Hit the Road, Joe

Now that I was leaving New York town, possibly for good after my stint in the army, it was time for one last visit with my old girlfriend of years past. Her name is Sally, and she's originally from England. She has the sexiest voice supplemented with a British accent, but I soon realized that she was really looking for someone much older, richer, and worldly-wise than me. Still, those bus rides way back when to school and back with Sally were great fun, and I knew I would miss her once this unavoidable parting of ways came to pass. Still, I had to see her one last time.

So I went straight to my usual bus stop with my faithful backpack, what little cash I was able to scrounge up, something to drink, and my trusty guitar. Then I waited. It seemed like forever. Finally, after what must have been an hour, here she came. Not Sally, no, the bus. It was a rattletrap of a double-decker bus, but it was all I had.

I didn't have a car, not only because I had little cash, but because parking your car in the city cost more over a short period of time than the car itself. And then trying to drive between all these maniac cab drivers was an impossibility. Add to that rain or snow and a commuter in New York is totally screwed. Hence, no matter how degrading and time-consuming it was, I took the bus everywhere.

Oh, don't even think about a bicycle. I've owned three bikes in my life. Guess how many of my bikes were stolen. Not by me, from me! That's right. Three! I gave up. At least I could insure the car against theft.

Finally, I was riding in the bus down the boulevard, and the place was pretty packed. Couldn't find a seat so I had to stand with the perverts in the back. It smelled like a locker room. There was junk all over the floor. We're already packed in like sardines, but we're stopping to pick up more. Look out! Another one comes on and another one comes on. Hey, he's gonna sit by you!

Then someone cried, 'Does this bus stop at 82nd Street?'

The reply wasn't short or sweet.

"Hey, bus driver, keep the change, bless your children, give them names. Don't trust men who walk with canes. Drink this and in a week you'll have wings on your feet. Broadway Mary, Joan Fontaine, advisor on the downtown train. Christmas crier busting cane. He's in love again.

"Where dock workers' dreams mix with Panthers' schemes to someday own the rodeo. Tainted women in Vista-vision perform for out-of-state kids at the late show. Wizard imps and sweat-sock pimps mixed with interstellar mongrel nymphs. Rex said his lady left him limp. Well, you know how love's like that.

"Well, Mary Lou found out how to cope. She rides to heaven on a gyroscope. The Daily News asks her for the dope, and she says, 'Man, the dope's that there's still hope'.

"Well now, queen of diamonds, ace of spades, newly discovered lovers of the everglades. They take out a full page ad in the trades to announce their arrival. Senorita, Spanish Rose, wipes her eyes and blows her nose. Uptown in Harlem, she throws a rose to some unlucky young matador.

"And that's all we have on 82nd Street!"

There's a suitcase poking me in the ribs. There's an elbow in my ear. There's a smelly old bum standing next to me, hasn't showered in a year. I think I'm missing a contact lens; I think my wallet's gone. And I think this bus is stopping again to let a couple more freaks get on. Look out!

The window doesn't open, and the fan is broke, and my face is turning blue. I haven't been in a crowd like this since I went to see The Who. Well, I should've got off a couple miles ago, but I couldn't get to the door. There isn't any room for me to breathe, and now we're gonna pick up more. Another one rides the bus.

When I was in third grade, they'd steal my bubble gum. When I was going on a date, they'd steal my condom. When I was going to church, they'd steal my offering. When I was going to confession, they'd add to my suffering. It was on the bus that I learned to cuss. If I listened to music, they'd raise a fuss and grind me into the dust. But we all learned to trust, the bus driver.

As was my usual habit, I calmed myself. The man sitting next to me smiled and revealed his thoughts.

"I am a passenger and I ride and I ride. I ride through the city's backsides. I see the stars come out of the sky. Yeah, the bright and hollow sky. You know it looks so good tonight.

"Oh, the passenger, how he rides. He looks through his window. What does he see? He sees the sign and the hollow sky. He sees the stars come out tonight. He sees the city's ripped backsides. He sees the winding ocean drive. And everything was made for you and me. All of it was made for you and me because it just belongs to you and me. So, let's take a ride and see what's mine!"

Suddenly, his expression was one of confusion as we passed the nuclear power plant.

"I can see the writing on the wall. I can hear the axe before it falls. I can really feel it getting through to me. I can see the sea begin to glow. I can feel it leaking down below. I can barely stand it, what you're doing to me. And in the morning will you still feel the same? How you going to keep yourself from going insane with glowing children and a barrel of pain?

"I don't want to hear it. I can feel the heat begin to rise. I can see the vapors in my eyes. Any way you look at this it's hard to take. I can feel my skin begin to peel. I can see the Dollar and the deal. I can see the companies that are on the make. And in the morning will you still feel the same? How you going to keep yourself from going insane?"

Soon we were well past the nuclear station, and our boy was back to his personal problems.

"Been dazed and confused for so long, it's not true. I wanted a woman. Never bargained for you. Lots of people talking, few of them know. Soul of a woman was created below.

"You hurt and abuse telling all your lies. Run around, sweet baby, Lord, how they hypnotize. Sweet little baby, I don't know where you been. Gonna love you, baby, here I come again.

"Every day I work so hard, bringing home my hard-earned pay. Try to love you baby, but you push me away. Don't know where you're going. Only known just where you been. Sweet little baby, I want you again.

"Oh, I don't like when you're mystifying me. Oh, don't leave me so confused, now. Take it easy, baby. Let them say what they will. Tongue wag so much when I send you the bill."

Finally, with the help of an angel, I got off that bus and with my transfer in hand I waited for the local bus that would drop me in front of Sally's house. Soon, an old man sat down next to me and told me that he was the local bus driver. Then, he began humming to himself.

"Have mercy, been waiting for the bus all day. I got my brown paper bag and my take home pay. Have mercy, old bus be packed up tight. Well, I'm glad just to get on and get on home tonight. Right on, that bus done got me back. Well, I'll be ridin' on the bus until I Cadillac."

Next he pulled out a roughly chewed cigar and settled back. After looking over all the baggage I was carrying, he asked me where I was going and why. For some reason the words flowed out of my mouth with ease.

"Every day I get in the queue, to get on the bus that takes me to Sally. I'm so nervous, I just sit and smile. Sally's house is only another mile. Thank you, driver, for getting me there; you'll be an inspector, have no fear. I don't want to cause no fuss. But, can I buy your magic bus?"

"Nooooo!" was all he said.

"I don't care how much I pay; I wanna drive this bus to my baby each day."

"Give me a hundred, I won't take under. She goes like thunder; it's a four-stage wonder. A magic bus."

"I want it, I want it, I want it," I cried.

"You can't have it!" he replied.

"Thruppence and sixpence every day, just to drive to my baby. Thruppence and sixpence each day, because I drive my baby every way. Magic Bus…I want the Magic Bus."

He just shook his head and muttered on.

"You ought to know by now that I don't wait around, drag my heels, hold my breath, and hang out underground. You think I think too much; I think we'll wait and see. From here to there I'll take a piece of all that's in between.

"Never say never and don't wait forever. It's an open mind that sees that now is the time to take a chance, to take a shot, take control of the situation. I can't stand around here telling you about the things I've done and what I got to do. So, are you on the bus or not 'cause we're leaving the station?

"Don't leave yourself behind and don't get in the way. Tomorrow's coming fast to take away today. You say I want too much, but I want you to see that if you want to come with me, you're going to have to leave."

The driver finished his cigar, laid an empty whiskey bottle on the bench, and staggered off after wishing me good luck. Then he stopped and pointed an accusing finger at me. "Son, you're going to need all the good luck you can find at work or on vacation! Beware that the burning desire you now feel does not turn into a burning sensation!"

That comment didn't bother me one bit, but I did wonder just what he meant. After all, I had what I needed. I said it aloud so he could hear me.

"Now I've got my Magic Bus. I drive my baby every day. Each time I go a different way. I want it, I want it, I want it. Every day you'll see my dust, as I drive my baby in my Magic Bus. Too much, the Magic Bus."

As I sat there, I relived those happy moments on what was really a magic bus. I spoke to an imaginary Sally sitting…riding beside me.

"On the bus, that's where we're riding. On the bus, O.K., don't say 'Hi', then. Your tongue, your transfer, your hand, your answer.

"On the bus, everyone's looking forward. On the bus I am looking forward and everything ain't okay. I might die before Monday. They're all watching us. Kiss me on the bus.

"If you knew how I felt now, you wouldn't act so adult now. Hurry, hurry, here comes my stop. On the bus, watch our reflection. On the bus I can't stand no rejection. C'mon, let's make a scene. Oh, Sally, don't be so mean. They're all watching us. Kiss me on the bus. Hurry, hurry, here comes my stop.

"Don't even think about what life would be, without you and me, riding on the bus. No seat to warm, no bees to swarm, no secret hugs and wrapped around arms. Life wouldn't be worth the ride without you."

When I finally got to Sally's house, on foot by the way, I could see her through the front window. There she was on the living room couch on her telephone sharing gossip with her girl friend, Alice. You could also tell by the way Sally waved her hands in the air during the conversation. It was enough to drive me crazy. I knew it was Alice because she was the only person Sally conversed with on the phone. Alice didn't particularly like me and my arrival in the middle of their girls' session didn't make things any better. I thought I would try the direct approach since this might be the last time I ever see Sally. There was no point in holding anything back.

I knocked on the front door and the window and began singing to her at the same time.

"Yeah, you got satin shoes! Yeah, you got nasty boots. You've got cocaine eyes. Yeah, you got speed-freak jive. Can't you hear me knocking on your window? Can't you hear me knocking on your door? Can't you hear me knocking down your dirty street, Yeah?

"Help me, Sally, I ain't no stranger. Are you safe asleep? Yeah, throw out the keys. All right now.

"Hear me ringing, big bell tolls. Hear me singing, soft and low. I've been begging on my knees. I've been kicking, help me please! Hear me prowling? I'm gonna take you down. Hear me growling? Yeah, I got flattened feet now. Hear me howling? And all around your street now. Hear me knocking? And all, all around your town."

Finally, she opened the front door to let me in. I continued my serenade with a smile.

"Friday night I crashed your party. Saturday I said I'm sorry. Sunday came and trashed it out again. I was only having fun. Wasn't hurting anyone. And we all enjoyed the weekend for a change. I've been stranded in the combat zone. I walked through Bedford Street alone. Even rode my motorcycle in the rain. And you told me not to drive, but I made it home alive. So, you said that only proves that I'm insane.

"You may be right. I may be crazy. But it just might be a lunatic you're looking for. Turn out the light. Don't try to save me. You may be wrong. For all I know you may be right.

"Remember how I found you there, alone in your electric chair. I told you dirty jokes until you smiled. You were lonely for a man. I said take me as I am because you might enjoy some madness for a while.

"Now, think of all the years you tried to find someone to satisfy you. I might be as crazy as you say. If I'm crazy, then it's true that it's all because of you, and you wouldn't want me any other way."

She had that puzzled look of hers on her face so I went on.

"Oh, sweet Sally, won't you come out tonight? I wanna take you walking way out in the clear moonlight. Oh, baby, come on take me by my hand. I don't wanna stop walking until we get up to the preacher man.

"I've been in love with you, baby, ever since you were back in Sunday school. And I knew right there and then, I just wanted to be your fool. Oh, sweet Sally, won't you come out tonight?

"Lay down, Sally, and rest here in my arms. Don't you think you want someone to talk to? Lay down, Sally, no need to part so soon. I've been trying all night long just to talk to you.

"The sun ain't nearly on the rise, and we still got the moon and stars above. Underneath the velvet skies, love is all that matters. Won't you stay with me? And don't you ever leave. I long to see the morning light covering your face so dreamily. So, don't let me go and say goodbye. You can lay your worries down and come with me."

I tried to tell her what my heart felt.

"Well, I'll make love to you, and Lord knows, you'll feel no pain. I said I'll make love to you in your sleep, and Lord knows you felt no pain, have mercy. Because I'm a million miles away, and at the same time I'm right here in your picture frame.

"Well, my arrows are made of desire from far away Jupiter's sulfur mines way down by the methane sea. I have a humming bird, and it hums so loud, you think you're losing your mind.

"Well, I float in liquid gardens and Arizona new red sand. I float in liquid gardens way down in Arizona red sand. I taste the honey from the flower named Blue way out in California, and then New York drowns as we hold hands. Yeah! Hey. Because I'm a Voodoo Chile. Lord knows, I'm a Voodoo Chile!"

Sally surprised me when she commenced to telling me about a new friend she met at the beach. His name was Hal, and he was a student at Cornell. She told me that he just left town today for school. As I remembered, roughly the same thing had happened last year, except that guy was in the military. I was honest.

"Nobody on the road. Nobody on the beach. I feel it in the air. The summer's out of reach. Empty lake, empty streets, the sun goes down alone. I'm driving by your house though I know that you're not at home. And I can see you, your brown skin shining in the sun. You got your hair combed back, sunglasses on. And I can tell you, my love for you will still be strong after the boys of summer have gone.

"Out on the road today I saw a dead head sticker on a Cadillac. A voice inside my head said, 'Don't look back, you can never look back.' I thought I knew what love was. What did I know? Those days are gone forever. I should just let them go.

"I will never forget those nights. I wonder if it was a dream. Remember how you drove me crazy? Remember how I made you scream? Now I don't understand what happened to our love. Now, Baby, gonna get you back, gonna show you what I'm made of.

"You know your walking real slow, smiling at everyone. Then, you got the top pulled down, radio on, Baby. My love for you will still be strong, after the boys of summer have gone."

Sally just stared at me with a blank look on her face. There was no love there for me. It was time to go.

"Well, you're dirty and sweet, clad in black, don't look back, and I love you. You're dirty and sweet, oh yeah. Well, you're slim and you're weak. You got the teeth of the hydra upon you. You're dirty sweet, and you were my girl. Well, you're built like a car. You got a hubcap diamond star halo. Well, you're an untamed youth. That's the truth with your cloak full of eagles.

"Well, you're windy and wild. You got the blues in your shoes and your stockings. Well, you dance when you walk, so let's dance, take a chance. Understand me. You're dirty sweet, and you were my girl. Get it on. Bang a gong. Get it on.

"Meanwhile, I'm still thinking…

"Sally, the truth is out so don't deny. Baby, to think I believed all your lies. Darlin', I can't stand to see your face. It's the truth, you understand, I got to get away.

"Baby, I don't want to live here in New York no more. Baby, though I tore your pictures off my walls, Darlin', my old room's fallin' in on me. You understand the truth now. I got to get away."

I paused and decided to try one last time.

"I get up in the morning, and I ain't got nothing to say. I come home in the evening; I go to bed feeling the same way. I ain't nothing but tired, Girl, I'm just tired and bored with myself. Hey there, Baby, I could use just a little help. You can't start a fire without a spark. This gun's for hire, even if we're just dancing in the dark.

"Message keeps getting clearer, radio's on and I'm moving around the place. I check my look in the mirror. I wanna change my clothes, my hair, my face. Girl, I ain't getting nowhere just living in a town like this. There's something happening somewhere. Baby, I know that there is.

"You sit around getting older. There's a joke here somewhere, and it's on me. I'll shake this world off my shoulders. Come on, Baby, the laugh's on me. Stay on the streets of this town, and they'll be carving you up all right. They say you gotta stay hungry. Hey, Baby, I'm just about starving tonight.

"I'm dying for some action. I'm sick of sitting around here trying to write this book. I need a love reaction. Come on now, Baby, gimme just one look.

"You can't start a fire sitting around crying over a broken heart. This gun's for hire even if we're just dancing in the dark. You can't start a fire about your little world falling apart. This gun's for hire!"

I could tell from the expression on her face that I was going to lose. She no more wanted to listen to my pleas than I wanted to lose her. But I kept trying.

"I got no time for corner boys down in the street making all that noise. Or the girls out on the avenue, because tonight I want to be with you. Tonight, I'm gonna take that ride across the river to the Jersey side. I'll take my baby to the carnival, and I'll take her on all the rides.

"Because down the shore everything's all right. Me and my baby on a Saturday night. You know all my dreams come true when I'm walking down the street with you. I'm in love with a Jersey girl!

"You know you thrill me with all your charms, when I'm wrapped up in my Sally's arms. My little girl gives me everything. I know that some day she'll wear my ring. Nothing else matters in this whole wide world when you're in love with a Jersey girl.

"I see you on the street, and you look so tired. I know that job you got leaves you so uninspired. When I come by to take you out to eat, you're lying all dressed up on the bed, fast asleep. Go in the bathroom and put your makeup on. We're gonna take that little brat you're babysitting and drop her off at your mom's. I know a place where the dancing's free. Now, Sally, won't you come with me? Because down the shore everything's all right. You and your baby on a Saturday night. Nothing else matters in this whole wide world."

She hesitated for a long moment. She had a strange pensive look in her eyes, one I'd never seen before. Then, slowly at first, she shook her head 'no'. Finally, reality kicked in as I headed for the street with a broken heart.

"First girl I loved...time has come, I will sing the sad goodbye song. I remember your long red hair falling in our faces as I kissed you.

"I just wanted you to know I just have to go. I just wanted you to know I just have to grow. And I will sometimes think of you as I lay there on a sad sick morning and on a lonely midnight.

"And I never slept with you though we must have made love a thousand times. Because we were just young and didn't have no place to go. So, it's goodbye first love, and I hope you're fine."

I guess I must have mentioned my dreams to visit California and Colorado. For some reason, Sally had a thing about Colorado. She jumped up to enthusiastically wave goodbye.

"Joey, the days of spring have just begun, and the melted snow begins to run. Aspen is a fine place where many people go, and so you're bound for Colorado. Don't send me cards from where you've been or tell me about the friends you win. But, send me a new leaf just begun to grow and hurry home from Colorado.

"You told me once that you would like to run away from all the tears and all the fears you felt this day. You should know no matter where you go you have your friends to lean upon when you're not sure what's goin' on.

"And, if you don't return by the summer, I will know you've found a home in Colorado, and you're doing fine in Colorado."

All I could say was, "Lord, I'm going to the river and get me a tangled rocking chair. And, if the blues overtake me, I'm gonna rock away from here."

Soon I was headed for the railway station with a heavy heart. Then I was standin' at the station out at the end of the line, feelin' mad, just a bit impatient. And I wish that you would make up my mind. Yes, I was out there on the platform, pay phone keeps eatin' my dimes. And I still don't have an answer, and the train's leavin' right on time.

I'm fallin' down, standin' at the station. Won the battle, here I am, standin' at the station like a general relieved of command.

See the old train go down the track. Hear the wheels go clicketty-clack. It's comin' home, comin' home. leavin' town, Baby, ain't comin' home no more.

Get the train, you know why I'm leavin'. No use in grievin'. Well, I'm leavin'. Train time, Baby, train time almost here. So, give me one more time, do dah yeah."

In the white room with black curtains near the station. Black roof country, no gold pavements, tired starlings. Silver horses ran down moonbeams in your dark eyes. Dawn light smiles on my leaving, my contentment. I'll wait in this place where the sun never shines; wait in this place where the shadows run from themselves.

You said no strings could secure you at the station. Platform ticket, restless diesels, goodbye windows. I walked into such a sad time at the station. As I rode out, felt my own need just beginning. At the party she was kindness in the hard crowd. Consolation for the old wound now forgotten. Yellow tigers crouched in jungles in her dark eyes. She's just dressing, goodbye windows, tired starlings.

I'll sleep in this place with the lonely crowd, lie in the dark where the shadows run from themselves.

Still, leaving my family and leaving Sally meant leaving New York. As much as I had learned to dislike it, New York was still my home, the place where I was born. I sat at the railway station and pondered my past and my future. Soon I again began talking to an imaginary Sally sitting next to me.

"Early in the morning when the sun begins to shine, you will see this poor boy leaving love behind. Seems it's just another day, guess I'm going another way, away from home.

"Sally, you're the cause of all the grief you see me wearing. Nobody thought that we would ever split apart. Seems it was an open door, one I haven't been through before. I've done some living, and for sure I'll do some dying. Your kind of woman almost makes me give up trying. Packed up everything I own, strapped it to my back. Seems what I've been looking for wasn't just an open door.

"So, I'll move on along, I'll go. This old road is all I will know. Down the road, away from home, I'm going."

The thought sent chills of excitement and fear through me. I pondered what might lie ahead and the home I was leaving.

"It's quiet now, and what it brings is everything. Comes calling back a brilliant night…I'm still awake. I looked ahead; I'm sure I saw her there. You don't need me to tell you now that nothing can compare. You might have laughed if I told you. You might have hidden a frown. You might have succeeded in changing me. I might have been turned around.

"It's easier to leave than to be left behind. Leaving was never my proud, leaving New York never easy. I saw the light fading out.

"Now life is sweet and what it brings I tried to take. But loneliness it wears me out. It lies in wait, and I've lost. Still in my eyes the shadow of a necklace across your thigh. I might've lived my life in a dream, but I swear that this is real. Memory fuses and shatters like glass. Mercurial future; forget the past. It's you; it's what I feel.

"I saw the life fading out. Leaving New York is never easy. The way you see me walking on, that's why I'm telling you in song. There's only one way to get ahead. I've got to give it up instead. Start all over again.

5
Off to Buffalo

I was lonely as I contemplated my fate. I had just left her, yet I began to miss Sally. I wondered how that could be when I hardly saw her at all over the last few years and I was right here, except for my military time, were I could have visited her every day. It was stupid of me to say the least. I remembered some of her words and my thoughts.

"So, you think you can tell heaven from hell, blue skies from pain. Can you tell a green field from a cold steel rail? A smile from a veil? Do you think you can tell?

"Joey, did they get you to trade your heroes for ghosts? Hot ashes for trees? Hot air for a cool breeze? Cold comfort for change? Did you exchange a walk on part in the war for a lead role in a cage?"

My mind responded.

"How I wish, how I wish you were here. We're just two lost souls, Sally, swimming in a fish bowl, year after year, running over the same old ground. What have we found? The same old fears. Wish you were here."

Waiting on a Sunday afternoon for what I read between the lines… your lies. Feeling like a hand in a rusted chain. So do you laugh or does it cry? Reply?

Leaving on a southern train. Only yesterday you lied. Promises of what I seemed to be only watch the time go by. All of these things you said to me. Breathing is the hardest thing to do with all I've said and all that's dead for you. You lied! Goodbye.

You see me standing on the bridge. I see the sunset in my view. The field looks colorful to me. I know there's more than I can see. I can start all over again.

Here comes my train!

I was wrong. It wasn't my train. I had two more hours to wait. Since I was in the neighborhood, I thought I'd stop and see my Cousin Dupree. His father, my uncle, had lived in Louisiana for quite a while, working in the oil business. Then, several years ago he returned to New York. I walked the two blocks to his house and rang the doorbell. Soon, there was Dupree standing in the doorway with a big smile on his face.

"Come in, Joey. With all that gear you're carrying, I'd say you were leaving town."

I didn't realize it right away, but what I needed most to begin my journey was to see a friendly and familiar face, especially someone who through personal experience might relate to my situation. My father never gave Dupree much credit for intelligence, but he had to admit that my cousin had the reputation of being very clever and a mite devious.

I confirmed his suspicions about my intentions and then, to be polite, I asked about my aunt and uncle. I would have been better off to let that subject rest. In his early days his father had made quite an impression on Dupree. He began to quote his father word for word.

"A word in your ear, Dupree, from father to son. Hear the words that I say. I fought with you. Fought on your side long before you were born. Joyful the sound! And the voice is so clear. Time after time it keeps calling you, calling you on. Don't destroy what you see, your country to be. Just keep building on the round that's been won. Kings will be crowned. The word goes around from father to son to son.

"Won't you hear us sing our family song? Now we hand it on. But I've heard it all before. Take this letter that I give you. Take it, Dupree, hold it high. You won't understand a word that's in it, but you'll write it all again before you die.

"A word in your ear from father to son. Funny that you don't hear a single word that I say. But my letter to you will stay by your side through the years until the loneliness is gone. Joyful the sound. Word goes around, father to son."

I could tell that Dupree had mixed emotions about his father just as I did about mine. It was probably a good thing to let him purge his soul to me.

"I left my life in New Orleans to return to my home nest. When I was there in the Southland, that move seemed like the best. Unfortunately for me, what I really needed was just a little rest, and my move to New Jersey and New York did not pass the litmus test. It must just be a family trait that came with my father's DNA and infected his mate. A bottle of bourbon and a handful of pills, mean more to my parents than any of my skills.

"Dad's been drinking all night long. So long, baby, he's gone. Well, Bloody Mary gives him shivers from a shot. Set up the shooters. It's time for a drop. Old Jamaica, running he comes. Down the hatch, Joey, the women and the fun. We drink a lot, that demon drops. This one's on Dad, and here's to you, Joey. Whiskey on the rocks, a double or a shot.

"Whiskey on the rocks. Elixir from the top. He drinks Mai Tais, Singapore sling. Beam him up, Jim. It's time to come in. He'll have one more before you close up the door. It's on the house, Dad, it's whiskey galore. This one's on me. Here's mud in your eye. Let's throw seven sheets to the wind. I'll have a whiskey on the rocks. Give my Dad whiskey on the rocks. Yeah, pour Dad a double, here comes trouble on the rocks.

"Joey, I know we aren't children any more and should be able to get along on our own. And my experience in living away tells me that I'm happier when I'm alone. New Orleans is not my birthplace, yet I love it the best. It feels like home; I don't feel like a guest. So, follow your feelings to the end of the line, and by hook or by crook everything will turn out fine."

I thanked him for his encouragement, and then he went on. First he warned me about Louisiana. He referred to it as Deep Elem.

"If you go down to Deep Elem, put your money in your shoes. The women in Deep Elem, they give you the Deep Elem blues. Once I had a girlfriend. She meant the world to me. She went down to Deep Elem. Now she ain't what she used to be. Once I knew a preacher, preached the Bible through and through. He went down to Deep Elem. Now his preaching days are through.

"When you go down to Deep Elem to have a little fun, have your ten dollars ready when the policeman comes. When you go down to

Deep Elem, put your money in your pants because the women in Deep Elem, they don't give a man a chance. Dupree's got the Deep Elem blues!

"I went to a garden party to reminisce with my old friends. A chance to share old memories and play our songs again. When I got to the garden party, they all knew my name. No one recognized me. I didn't look the same.

"People came from miles around. Everyone was there. Yoko brought her walrus. There was magic in the air. And over in the corner much to my surprise, Mister Hughes hid in Dylan's shoes wearing his disguise.

"Played them all the old songs, thought that's why they came. No one heard the music. We didn't look the same. I said hello to Mary Lou; she belongs to me. When I sang a song about a honky-tonk, it was time to leave.

"Someone opened up a closet door, and out stepped Johnny B. Goode, playing guitar like ringing a bell and looking like he should. If you gotta play at garden parties, I wish you a lotta luck. But if memories were all I sang, I'd rather drive a truck.

"But it's all right now. I learned my lesson well. You see, you can't please everyone, so you've got to please yourself!"

Before I could ask him a question, he moved back to the subject of his father.

"Daddy don't live in that New York City no more. He don't celebrate Sunday on a Saturday night no more. Daddy don't need no lock and key for the piece he stowed out on Avenue D. Daddy don't drive in that Eldorado no more. He don't travel on down to the neighborhood liquor store. Your Aunt Lucy still loves her coke and rum, but she sits alone because her daddy can't come. Daddy don't drive in that Eldorado no more.

"Driving like a fool out to Hackensack, drinking his dinner from a paper sack. He says, 'I gotta see a joker, and I'll be right back.' Daddy don't live in that New York no more. He can't get tight every night, and pass out on the barroom floor. Daddy can't get no fine cigar no more, but we know you're smoking wherever you are, that's for sure. Daddy don't live in that New York City no more.

"Baby, oh, no, I've been stuck here. I've been searching so long. Don't go. Millions of people were wrong in the dark of the cold light of day. I will still be here. If my heart and my soul have their way, you would still be here."

I wasn't sure who Dupree was talking about, but I was willing to listen.

"Another lonely night in New York. The City of Dreams just keeps on getting me down because my baby's no longer around. And my feeling can never be found. Another lonely night in New York. And my sorry eyes are looking out on the world.

"Janine, you said, 'A guy like me was way out of line'. And knowing today, your leaving was a question of time. In the mist of the sweet summer rain, you will find me here. Should the sparkle of the stars lose their way, I'll be holdin' near. Just another lonely night in New York."

Dupree reached over into a desk drawer and pulled out an envelope, which he proceeded to hand to me.

"It's the note Daddy left. It was addressed to mom, but I can't think of a reason why you shouldn't read it."

I pulled out the note and began reading the scrawled text.

"Is it my imagination or have I finally found something worth living for? I was looking for some action, but all I found was cigarettes and alcohol. You could wait for a lifetime to spend your days in the sunshine. You might as well do the white line because when it comes on top, you've got to make it happen.

"Is it worth the aggravation to find yourself a job when there's nothing worth working for? It's a crazy situation, but all I need are cigarettes and alcohol. You've got to make it happen!"

As I said, I knew my Uncle Rodney was a heavy drinker just like my dad, but no one at home told me that he had disappeared. And it was hard to tell if Dupree was happy or sad. This note gave no hope for his early return. To change the subject I asked Dupree how he himself was doing. I didn't really want to tell him that I was running away from home today, but that I was just pondering the possibility. There was always the chance that he might want to go with me. I figured my chances of survival were better if I were alone.

"Well, I've kicked around a lot since high school," said Dupree. "I've worked a lot of nowhere gigs from keyboard man in a rocking band to hauling boss crude in the big rigs. Now, I've come back home to plan my next move from the comfort of your Aunt Lucy's couch. When I see my little cousin Janine walk in, all I could say was ow-ow-ouch!"

I last saw Janine at a family reunion three years ago. Before I could ask about her, Dupree continued after telling me that he called her 'Layla'. He told me exactly what he said to her a while back.

"What do you do when you get lonely and nobody's waiting by your side? You've been running and hiding much too long. You know it's just your foolish pride. I tried to give you consolation when your young man had let you down. Like a fool, I fell in love with you. You turned my whole world upside down.

"Let's make the best of the situation before I finally go insane. Please don't say we'll never find a way or tell me all my love's in vain. Layla, you got me on my knees. Layla, I'm begging, darling, please! Layla, darling, won't you ease my worried mind?"

He really seemed to like her as strange as it was. Before I could stop him, Dupree went into more details on the subject.

"She turned my life into a living hell in those little tops and tight capris. I pretended to be reading Sports Illustrated as I was watching her wax her skis. On Saturday night she walked in with her date and backs him up against the wall. I tumbled off the couch and heard myself sing in a voice I never knew I had before.

"Honey, how you've grown, like a rose. Well, we used to play when we were three. How about a kiss for your Cousin Dupree?

"One night we're playing gin by a crackling fire, and I decided to make my play. I said, 'Babe, with my boyish charm and good looks, how can you stand it for one more day?' She said, 'Maybe it's the skeevy look in your eyes or that your mind has turned to applesauce the dreary architecture of your soul.' I said, 'But what is it exactly that turns you off? I'll teach you everything I know, if you teach me how to do that dance. Life is short and quid pro quo. And what's so strange about a down-home romance?

"They picked me up, put me in the county jail. They wouldn't let my woman come and post my bail. There I was in prison, almost done with my time. They gave me six months; I had to work out nine. I know my baby, she was gonna jump and shout when the train comes in and I come walking out. Take these stripes from around me, chains from around my legs. The stripes didn't hurt me. The chains could kill me dead."

Dupree seemed ready to leave town, too.

"Well, I can't live here like this anymore because my girl, she ain't gonna like it. What's my momma gonna say when I get home. She's gonna whip my butt for sure now. She's gonna wonder what I do now. I'd better slip across the fence where I belong. I'd better get on back to Orleans quick before they know I'm gone. No, I can't live here like this because my people ain't gonna like it. No, I can't live here like this anymore."

It was clearly time for me to leave so I wished Dupree well and trudged back to the rail station. I began to realize that not being near my family might actually be an advantage. I realized that some strange things were going on back there. Suddenly, I felt better about leaving.

When I reached the station, I queried the station man about my train because I had completely forgotten the departure times.

"Station man, I've been waiting. Can you tell me when we're leaving?"

He said "Midnight train, now is leaving. Engine screaming, ah ah, ah, ah."

"Where I'm going I don't know. But you tell me I must go. When we're leaving, I don't know, but you tell me now.

"I see it's coming and bringing something, this train of loving. I see it's coming; I feel it's running, this train of loving from ages past. Station man, I've been waiting. Can you tell me when we're leaving?"

Just then my Cousin Dupree appeared on the platform and made his best effort to keep me from going just yet. He told me he was catching the next train for the city and that I should go with him... back home. He wanted to talk to my father about his father. That's when he began his song and dance.

"Start spreading the news, I'm leaving today. I want to be part of it, New York, New York. These vagabond shoes are longing to stray right through the very heart of it, New York, New York.

"I wanna wake up in a city that doesn't sleep and find I'm king of the hill, top of the heap. These little town blues are melting away. I'll make a brand new start of it in old New York. If I can make it there, I'll make it anywhere. It's up to you, New York, New York."

As he finished, he looked deep into my eyes. He could see that I didn't agree, at least for myself. Shaking his head, he just shrugged his shoulders, wished me good luck, and then turned around to walk back home here in Jersey. Obviously, he didn't want to face my father alone.

I looked around and here came my train up the track. I was ready! But I was also very nervous. I was finally on my way into the unknown. I tried to organize my fears positively by pushing them into new songs I might write. I patted my trusty guitar. It was clumsy for me at first. I found myself chanting under my breath.

"Pressure pushing down on me, pressing down on me, and I didn't ask for it. Under pressure that tears a building down, splits a family in two, puts people on the streets like me and Dupree. It's the terror of knowing what this world's about, watching some good friends screaming 'Let me out!' Pray for tomorrow. It gets me higher. Pressure on people. Pressure on streets. That's okay.

"Chipping around. Kick my brains around on the floor. These are the days it never rains, but it pours. Turned away from it all like a blind man. Sat on a fence, but it didn't work. Keep coming up with love, but it's so slashed and torn. Why, why, why?

"Insanity laughs. Under pressure we're cracking. Can't we give ourselves one more chance? Why can't we give love that one more chance? Because love's such an old-fashioned word. And love dares you to care for the people on the edge of the night. And love dares you to change our way of caring about ourselves. This is our last dance! This is me, under pressure."

Soon, I found myself on the ground in Buffalo. As I was walking down the street, a pretty girl I chanced to meet. She was going to a party right here at the station. She asked me to accompany her, and we danced by the light of the moon. I danced with a gal with a hole in her stocking, and her knees were a-knocking and her shoes was a-rocking. Buffalo gals won't you come out tonight, and we'll dance by the light of the moon.

Well, she told me that her brother was coming back to Buffalo after a stint in the military. She called him her gypsy biker.

"The speculators made their money on the blood he shed. His momma pulled the sheets up off his bed. Profiteers on Flatbush Avenue sold his shoes and clothes. Ain't nobody talking because everybody knows. We pulled his cycle from the back of the garage and polished up the chrome. Our gypsy biker is coming home.

"Sister Mary sits with his colors, but Johnny's drunk and gone. This old town's been rousted, which side are you on? They would march up over the hill, this old fools' parade, shouting victory for the righteous for you must hear the grace. Ain't nobody talking, just waiting on the phone. Gypsy biker is coming home.

"To the dead, well it don't matter much about who's wrong or right. You asked me that question; I didn't get it right. He slipped into his darkness, now all that remains is my love for you, brother, life's still unchanged. To those that threw him away, he ain't nothing but gone. My gypsy biker's coming home.

"We rode into the foothills. Bobby brought the gasoline. We stood around in a circle while he lit up the ravine. The spring hot desert wind rushed down on us all the way back home.

"And now I'm counting white lines and getting stoned. My gypsy biker's coming home."

Well, the sadness in her voice said it all.

"I'm here at Fourth and Main. Been standing in the rain. I feel no joy. I feel no pain. I got nothing to lose, nothing to gain. I'm at Fourth and Main.

"Been down at City Hall. Been writing on the wall. The grass is wet and the trees are tall. I listen to the pigeons, to the raindrops fall. I'm at City Hall.

"Been down at Market Square. I can't seem to care if the people stop or the people stare. I don't care if I'm leaving, I'm going somewhere. I'm at Market Square."

The street party in honor of her brother ended around midnight as my train pulled into the station. My stay in Buffalo was short and ultimately sad. I waved goodbye to Emily and wished her good luck. She did the same. I saw tears in her eyes. I had to pull myself together.

I'm moving. I'm gonna see the world while I can. I'm moving, I'm gonna be a well rounded man. And there ain't no room for no one else. I've got to learn it all for myself. I'm hungry. I wanna taste the fruits of the world. So hungry, and assure I did love a girl. But, if she was what I was searching for, my heart will lead me back to her door.

No excess baggage there to worry me. No excess baggage there to hurry me. I must roam all alone, on my own. Suddenly a surge of confidence came over me as I realized that I was finally free! I stood on the platform and shouted the words to the stars above.

"I'm the one who flew! Sally, you're the one who fell. When you let me go, well, didn't that work out well. You said you wanted your freedom, but I'm the one with nothing to lose. Well, it got cold when the sun went down, but, Sally, bring on the night. Because starting from right now, deal'em down and dirty. Feeling all right! Line'em up. Daddy's getting numb tonight. Gonna act like a fool who can't say no to nothing!

"So what, if she don't want me back. Tonight I'm getting lucky like a one-eyed Jack. And it's a perfect night for shouting out loud. I'm a free man now!

"Sally, you're the one who said this will work out fine. You got what you wanted, now I'll get mine. And it serves you right if my heart works better than ever. If this is the dark before the dawn, then, Sally, bring on the night because life goes on forever.

"I bet you didn't think I'd survive. I may be broken, but I'm still alive. When this crying is over, I'll be laughing out loud. Because I'm a free man now!"

My train was coming. I could see the light quite a distance away. With it, I would be on my way into the mystic, as my mother would say. She used to sing to me when I was still a small child. I remembered the words.

"We were born before the wind. Also younger than the sun. Ere the bonny boat was won as we sailed into the mystic. Hark, now hear the sailors cry. Smell the sea and feel the sky. Let your soul and spirit fly into the mystic.

"And when that fog horn blows, I will be coming home. And when the fog horn blows, I want to hear it. I don't have to fear it. And I want to rock your gypsy soul, just like way back in the days of old. And magnificently we will flow into the mystic."

6
On My Way

Well, my first few weeks on the road were uneventful. I got a job at a grocery store bagging groceries just to keep food on my plate. I found a warm spot near a bridge in a city park, but I knew that couldn't last forever. One night, as I was staring up at the stars, I began to review my situation.

I'm gonna take a freight train down at the station, Lord, I don't care where it goes. Gonna climb a mountain, the highest mountain, Lord, and gonna jump off, ain't nobody gonna know. I'm gonna find me a hole in the wall. I'm gonna crawl inside and die, 'cause my lady, now a mean old woman, never told me goodbye. I'm gonna buy me a ticket as far as I can. I ain't never coming back! I'm gonna take me that southbound all the way to Georgia now until the train it runs out of track. Can't you see what that woman's been doing to me?

Well, since I was in Buffalo and the main railway ran southwest from here, I quickly abandoned my dream of going south to Atlanta or Miami, at least for now. Besides, with a search of the internet and a few calls, I found myself with a gig in Detroit. I had enough money for a train ticket and a bottle of white lightning so there was no reason to hesitate.

On a warm summer's evening on a train bound for Cleveland, I met up with the son of a sea cook, an old 60's hippie, a little old lady and a gambler. We were all too tired to sleep. So we took turns staring out the window at the darkness until boredom overtook us, and the cook began to speak.

"We were forty miles from Albany, forget it I never shall. What a terrible storm we had one night on the Erie Canal. Oh, the Erie was arising, and the gin was getting low, and I scarcely think we'll get a drink until we get to Buffalo.

"We were loaded down with barley. We were chock full up on rye. The captain, who was called the Monkey Man by other sailors, he looked down at me with his shiny gol-durned wicked eye. Two days out from Syracuse the vessel struck a shoal. We like to all be foundered on a chunk of Lackawanna coal.

"We hollered to the captain on the towpath, treading dirt. He jumped on board and stopped the leak with his old red flannel shirt. The other cook, she was a grand old gal, stood six foot in her socks, had a foot like an elephant and her breath would open locks.

"The wind begins to whistle and the waves begin to roll. We had to reef our royals on that raging canal. The cook she came to our rescue, she had a ragged dress. We heisted her up on the pole as a signal of distress.

"When we got to Syracuse, off-mule, he was dead. The nigh-mule got blind staggers. We cracked him on the head. The cook is in the Police Gazette. The captain went to jail. And I'm the only son-of-a-sea-cook who was bailing with a pail."

The lad shook my hand and got up from his seat to get off at the next stop. Inspired by his words, the gambler smiled and began his tale.

He said, "Son, I've made a life out of reading people's faces, and knowing what their cards were by the way they held their eyes. And, if you don't mind my saying, I can see you're out of aces. For a taste of your whiskey, I'll give you some advice."

It was obvious that he could see the outline of my Jack Daniels bottle in my backpack.

So, I handed him my bottle, and he drank down my last swallow. Then, he bummed a cigarette and asked me for a light. And the night got deathly quiet, and his face lost all expression.

He said, "If you're gonna play the game, boy, ya gotta learn to play it right. You gotta know when to hold'em, know when to fold'em, know when to walk away, and know when to run. You never count your money when you're sitting at the table. There'll be time enough for counting when the dealing's done.

"Every gambler knows that the secret to surviving is knowing what to throw away and knowing what to keep, because every hand's a winner and very hand's a loser. And the best you can hope for is to die in your sleep."

And when he'd finished speaking, he turned back towards the window, crushed out his cigarette, and faded off to sleep. And somewhere in the darkness, the gambler, he broke even. But in his final words I found an ace that I could keep.

The hippie finally spoke up. He was very mellow.

"All aboard. Ha, Ha, Ha, Ha,ha! I, I, I, I, I, I . . .

"Sometimes I can't help the feeling that I'm living a life of illusion. And, oh, why can't we let it be and see through the hole in this wall of confusion? I just can't help the feeling that I'm living a life of illusion.

"Pow, right between the eyes. Oh, how nature loves her little surprises. Wow, it all seems so logical now. It's just one of her better disguises. And it comes with no warning. Nature loves her little surprises…continual crisis.

"Hey, don't you know that it's a waste of your day, caught up in endless solutions that have no meaning. Just another hunch based upon jumping conclusions. Caught up in endless solutions backed up against a wall of confusion. Living a life of illusion."

He paused and pointed out the window.

"Crazy, but that's how it goes. Millions of people living as foes. Maybe it's not too late to learn how to love and forget how to hate? Mental wounds not healing. Life's a bitter shame. I'm going off the rails on this crazy train!

"I've listened to preachers. I've listened to fools. I've watched all the dropouts who make their own rules. One person conditioned to rule and control. The media sells it, and you live the role. Mental wounds still screaming. Driving me insane.

"I know that things are going wrong for me. You gotta listen to my words. Yeah, yeah, yeah. Heirs of the cold war. That's what we've become. Inherited troubles, I'm mentally numb. Crazy, I just cannot bear. I'm living with something that just isn't fair.

"Mental wounds not healing. Who and what's to blame? I'm going off the rails on a crazy train."

The little old lady smiled briefly and picked up the conversation, all the time looking directly at me as if she had known me her whole life.

"Well, you've been on a fast train, and it's going off the rails. And you can't come back, can't come back together again. And you start breaking down in the pouring rain. Well, you've been on a fast train.

"When your lover has gone, don't it make you feel so sad? And you go on a journey way into the land. And you start breaking down because you're under the strain. And you jump on a fast train."

I was trying to figure out how she knew about Sally and I.

"You had to go on the lam. You stepped into no-man's land. Ain't nobody here on your waveband. Ain't nobody gonna give you a helping hand. And you start breaking down and go into the sound when you hear that fast train.

"And you keep moving on to the sound of the wheels, and deep inside your heart you really know just how it feels. You're way over the line. Next thing, you're out of your mind. And you're out of your depth. In through the window she crept. Oh, there's nowhere to go in the sleet and the snow. Just keep on moving on a fast train. Trying to get away from the past, going nowhere, across the desert sand, through the barren waste, on a fast train going nowhere."

Well, I somehow made it to Cleveland in one piece in spite of all my new friends. Actually, I ended up standing in a truck stop in Brook Park, Ohio, talking with a girl named Nelda. I told her about my gig in Detroit, and her eyes lit up. She could see I needed a ride real bad. Soon, I was conferring with her friend, Floyd Miller, who was an over the road trucker. He offered me a ride. Turns out, he's a former musician and when he saw my guitar, that's all it took. He asked me how I got started.

"My Uncle Bill played the fiddle in his New Jersey home. And I backed him on the banjo so he didn't play alone. We've got five generations of a fiddle-playing clan. And it's nice to hear a fiddle by a fiddle-playing man. Here's another song for Uncle Bill written on the road by the light of the moon. I'm thinking about fiddling somewhere up in Michigan. Then I hope to make it to Colorado soon.

"Well, my uncle had his fiddle, and he laid it on me saying, 'Son, play the fiddle like your fiddling folks done'. Well, it's hard to learn to fiddle when you're fiddling on the run. But, fiddling is fiddling and fiddling is fun!"

I explained to Floyd that early on I switched to my Les Paul six-string. As we talked, Floyd commenced to telling me of his experiences on the road.

"Truckin', got my chips cashed in. Keep truckin' like the doodah man. Together, more or less in line. Just keep trucking on.

"Arrows of neon and flashing marquees out on Main Street. Chicago, New York, Detroit, it's all on the same street. Your typical day involved in a typical daydream. Hang it up, and see what tomorrow brings. Dallas, got a soft machine. Houston, too close to New Orleans. New York, got the ways and means, but just won't let you be."

I vigorously agreed with the last statement as he went on.

"I'm a traveling man who made a lot of stops all over the world. And in every port I owned the heart of at least one lovely girl. I've a pretty senorita waiting for me down in old Mexico. If you're ever in Alaska, stop and see my cute little Eskimo.

"Oh, my sweet fraulein down in Berlin town makes my heart start to yearn. And my China doll down in old Hong Kong waits for my return. Pretty Polynesian baby, over the sea. I remember the night when we walked in the sands of Waikiki, and I held you oh so tight! Yes, I'm a traveling man."

Floyd laughed because he'd never ventured outside North America. But his stories were fun to listen to. He had a good heart.

"Most of the cats you meet on the street speak of true love. Most of the time they're sitting and crying at home. One of these days they know they've got to get going out of the door and down the street all alone.

"Truckin', like the doodah man once told me, you've got to play your hand sometime. The cards ain't worth a dime if you don't lay them down.

"Sometimes the light's all shining on me. Other times, I can barely see. Lately, it occurs to me what a long strange trip it's been.

"What in the world ever became of sweet Jane? She lost her sparkle. You know she isn't the same. Living on reds, vitamin C, and cocaine. All a friend can say is, 'Ain't it a shame.'

"Truckin', up to Buffalo. Been thinking, you've got to mellow slow. Takes time. You pick a place to go and just keep trucking on. Sitting and staring out of a hotel window. Got a tip they're gonna kick the door in again. I'd like to get some sleep before I travel. But, if you've got a warrant, I guess you're gonna come in. Busted down on Bourbon Street. Set up like a bowling pin. Knocked down, it gets to wearing thin. They just won't let you be!"

Next, Floyd pulled his rig into a state weighing station. The attendants knew him by sight. They called for a quick tune. Floyd obliged. He grabbed my guitar and started strumming.

"I stopped at a roadhouse in Texas at a little place called Hamburger Dan's. I heard that jukebox start playing a tune called a Truck Driving Man. The waitress brought me some coffee. I thanked her then called her again. I said, 'That old song sure does fit me because I'm a truck driving man'. Well, pour me another cup of coffee for it is the best in the land. I'll put a nickel in the jukebox and play the Truck Driving Man.

"I climbed back aboard my old semi, and then like a flash I was gone. I got them old truck wheels a-moving. Now I'm on my way to San Antone. When I get my call up to glory, they'll take me away from this land. I'll head this old truck up to heaven because I'm a truck driving man. Well, pour me another cup of coffee…"

After the applause and a few minutes worth of forms, we were on our way again. Floyd could see that I was enjoying our conversation so we pulled into a nearby truck stop for some coffee. It was there at the counter that he told me a special story of one of his friends.

"Straight-laced, leather-faced he rolled in like he owned the two-bit town, dollar bills bulging from his bell-bottomed jeans. The population they gathered 'round. Nothing this exciting since a fertilizer truck blew a front tire and landed in the creek. Everybody talking, everybody straining, tryin' to get a little peek.

"Paying for the gas, he wickedly shouted thanks and continued on his journey all once again just about the time a siren fast-approached and the pot bellied sheriff he whizzed right in. With his self inflicted grammar, he started shouting accusations at the long haired greasy looking ape while a local d.j. from the fifty watt station got the whole damn thing on tape.

"The holy roller preacher told the eager congregation that the devil had passed right through their nest. But the teenage girls with their locks in curls were a talkin' 'bout that hair upon his chest. Now the kids got their cookies while the preacher saved some souls, and the story spread to everyone in sight. Commotion was the word, and everybody heard he was gone before the night.

"It's just the world they'll never know, not a country fair side show. Reality they'll somehow never see. He's what they've tried to kill with their Bibles and their stills. But he's not weird, just a man that's being free. He's the Monkey Man!"

Floyd was laughing to beat the band as he finished his story. We still had a ways to go so I asked for more. He pointed to a fellow sitting at the end of the counter telling me that the driver was once in love with a waitress who worked at this very truckstop.

"A truck stop in Dayton with no where to go. Too many days without any shows. It was 4 AM, and he sipped from his cup. At 5 AM the sun's coming up. His body has shifted from the touring mode, trying to sleep in the van on the road. He had to find a place to sleep. He had the truck stop blues, taking care of himself, paying his dues. Living life, day by day. He had the truck stop blues. Don't think he'd have it any other way.

"He called his girl, a waitress working right here. He said he couldn't take this life for another year. Up to Canada he was going to fly. On the other end of the phone he could hear his girl cry. She couldn't face life without his touch. She loved him so very, very much. But he didn't know exactly what to say except that he couldn't stay.

"The waitress was sliding down the wall. You could see her chest rise and fall. Her mascara was running thin, and the payphone was swinging against the wall. Don't ask her about the call. You know she's only trying to begin again.

"And her manager was yelling something about her hair being in her face. A customer was complaining, but he really had no case. And the counter-queens didn't even look up from their magazines. But the waitress stares straight ahead saying something she never said.

"And the waitress had them backing against the wall until they were white in the face. She had them going and praying, but they never knew the role they would play. And the manager was quiet as he fumbled with the drawer. 'No', he said, 'you will never get away with this'.

"Because, today when the door opens, the rain slants in, and there's water all over the floor. The buss boy waves to the meter maid, who didn't wave back no more. We're all searching for something. We'll all find a place to stay. Though we may have next to nothing, oh, Lord, we'll find a way."

Floyd waved to the man who waved back but didn't smile.

"There's a place in the world for the angry young man with his working class ties and his radical plans. He refuses to bend. He refuses to crawl. He's always at home with his back to the wall. And he's proud of his scars and the battles he's lost. And he struggles and bleeds as he hangs on the cross. And he likes to be known as the angry young man.

"Give a moment or two to the angry young man, with his foot in his mouth and his heart in his hand. He's been stabbed in the back. He's been misunderstood. It's a comfort to know his intentions are good. And he sits in a room with a lock on the door, with his maps and his medals laid out on the floor. And he likes to be known as the angry young man."

Floyd paused to consider his thoughts.

"I believe that I've passed the age of consciousness and righteous rage. I found that just surviving was a noble fight. I once believed in causes, too. I had my pointless point of view. And life went on no matter who was wrong or right.

"And there's always a place for the angry young man with his fist in the air and his head in the sand. And he's never been able to learn from mistakes, so he can't understand why his heart always breaks. But his honor is pure and his courage as well. And he's fair and he's true and he's boring as hell. And he'll go to the grave as an angry old man."

It was time to change the subject, and I knew better than to ask what happened to the waitress. Floyd went back to his musician days.

"Highways and dancehalls, a good song takes you far. You write about the moon, and you dream about the stars. Blues in old motel rooms; girls in daddy's car. You sing about the nights, and you laugh about the scars. Coffee in the morning, cocaine afternoons. You talk about the weather, and you grin about the rooms. Phone calls long distance to tell how you've been. Forget about the losses; you exaggerate the wins. And when you stop to let 'em know you've got it down, it's just another town along the road.

"The ladies come to see you if your name still rings a bell. They give you damn near nothing, and they say they knew you well. So you tell them you remember, but they know it's just a game. And along the way their faces all begin to look the same. And when you stop to let 'em know you got it down, it's just another town along the road.

"Well, it isn't for the money, and it's only for a while. You stalk around the rooms and you roll away the miles. Gamblers in the neon clinging to guitars. You're right about the moon, but you're wrong about the stars. And when you stop to let 'em know you got it down, it's just another town along the road.

"I've witnessed those one night stands, must have played in a thousand bands. But, I'm just here tonight, tomorrow I'll be gone. Seen folks show their blacker sides. Seen them die just for foolish pride. And those drivers always ask to hear that same old song.

"I've heard all those hard luck tales from all of you U.S. males. I've heard you tell those lies about the love you've known. And I've followed those highway signs, and I've run down those thin white lines. Like those drivers, this old road is all I call my own.

"That's a big ten-four from your back door. Just put that hammer down. This young man feels those eighteen wheels that keep turning 'round to take me to Shaky Town…Detroit."

We were on our way. I asked Floyd to tell me more about life on the road. I could certainly use the advice.

"On a long and lonesome highway, east of Omaha, you can listen to the engine moaning out its one lone song. You can think about women or the girl you knew the night before. But your thoughts will soon be wandering the way they always do when you're riding sixteen hours and there's nothing much to do. And you don't feel much like riding, you just wish the trip was through. Say, here I am on the road again. There I am up on the stage. Here I go playing star again. There I go, turn the page.

"Well, you walk into a restaurant strung out from the road. You can feel the eyes upon you as you're shaking off the cold. You pretend that it doesn't bother you, but you just want to explode. Most times you can't hear them talk, other times you can. Oh, the same old cliché, is that a woman or a man? You always seem outnumbered. You don't dare make a stand.

"Out there in the spotlight you're a million miles away. Every ounce of energy you try to give away, as the sweat pours out of your body like the music that you play. Later in the evening as you lie awake in bed, with the echo from the amplifiers ringing in your head, you smoke the day's last cigarette remembering what she said. Now here I am on the road again. There I go. There I go."

Floyd went on.

"I've been warped by the rain, driven by the snow. I'm drunk and dirty, don't ya know, and I'm still, willin'. Out on the road late at night, seen my pretty Alice in every headlight. Alice, Dallas Alice.

"I've been from Tucson to Tucumcari, Tehachapi to Tonapah, driven every kind of rig that's ever been made. Driven the back roads so I wouldn't get weighed. And if you give me weed, whites, and wine, and you show me a sign, I'll be willin' to be movin'. I've been kicked by the wind, robbed by the sleet, had my head stoved in, but I'm still on my feet, and I'm still willin'.

"Now I smuggled some smokes and folks from Mexico, baked by the sun every time I go to Mexico, and I'm still willin' to be movin'."

I noticed a picture in the cab. It was a photo of Floyd's son, Jake. Unfortunately, what I didn't realize was that Jake had died in Vietnam. Floyd was philosophical about it.

"Us and them. And after all we're only ordinary men. Me and you. God only knows it's not what we would choose to do. 'Forward' he cried from the rear, and the front rank died. The General sat, and the lines on the map moved from side to side.

"Black and blue. And who knows which is which and who is who. Up and down. And in the end it's only round and round and round. 'Haven't you heard? It's a battle of words,' the poster bearer cried. 'Listen, son,' said the man with the gun, 'there's room for you inside.'

"Down and out. It can't be helped, but there's a lot of it about. With, without. And who'll deny it's what the fighting's all about. Out of the way, it's a busy day. I've got things on my mind. For want of the price of tea and a slice, the young man died."

Well, with Floyd at the wheel we rolled on up that road and soon I was in Detroit. I bid Floyd goodbye and told him I hoped we'd meet again some day. Somewhere, deep down inside, I had this strong feeling that we would.

7
Detroit Breakdown

I've got this place I'm renting. It cost me next to nothing downtown. Nobody comes around telling me I've got to turn the sound down. Broadway, down on the corner, the Bible screamer, the plasma donor, buses, car horns, ghetto blasters, the shouts and cries of the human disasters.

I feel all right when I'm downtown. My feet are light when I'm downtown. I cast my hopes on the human tide. I place my bet, and I let it ride. I'm open wide when I'm downtown.

Eight blocks south of city hall, the rats run free and the winos crawl. Darkness falls on the vast machine where the future stalks the American dream. I feel all right when I'm downtown. My head feels light when I'm downtown. It's all in sight when I'm downtown.

I did have to do a lot of things I never worried much about before. For some reason I have never divined, my mom loved to do the laundry. Those happy days were over. Soon, I got the all night Laundry Mat blues. Washing everything I own except my shoes. I got makeup around the collar, and it smells like sweat, a dollar in the dryer, and it ain't dry yet. If you wear clothes, you got to pay the dues and sing the all night Laundry Mat blues.

But worse than the petty concerns I had, it was tough overcoming the homesickness that eventually set in on my psyche. It wasn't that I wanted to return to New York. Far from it. It was the absence of familiar sights and familiar faces.

I don't mind the quiet or the lonely nights. I don't miss the funky attitudes, and I don't miss the fights. I lie on the couch until suppertime and hunker down and read the Post. And that's when I remember the things I miss the most.

I kinda like frying up my sad cuisine, getting in bed and curling up with a girlie magazine. But sometimes in the corner of my eye I see that adorable ghost, and then, ba-boom, I remember the things I miss the most.

I'm learning how to meditate, so far so good. I'm building the Andrea Doria out of balsa wood. The days don't really last forever, but it's getting pretty damn close. And that's when I remember the things I miss the most.

The talk. The sex. Somebody to trust. The comfy Eames chair. The good copper pans. The '67 Chevy. The Go-Go Sox. Brad Park's slap shot. These are the things I miss the most.

After I got my bearings in Detroit town I was told that they needed me to play piano for a few weeks at another bar until the usual guy recovered from a ruptured appendix. That was okay with me because I was okay on keyboards, and it gave me an opportunity to sing some of my favorite tunes. I'll never forget that final night at the Last Whiskey Bar.

It's nine o'clock on a Saturday, the regular crowd shuffles in. There's an old man sitting next to me making love to his tonic and gin. He says, 'Son, can you play me a memory? I'm not really sure how it goes. But it's sad and it's sweet and I knew it complete when I wore a younger man's clothes.'

Then he stood up and led the bar clientele in a chorus.

"Sing us a song, you're the piano man. Sing us a song tonight. Well, we're all in the mood for a melody, and you've got us feeling all right."

Now John at the bar is a friend of mine. He gets me my drinks for free. And he's quick with a joke or to light up your smoke, but there's some place that he'd rather be. He said, 'Joe, I believe this is killing me' as the smile ran away from his face. 'Well, I'm sure that I could be a movie star if I could get out of his place.'

"Have you ever been mistreated?" asked John with a serious look on his face. "You know what I'm talking about. I worked five long years for one woman; she had the nerve to put me out. I got a job in a steel mill, shucking steel like a slave. Five long years, every Friday, I come straight back home with my pay.

"I finally learned my lesson, should have a long time ago. The next woman I marry, she gonna work and bring me the dough. Have you ever been mistreated? You know just what I'm talking about. She had the nerve to put me out!"

I told John that better times lay ahead for him. He had more to say so I gave him my full attention.

"Joey, if I could hold on to just one thought for long enough to know why my mind is moving so fast and the conversation is slow. Burn off all that fog and let the sun through to the snow. Let me see her face again before I have to go.

"I have seen her in the movies and in those magazines at night. I saw her on the barstool when she held that glass so tight. And I saw her in my nightmares, but I'll see her in my dreams. And I might live a thousand years before I know what that means.

"Once there was a friend of mine who died a thousand deaths. His life was filled with parasites and countless idle threats. He trusted in a woman, and on her he made his bets. Once there was a friend of mine who died a thousand deaths."

His voice was so sad near the end. I got the impression that John was referring go himself. Luckily, a customer called him away before I could ask him that question.

Now Paul is a real estate novelist who never had time for a wife. And he's talking with Davy who's still in the navy and probably will be for life. And the waitress is practicing politics as the businessmen slowly get stoned. Yes, their sharing a drink they call loneliness, but it's better than drinking alone.

It's a pretty good crowd for a Saturday, and the manager gives me a smile because he knows that it's me they've been coming to see to forget about life for a while. And the piano sounds like a carnival, and the microphone smells like a beer. And they sit at the bar and put bread in my jar and say, "Man, what are you doing here?"

Well, after that I played my guitar and sang for my supper every night at a downtown bar in Detroit called O'Shea's. Bill Green and his wife were the owners, and they were very kind and understanding.

I spent quite a bit of time talking to a waitress named Colleen mainly because she seemed willing to listen and smooth over my obvious homesickness. After a few conversations she began to tell me about her personal problems which sounded quite a bit like mine.

"I've been run down; I've been lied to. I don't know why I let that mean man make me a fool. He took all my money, wrecked my new car. Now, he's with one of my goodtime buddies; they're drinking in some cross-town bar.

"My friends tell me that I've been such a fool. And I have to stand by and take it, Baby, all for loving him. Drown myself in sorrow, and I look at what he's done. But nothing seems to change, the bad times stay the same, and I can't run.

"Sometimes I feel like I've been tied to the whipping post. Good Lord, I feel like I'm dying."

I tried my best to comfort Colleen, but I said some of the dumbest things to her.

"Let me ask you, Baby, do you lie here every day of your life in a burned out war zone just like Beruit or something, Man? It hurts my eyes; got my whole damn head on fire. Detroit breakdown. What a surprise! Motown, schmotown, ain't nothing left. No more Iggy or the MCS. Wayne's been doin' it in L.A. now, so you're just living a lie.

"Let me ask you, Baby. Do you live here every day of your life? This is a town that makes a career out of waiting for hell night."

I had a sip of my beer and went on about Detroit when I probably should have just shut up.

"Ted and Seger were burning with fever and let the Silver Bullets fly. The Kid was in his crib. Shady wore a bib, and the Posse wasn't even alive. Shock rock choppin' block, sort of make your heart stop. Shoving into overdrive, playing loud and fast. Make that guitar blast. Playing like today will be your last.

"Well, I wasn't born here. I ain't gonna die here with all my long hair. Detroit City. You feel your heart beat. You hit the concrete to get to mean street. Detroit City. There's a riot raging downtown. Trying to burn the place down. Skies glowing red and gray. But the Riff kept a-rocking, the Greek kept a-talking. And the streets are still smoking today."

I got back to Colleen and me.

"Comes a time when you're drifting. Comes a time when you settle down. Comes a light, feelings lifting. Lift that baby right off the ground. Oh, this old world keeps spinning round. It's a wonder tall trees ain't laying down. There comes a time.

"You and I, we were captured. We took our souls, and we flew away. We were right. We were giving. That's how we kept what we gave away. Oh, this old world keeps spinning round. There comes a time.

"Baby, can't wait; baby, gotta go. Gotta do a number on a late night show. Do a little song, do a little dance, gonna make the best of this big chance. It don't really matter if I don't or I do, just trying to make the best of the hometown blues.

"I had a little friend named Sally, had a little girl, said she was the best in the whole wide world. Said it's so good, said it so unreal; it didn't last, but it's no big deal. It don't really matter if she don't or she do; I'm just trying to make the best of the hometown blues.

"Colleen, save me, save me, save me with your sweet smile. Honey, I really need your attention to help me kill a little bit of time.

"All of the girls run with the crowd. They go wild when the lights go down. They got a little money, little in a dream, wanna be the queen of their little scene. Don't really matter if they don't or if they do; they're trying to make the best of the hometown blues."

With Colleen's help my gig went well, and the owner, Bill Green, even offered to sell me his Harley. The price was fair; he just took it out of my wages. It was just what I was looking for.

I was so proud of my Harley. It had seen better days, yet because I earned it with the sweat of my brow, playing a three-month gig with my guitar in the City of Detroit, I fell in love with the machine. I rode the bike around a city block several times and that was enough to convince me. Besides, my father hated motorcycles, which might be one reason I love this one so much. I call her the 'Detroit Demolition'.

I went back to Colleen and asked her if she wanted to go with me.

"Copycats ripped off my words. Copycats ripped off my songs. Copycats ripped off my melody. It doesn't matter what they say. It doesn't matter what they do. All that matters is my relationship to you. Gonna take you out, get you on my bike. We're going for a long, long ride. We're going down to a town called Paradise. Down where we can be free. We're gonna drink that wine. We're gonna jump for joy.

"We're going up the mountainside, child, you can see for miles and see the vision on the west. We're gonna swing around and look from north to south. Swing around from east to west and go round in a circle, too. And we're gonna start dancing like we've never done before.

"I'm gonna take you in my arms. I'm gonna squeeze you tight. Everything will be all right. We're gonna get that squealin' feelin'. Gonna take you down to a town called Paradise, down where we can be free.

"By the river we will linger, as we drive down to be free. We're gonna ride all night long all along the ancient highway."

But there was a restriction. I had to be honest.

"It's a hard world to get a break in. All the good things have been taken. But, Colleen, there are ways to make certain things pay. Though I'm dressed in these rags, I'll wear sable some day.

"Hear what I say. I'm going to ride the serpent. No more time spent sweating rent. I'm breaking loose. It ain't no use holding me down. Stick around. It's my life, and I'll do what I want. It's my mind, and I'll think what I want. Show me I'm wrong. Hurt me sometimes. But someday I'll treat you real fine.

"There'll be women and their fortunes that just won't do. Are you gonna cry when I'm squeezing the rye? Taking all I can get, no regrets? When I openly lie and leave only money, can you believe I ain't no saint? No complaints? And, baby, remember, it's my life and I'll do what I want."

I saw a tear running down her cheek. She kissed me softly and walked away. I would never see Colleen again.

When I went to see Bill Green and get my final check, I had to wait at the bar for him to return from an errand. Soon, my attention was drawn by the TV set behind the bar. The news was on.

"The President says he's disappointed with Congress's performance. In Detroit, a youth was reported dead at the scene of a head-on collision. The youth was reportedly driving on the wrong side of the boulevard when he struck a delivery truck and was catapulted through the windshield of his car. County representatives today are expected to rally to the aid of striking longshoremen in hopes of ending a nine month deadlock…"

I must have dozed off for a while. Suddenly someone nudged me back to consciousness.

"I feel uptight on a Saturday night. Nine o'clock, the radio's on, the only light. I hear my song, and it pulls me through. Comes on strong, tells me what I got to do."

It was Charlie, a drummer I'd worked with last week.

"I got to get up, everybody's gonna move their feet. Get down, everybody's gonna leave their seat. You gotta lose your mind in Detroit rock city.

"Getting late, I just can't wait. Ten o'clock and I know I gotta hit the road. First, I drink. Then, I smoke, start up the car and try to make the midnight show. Moving fast, doing 95. Hit top speed, but I'm still moving much too slow.

"Twelve o'clock, I gotta rock! There's a truck ahead, light staring at my eyes. Oh, my God, no time to turn. I gotta laugh because I know I'm gonna die. I feel so good, I'm so alive. I hear my song playing on the radio. Get up, everybody's gonna move their feet. Get down, everybody's gonna leave their seat."

By this time Charlie was laughing hysterically as he downed his beer, and Bill Green was grinning from ear to ear.

"Caught you daydreaming, Joey," Bill whispered. "What's her name?" I just shrugged my shoulders.

Bill smiled again and handed me my check. It had a bonus, which I really appreciated. Then, the strangest thing happened. There in his other hand was a letter addressed to me! It had a Boston postmark. I didn't know anyone in Boston. So, what could I do? I opened it!

It was a letter from the last person I ever thought I'd hear from. Sally! This is what it said.

"Please come to Boston for the spring time. I'm staying here with some friends, and they've got lots of room. You can sing your music on the sidewalk or in a café where I hope to be working soon. Please come to Boston.

"Hey, rambling boy, now won't you settle down? Detroit ain't your kind of town. There ain't no gold, and there ain't nobody like me. I'm the number one fan of the man from New York City.

"We could go to Denver with the snowfall. We'll move up into the mountains so far that we can't be found, and throw 'I love you' echoes down the canyon. And then lie awake at night until they come back around. Let's go to Denver.

"Now this drifters' world goes 'round and 'round. And I doubt that it's ever gonna stop. But of all the dreams I've lost or found and all that I ain't got, I still want to lean on someone who will sing to me.

"We could go to L.A. to live forever. California life alone is just too hard to build. We'd live in a house that looks out over the ocean. And there's some stars that fell from the sky. And we'd be living up on the hill. Please meet me in L.A."

Then I put the letter in my pocket. I promised myself that I'd reply, but I needed some time. Colleen taught me that Sally might not be the girl for me. Sally was very fickle. How long would we last together with no home and no money? That's one of the questions I would ask when I wrote back to her. If I wrote back to her.

8
Roll Me Away

When my gigs in Detroit finally ended, I took a look down a westbound road out of the city, and right away I made my choice. I jumped on my big two-wheeler with my trusty guitar strapped to my back and hit that road. I was tired of hearing my own voice so the sound of the bike on the road and the wind rushing through my hair was enough to begin the cleansing of my soul. I had always wanted to see the northern plains so I drew a bead on them and just rolled that power on.

Not that I didn't enjoy working for the Greens and playing the piano once in a while. I also got to work on my harmonic playing which was pretty pathetic before I got here. I discovered that Detroit people are very friendly and supportive. Plus, the Red Wings are a great hockey team. But, I couldn't envision living and working here on a permanent basis. I hadn't seen and flown enough of the road yet to decide where to land on a permanent basis. I was still alone.

Well, I'm so tired of crying, but I'm out on the road again. I ain't got no woman just to call my special friend. You know, the first time I traveled out in the rain and snow, I don't have no payroll. Not even no place to go.

The land here is flat. The sky, she is blue. The road is straight with just a little hill or two. The beer tastes good, and the birds sing happily in the woods. I've seen cows in the fields, and flocks of birds at their heels. Nature is certainly having her say. I don't believe she would have it any other way.

I thought back to New York and my mother, trapped in the city. My Cousin Dupree had promised to look in on her once in a while. I wished I could see her now.

And I left my mother while I am quite young. She said 'Lord, have mercy on my wicked son.' Take a hint from me, mama, please. Don't you cry no more. 'Cause it's soon this morning down the road I'm going. But I ain't going down that long old lonesome road all by myself. If I can't carry you, Colleen, Baby, gonna carry somebody else.

Twelve hours out of Mackinaw City I was pretty tired and thirsty so I pulled into the parking lot of a friendly looking roadhouse called Johann's Bar & Grill. As I parked my Harley, I was surprised to see that of the forty or so vehicles parked in the lot that over half were two-wheelers…bicycles! There were a few motorcycles, but I finally figured out that a local bicycle club had stopped for some libation. With all of the open country around here there are probably some great places to ride a bicycle.

It felt natural for me to stop into a bar for a brew even though I wasn't much of a beer drinker at the time. I needed to see a friendly face or two and see what the locals did for entertainment. This was the opposite of a big city. Madison was the closest metropolis of any size. I was curious to learn how these people differed from those I encountered in a big city like Detroit or Buffalo. After I dusted myself off and walked inside, I was glad for my decision. It was definitely a friendly place so I pulled up a stool at the bar and ordered a drink. Well, sitting next to me was one of the locals whose attention was drawn by the television set that sat behind the bar. His name was Frank, and he was not very sociable at first. He seemed down in the mouth about something. Out in this beautiful Wisconsin countryside with its open spaces and clean air, it was hard to understand how anyone could be down.

Just then a waitress bumped into me and dropped a piece of paper on my lap. She was gone before I could retrieve it so I put it in my pocket. I was going to give it to her next time she went by.

I asked Frank how things were going. He was hesitant to engage in conversation at first, but he finally gave in.

"I drink alone, yeah! With nobody else! You know, when I drink alone, I prefer to be by myself. Every morning just before breakfast, I don't want no coffee or tea. Just me and my good Buddy Wiser. That's all I'll ever need.

"The other night I lay sleeping, and I woke from a terrible dream. So, I caught up with my pal, Jack Daniel's and his partner Jimmy Beam, and we drank alone. The other day I got invited to a party, but I stayed home instead. Just me and my pal Johnny Walker and his brothers, Black and Red. And we drank alone.

"My whole family done give up on me, and it makes me feel, oh, so bad. The only one who will hang out with me is my Old Granddad. And we drink alone, with nobody else!"

Suddenly, he paused and looked at me, and his attitude began to change. I guess he wasn't used to strangers coming up to him at the bar. He grabbed his beer and chugged a sizeable gulp. He wiped his chin on his flannel shirt and began.

"Sitting on this barstool talking like a damn fool, got the twelve o'clock news blues. And I've given up hope on the afternoon soaps and a bottle of cold brew. Is it any wonder I'm not crazy? Is it any wonder I'm sane at all?

"Well, I'm so tired of losing, I got nothing to do and all day to do it. I go out cruising, but I've got no place to go and all night to get there. Is it any wonder I'm not a criminal? Is it any wonder I'm not in jail? Is it any wonder I've got too much time on my hands, and it's ticking away from me? It's ticking away with my sanity. It's hard to believe such a calamity.

"Well, I'm a jet fuel genius; I solve all the world's problems without even trying. I have dozens of friends, and the fun never ends. That is, as long as I'm buying. Is it any wonder I'm not the president? Is it any wonder I'm null and void? Is it any wonder I've got too much time on my hands?

"Well, my new friend, Joe, you look like a traveling man. You relax, sit back, set a course, and go wherever you can. Me, I'm just a poor rural boy. In my life, Mother Nature hasn't blessed me with a single solitary toy. To be free as a bird like you, even if I had the necessary skills, my soul would be found quite wanting, because I lack the necessary will… to be free.

"Compared to me, Joe, without actually knowing, you must have a wonderful life and your enjoyment is still growing. Compared to me,

Joe, you must spread your wings and fly. I just sit here in this one horse town and cry."

Frank finished his beer and thanked me for listening to his problems. I didn't mind because I needed the companionship. He wished me the best of luck on my trip and got up quietly from his barstool. All of a sudden he began talking with a girl around the corner of the bar. I couldn't see her face.

"You've got to change your evil ways, Janie, before I stop loving you. You've got to change, Janie, and every word that I say, it's true. You've got me running and hiding all over town. You've got me sneaking and peeping and running you down. This can't go on. Lord knows, you've got to change.

"When I come home, baby, my house is dark and my pots are cold. You're hanging around, baby, with Jean and Joan and who knows who. I'm getting tired of waiting and fooling around. I'll find somebody who won't make me feel like a clown. This can't go on. Lord knows you've got to change."

Then he walked out of Johann's. I felt sorry for Frank, but somehow I hoped that our chance meeting had encouraged him to try harder. Now I was alone again. I ordered another beer.

From where I sat I couldn't see the girl Frank was talking to. But around the corner of the bar there she sat, a very pretty girl who was wearing a Panama hat. She seemed to be alone and also had that same sad look on her face as I saw on Frank's face. She obviously had some sort of falling out with Frank. This was Central Wisconsin, which is a beautiful place, especially for nature lovers. It was hard to understand how anyone living here could be sad. I glanced at her several times hoping to gain her attention.

It didn't take long for her to notice me. We had a few drinks and one thing led to another, and finally we were talking about the weather, politics, our lives and her recently deceased Saint Bernard dog. She told me that her name was Jane and that she had lived here in the upper Midwest for her whole life. But, as I said, her words weren't accompanied by a smile. I listened patiently because she, like Frank, seemed to need someone to pay attention to her problems. I was getting a lot of practice being a good listener. Soon, she began telling me her problems.

"People try to put us down just because we get around. Things they do look awful cold. I hope I die before I get old. Why don't they all just fade away and don't try to dig what we all say. I'm not trying to cause a big sensation. I'm just talking about my generation. This is my generation, Joey!"

I couldn't help but agree with her, yet she had much more to say.

"I said blow away, blow away, this cruel reality, and keep me from its storm. Suspicion has crept in and ruined my life. I'm messed up and hassled and worn. Well, it's pure indignation, just another sensation, and I'd like to knock on that door. But the boy, he keeps calling for more.

"Yes, and my China White, he ain't here tonight, and love has robbed me blind. So, cast away, cast away, from this ball full of pain before it sinks beneath the waves. Yes, and my sweet China White, he ain't here tonight. Oh, and love has robbed me blind. Some sweet Sergio has robbed me blind!"

She was almost crying. I wasn't sure who Sergio was, but I was sure she would tell me.

"Sergio and I grew up together on the farm. He promised me as a boy that he'd never do me any harm. And then, as time went by, he became my first true love, and for our first kiss neither of us needed a shove.

"He's the kind of person you meet at certain dismal dull affairs... center of a crowd, talking much too loud, running up and down the stairs. Well, it seems to me that he has seen too much in too few years. And although I've tried, I just can't hide, my eyes are edged with tears. I'd better stop and look around; here it comes, my nineteenth nervous breakdown!

"When Sergio was a child, he was treated kind, but he was never brought up right. He was always spoiled with a thousand toys, but still he cried all night. His mother, who neglected him, owes a million dollars tax, and his father's still perfecting ways of making sealing wax.

"Oh, who's to blame, that boy's just insane. Well, nothing I do don't seem to work. It only seems to make matters worse. Oh, please!

"He was still in school when he had that fool who really messed his mind. And after that he turned his back on treating people kind. On our first trip I tried so hard to rearrange his mind. But, after a while I realized, he was disarranging mine. Here comes my nineteenth nervous breakdown!"

She caught her breath and turned to look at me.

"I'm done with Sergio," she whispered. "He treats me like a rag doll. But if he comes back again, tell him to wait right here for me, or just try again tomorrow. I'm gonna kick tomorrow!

"Standing on the corner suitcase in my hand. Sergio's in his corset, Jane…I'm in my vest. You, honey, you're in a rock 'n' roll band… playing in a traveling band. Riding in a Stutz Bearcat, my old flame, Jim. You know those were different times. All the poets, they studied rules of verse and those roadies they just rolled their eyes."

I was confused by her commentary, but I wanted to give her a shoulder to lean on so I began to ad lib.

"Sergio, he is a banker and Jane, you are a clerk, and both of you save your money when you come home from work. Sitting down by the fire the radio does play, look classical music there, kids. 'The March of the Wooden Soldiers' you can hear Sergio say.

"You sing and dance together, and all you have is fun. Through the sleet and snow, the hail, and the brightly shining sun, you have no need to be packing a gun. That's all because he knows that you are, and you know that he is, the one."

I noticed that Janie winced when I mentioned the word 'gun'. Then she smiled for a brief moment and picked up where I left off.

"Some people like to go out dancing and other people like us, we gotta work. And there's even some evil mothers; they're gonna tell you that everything is just dirt. And you know that women never really faint and that villains always blink their eyes, that children are the only ones who blush and that life is just to die.

"Anyone who ever had a heart and wouldn't turn around and break it. Anyone who ever played a part and wouldn't turn around and hate it…they call me, Sweet Jane."

Jane stopped and with a blush on her face, she began searching her purse frantically. She was obviously missing something.

"Joey, have you seen my wig around? I feel naked without it. I know all these people want me to go, but that's okay, man. I don't like them anyway. I'm goin' away to Spain when I get my money saved. I'm gonna start tomorrow. I'm gonna kick tomorrow!

"Out there in the fields I fought for my meals. I get my back into my living. I don't need to fight to prove I'm right. I don't need to be forgiven. Don't cry. Don't raise your eye. It's only teenage wasteland.

"Sergio take my hand, travel south across this land. Put out the fire and don't look past my shoulder. The exodus is here; the happy ones are near. Let's get together before we get much older. Teenage wasteland. It's only teenage wasteland."

It was clear that Janie was still hung up on this Sergio fella. But eventually the conversation shifted back to me and my plans for the near future. I told her about leaving home and my attempts at being a musician. I was a traveling band, all right, a one-man traveling band. I must have sounded enthusiastic because she seemed to hang on my every word about traveling west, free as a bird. Then, without warning, she asked me if I was staying in town. I had to tell her the truth.

"If I leave here tomorrow, would you still remember me? For I must be traveling on now, because there's too many places I've got to see. But, if I stayed here with you, girl, things just couldn't be the same because I'm as free as a bird now. And this bird you cannot change. Lord knows, I can't change!"

I decided to tell Janie exactly how I felt.

"In the day we sweat it out in the streets of a runaway American dream. At night we ride through mansions of glory in suicide machines sprung from cages out on Highway 99. Chrome wheeled, fuel-injected, and stepping out over the line. Baby, this town rips the bones from your back. It's a death trap. It's a suicide rap. We gotta get out while we're young because tramps like us, Janie, we were born to run.

"Janie, let me in, I wanna be your friend. I want to guard your dreams and visions. Just wrap your legs around these velvet rims and strap your hands across my engines. Together we could break this trap. We'll run until we drop. Baby, we'll never go back. Will you walk with me out on the wire, because, Baby, I'm just a scared and lonely rider, but I gotta know how it feels. I want to know if your love is wild. Girl, I want to know if love is real.

"Back in New York, hemi-powered drones scream down the boulevard. The girls comb their hair in rearview mirrors, and the boys try to look so hard. The amusement park rises bold and stark. Kids are huddled on the beach in a mist. I wanna die with you, Janie, on the streets tonight in an everlasting kiss.

"The highway's jammed with broken heroes on a last chance power drive. Everyone's out on the run tonight, but there's no place left to hide. Together, Janie, we can live with the sadness. I'll love you with all the madness in my soul. Someday, girl, I don't know when, we're gonna get to that place where we really want to go, and we'll walk in the sun. But, until then, tramps like us, Janie, we were born to run."

Janie seemed to understand where I was coming from.

"Have you ever thought about what it would be like to go back the way you came? I have nothing cooking. I could go with you. What would that be like?

"Joe, it must have been my lucky Thursday. Sergio went on that spree. Before the crew could put out the fires, we hopped a bus for New York City. Down in Detroit, the future looked desperate and dark. Now, I'm the wonder waif of Gramercy Park.

"Let's grab some takeout from Dean and Deluca, a hearty gulping wine. I'll be the showgirl, and you be Sinatra way back in '59. Sweetness in heels…look at me in long black gloves. I'm coming to old blue eyes to ask him…who do you love?

"Let's plan a weekend alone together, drive out to Binky's place, the sugar shack in Pennsylvania or would that be a federal case? We'll take the Big Red, the Blazer. It's nice inside and guess who's coming along for the ride?

"Who has a friend named Melanie? Who's not afraid to try new things? Who gets to spend her birthday in Spain? Possibly me…Janie Runaway!"

Binky's place? I didn't know anybody named Binky. What a sense of humor Janie had! Or was it the alcohol or the drugs? What difference does it make? She's certainly alive so I kept the conversation going.

After I mentioned my dreams of our future and talked more about my new old Harley, Janie looked out of the window behind the bar for a long, long moment. I pointed to my Harley through the bar window and asked her whether she had ever ridden cross-country on one. She sort of nodded affirmatively and told me Sergio had a motorcycle, but she said that it was much smaller than my Harley.

All of a sudden she was very quiet. She turned to whisper to me.

"Don't get me wrong, if I'm looking kind of dazzled. I see neon lights in your blue eyes. Don't get me wrong if you say 'Hello', and I take a ride upon a sea where the mystic moon is playing havoc with the tide. Don't get me wrong if I'm acting so distracted. I'm thinking about the fireworks that go off when you smile. Don't get me wrong if I split like light refracted. I'm only off to wander across a moonlit mile.

"Once in a while two people meet, seemingly for no reason. They pass on the street. Suddenly, thunder showers everywhere. Who can explain the thunder and rain? But there's something in the air. Don't get me wrong if I come and go like fashion. I might be great tomorrow but hopeless yesterday.

"Don't get me wrong if I fall in the mode of passion. It might be unbelievable, but let's not say, 'So long.' It might just be fantastic. Don't get me wrong."

Then she turned slowly and looked into my eyes. She didn't have to say a thing. I knew exactly what she was thinking!

"Roll, roll me away. Won't you roll me away tonight? I too am lost. I feel double-crossed. And I'm sick of what's wrong and what's right. I've never been in love. I don't know what it is. I only know if someone wants me. I want them if they want me. When I get mad, I start to cry, and I take a swing, but I can't hit anything. I don't mean no harm. I just don't know what else to do about it."

I was feeling better and better with each passing moment. Janie seemed to be a true kindred spirit. Then, she spoke some words that reminded me of Sally.

"Spent the last year, Rocky Mountain way, couldn't get much higher," Janie whispered as she dreamed of Colorado. "Out to pasture, think it's safe to say…time to open fire. And we don't need the ladies crying because the story's sad. Because the Rocky Mountain way is better than the way we had."

We didn't say another word. We paid for our drinks. We just walked out hand in hand and there on the sidewalk blocking our way stood this man, and he exclaimed that his name was Sergio. He grabbed Janie and pulled her aside as he spoke to me.

"Oh, my, Janie's sitting in the sun. Go buy a candy and a currant bun. I'm high! Don't try to spoil my fun. Don't cry, we'll roll another one."

He looked at her.

"You got your book, baby, with all your fears. Let me, honey, and I'll catch your tears. I'll take your sorrow if you want me to. Come tomorrow, that's what I'll do.

"Well, you say you got no dreams to touch. You feel like a stranger, babe, who knows too much. Well, you come home late and get undressed. You lie in bed, feel this emptiness. Well, listen to me. Janie, don't you lose heart!

"Until every river runs dry. Until the sun's honey is torn from the sky. Until every fear you felt bursts free and goes tumbling down into the sea. Listen to me. Janie, don't you lose heart."

Sergio's voice was now a seductive whisper.

"Oh, don't touch me, child. Please, you know you drive me wild. Please, you know I'm feeling frail. Oh, don't talk to me. Please, just walk with me. It's true, the sun's shining very bright. It's you I'm gonna love tonight. Ice cream tastes good if you eat it right. Ice cream tastes good if you treat it right.

"I'm high, don't try to spoil the fun. Go cry, Janie, or I'll have another one."

By now I was really confused. Before I could ask any of the pertinent questions, Sergio went on.

"Her whole world's come undone from looking straight at the sun. What did her daddy do? What did he put her through?"

Sergio was talking to both of us as if he knew we were leaving for good.

"They say when Janie was arrested, they found him underneath a train. But, man, he had it coming. Now that Janie's got a gun, she ain't never gonna be the same."

Both Sergio and Janie were staring at Janie's purse. She hadn't said that she was packing a weapon, but I wanted an explanation before making any judgments.

"Her dog days just begun. Now everybody is on the run. Tell her now it's untrue. What did her daddy do? He jacked the little bitty baby. The man has got to be insane! They say the spell that he was under, the lightning and the thunder, knew that someone had to stop the pain. Run away, run away from the pain.

"She had to take him down easy and put a bullet in his brain. She said that nobody believes me. The man was such a sleeze. He ain't never gonna be the same.

"Honey, Honey, what's your problem? Tell me it ain't right. Was it daddy's cradle robbing that made you scream at night?

"Her dog days have just begun. Now, everybody's on the run. Janie's got a gun!"

Janie gritted her teeth and growled at Sergio.

"You're trying to make your mark in society. You're using all the tricks that you used on me. You're reading all them high fashion magazines. The clothes you're wearing, Sergio, are causing public scenes.

"When I first met you, Sergio, you didn't have no shoes. Now you're walking around like you're front page news. You've been awful careful about the friends you choose. But you won't find my name in your book of who's who. I'm not your stepping stone!"

Sergio pumped his right hand in the air with his index finger extended, and then he pointed that finger straight at Janie.

"Well, Janie's got a doctor who tears apart her insides. He investigates her, and he silently abates her sighs. He probes with his fingers, but he knows her heart only through his stethoscope. Hands are cold and his body's so old. Janie turns him down like a dope.

"Well, Janie's got a priest. From his marble pulpit he smiles. He provides conciliations and confessions at any time. Through the pages of his Bible he holds from what Janie hides. With her doors open wide she begs him to come inside. But he's frozen in the clear on the outside.

"Well, Janie's got a cop who lives around the block and checks on her every night. From at the jail outside her house his siren roars when he knows that I'm inside. Well, Janie's small, and sometimes he scares her. So, I held her real close. She flowed like a ghost. And I told her goodbye, so long, I can't play that dope.

"Janie needs a shooter, Joey, a shooter like me on her side. Janie needs a shooter, Joey, a shooter man who knows her style the way I know her style.

"Further on up the road, someone's gonna hurt you like you hurt me. You gotta reap just what you sow. That old saying is true. Just like you mistreat someone, someone's gonna mistreat you.

"You been laughing pretty baby, someday you're gonna be crying. Further on up the road, you'll find out I wasn't lying. Further on up the road, Baby, just you wait and see."

Sergio turned around and without another word he walked away. I looked at Janie, and she just shrugged her shoulders.

"Get your motor running. Head out on the highway looking for adventure and whatever comes our way. Yeah, darlin', go make it happen. Take the world in a love embrace. Fire all of your guns at once and explode into space.

"I like smokin' lightning, heavy metal thunder, racing with the wind, and this feeling that I'm under. Like a true nature's child, we were born to be wild. We can climb so high. I never want to die! Born to be wild."

I didn't want to know what was in her purse. After a few moments, we got on that bike, and we rolled. And we rolled clean out of sight. We rolled across the high plains deep into the mountains. It felt so good to me finally feeling free.

9
Black Diamond Bay

It seems just like yesterday, but it was long ago. Janie was lovely, she was the queen of my nights, there in the darkness with the radio playing low. And the secrets that we shared, the mountains that we moved, caught like a wildfire out of control 'till there was nothing left to burn and nothing left to prove.

She is my low rider. Some say she's bad, but she's better than no rider. She carries a .45 on her hip. She takes no bother. She takes no lip. So put your hands on my rider today. In the morning I get my kicks, when she shows me all her tricks. A love of mine. You know she's fine. She is my low rider.

And I remember what she said to me, how she swore it would never end. I remember how she held me, oh so tight. Wish I didn't know now what I didn't know then. Against the wind, we were running against the wind. We were young and strong; we were running against the wind.

I know there's a place you walked where love falls from the trees. My heart is like a broken cup; I only feel right on my knees. I spit out like a sewer-hole, yet still receive your kiss. How can I measure up to anyone now after such a love as this.

Janie had her own vision of the future.

"When the sun is in the mid-sky, he wears a golden crown, and he soaks the world with sunshine as he makes another round. It's been a faster year than yesterday, all the things that I had planned, and when I think I might be gaining, I'm in the sunshine again. Well, I walk the road of life among the strong, among the weak, and I ask them for the shortcut to the answers that I seek. But, it seems nobody understands what is and what will be. Oh, the questions of my childhood weave a web of mystery.

"Can you get me through these changes? Well, I sure don't know about life, but one thing for sure. We got to get the golden key to unlock the door. I don't need to face a world of disillusion. I've come to one conclusion that I know you know is true. In the game of silent searching, the cost of love is rising. And I'm just now realizing that it's between Sergio and you.

"It's a game that I've been living now. I need to know what's real. Can you help me find the answers? Can you tell the way I feel? Will you stay with me forever? Just stay with me tonight. And we can talk about tomorrow if it all works out all right."

Somewhere along a high road the air began to turn cold. She said she missed her home. Eventually, she showed me a letter from Sergio asking her to come back to him. He wanted her to meet him at a place called Black Diamond Bay. She wouldn't tell me where it was, but my best guess was somewhere in Montana or Washington State. I was wrong. It was Hawaii! She also had a one-way airline ticket. I told her I would take her to the nearest bus station, but first I said goodbye.

"Jane, you say it's all over for you and me, girl. There's a time for love and a time for letting it be, baby. Jane, you're playing a game called…called hard to get by its real name. Making believe that you still don't feel the same. Oh, Jane.

"Jane, you're playing a game you never can win, girl. You're going away just so I can ask you where you been, baby. Like a cat and a mouse, from door to door, from house to house. Don't you pretend you don't know what I'm talking about.

"Were all those nights we spent together only because you didn't know better? I've got to know, Jane. You're playing a game. Jane, you're playing a game of hide and go seek. You're playing for fun, but I play for keeps. Yes I do!"

I knew it was over. It was time to make the break.

"Loving you isn't the right thing to do. How can I ever change things that I feel? If I could, maybe I'd give you my world. How can I when you won't take it from me? Tell me why everything turned around. Packing up, shacking up is all you wanna do. If I could, Janie, I'd give you my world. Open up, everything's waiting for you.

"You can go your own way, go your own way. You can call it another lonely day. You can go your own way..."

The words made me feel terrible, but they had to be voiced.

"Goodbye, Girl. It's time to part. When you leave me, you take my heart. Better get a start and get back, get back to the one you love. No one told me, I just knew there was nothing I can do to make you stay true. Well, it's time that you do get back to the one you love.

"Goodbye, Girl, this might sound strange, but I told you when I met you that you'd change. Better get that plane and make it home, get back to the one you love."

And then, I turned away and headed on alone.

I was tired of the road so I stopped at a motel in Twin Peaks. I must have really been tired because I slept for almost eighteen hours the first night and fourteen the next. Finally, I dragged myself to the couch and decided to watch television for a while. But it was the dream about Janie I had that bothered me most. It went something like this.

Up on the white veranda Jane wears a necktie and a Panama hat. Her passport shows a face from another time and place, she looks nothing like that. And all the remnants of her recent past are scattered in the wild wind. She walks across the marble floor where a voice from the gambling room is calling her to come on in. She smiles, walks the other way as the last ship sails and the moon fades away from Black Diamond Bay.

Sergio appears in the doorway and calls to Jane.

"Like a fool I went and stayed too long. Now I'm wondering if your love's still strong? Then that time I went and said goodbye. Now I'm back and not ashamed to cry. Done a lot of foolish things that I really didn't mean. Oh-wee, baby, you set my soul on fire. That's why I know you're my one desire. I could be a broken man, but here I am."

Sergio strides across the intervening distance a smile on his face.

"Here I am, Janie, signed, sealed and delivered, I'm yours!"

He took Janie in his arms and gave her a hug.

"When I lost you, Janie, sometimes I think I lost my guts, too. And I wish God would send me a word, send me something I'm afraid to lose. Lying in the heat of the night like prisoners all our lives. I get shivers down my spine, and all I want to do is hold you tight."

Just then Sergio hesitated for a moment when he felt a slight shaking in the floor.

"Tonight there are fallen angels, and they're waiting for us down in the street. Tonight they are calling strangers, hear them crying in defeat. Let them do their dances of the dead. You just dry your eyes, Janie, and come, let's go to bed.

"There are machines and there's fire waiting on the edge of town. They're out there for hire, but, Janie, they can't hurt us now because you've got my love. Through the wind, through the rain, the snow, the wind, and the pain, you've got my love."

Again there was a slight shaking in the building as if some construction work were being performed nearby with a jack-hammer. Sergio went on.

"When I was very young, so many songs were sung, so much wasted time on an uphill climb. But you were always there, a feeling in the air. There was nothing to fear. You were so near. Now you are here once again. As I stand in your presence, I can feel the quiet patience of your gaze. Like an old superstition, you are haunting all my dreams and waking days.

"There's no resisting you among the chosen few. It's hard to be sure; it's hard to endure. And when I hear your voice I know I have the choice to pursue an ideal, something so real. Now I've got nothing to lose. As I see your reflection, all the answers I desire become so clear. Like a page that is turning, I can look into the future without fear.

"You're in my rock and roll. You're in my very soul. Though it's heavy to bear, it's a feeling so rare. And it's a mystery, the way it's meant to be. Can we ever know; we're moving so slow. There ain't enough time in the world.

"As I reach up the ladder, there is something ever higher to perceive. Like a fire that is burning, in my heart I know I surely must believe."

Janie smiles at Sergio and starts to walk away. He grabs her by the arm and issues a warning.

"I'm tired of putting up with your sober ways. Tired of looking at you through an alcoholic haze. You'd better change. I'm begging you please. Because if you don't start drinking, I'm gonna leave!

"I wake up in the morning. I'm under the roof. But, I get no sympathy, Janie, you're too aloof. You better change. Yes, I'm begging you please. Budweiser, Budweiser, Miller Lite. Take a little nip, Janie, it's all right. All a fellow wants is company. Come on, Janie, have a taste with me.

"Yeah, you say it's all right, Janie, you don't care. But as soon as I indulge, I get that icy stare. Don't give me no lectures about stress and strife. Sobriety just ain't my way of life. You better change. Yes, I'm begging you please. Because if you don't start drinking, I'm gonna leave."

Janie loved to drink, but she shook her head anyway, and she turned her back on Sergio and walked away.

As the morning light breaks open, the Greek come down, and he asks for a rope and a pen that will write. "Pardon, Monsieur," the desk clerk says, carefully removing his fez. "Am I hearing you right?" And as the yellow fog is lifting, the Greek is quickly heading for the second floor. Janie passes him on the spiral staircase thinking he's the Soviet Ambassador. She starts to speak, but he walks away as the storm clouds rise and the palm branches sway on Black Diamond Bay.

Sergio sits beneath the fan doing business with a tiny man who sells him a ring.

"Women think I'm tasty, but they're always trying to waste me and make me burn the candle right down. Little man, I don't need no jewels in my crown. 'Cause all them women is low down gamblers, cheating like I don't know how. There's fever in the funk house now. This low down bitchin' got my poor feet itchin'. You know, you know the deuce is still wild. Can't stay! You gotta roll me and call me the tumbling dice.

"Always in a hurry. I never stop to worry. Don't you see the time flashing by? I got no money. I'm all sevens and sixes and nines. Say, little man, I'm the rank outsider. You can be my partner in crime. I'm the lone crap shooter playing the field every night. You gotta roll me and call me the tumbling dice."

Suddenly, lightning strikes and the lights blow out. The desk clerk awakes and begins to shout, "Can you see anything?"

Then the Greek appears on the second floor in his bare feet with a rope around his neck, while the loser in the gambling room, lights up a candle and says, "Open up another deck." But the dealer says, "Attendez-vous, s'il vous plait," as the rain beats down and the cranes fly away from Black Diamond Bay.

The desk clerk heard Janie laugh, as he looked around the aftermath, and Sergio got tough. He tried to grab Janie's hand and said, "Here's a ring; it cost a grand." She said, "That ain't enough." Right there, Sergio realized his fate and began to lament it.

"Riding the storm out. Waiting for the thaw out on a full moon night just like in the Rocky Mountain winter. My wine bottle's low. I'm watching for the snow. I've been thinking lately of what I've been missing in the city. And I'm not missing a thing. Watching the full moon crossing the range. Riding the storm out.

"My lady's beside me. She's here to guide me. She says that alone we've finally found home. The wind outside is frightening, but it's kinder than the lightning. This is a hard life to live, but it gives back what you give.

"I'm so hot for her, and she's so cold. I'm the burning bush; I'm the burning fire; I'm the bleeding volcano!

"Yeah, I tried re-wiring her, tried re-firing her. I think her engine is permanently stalled. She's so cold, like a tombstone. She's so cold, cold, cold like an ice cream cone, and when I touched her, my hand just froze.

"Janie was born in an artic zone. Who would believe you were a beauty indeed when the days get shorter and the nights get long. Lie awake when the rain comes, nobody will know when you're old. When you are old, nobody will know that you were a beauty, a sweet, sweet beauty, but stone, stone cold.

"I'm so hot for you, and you're so cold. I'm the burning bush; I'm the burning fire; I'm the bleeding volcano."

Janie just turned away and cast a casual glance at her gold watch, one that Sergio hadn't seen before. Sergio had more to say.

"Rock on, gold dust woman, take your silver spoon, dig your grave. Heartless challenge, pick your path and I'll pray. Wake up in the morning, see your sunrise loves to go down. Lousy lovers, pick their prey, but they never cry out loud.

"Well, did he make you cry, make you break down, shatter your illusions of love? And is it over now, do you know how to pick up the pieces and go home? Rock on ancient queen, follow those who pale in your shadow. Rulers make bad lovers; you better put your kingdom up for sale.

"Black shadow of a woman, black widow. Pale shadow of a dragon, death woman. Pale shadow of a woman, black widow. Pale shadow, you're a dragon, a death woman."

With those words Sergio went back and sat by the little man in the corner. Janie just stood there seemingly mesmerized by Sergio's words. The little man shook his head as he thought of days past.

"Frank Zappa and the Mothers were at the best place around. But someone stupid with a flare gun burned the place to the ground. Smoke on the water. Fire in the sky."

Just then a bolt of lightning struck a nearby hill causing Sergio to jump into the air. The little man laughed and pointed to the casino.

"They burned down the gambling house. It died with an awful sound. And Funky Claude was running in and out pulling kids out to the ground. When it was all over, we had to find another place, but time was running out. It seemed that we would lose the race.

"We ended up here at Black Diamond Bay. Then it was empty, cold, and bare. With a few red lights and a few old beds, we made a place to sweat. No matter whether or not we get out of this, I know we'll never forget. Smoke on the water! Fire in the sky!"

"Well, little man, it seems it's happening again," whispered Sergio. "There is smoke on the water. There is fire in the sky."

The little man pulled a bottle out of his pocket and dumped he contents on the floor. Sergio saw a number of colored pills rolling toward him. The little man explained that he had been saving these for a special occasion.

"One pill makes you larger, and one pill makes you small. And the ones that mother gives you don't do anything at all. Go ask Alice, when she's ten feet tall.

"And if you go chasing rabbits and you know you're going to fall, tell 'em a hookah-smoking caterpillar has given you the call. Call Alice when she was just small.

"When the men on the chessboard get up and tell you where to go, and you've just had some kind of mushroom and your mind is moving slow, go ask Alice, I think she'll know.

"When logic and proportion have fallen sloppy dead and the white knight is talking backwards and the red queen's off her head, remember what the dormouse said, 'Feed your heads, feed your head!'"

Then Janie ran upstairs to pack her bags, while a horse-drawn taxi waited at the curb. She passed the door that the Greek had locked, where a handwritten sign read, *Do Not Disturb.* Janie knocked upon it anyway as the sun went down and the music did play on Black Diamond Bay.

"I've got to talk to someone quick!", but the Greek said, "Go away," and he kicked the chair to the floor. He hung there from the chandelier. She cried, "Help, there's danger near. Please open the door!" Then the volcano erupted and the lava flowed down from the mountain high above. Sergio and the tiny man were crouched in the corner thinking of forbidden love. But the desk clerk said, "It happens every day," as the stars fell down and the fields burned away on Black Diamond Bay.

As the island slowly sank, the loser finally broke the bank in the gambling room. The dealer said, "It's too late now. You can take your money, but I don't know how you'll spend it in the tomb." Then the tiny man bit Sergio's ear, as the floor caved in and the boiler in the basement blew. Meanwhile, Janie's out on the balcony where a stranger tells her, "My darling, je vous aime beaucoup." She sheds a tear and then begins to pray as the fire burns on and the smoke drifts away from Black Diamond Bay.

But the man persists with his plea.

"I don't want to be your friend. I just want to be your lover. No matter how it ends. No matter how it starts. Forget about your house of cards and I'll do mine. The infrastructure will collapse. Voltage spikes. Throw your keys in the bowl. Kiss your boyfriend goodnight. Your ears should be burning. Fall off the table. Get swept under. Forget your house of cards."

Janie just shook her head negatively and goes back to praying.

"Now I don't know where I'm gonna go when the volcano blows." She paused for a moment and pondered her fate.

"Ground she's moving under me, tidal waves out on the sea. Sulfur smoke up in the sky. Pretty soon we learn to fly. Now, that stranger quickly say to me, Madam, you better watch your feet. Lava come down soft and hot. You better lava me now or lava me not.

"No time to count what I'm worth because I just left planet earth. Where I go I hope there's rum. Not to worry, Mon, soon come. But I don't want to land in New York City, don't want to land in Mexico… no, no, no. Don't want to land on no Three Mile Island; don't want to see my skin aglow…no, no, no.

"Don't want to land in Commanche Sky Park or in Nashville, Tennessee…no, no, no. Don't want to land in no San Juan airport or the Yukon Territory…no, no, no. Don't want to land no San Diego; don't want to land in no Buzzards' Bay…no, no, no. Don't want to land on no Ayotollah.

"I got nothing more to say!"

In her final moment Janie sadly watched as her Panama hat blew away. She recalled some of the final words Sergio whispered to her.

"Your breath is sweet. Your eyes are like two jewels in the sky. Your back is straight. Your hair is smooth on the pillow where you lie. But I don't sense affection. No gratitude or love. Your loyalty is not to me, but to the stars above. One more cup of coffee for the road. One more cup of coffee before I go to the valley below.

"Your daddy, he was an outlaw and a wanderer by trade. He taught you how to pick and choose and how to throw the blade. He oversaw his kingdom. No stranger could intrude. His voice it did tremble as he called out for another plate of food.

"Your sister sees the future like your momma and yourself. You've never learned to read or write. There's no books upon your shelve. And your pleasure knows no limits. Your voice is like a meadowlark. But, your heart is like an ocean, mysterious and dark. One more cup of coffee before I go to the valley below."

It was too late for that last cup of coffee. In seconds Black Diamond Bay was a smoldering mass of volcanic lava.

I was sitting alone in my room at Twin Peaks watching old Cronkite on the seven o'clock news. It seems there was an earthquake that left nothing but a Panama hat and a pair of old Greek shoes. The place sounded familiar, but I couldn't put a finger on it.

Didn't seem like much was happening, so I turned it off and went to grab another beer. Seems like every time you turn around there's another hard-luck story that your gonna hear, and there's really nothing anyone can say. And I never did plan to go anyway to Black Diamond Bay.

Eventually, I stood alone on a mountain top staring out at the great divide. I could go east; I could go west. It was all up to me to decide. Just then I saw a young hawk flying overhead, and my soul began to rise. The answer was clear.

Well, east coast girls are hip. I really dig the styles they wear. And, the southern girls with the way they talk, they knock me out when I'm down there. The Midwest farmers' daughters really make you feel all right. And the northern girls with the way they kiss, they keep their boyfriends warm at night. I wish they all could be California girls.

The west coast has the sunshine, and the girls all get so tanned. I dig a French bikini on a Hawaii island, dolls by a palm tree in the sand. In my dreams I've been all around this great world, and I seen all kind of girls. But I shouldn't wait to get to the cutest girls in the world. I wish they all could be California girls.

And pretty soon my heart was singing.

"Roll, roll me away. I'm gonna roll me away tonight. I've gotta keep rolling, gotta keep riding, keep searching until I find what's right."

And as the sunset faded, I spoke to the faintest first starlight and I said:

"Next time we'll get it right!"

And in my dream the years rolled slowly past, and I found myself alone, surrounded by strangers I thought were my friends. I found myself further and further from my home. And I guess I lost my way, there were oh so many roads. I was living to run and running to live, never worried about paying or even how much I owed, moving eight miles a minute for months at a time. Breaking all of the rules that would bend I began to find myself searching, searching for shelter, again and again.

Spent my days with a woman unkind, smoked my stuff and drank all my wine. Made up my mind to make a new start. Going to California with an aching in my heart. Someone told me there's a girl out there with love in her eyes and flowers in her hair. Not taken my chances on a big jet plane. Never let them tell you that they're all the same.

The sea was red and the sky was gray, wondered how tomorrow could ever follow today. The mountains and canyons started to tremble and shake as the children of the sun began to awake. Seems that the wrath of the gods got a punch in the nose, and it started to flow. I think I might be sinking!

Throw me a line. If I reach it in time, I'll meet you up there where the path runs straight and high.

To find a queen without a king; they say she plays guitar and cries and sings. Ride a white mare in the footsteps of dawn, trying to find a woman who's never, never, never been born.

Standing on a hill in my mountain of dreams, telling myself it's not as hard, hard, hard as it seems.

Driving on a beat-up Harley, better than a car. The highway is long, but I've come so far. Two thousand miles from home, I've got to find some place where I belong.

Heading out into the sun, I've been to the stars, and I've only begun. Nothing's gonna change my mind. There are songs to be sung, but I've left them behind.

I'm going to California!

But, first, all the way to Reno. Dusted the non-believers and challenged the laws of chance. Now sweeter, I'm so sugar sweet. I might as well have 'kick me' fastened on my sleeve. I know what I am. I'm gonna be a star.

Wing is written on my feet. My Achilles heel is my tendency to dream. But I've known from the beginning that I didn't have to go so far. I'm gonna be a star! I've written my own directions and whistles the rules have changed. I know what I am. I'm gonna be a star.

I decided to follow the sun toward a meaningful life or at least one where I could have some fun. The decision wasn't hard to make.

There was nothing or no one I had to fake. Just pick up my guitar and turn my bike west. And there, over the mountains, I would renew my quest.

10
Wild Thing

I went walking in the park just the other day, Janie. What do you think I saw? Crowds of people sitting on the grass with flowers in their hair said, 'Hey, Boy, do you wanna score?' And you know how it is. I really don't know what time it was. So I asked them if I could stay awhile. I didn't notice, but it had gotten very dark, and I was really out of my mind.

Just then a policeman stepped up to me and asked if we would all get in line. They asked us to stay for tea and have some fun. He said his friends would all drop by. He said 'Why don't you take a good look at yourself and describe what you see. Do you like it? There you sit like a book on a shelf rusting, not trying to fight it. You really don't care if they're coming. I know that it's all a state of mind.'

If you go down in the streets today, you better open your eyes. Folk down here really don't care which way the pressure lies. So, I've decided what I'm gonna do now. So, I'm packing my bags for the misty mountains where the spirits go. Over the hill where the spirits fly.

As I checked out of the motel in Twin Peaks, I asked one of the clerks what the best route to California was. He said that if he were going, he'd head straight for San Francisco. And he had some advice for me.

"If you're going to San Francisco, be sure to wear some flowers in your hair. If you're going to San Francisco, you're gonna meet some gentle people there. For those who come to San Francisco, summertime will be a love-in there. In the streets of San Francisco, gentle people with flowers in their hair.

"All across the nation such a strange vibration, people in motion. There's a whole generation with a new explanation. People in motion beget people in motion. If you come to San Francisco, summertime will be a love-in there."

I thanked him and gave him a big tip. He made me feel a lot better when he told me of some of his experiences.

"Sitting in a park in Paris, France. Reading the news, and it sure looks bad. They won't give peace a chance. That was just a dream some of us had. Still a lot of lands to see, but I wouldn't want to say there. It's too old and cold and settled in its way there. Oh, but California, I'm coming home. I'm going to see the folks I dig. I'll even kiss a sunset pig.

"I met a redneck on a Grecian isle who did the goat dance very well. He gave me back my smile, but he kept my camera to sell. He cooked good omelettes and stews, but my heart cried out for you, California.

"So, I bought me a ticket. I caught a plane to Spain. Went to a party down a red dirt road. There were lots of pretty people there reading Rolling Stone and Vogue. They said, 'How long can you hang around?' I said, 'A week, maybe two. Just until my skin turns brown. Then I'm going home to California.'

"California, I'm coming home!"

Soon, as I sat on my bike, I started analyzing my situation.

It's a long, long highway. Will this road of life lead me to someone who sees the world in a grain of sand, who holds the future in the palm of her hand? Oh, no one else can see things like I do.

It's a long, long highway looking for a home where the seed was sown and the harvest was young. Will this road of life lead me to someone?

The rays of the sun and the light of dawn, my inspiration since the day I was born. But don't make the start on an empty heart. When I think I've begun, let the road of life lead me to someone.

Nothing is serious to me. I live for what will be. I can always be a dreamer, so trust my heart, don't fall apart. I touched the dream that was in my eyes. I took so long only to realize, oh, no one else can love like I do.

Rocking Robin in the tree. Won't you come down here and rescue me. Because there's someplace else I gotta see, and you can stand in for me...for a while. Come on now, hurry down. No time to play around.

I need someone to walk this mile, I jumped and said like a child. Love is gone, but now I see, you've got to capture me to set me free.

Miss Sally came to me in a dream. She said, 'Boy, come and walk with me. There's some place I've got to see.' So, we strolled along the mountain high. She called me 'Boy', my friend. And I wondered if or even when I'd see Colleen and my Janie again. The time has come for dealing.

Lessons learned, but now I see. You've got to capture me to set me free. I flew on the wings of a bird. And I whispered names of girls I once knew. Then they disappeared into a fallen stream.

I thought about Janie one last time. I imagined her face and shape sitting next to me.

"I wonder where you are tonight? You're probably on the rampage somewhere. You have been known to take delight in getting in somebody's hair. And you always had the knack…fade to black.

"I bet you already made a pass. I see a darkened room somewhere. You run your finger around the rim of his glass. You run your fingers through his hair. They scratch across his back…fade to black.

"Well, maybe it's all for the best. But I wish I'd never been lassoed. Maybe it's some kind of test. But I wish I'd never been tattooed or been to hell and back…fade to black."

I rolled down the road for a few hours, and then stopped at a café similar to the one in Wisconsin where I met Janie. There were a couple single what I would call biker girls at the bar. I know it was a stupid thing to do, but I thought I'd just come right out and ask if one of them wanted to hit the road with me to California. They realized that I had arrived on a Harley so at least I had the minimum qualification to ask the question.

I pulled out my guitar, which at least caused them to smile as they awaited my proposal.

"If I strum chords, would you sing a song with me? If I leave town, would you leave along with me. We can fly away to outer space. We can find a way to leave this place.

"We don't need a map, and you can throw your phone away. We don't wanna hear the things we know they're gonna say. You don't trust yourself, but girl trust in me. Don't look in the mirror, the past you don't wanna see. If we leave our friends, then we can be together. We can leave this town if only for the weather.

"What do you say we leave for California. If we drive all night, we can make it by the morning. And no one has to know if we decide to go. What do you say we leave for California?"

The members of my audience of three biker girls were all shaking their heads negatively. But they gave me credit for a nice try, and one of them named Alice even suggested one of her girlfriends as my possible companion on this trip. I guess I just wasn't up for a blind date so I politely declined.

I wished Alice and her friends goodbye. They were very kind because they said that if I happened back this way, I should look them up. They even gave me a card bearing their names and telephone numbers. I had a warm feeling as a walked away. I began to realize that people out west are more friendly than those back home.

Yet, happily, I was on the road again! Just couldn't wait to get on the road again. The life I love is making music with my friends. And, I can't wait to get on the road again. Going places that I've never been. Seeing things that I may never see again.

Like a band of gypsies, my imaginary friends and I go down the highway. We're the best of friends insisting that the world keep turning our way. And our way is on the road again. One of them began singing his song to me.

"Well, you can tell by the way I use my walk, I'm a woman's man, no time to talk. Music loud and women warm. I've been kicked around since I was born. And now it's all right, it's O.K. And, you may look the other way. We can try to understand the New York Times' effect on man. Whether you're a brother or whether you're a mother, you're stayin' alive, stayin' alive.

"Feel the city breakin' and everybody shakin', and we're stayin' alive! Well, now, I get low and I get high. And if I can't get either, I really try. Got the wings of heaven on my shoes. I'm a dancin' man, and I just can't lose. You know, it's all right, it's okay. I'll live to see another day. I'm stayin' alive."

Suddenly, my imaginary friends disappeared, but I was still humming the tune as my Harley and I headed south toward Lodi, California.

"Life goin' nowhere. Somebody help me! I'm stayin' alive."

This whole fiasco began in earnest when I decided that I needed a steadier job than my music allowed. As it turned out, that was a big mistake. This decision would evolve into a huge problem for me. It turned out to be something completely different than I expected, as you will soon see. I came into town on a Greyhound bus, but as it soon became clear, if I left town, I was going to be walking out. My Harley was just down the road from Lodi getting some much needed repairs.

With some luck that involves a long story of its own, I got a gig replacing a sick guitar player in a local band in Lodi. Naturally, I asked the band members about the local job market, and they were unanimous in suggesting that harvest season meant I could easily get a job on a local farm. The drummer, Earl, was very enthusiastic about his spread.

"Bought myself a farm way out in the country. Took to growing lettuce, milking cows, and honey. Spent some time in the hayloft with the mice and the bunnies. Spent time in the country. Yes, it's good living on the farm.

"Here comes my next door neighbor coming down the road. He always looks so regal riding on his toad named Lightning. Really, the toad's name is Lightning. He's ten hands at the shoulder. And if you give him sugar, you know he'll whinny like a boulder, yes, he will.

"Well, I gotta get back to work now and clear away some logs. Ah, the sun is shining westwards. Yeah, I think I'll saddle up my frog and get outta here."

I immediately made a note to myself to ask the boys for help only when they are sober and not doing drugs, which Earl was not. But, his remarks didn't hurt. I was out of sorts and out of cash and my Harley was in the shop for repairs for a blown head gasket, so in desperation I answered an ad in the local newspaper for a job as a farm hand near Lodi.

Lodi is in California for those of you who are geographically challenged. The owner of the spread that ran the newspaper ad was a very mean middle-aged woman everyone called Maggie McGuire. She lived there with her mother, her father, her sister and her brother. There were already several farm hands working the land at the place when I arrived, probably because they were as broke as I was because no one in their right mind would do that kind of work voluntarily. But, as fate would have it, one of them was a beautiful, bright-eyed young girl named Linda Lou.

I'll never forget the first time I saw her. It wasn't on the farm. It happened a few weeks earlier on a night when I was playing guitar for the band I mentioned before in a local bar. I know that I'm repeating myself, but how I got into the band is a whole 'nother story for later.

Linda Lou had the prettiest smile, and I couldn't forget her deep dark eyes. In my head I knew right then and there that she could and should be the love of my life. I had never thought that way about anyone before.

"Winding paths through tables and glass. First fall was new. Now watch the summer pass so close to you. Too late to keep the change. Too late to pay. No time to stay the same. Too young to leave. No pass out sign on the door set me thinking. Are waitresses paying the price of their winking? While stars sit in bars and decide what they're drinking, they drop by to die because it's faster than sinking.

"Find out that now was the answer to answers that you gave later. You did the things that we both did before now, but who forgave you? If I could stand to see you crying, I would tell you not to care. When you learn of all my problems, will you join me there?

"Country girl, I think you're pretty. Got to make you understand, I have no lovers in the city. Let me be your country man. Got to make you understand. I like the way your sparkling earrings lay against your skin so brown, to sleep with you in the desert tonight with a billion stars all around. Because I got a peaceful, easy feeling, and I know you won't let me down because I'm already standing on the ground.

"And I found out a long time ago what a woman can do to your soul. Ah, but she can't take you anyway you don't already know how to go. I get this feeling I may know you as a lover and a friend, but this voice keeps whispering in my other ear, tells me I may never see you again."

I was broke and all I had was my Harley and my guitar, and working a temporary gig far from home. I never thought that I could get that so wrong. But for the very short time that things were clicking for me, it was wonderful.

Linda Lou and I had a few drinks…well, maybe more than a few. Almost immediately I began to tell her exactly what my heart felt about her.

"Wild Thing, you make my heart sing. You make everything… groovy!"

It sounded so good and so right that I said it again.

"Wild Thing…I think I love you. But I wanna know for sure. Come on, hold me tight. I love you. Wild thing, you make my heart sing; you make everything groovy. Wild Thing, I think you move me, but I wanna know for sure. So come on, hold me tight! You move me."

Somehow I knew right then and there that this was the woman for me. She just had that look on her face. I met a devil woman; she took my heart away. She said I had it coming to me, but I wanted it that way. I think that any love is good lovin', and so I took what I could get. Mmmm, Oooh, Oooh. Linda Lou looked at me with those big brown eyes and said, "You ain't seen nothing yet!"

"B-B-B-Baby, you just ain't seen nothing yet. Here's something that you're never gonna forget. B-B-B-Baby, you just ain't seen nothing yet."

And then I was feeling better because I found out for sure. She took me to her doctor, and he told me of a cure. He said that any love is good love, so I took what I could get, yes, I took what I could get. Oooh, and she looked at me with those big brown eyes and said, "You ain't seen nothing yet!"

"But it's gonna take money," I said, "a whole lot of spendin' money to do it right, child. It's gonna take time, a whole lotta precious time to do it right, child. It's gonna take patience and time. I got my mind set on you.

"And this time I know it's for real, the feelings that I feel. I know if I put my mind to it, I know that I really can do it. I got my mind set on you!"

As the evening wore on, I realized that I had to return to get to a band rehearsal. But I wanted her to know that I'd be back in a few hours.

"It's getting near dawn when lights close their tired eyes. I'll soon be with you my love to give you my dawn surprise. I'll be with you, darling, soon. I'll be with you when the stars start falling. I've been waiting so long to be where I'm going in the sunshine of your love.

"I'm with you my love; the light shining through on you. It will be the morning and just we two. I'll stay with you until my seeds are dried up. I've been waiting so long to be where I'm going in the sunshine of your love."

The spirit was moving me. I had to tell her.

"Hey there, woman, I came to California to find a dream. I found you, girl! Hey there, baby, you pointed in my direction with tender love, changed my world. I've been reaching for love so long. I've just had a holiday to have you here. I've been running down avenues so filled with solitude and restless fears.

"I set sail on a rainy day steering my way through a cloudy sky. In this heaven my dreams are never ending. They're sending me through space and time. You're the center of all my inspiration. It's wonderful. It's so divine. I can't escape from this energy. You put a spell on me. No turning around. Power of love has no gravity. It's got a hold on me. I'm paralyzed.

"Danger, slow down, haunting me. Your love, turning me around, rescued me. Distant dreams of yesterday, when I was down and far away. You promise me love, but I'm scared of losing what I've got today. Danger! Slow down!"

11
Down on the Farm

Out in the middle of nowhere gathered around in the barn, animals all in agreement. They were down on the farm. There was talk of all the boring hours standing around with nothing to do. It was just another boring evening with a pail of boring things to chew. There were cows and horses and sheep and pigs. They were tired of the daily routine. They were planning on having themselves a bash. Gonna throw a great big wing-ding.

So, they said, 'Let's do it, play some rock and roll!' And they got all loose and had a few. And before they knew it, they were out of control. Turned into a regular zoo. They were tired of the daily routine. Having themselves a great big bash, they were gathering steam.

And a pig grabbed a chicken and said, 'Come on over. Let's doe-see-doe a few'. And the chick said, 'No, you're covered with mud'. Called him a pig, and it was true. And every gol' dang one of their tails was a-wagging under the old horseshoe.

That night the animals fell off the wagon and a tractor or two. Well, they were out in the middle of nowhere. They were rocking out in the barn. They were tearing it up in the hayloft, getting down on the farm.

But, working on Maggie's farm wasn't what I expected it to be despite the hip animals and the presence of Linda Lou. I used to wake up in the morning with my hands folded and pray for rain. I particularly remember my first day there. It was spent not in the field with the crops or in the barn with the animals. No, I was scrubbing floors in the house! The owners sang and drank while I slaved so I just got bored. Then they would tell me that I should strive to be just like them! It was total madness.

Every day that I awake I must be mindful that every day is all I have to call my own. It's every day the sun will rise even though the dark clouds seem so low. It will only tell the truth. I am alone.

Every day that I believe I must be mindful that every belief I have is all I own. Ten thousand roads will all return here only reaping what they've sown. And it will only tell the truth. I am alone.

Every day that I awake I must be mindful that every day is all I have for me to change, to see everything as it really is. Everything I have, I have to give, and it will only tell the truth. I am alone. We are alone together. We are all alone with each other.

It didn't take me long to realize that Maggie's Farm was not the answer to my financial problems. For a number of good reasons after a short while I decided not to work there anymore.

All Maggie wanted me to do was scrub the floor. It was never clean enough for her. And she would take liberties with me when I was down on my hands and knees. Every time she would walk past me she would pat me on the butt and call me 'honey'. I got a head full of ideas from those experiences that were driving me completely insane! Right then and there I realized that I shouldn't ever work on Maggie's farm no more.

Maggie's brother wasn't much better. After I finished my chores he would hand me a nickel and then hand me a dime and with the stupidest grin on his face he would ask if I was having a good time? He was a sadistic bastard. Then, he would take the money back because he would fine me every time I slammed the door! I'm definitely not gonna work for Maggie's brother no more.

But Maggie's father was even worse. Everyone referred to him as 'Pa'. He would put his cigar out right in my face just for kicks. And his bedroom window was made out of bricks of all things. But to top it off, the National Guard stands around his door! You guessed it. I ain't gonna work for Maggie's Pa no more.

Still, Maggie's mother…they called her 'Ma', of course, was the hardest to deal with. She was definitely the brains behind Pa. She would lecture all of us servants about man and God and law. What was worse though was the fact that she was sixty-eight years old but said she was twenty-four! I almost couldn't take it any more…Maggie's Ma that is.

I cornered one of the other farmhands, a thirty year old named Eddie who spoke with a light lisp. I needed to know whether I was making a gigantic mistake by working at Maggie's Farm. I explained my situation and that I wanted to be a musician. I wanted to know how he was doing since we seemed to be in the same boat.

"Taking chances, and your reputation is going down. Going out in the night time, good thing you make no sound. But you don't fool anyone because they know what you feel. If you ignore the things you see, someday soon you'll find your way down to Beggar's Farm.

"You pay your money for no returns. You think you gotta find someone. When you go wild, and you ask yourself why, don't worry when you find yourself lying down on Beggar's Farm.

"But they're on to you, gonna turn away. Won't even listen when you try to say that you were only kidding around. But, if you ask them nicely, they'll wake up early one day and come and visit you on Beggar's Farm."

Even with all these obvious faults there was still one good reason why I wanted to stay. It was bearable because Linda Lou was there. She seemed to like me…a lot. But then the worst possible thing happened for no apparent reason. One day, without a word, she was gone!

I found out when I went to the main barn to visit with her. The animals looked so sad. After a while I figured out why. The cows asked, the pigs asked and the horses asked, too. They all wanted to know why to the city she moved and changed her name to 'Kitty'. I was stunned so I immediately called her on the phone. When I heard her voice, I just let go.

"I went to town to see you yesterday, but you were not at home. So I talked to some old friends for a while before I wandered off alone. Well, I miss you more than ever, since you're gone I can hardly maintain. Things are different around here every night. My tears fall down like rain.

"It's so hard for me now, but I'll make it somehow. Though, I know I'll never be the same. Won't you ever change your ways? It's so hard to make love pay when you're on the losing end. And I feel that way again."

I looked around at the animals knowing they had a stake in this situation, too.

"Say it ain't true, Linda Lou! They's all bawling 'bout you down on Maggie's farm. The cows bawl, the pigs bawl, the horses bawl, too. We miss you so much, crying's all we can do. We are all weeping and wailing, praying you'll come home soon."

She told me she was working in a saloon. That was bad enough, but I almost passed out when she told me that her hours were from midnight 'till noon! I might be from the woods, but them hours don't sound so good. What could she be doin' in that barroom?

"Please say it ain't true, Linda Lou. You can't dance a lick and in a bag you can't carry a tune...!

"What I feel, I can't say. But my love is there for you any time of day. But if it's not love that you need, then I'll try my best to make everything succeed. Tell me, what is my life without your love? Tell me, who am I without you by my side.

"What I know, I can do if I give my love now to everyone like you. But if it's not love that you need, then I'll try my best to make everything succeed.

"Well, I gave you everything I had, but you left me sitting on my own. Did you have to treat me oh so bad? All I do is hang my head and moan. If there's something I have said or done, tell me what and I'll apologize. If you don't, I really can't go on holding back these tears in my eyes.

"Well, I beg you on my bended knees, if you'll only listen to my pleas. Is there anything I can do because I really can't stand it. I'm so in love with you.

"Tell me why you cried, and why you lied to me."

Linda Lou came back with her story.

"I bought a toothbrush, some toothpaste, a flannel for my face, pajamas, a hairbrush, new shoes and a case. I said to my reflection, 'Let's get out of this place!' Passed the church and the steeple, the laundry on the hill, billboards and the buildings. Memories of it still keep calling and calling. But, forget it all I know I will.

"I'm at the carpark, the airport, the baggage carousel. The people keep on grabbing, ain't wishing I was well. I said, 'It's no occasion. It's no story I can tell.' At my bedside, empty pocket, a foot without a sock. Your body gets much closer, I fumble for the clock. Alarmed by the seduction, I wish that it would stop.

"I bought a novel, some perfume, a fortune all for me. But it's not my conscience that hates to be untrue. I asked of my reflection, 'Tell me, what is there to do?' Tempted by the fruit of another. Tempted, but the truth is discovered, what's been going on. Now that I have gone, there's no other."

Linda Lou said she was tired of the farm and Lodi for that matter and that she wanted the excitement of the big city. I could tell from her voice that she had met someone else.

"Well, the times are getting hard for you little girl. I'm a hummin' and a strummin' all over God's world. You can't remember when you got your last meal, and you don't know just how a woman feels. You didn't know what rock-n-roll was until you met that drummer on the gray tour bus. I got there in the nick of time before he got his hands across your state line.

"Now it's the middle of the night on the open road. The heater don't work, and it's oh so cold. You're lookin' tired; you're lookin' kinda beat. The rhythm of the street sure knocks you off your feet. You didn't know how rock-n-roll looked until you caught your sister with the guys from the group halfway home in the parking lot. By the look in her eye, she was giving what she got.

"Woman, you're a mess, gonna die in your sleep. There's blood on my amp, and my Les Paul's beat. Can't keep you on the farm; you're messing around. My best friend told me you were the best lick in town. You didn't know that rock-n-roll burned, so you bought a candle and you lived and you learned. You got the rhythm; you got the speed. Mama's little baby likes it short and sweet.

"You told me I was the only one. But, look at you now; it's dark as it's dawn. I'm once bitten, twice shy."

When she didn't respond, I warned her of the temptations my mother had warned me of.

"Seven, seven, seven deadly sins. That's how the world begins. Watch out when you step in for the seven deadly sins. Seven deadly sins, that's when the fun begins. Once it starts, it ever ends. Watch out around the bend.

"Sin number one was when you left me. Sin number two…you said goodbye. Sin number three was when you told me a little white lie. Sin number four was when you looked my way. Sin number five was when you smiled. Sin number six was when you let me stay. Sin number seven was when you touched me and told me why.

"Seven deadly sins, so many rules to bend, time and time again."

With those words, Linda Lou hung up on me.

There's a lady who's sure all that glitters is gold, and she's buying a stairway to heaven. When she gets there she knows, if the stores are all closed, with a word she can get what she came for.

There's a sign on the wall, but she wants to be sure because you know sometimes words have two meanings. In a tree by the brook there's a songbird who sings. Sometimes all of our thoughts are mistaken. Oh, it makes me wonder.

There's a feeling I get when I look to the west, and my spirit is crying for leaving. In my thoughts I have seen rings of smoke through the trees and the voices of those who stand looking. Oh, it makes me wonder.

And it's whispered that soon if we all call the tune, then the piper will lead us to reason. And a new day will dawn for those who stand long, and the forests will echo with laughter. If there's a bustle in your hedgerow, don't be alarmed now; it's just a spring clean for the May queen.

Yes, there are two paths I can go by, but in the long run there's still time to change the road I'm on. And, it makes me wonder.

"Dearest Linda Lou, your head is humming, and I won't go. In case you don't know, the piper's calling you to join him. Dear Lady, can you hear the wind blow, and did you know your stairway lies on the whispering wind.

"And as she winds on down the road, her shadow's taller than her soul. There walks a lady we all know who shines white light and wants to show how everything still turns to gold. And if you listen very hard, the tune will come to you at last. When all are one and one is all, to be a rock and not to roll. And she's buying a stairway to heaven."

And the animals on Maggie's farm all agreed.

Little did I realize that my troubles had just begun. I went back to the local bar and got a gig playing the midnight to closing shift. I was just trying to forget.

I worked the bars and sideshows along the twilight zone. Only a crowd can make you feel so alone. And it really hit home. Booze and pills and powders, you can choose your medicine. Well, here's another goodbye to another good friend.

After all is said and done, gotta move while it's still fun. Let me walk before they make me run. After all is said and done, I gotta move. It's still fun! I'm gonna walk before they make me run.

Watched the taillights fading. There ain't a dry eye in the house. They're laughing and singing. Started dancing and drinking as I left town. Gonna find my way to heaven because I did my time in hell. I wasn't looking too good, but I was feeling very well.

After all is said and done, I did all right. I had my fun. I will walk before they make me run.

12
Cold Steel .44

I found myself down in L.A. standing in line at the Bank of America to get some cash out of my checking account. My account balance was around five hundred dollars, and I needed a quick two hundred in cash. I was so mad that for one time in my life the amount of money wasn't important. But I did remember what my father used to say about the money he had after he'd had a little too much to drink.

"Money, get away! Get a good job with good pay and you're okay. Money, it's a gas! Grab that cash with both hands and make a stash. New car, caviar, four star day dream. Think I'll buy me a football team. Money, get back! I'm all right, Jack, keep your hands off of my stack.

"Money, it's a hit! Don't give me that do goody good bullshit. I'm in the high-fidelity first class traveling set, and I think I need a Lear Jet. Money, it's a crime! Share it fairly, but don't take a slice of my pie. Money, so they say, is the root of all evil today! But if you ask for a raise it's no surprise that they're giving none away."

The teller must have seen me mumbling to myself, but she was very polite and with a swipe of my bank card and the input of my personal code I had the money in a matter of seconds. Ten crisp twenty dollar bills flowed into my hands, and I was on my way out the door. Just as I reached the door to the front lobby a familiar voice stopped me in my tracks.

"Hey, Joe! Where you goin' with that money in your hand?"

It was the voice of Don Eleveld, the lead singer and blues harmonica player in a band I heard play a few times here in L.A. Don and I had become friends mostly because our common interest in music.

"I'm...Don, it's good to see you," I gasped. "You're right. I shouldn't be walking around with this money in my hand."

"Especially the way you're holding it rolled up like that with your index finger stuck out. Looked like a gun to me...at first." Don's serious facial expression slowly turned to a laugh.

"A...gun?" I almost gagged on the word. "What would I be doing with a gun?"

"I got an idea of something we can do with a gun. Sink load and fire until the empire reaps what they've sown. Shoot, shoot, shoot until their minds are open. Shoot, shoot, shoot until their eyes are closed. Push, push, push until we get some motion. Push, push, push until the bombs explode.

"I got an idea. We can do it all on our own. Nothing to worry. Regret must weigh a ton. Kick, kick, kick until the laws are broken. Kick, kick, kick until the boots are worn. Hit, hit, hit until the truth is spoken. Hit, hit, hit until the truth is born.

"It looks like you just robbed a bank with..." Don's laughter overtook his words. "With their own money!

"The best things in life are free, Joe. But you can keep it for the birds and bees. Now, gimme money...that's what I want. Money don't get everything, it's true. What it don't get, I can't use. So gimme money, a little money! That's what I want.

"My girl's loving gives me a thrill, but her loving don't pay my bills. Money don't get everything, it's true. But until they invent something better, it will do."

His logic was irrefutable. Cash is still king.

I asked Don how he and his band were doing. He was eager to respond.

"Seven-thirty-seven coming out of the sky. Oh! Won't you take me down to Memphis on a midnight ride. I wanna move. Take me to the hotel. Baggage gone, oh, well. Come on, won't you get me to my room?

"Listen to the radio. Talking about the last show. Somebody got excited. Had to call the State Militia. Here we come again on Saturday night. Oh, with your fussing and a fighting. Won't you get me to the rhyme?

"Oh, I'm playing in a traveling band. Won't you get me, take my hand? Well, I'm flying across the land. Trying to get a hand playing for a traveling band!"

Don flapped his arms like they were wings.

"In a matter of time, there'll be a friend of mine gonna come to the coast. You're gonna see him up close for a minute or two while the ground cracks under you. By the look in your eyes you'd think that it was a surprise. But you seem to forget something somebody said about the bubbles in the sea and an ocean full of trees. And you're now in L.A., uptight city in the smog. Don't you wish you could be here too?

"Well, it's hard to believe so you get up and leave, and you laugh at the door that you've heard it all before. Oh, it's so good to know that it's all just a show for you. But when the suppers are planned and the freeways are crammed and the mountains erupt and the valley is sucked into the cracks in the earth, will I finally be heard by you? L.A. Uptight, city in the smog.

"You get up every morning from your alarm clock's warning. Take the 8:15 into the city. There's a whistle up above and people pushing, people shovin' and the girls who try to look pretty. And, if your train's on time, you can get to work by nine and start your slaving job to get your pay.

"If you ever get annoyed, look at me, I'm self employed. I love to work at nothin' all day. And, I'll be…takin' care of business, every day. I've been takin' care of business, every way. I've been takin' care of business; it's all mine. Taking are of business, and working overtime. Work out!

"If it were easy as fishin', you could be a musician if you could make sounds loud and mellow. Get a second-hand guitar, chances are you'll go far, if you get in with the right bunch of fellows. People see you having fun just a-lying in the sun. Tell them that you like it this way. It's the work that we avoid, and we're all self-employed. We love to work at nothin' all day. I've been takin' care of business; it's all mine. Takin' care of business and working overtime.

"I want to be a cowboy star up on the screen. Oh, hey, I want to drive my cowboy car across the scene. Oh, hey, I want to write the magazines the housewives read. And I want to be in control of everything. I want to be king.

"I want to make the toys you buy for Christmas Eve. Yeah, and I want to be the father of the ethnic child who stars on TV. Oh, hey, and I want all the leaders of the third world to answer to me. So, maybe now the pope will bow and kiss my ring. I wanna be king!"

Don also played a mean bass guitar on occasion, and I remembered that the last time I saw him, he was looking for a new one. I asked him what happened to the old one.

"Remind me to tell you about the old silver miner name of Hard Rock Pete. He had his house built on a slope. They say one of his legs lived in Calico. There's a rumor going around that the other lived in hope. So, I walked into the room and I stopped. I turned around and looked over my shoulder and a voice close beside me said, 'You better watch your head, the party's over!'

"It wasn't long before the waitress came over and said, "Can I freshen up your drink and have you heard these boys and if you feel included to buy some cowboy boots?' Well, it's not that bad. We can talk above the noise. So, I sucked on my beer and shut my eyes and tried to listen to the words. I know I missed the meaning, but the message was something I'd already heard.

"Johnny Ringo's voice is getting deeper, and now he's going to put another lock on the door. The night was getting later. My head was getting lighter. The mood is getting darker. Tequila's being poured. So, I smile at the old gunslinger in his frame on the wall as he pushed back his hat. And it's all coming back. I'd cut a long story short, but it's much too late for that.

"Somebody stole my bass guitar! They took it from the back seat of my car. I was sleeping in Pasadena in my hotel room, and somebody stole my guitar."

Don had a sheepish smile on his face.

"I was all my fault, Joe. I was drunk as a skunk. I need a new sound anyway. How about you? What's up?

We shook hands vigorously. He asked me how I liked California so far. Then there was a pregnant pause in the conversation before I tried to explain myself.

"Some people get a cheap laugh breaking up the speed limit, scaring the pedestrians for a minute, crossing up progress, driving on the grass, leaving just enough room to pass. Sunday driver never took a test. Oh, yeah, once upon a time in the west.

"Yes, it's no use saying that you don't know nothing. It's still gonna get you if you don't do something. Sitting on a fence, that's a dangerous course. You could even catch a bullet from the peacekeeping force. Even the hero gets a bullet in the chest, once upon a time in the west.

"Mother Mary, your children are slaughtered. Some of you mothers ought to lock up your daughters. Who's protecting the innocenti? Heap big trouble in the land of plenty. Tell me how we're gonna do what's best? You guess once upon a time in the west."

Don could only laugh and nod his head.

"I'm going down to the Monkey Man's Pawn Shop and buy me a cold steel .44," I said before I could stop myself. I filled him in on the details, and surprisingly he seemed to understand perfectly.

He told me that I seemed to be a peaceful man, and then he started into a story. Don liked to tell stories to make his point. That was obvious even after only a few conversations. This story was about a boyhood friend of his.

"Everyone considered my friend Tommy to be the coward of the county. He never stood one single time to prove the county wrong. His mama named him Tommy. The folks just called him 'Yellow'. But something always told me they were reading Tommy wrong.

"Now, he was only ten years old when his daddy died in prison. I looked after Tommy because he was my uncle's son. I still recall the final words my uncle said to Tommy. 'Son, my life is over, but yours has just begun. Promise me, son, not to do the things I've done. Walk away from trouble if you can. Now, it don't mean you're weak, if you turn the other cheek. I hope you're old enough to understand. Son, you don't have to fight to be a man!'

"There's someone for everyone, and Tommy's love was Becky. In her arms he didn't have to prove he was a man. One day while he was working, the Gatlin boys came calling. They took turns at Becky… there were three of them!

"Tommy opened up the door and saw his Becky crying. The torn dress, the shattered look, was more than he could stand. He reached above the fireplace and took down his daddy's picture. As the tears fell on his daddy's face, I heard these words again: 'Promise me, Son, not to do the things I've done. Walk away from trouble if you can. Now, it don't mean you're weak, if you turn the other cheek. I hope you're old enough to understand. Son, you don't have to fight to be a man.

"The Gatlin boys just laughed at him when he walked into the barroom. One of them got up and met him half way across the floor. When Tommy turned around, they said, 'Hey, look, old Yellow's leaving'. But, you could have heard a pin drop when Tommy stopped and locked the door.

"Twenty years of crawling was bottled up inside of him. He wasn't holding nothing back; he let'em have it all. When Tommy left the barroom, not a Gatlin boy was standing. He said, 'This one's for Becky, as he watched the last one fall. And I heard him say, 'I promised you, dad, not to do the things you've done. I'll walk away from trouble when I can. Now, please don't think I'm weak. I didn't turn the other cheek. I hope you understand.'

"Sometimes you've got to fight when you're a man.

"Well, now, give me my pistol, man, and three round balls. I'm gonna shoot everybody that I don't like at all. Got a .38 special, man, and a .45 frame. You know the thing don't miss because I got dead aim. Well, the world is a drag and my friends can't vote. Gonna make me a connection and score some dope and go get high."

We laughed. Don's story made his point. I thanked him for the encouragement, and asked if he knew anything about this Monkey Man fellow.

"The Monkey Man's place?' asked Don. "You've heard of the Monkey Man haven't you? He's from Jersey, I believe. Has a glass eye and a scar across his face."

I had to admit that I'd never heard of the man before today unless…

"When I was on a train near Buffalo, I met a young man who told me he was a cook. He told me a story about a barge on the Erie Canal.

I could swear that he called the captain of the barge 'The Monkey Man'!

"Did he have a glass eye?" asked Don immediately. From the tone of his voice, it seemed as if Don was familiar with this Monkey Man. As far as I could remember, the kid did mention something about the captain's eye. I just couldn't remember exactly what he said. After some reflection I ascribed the similarity to mere coincidence.

Don grabbed me by my shoulders and commenced the telling of another story that might shed some light on the situation.

"Tweeter and the Monkey Man were hard up for cash. They stayed up all night selling cocaine and hash, to an undercover cop who had a sister named Jan. For reasons unexplained she loved the Monkey Man.

"Tweeter was a boy scout before she went to Vietnam and found out the hard way nobody gives a damn. They knew that they found freedom just across the Jersey line, so they hopped into a stolen car and took Highway 99.

"The undercover cop never liked the Monkey Man. Even back in childhood he wanted to see him in the can. Jan got married at fourteen to a racketeer named Bill. She made secret calls to the Monkey Man from a mansion on the hill.

"It was out on Thunder Road, Tweeter at the wheel. They crashed into paradise; they could hear them tires squeal. The undercover cop pulled up and said, 'Everyone of you's a liar. If you don't surrender now, it's gonna go down to the wire.'

"The ambulance rolled up, a state trooper close behind. Tweeter took his gun away and messed up his mind. The undercover cop was left tied up to a tree, near the souvenir stand by the old abandoned factory.

"Next day the undercover cop was in hot pursuit. He was taking the whole thing personal; he didn't care about the loot. Jan had told him many times, 'It was you to me who taught, in Jersey anything's legal as long as you don't get caught.'

"Someplace by Rahway Prison they ran out of gas. The undercover cop cornered them and said, 'Boy, you didn't think that this could last.'

Jan jumped out of bed and said 'There's someplace I gotta go!' She took a gun out of the drawer and said, 'It's best if you don't know!'

"The undercover cop was found face down in a field. The Monkey Man was on the river bridge using Tweeter as a shield. Jan said to the Monkey Man, 'I'm not fooled by Tweeter's curl. I knew him long before he ever became a Jersey girl.'

"Now the town of Jersey City is quieting down again. I remember sitting in a gambling club called the Lion's Den. The TV set was blown up, every bit of it was gone, ever since the nightly news show that the Monkey Man was on.

"I remember deciding to come to California and get myself some sun. There ain't no more opportunity in Jersey, everything's been done. Sometimes I think of Tweeter. Sometimes I think of Jan. Sometimes I don't think about nothing but the Monkey Man.

"And the walls came down all the way to hell. Never saw them when they were standing. Never saw them when they fell."

All of a sudden, Don stopped, wondering whether he had gone too far. He warned me to be careful of the Monkey Man and then pointed to the south.

"Down there at the pawn shop it's the only way to shop," Don exclaimed. "Down there at the pawn shop if it's not in stone. So, why I'm down here at the pawn shop? What has been sold, not strictly made of stone, just remember that it's flesh and bone."

While I was trying to decipher what Don said, he proceeded to tell me the gory details of his relationship with a girl named Gail.

"Pawn shop wedding rings, so many shattered dreams. Broken vows from lovers who gave up. 'But you can count on me', I told Gail, 'to be yours faithfully and stand beside you when push comes to shove'. And these pawn shop wedding rings are gonna learn about love."

Suddenly Don's face turned sad.

"I couldn't give you a ring that's new, but I can give you a ring of truth and a love that won't grow old, shining like that band of gold. Put your hand in mine and everything will work out fine. Together I know we can rise above and these pawn shop wedding rings are gonna learn about love.

"I imagine on our wedding day, when we stand in front of the preacher and say, 'We'll be together until death do us part,' and give those rings a brand new start.

"Pawn shop wedding rings, so many shattered dreams."

I understood his sadness because Gail was gone. His words said it best.

"Gail, you might have forgot, the journey ends. You tied your knots, and you made your friends. You left the scene without a trace, one hand on the ground, one hand in space. Oh, you passed on mercy. You tried the rest. You gave your body. You gave your best. Stare at the green door living in the sky. You don't want to know it. You just want to fly.

"I know you're a dreamer who's under the gun. I know you're a dreamer who's only just begun. Hello again!"

He sensed my loss, too. Don knew that I was losing Linda Lou. He put his hand on my shoulder and proceeded to give me some fatherly advice as he glanced down at my feet.

"Well, Joe, you say you got the blues; you got holes in both your shoes. You're feeling alone and confused, you gotta keep on smilin'.

"You're about to go insane, 'cause your woman's playing games, and she says that you're to blame, yet you try to keep on smilin'.

"Keep on smilin' through the rain, laughing at the pain, just flowing with the changes till the sun comes out again.

"I heard you been singing in a honky tonk café, nobody's hearing what you play, they're too busy drinkin' anyway…still, you gotta keep on smilin'.

"Say you found a piece of land, gonna change from city boy to country man, and try to build your life with your hands, and just keep on smilin'.

"You're just hanging out in a local bar, and you're wondering who the hell you are. Are you a farmer…are you a star? Smile through the rain, laugh through all the pain, flow through to changes till the sun comes out again!"

I knew he was right, then and there. He could see it so he changed the subject to something more pleasant.

"Well, Joe, doin' any gigs lately? Frank and I are playin' over at the Roadhouse Friday through Sunday. "We're doin' mostly Zepplin, Stones and Hendrix."

I made it a point to go see them play. They had a good sound, and I could visualize me playing in the band.

"I was in Lodi for three months. Mostly country...for the cows and pigs.

"I woke up in a Soho doorway, a policeman knew my name. He said, 'You can go sleep at home tonight if you can get up and walk away.' I staggered back to the local bar, and the breeze blew back my hair. I remember throwing punches around and preaching from my chair. I took my Harley back out of town back to the Rolling Pin. I felt a little like a dying clown with a streak of Rin Tin Tin.

"I stretched back, and I hiccupped and looked back on my busy day. Eleven hours in the Tin Pan at Maggie's Farm; God, there's got to be another way."

"Glad you haven't lost your sense of humor," Don responded. "We could use your guitar on this gig. Are you free? I know that you're a fellow traveling wilbury."

The word 'free' rang a special chord in my brain. I wondered for just how long I would be free.

"I'll drop by Friday with my guitar. Then we can see what the situation is."

Don agreed and wished me a good day as he entered the crowded bank. One thing he said as we parted always stuck in my mind.

"We'll always be friends. We'll always look out for one another. No matter where. No matter when. That's a promise."

Little did I know at the time how well Don kept his promises.

I got on my Harley after stashing the cash in my vest pocket. Then I remembered something my mother told me about pawn shops...she called them second-hand stores. She loved to use analogies. I recalled exactly what she said.

13
The Monkey Man

I recalled something my mother once told me.

"You lost your color when you painted the town. Painting by the numbers. You headed for the lobby, but you never came down. Is it any wonder?

"You end up sitting in a second hand store on display in a window. Wind up sitting in the bottom of a drawer any way the wind blows.

"So, you burned your bridges and headed downstream. Never know until you try. Spent your fortune on a riverboat queen, then the river ran dry. You end up sitting on a sandbar down to a handful of treasures. Another shot of gold won't get you very far. When you got forever, any way the wind blows.

"And so you keep on following directions until pretty soon you've passed it. Guess you should'a known better, and still it was fun while it lasted. You end up sitting in a second-hand store on display in a window. Wind up sitting in the bottom of a drawer, any way the wind blows."

My mom was right. I had to be careful not to end up in that window. I can't spend my life in a second-hand store. My life in its living can be like a ball of fuzzy yarn. I could unroll myself slowly or just be torn. The sky is the limit, and each day it gets higher, as the yarn runs out and all that's left is desire.

I want to be loved. Don't want to be hated. I just have to figure out how my hook should be baited. Should it be dressed shiny to attract more curious eyes or should it be dull in texture so that I can surprise? Who knows the ultimate answer? Step forward and give me the news. I want my life to be as smooth as a Sunday afternoon cruise.

Maybe I should give this some thought. Tonight, I'm going to spring a surprise visit on Linda Lou, ah…Kitty or whatever she calls herself now, and see what's up with her. Then, maybe, I'll have some kind of answer.

I drove my Harley down to the Monkey Man's Pawn Shop. There he stood behind the counter. He had a huge mop of black hair on his head, a nasty scar across his face and, as I would soon learn, a glass eye. I wanted to ask him whether he ever captained a barge on the Erie Canal, but I thought better of it.

"They call me the Monkey Man. Part man, part monkey. They prosecuted some poor sucker in these United States for teaching that man descended from the apes. They could have settled that case without a fuss or fight if they'd seen me chasing my girl through the jungle last night. They would have called in that jury and a one two three said, 'Part man, part monkey, definitely.'

"Well, the church bell rings from the corner steeple. Man in a monkey suit swears he'll do no evil. Offers his lover's prayer, but his soul lies dark and drifting and unsatisfied. Well, ask any bartender what he sees. Looks like part man, part monkey to me.

"Well, the night is dark, the moon is full. The flowers of romance exert their pull. We talk a while, my fingers slip. I'm hard and cracking like a whip. Well, did God make man in a breath of holy fire, or did he crawl on up out of the muck and mire? Well, the man on the street believes what the Bible tells him so. But you can ask me, Joey, because I know. Tell them soul-sucking preachers to come on down and see. Part man, part monkey, that's me!"

As I looked at the Monkey Man, I could see what he meant. He had a certain caveman aura about him. As he kept on going, I wondered how he knew my name?.

"Shock the Monkey Man to life. Cover me when I run. Cover me through the fire. Something knocked me out of the trees. Now I'm on my knees. Don't you know when you're going to shock the monkey? Fox the fox. Rat the rat. You can ape the ape. I know about that. There is one thing you must be sure of. I can't take any more. Wheels keep turning. Something's burning. Don't like it, but I guess I'm learning.

"So, let me tell you, Joe, why you need this cold steel .44. You see, there is a sheriff whose name is John Brown, but he could have been so much more. And he has a brother named Leroy Brown. And a more closely-knit set of brothers will never be found.

"Well, the south side of L.A. is the baddest part of town. And, if you go down there, you better just beware of a man whose name is Leroy Brown. Now Leroy's more than trouble, you see he stands about six foot four. All the downtown ladies call him treetop lover. All the men just call him 'Sir'.

"Now, Leroy he's a gambler, and he likes his fancy clothes. And he likes to wave his diamond rings in front of everybody's nose. He's got a custom Continental. He's got an Eldorado, too. He's got a .32 gun in his pocket for fun. He's got a razor in his shoe.

"And, it's bad, bad Leroy Brown. The baddest man in the whole damn town. Badder than old King Kong, and meaner than a junkyard dog.

"Well, Friday about a week ago, Leroy was shooting dice. And at the edge of the bar sat a girl named Linda Lou. And, oh that girl looked nice. Well, he cast his eyes upon her, and the trouble soon began. And, Leroy Brown learned a lesson about messing with the girl of a jealous man. Leroy went up to Linda Lou and made his proposal. This is what he said.

"On the day I was born the nurses all gathered around, and they gazed in wide wonder at the joy they had found. The head nurse spoke up, said, 'Leave this one alone'. She could tell right away that I was bad to the bone.

"I broke a thousand hearts before I met you. I'll break a thousand more, baby, before I am through. I wanna be yours, pretty baby. Yours and yours alone. I'm here to tell you honey that I'm bad to the bone.

"I make a rich woman beg. I'll make a good woman steal. I'll make an old woman blush. And make a young girl squeal. I wanna be yours, pretty baby, yours and yours alone. I'm here to tell you honey that I'm bad to the bone.

"And when I walk the streets, kings and queens step aside. They all stay satisfied. Well, you see I make my own. I'm here to tell you that I'm bad to the bone."

Suddenly, the tone of the Monkey Man's voice changed.

"Well, this Linda Lou girl stood up and pointed toward the back of the bar. And man in a motorcycle jacket, something like the one you're wearing, was striding forward to meet his fate. Linda Lou began describing him to Leroy. 'He's a rebel and an angel of the devil. You can't see him, but he's always on the level. He's a traveler and survivor from below. If you cheat him, he'll even up the score. He's a traveler and an unraveler of your mind. He's the High Priest, you can worship at his shrine. He's the shadow. He can read between the lines. He's got the power. He's like lightning from the sky. He's been down in the ground. He's been kicked and pushed around. Now he's coming back, coming back to claim his crown.'

"Well, the two men took to fighting, and when they pulled them from the floor, Leroy looked like a jigsaw puzzle with a couple of pieces gone.

"Well, soon Sheriff John Brown came along, and Leroy told his brother in a song. As it turned out, his assailant was a man named Joe. And with his girl, Linda Lou, this man named Joe did go. Now the word on the street is that Leroy is disabled for life. Linda Lou was never to be seen again. They say she lost her life. They tell that Joe shot her dead in the alley behind the bar.

"And forget about getting ammo next door. Pressed Rat and Warthog have closed down their shop. They didn't want to, 'twas all they had got. Selling atonal ammo, amplified heat, and Pressed Rat's collection of dog's legs and feet.

"Sadly, they left, telling no one goodbye. Pressed Rat wore red jodhpurs, Warthog a striped tie. Between them, they carried a three-legged sack, went straight around the corner and never came back.

"The bad captain landlord had ordered their fate. He laughed and stomped off with a nautical gait. The gait turned into a deroga tree, and his peg-leg got wormwood and broke into three."

I couldn't believe what I just heard. The Monkey Man said I was wanted for the murder of Linda Lou! I didn't fight Leroy Brown. That's impossible! That's absurd! Linda Lou is alive! But suddenly a dark cloud appeared in my mind. I had to find Linda Lou and Sheriff John Brown and straighten this whole thing out. The Monkey Man had more to say.

"Making no deposit, no return. Making the same mistakes, I never learn. All of the pain in those faces trying not to show concern. Spent and broken like a worn out subway talking in the city. Hanging in the closet. Waiting in line. When you go by the laws, you pay the fine. I'm burning the candle at both ends. Twice the light in half the time. Damn the calling, feel like I'm falling.

"Oh, and as the rain doesn't have to hurry in the city, it falls sadly to the ground. Rain doesn't have to hurry in the city, the only way to fall is down. Falling down.

"But, still I'm running in a race that can't be won, aiming hard to fill the spaces when they're gone. Worn out shoes with no laces getting too loose to stay on. I'm back to crawling. Feel like I'm falling."

He looked down at his shoes and tied a loose shoelace. Then, the Monkey Man had still more to tell me.

"You gotta be crazy. You gotta have a real need. You gotta sleep on your toes. And when you're on the street, you gotta be able to pick out the easy meat with your eyes closed. And then, moving in silently, down wind and out of sight, you gotta strike when the moment is right without thinking.

"And after a while you can work on points for style, like the club tie and the firm handshake, a certain look in the eye and an easy smile. You have to be trusted by the people you lie to, so that when they turn their backs on you, you'll get the chance to put the knife in.

"You gotta keep one eye looking over your shoulder. You know it's gonna get harder, and harder, and harder as you get older. And, in the end you'll pack up and fly down south, hide your head in the sand, just another sad old man, all alone and dying of cancer.

"And when you lose control, you'll reap the harvest you have sown. And as the fear grows, the bad blood slows and turns to stone. And it's too late to lose the weight you used to need to throw around. So, have a good drown, as you go down, all alone, dragged down by the stone."

I stopped the Monkey Man for a moment.

"I gotta admit, Mister Monkey Man, that I'm a little bit confused. Sometimes it seems to me that I'm just being used. Gotta stay awake. Gotta try and shake off this creeping malaise. If I don't stand my own ground, how can I find my way out of this maze?"

He had an answer.

"Deaf, dumb, and blind, you just keep on pretending that everyone's expendable, and no one has a real friend. And it seems to you the thing to do would be to isolate the sinner. And everything's done under the sun. And you believe at heart that everyone's a killer."

He stopped and pointed an accusing finger at me.

"Who was born in a house full of pain? Who was trained not to spit in the fan? Who was told what to do by the man? Who was broken by trained personnel? Who was fitted with a collar and chain? Who was given a pat on the back? Who was breaking away from the pack? Who was only a stranger at home? Who was ground down in the end? Who was found dead on the phone? Who was dragged down by the stone?"

I was understandably depressed. The Monkey Man's face wore a wry smile. He had a further suggestion.

"It's a mystery to me. The game commences for the usual fee plus expenses. Confidential information. It's in a diary. This is my investigation. It's not a public inquiry.

"I go checking out the report, digging up the dirt. You get to meet all sorts in this kind of work. Treachery and treason. There's always an excuse for it. And when I find the reason, I still can't get used to it.

"And what have you got at the end of the day? What have you got to take away? A bottle of whiskey and a new set of lies, blinds on the window, and a pain behind the eyes. Scarred for life, no compensation. Private investigations.

"All you women who want a man of the street, but you don't know which way you wanna turn. Just keep a coming, and put your hand out to me. Because I'm the one who's gonna make you burn. I'm gonna take you down, down, down. So, don't you fool around. I'm gonna pull it, pull it, pull the trigger. Shoot to thrill, play to kill. I got my gun at the ready. Gonna fire at will. Because I shoot to thrill, and I'm ready to kill.

"I'm like evil. I get under your skin. Just like a bomb that's ready to blow. Because I'm illegal, I got everything that all those women might need to know. Too many women with too many pills. I can't get enough. I can't get my fill. I'm gonna get you to the bottom and shoot you. Yeah, pull the trigger."

So now I realized what the Monkey Man was up to in his free time.

"Joey, if you're having trouble with your high school head; he's giving you the blues. You want to graduate but not in his bed, here's what you gotta do. Pick up the phone; I'm always home. Call me any time. Just ring: three-six-two-four-three-six, hey. I lead a life of crime. Dirty deeds done dirt cheap.

"You got problems in your life of love. You got a broken heart. She's double-dealing with your best friend. That's when the teardrops start, Joey. Pick up the phone; I'm here alone. Or make a social call. Come right in; forget about her. We'll have ourselves a ball, eh.

"You got a lady, and you want her gone, but you ain't got the guts. She keeps nagging at you night and day, enough to drive you nuts. Pick up the phone; leave her alone. It's time you made a stand. For a fee, I'm happy to be your back door man, hey.

"Dirty deeds done dirt cheap. Concrete shoes? Cyanide? T.N.T.? Neckties? Contracts? High voltage? Dirty deeds, I'll do anything you want me to…done dirt cheap!"

I appreciated the Monkey Man's offer, but I had to decline. I took the cold steel .44 instead. After all, this was my responsibility. He was still talking as I backed toward the door.

"They sentenced me to twenty years of boredom for trying to change the system from within. I'm coming now. I'm coming to reward them. First we take Manhattan, then we take Berlin.

"I'm guided by a signal from the heavens. I'm guided by this birthmark on my skin. I'm guided by the beauty of our weapons. First, we take Manhattan, then we take Berlin."

When the Monkey Man mentioned his birthmark, he pointed to the nasty scar that ran across his face. When he mentioned weapons, he pointed toward the cold steel .44. He then showed me a photo of his former girlfriend. Her name was Natasha.

"I'd really like to live beside you, Natasha. I love your body and your spirit and your clothes. But, you see that line there moving through the station. I told you I was one of those."

I saw the packed suitcases sitting near the counter. He must have been planning to hit the road soon. I asked him if he was leaving, too?

"There is a house down in New Orleans they call the Rising Sun. And it's been the ruin of many a poor girl, and Natasha, oh God, is one.

"Her mother was a tailor. She sewed these new blue jeans. Her father was a gambler, Lord, down in New Orleans. Now, the only thing a gambler needs is a suitcase and a trunk. And the only time he's satisfied is when he's on a drunk. He fills his glasses up to the brim and helps pass the cards around. And the only pleasure he gets out of life is rambling from town to town. Natasha told me to tell her baby sister not to do what she has done. Please shun that house in New Orleans they call The Rising Sun.

"Well, it's one foot on the platform and the other foot on the train. I'm going back to New Orleans where Natasha wears that ball and chain. I'm going back to New Orleans, my race is almost run. I'm going back to end my life down in The Rising Sun."

He hesitated as if he were talking with Natasha.

"She had the word. She had the way. The way of letting me know she knew the game. She called the play. Oh, she hit me low. She said, 'Now you go your way. I'll go mine. And, that's a start. Doctor, doctor, ain't no cure for the pain in my heart.

"Gimme a bullet to bite on. Something to chew and I'll make believe it's you. Don't need no drink. Don't need no drug. Don't need no sympathy. Sooner or later send me the bill for what she's doing to me. Operator, long distance lips on the telephone. Come tomorrow, come to grips with me…all alone."

For a moment I thought he was going to cry. But I let him rave on.

"You loved me as a loser, but now you're worried that I just might win. You know the way to stop me, but you don't have the discipline. How many nights I prayed for this, to let my work begin.

"I don't like your fashion business, Natasha. I don't like these drugs that keep you thin. And I thank you for those items that you sent me.

The monkey and the plywood violin. Remember me, I used to live for music. Remember me, I brought your groceries in."

The Monkey Man turned to look at me with his one good eye.

"Good luck, Joey, with your new pal, the cold steel .44. You're going to need it."

I was about to leave the Monkey Man's establishment when I realized that I still had a question for him. So, I stepped back inside to ask.

"Mister Monkey Man, how did you come to know this Sheriff John Brown?"

A perplexed look covered his scarred face. He told me to come in and sit down.

14
Sheriff John Brown

The Sheriff pulled up in front of Linda Lou's residence in his big black limousine. He stepped confidently out of the vehicle and entered the apartment without knocking. There sat Linda Lou in the living room watching television. Sheriff John Brown walked over and silenced the TV. Then he faced Linda, a serious look on his face.

"The word is out that I'm about, and I've come gunning for your little friend, Joey. I'm a real entertainer, a mischief maker, a lover of no fixed abode. Quick draw on the floor, no law gives you more. Sweet talker, lover of sin, you are what you got, you get what you want. Look out, woman, I got guns for hire! Shoot you with desire, the guns for hire.

"I'm a wanted poster, a needed man running right across the land. I'm a smooth operator, a big dictator. Gonna mark you with my brand. Hot to trot, big shot, take a lot, never get the drop on me. My gun's for hire, shoot you with desire. What you get, but shot, you can't get the drop on me, girl.

"Hey, I'm the hitman. Stand aside. I'm the hitman. I want Joey's life. Ain't no escaping. Don't run and hide. There goes the neighborhood. I'm gonna kill for your love. That's right.

"Hitman! Now, Linda Lou, don't you cry. I'm just it, woman. And you might get fried. Gun in my pocket. Don't get me wrong. I'll be your hitman. I'm a fool for your love. I'm a head shredder. That's better.

"Trouble in the east. Trouble in the west. Struggle with the beast. What a thief. What a pest. Come back, mother, nuke that sucker. Waste that brother. That's the way to do it.

"I'm the hitman. I'm your prize. But this hitman can cut you down to size. Love me, don't be so cool. I've been to the hitman school. You're gonna make my day. Gonna blow Joey away. That's when the fun begins. Are you ready for the sting? Gonna waste that thing. Hitman is king!"

All this time I was several miles from Linda Lou's apartment. I remembered laying down on the couch for a rest. I started to dream again.

Big kid Joey rode away in the sunset covered sky. A lynching mob had strung his girlfriend up right before his eyes. He didn't know what they'd both done. He, sure as hell, would end up hung, a hot tin notch on the sheriff's gun if he didn't move on, get out of here.

The sheriff followed Joey's trail from L.A. southwest. He said he'd put a bullet through poor Joey's chest. But Joey wasn't like the rest. He don't like bullet holes in his vest. In fact, he'd do his very best to avoid any arrest. Doesn't want to be a guest of the sheriff.

The nights got so damn hot. He couldn't stand the pace. He looked again for sheriff's men, but couldn't see a trace. Joey found a nice cool place. But then the sheriff solved the case. Poked a gun at Joey's face and said,'Lookie here…'.

Sheriff rode him into town with Joey looking sad. He didn't know about the six-gun big kid Joey had. Then Joey drew his gun real fast and gave the sheriff one big blast. Now, Joey runs the town at last, a legend from the past. Nobody ever messed with the sheriff.

I woke up. It was my recurring dream. It ends differently every time, but I'm always alive when it ends. At least I can feel happy about that. Let's hope it stays that way.

It was time for me to try to find Linda Lou. If someone's trying to steal her from me or kill her, my cold steel .44 will teach him otherwise and show me what to do. As I stood by the door, I planned my every move.

Gonna go downtown. Gonna get my gun. Gonna dress real sharp. Gonna beat my drum. I ain't gonna lie. Gonna walk so slow. Gonna talk just right. And my diamond ring gonna shine so bright. I ain't gonna lie.

I've got a debt to repay. I ain't gonna cry. I put a gun in your face; you'll pay with your life. And I got my ears. And I got my eyes. And I got my narks and my alibis. I won't waste your time.

You make one false move, you make one mistake, when the juice is squeezed that's the way it breaks. You'll pay for your crime.

Your tongue licking way out of place, I'll rip it out. I'll stick a gun in your face. You'll pay with your life.

I taught Linda Lou everything; I taught her how to dream. I taught her everything; I'm gonna teach her how to scream. I taught her all she knows; I taught her how to lie. I taught her everything; I'm gonna teach her how to cry.

I taught her how to speak. I taught her how to eat. I half invented her, and now she acts so chic. I taught her everything, but now she's obsolete.

I taught her how to read and write. She was a neophyte. I loved to watch her grow, and now I want to see her go.

I taught her how to cheat. She was so indiscreet. I taught her how to lie. I'm gonna teach her how to cry.

And you cause me hurt, and you cause me pain. And you turned the tap on my burning rage. And I can't put it out.

Gonna leave no sign; gonna leave no trace. Gonna leave this town in a state of grace. Give me the power.

I got a debt to repay; I ain't gonna lie. I put a gun in your face; you'll pay for the crime.

Finally, I got up the courage and walked down to Linda Lou's address. How she could afford such a beautiful accommodation on her meager salary made me wonder. As I prepared to knock open her door, the door swung open. There stood Linda Lou, as beautiful as ever. She wasn't dead! Before she could say a word, I stated my case.

"I'll never be your beast of burden. My back is broad, but my mind is uncertain. All I want is for you to make love to me. I've walked for miles, my feet are hurting. So, let's go home and draw the curtains. Music on the radio; come on, Baby, make sweet love to me.

"Am I hard enough? Am I rough enough? Am I rich enough? I'm not too blind to see. I'll tell ya, you can put me out on the street, put me out with no shoes on my feet. but, put me out of misery!

"Yeah, all your sickness, I can suck it up. Throw it all at me; I can shrug it off. There's one thing baby that I don't understand. You keep on telling me I ain't your kind of man. Still, I'll never be your beast of burden."

Surprisingly, Linda Lou pushed the door open and invited me in. I was nervous, but I sat down on the couch and she took a spot next to me. She held my hand as she spoke.

"Take off your hat, kick off your shoes, I know you ain't going anywhere. Run around the town singing your blues, I know you ain't going anywhere. You've always been a good friend of mine, but you're always saying farewell. And the only time that you are satisfied is with your feet in the wishing well."

Linda Lou was always speaking in metaphors so I had to listen carefully. As I sat on the couch, I realized that she had detected the presence of my cold steel .44.

"Throw down your gun. You might shoot yourself. Or is that what you're trying to do? Put up a fight, you believe to be right, and some day the sun will shine through. You have always got something to hide. Something you just can't tell. And the only time that you are satisfied is with your feet in the wishing well.

"Oh, but I know what you're wishing for…love and a peaceful world. You have always been a good friend of mine. Yes, I wish you well!"

She was always so right, but she had a sad look in her eyes.

"I can feel it floating away," I whispered. "Inch by inch, day by day. The love boat has set itself free. Castaway, slipping out to sea.

"I can feel it coming adrift. Even a blind man could see the rift. From an ocean liner to a Chinese junk, there ain't been a ship that can't be sunk.

"I used to dream it could last forever. But pipedreams never come true. I'd be fooling myself if I never thought something like this couldn't happen to you.

"It's not something you can hide away. Sooner or later it starts to show. It's written on your face. You've been betrayed. Do you really think that I don't know?

"He's already fallen so it's no use to fight. And if he starts calling, let him know you're with me for the rest of the night.

"You've got a man on your mind. You've got a weight on your shoulders. How you ever gonna find the words to say goodbye?

"I know you know all the pros and cons. They help you get to everything you want. Greasing policemen, bending all the rules. Make them an offer they can't refuse. One crime, Linda Lou, I can't forgive. The kind that hurts where I live. I'm a nice guy. I try to wait and see if you'll get caught or go free.

"Beat the heat, but you couldn't pay me off. You're staying cool no matter what it costs. If you get caught, you'll never do the time. I have to say you've got away with one crime, Linda Lou, I can't forgive. The kind that hurts where I live. It's all too clear, but I still don't see why all the guilty go free?

"Catch a thief, and let her go. You won't get back the love she stole. Shake her down, but she doesn't mind because she's committed the perfect crime. You know that I know that you're a con artiste. Oh, Linda Lou, you're a false alarm. Why do I try to play it by the rules? I was the victim, but I'm not a fool.

"You stole my heart and left me blue. It looks like crime pays for you. You do it, and you get away. It seems like the perfect crime. Crime pays!"

"Joey," said Linda Lou in a sorrowful voice. "I met a stranger..."

"Well, we all have a face," I said firmly, "that we hide away forever. And we take them out and show ourselves when everyone has gone. Some are satin, some are steel, some are silk, and some are leather. They're the faces of the stranger, but we love to try them on.

"Well, we all fall in love, but we disregard the danger. Though we share so many secrets there are some we never tell. Why were you so surprised that you never saw the stranger. Did you ever let me see the stranger in yourself?

"Don't be afraid to try again; everyone goes south every now and then. You've done it; why can't someone else? You should know by now, you've been there yourself.

"Once I used to believe I was such a great romancer. Then I found myself with a woman that I could not recognize. When I pressed her for a reason, she refused to even answer. It was then I felt the stranger kick me right between the eyes.

"You may never understand how the stranger is inspired, but he isn't always evil, and he isn't always wrong. Though you drown in good intentions, you will never quench the fire. You'll give in to your desire when the stranger comes along."

Fear flashed across Linda Lou's face. She seemed concerned for Joey's safety as well as her own.

"I must be crazy. They don't know what we've done. You are my lover even though I know it's wrong. I hear them talking, but whatever they do, I need to love you. And if I love you, couldn't we make it?"

Then, all of a sudden, her attitude started wavering.

"Got someone loving me. He won't say goodbye. He's been so good to me. I don't wanna make him cry. I need you both to love me. It's up to you. You can help me. You're the reason, Joey, I can't decide.

"Breaking my bones and shaking my nerves until I just can't see tomorrow. Looking at him and looking at you, and I don't know who to follow. I'll never win in the state I'm in. It's a crime of passion. I'm bad to love you. Whenever I'm with you, I lose control. It's a crime of passion for me and or you.

"Whatever I give you, it's just too late to save my soul. I need to love you. My desperation is the power to go on. Each night I prayed for love I'm at the mercy of. And if you don't hear me now, then I'll be the only one. Don't wanna be the only one.

"I saw Sheriff John Brown yesterday. The questions he asked…I think he knows about us. Did we move too fast? How can we hide it when we know it's a lie? Keep our love under the covers? The pressure's too high."

Linda Lou stopped, then continued muttering to herself.

"Why do I get myself tied up? Why tangle with love you borrow? I should have been known as a one-man woman! Should have been one love, but oh, no. Never be a cure for the human law!"

She turned and looked me right in the eyes. It was a warning.

"Riot on the radio, pictures on TV. Invader-man takes what he can, shootout on the silver screen. Sticking 'em up and knocking 'em down, living out a fantasy. There's a bad man cruising around in a big black limousine. Don't let it be wrong. Don't let it be right. Get in Sheriff John Brown's way, you're dead in his sights.

"Terminators, Uzi makers, shooting up Hollywood. Snakes alive with a .45 setting off and doing no good. If you ain't wise, they'll cannibalize, tear flesh off you. Classified lady-killer preying in the human zoo. He'll saddle you up and take you to town. Better look out when he comes around.

"Big gun, got a hot one. Big gun, got a number one. Big gun, loaded and cocked. Big gun, hot, hot, hot. Got a big gun, ready or not. A big gun, give it, give it a shot!"

Sheriff John Brown was outside the door. I had to decide what to do and fast. Linda Lou wanted me to run and fast! I thought about what I would say. I thought about what the Monkey Man told me.

"Law man…I'm afraid you just walked in here at the wrong time. My cold steel .44 has never been fired, but there's a first time and this could be the first time. Law man…you know you look a lot older than me, and I know you'd hate to shoot a baby. I've got a long way to go before I'm old and slow, and it could be, it could be a good time if you change your mind.

"Well, I'm tired and sweet from making love, and it's just too late, you'll have to wait, bring your business around here in the morning.

"Well, I've heard your line and you've heard mine and I'm just too tired to take a side. Bring your business around here in the morning. Don't you want to be easy. Look there, let some of the things you see go on by, or you can burn them into your brain. Go on home. Don't you see the children? They're just like you. They want everything to be fine, but they let it slide, and the laughing lets you know that smiling breaks the rules.

"Law breaker? You know it could be me, and if you had your way, we'd all be down under the face of a clock that's just too old to be wound. And you can see now, the old hands won't move around.

"One way or the other, fool card, brother, this could be. This could be the first time."

Well, my mind has been overflowing about some things that don't seem right. And my gun is cocked and loaded, I hope I get me some sleep tonight. Well, I don't know what went wrong. It seems like nothing is right. So, take it nice and easy. Leave the coals in the pit. Don't let your mind post-toastee, like a lot of my friends did.

15
Man on the Run

I was born a rambling man. And I never got the chance to settle down and get a hold on love. Taking air and moving around is all I can see that I'm doing. And it is bringing me down, driving on a highway going nowhere. Desolation destination. Guess I'll find it somewhere. I know that if there's trouble, I ain't taking the blame. That's why I keep moving so nobody knows my name.

Born a loser. I'm beyond the law. Women behind me never can find me. They can never put together what I've been here for because I'm a drifter. Rolling on. Ain't wasting my time no more.

It's all the same, only the names will change. Every day it seems like I'm wasting away. Another place where the faces are so cold. I'd drive all night just to get back home. Sometimes I sleep, sometimes it's not for days. And the people I meet always go their separate ways. Sometimes you tell the day by the bottle that you drink. And times when you're all alone, all you do is think.

I walk these streets, a loaded six-string on my back. I play for keeps because I might not make it back. I've been everywhere. Still I'm standing tall. I've seen a million faces, and I've rocked them all.

I'm a cowboy. On a steel horse I ride. I'm wanted...Dead or Alive!

I lovingly looked down at my Harley and patted the gas tank. It was saving my life, and I appreciated it. I was headed south out of L.A.

One foot on the brake and one on the gas. Well, here's too much traffic. I can't pass. So I tried my best illegal move. To think that a black and white came and touched my groove, again! So I signed my name on number twenty-four. 'Yeah', said the judge. 'Boy, just one more and we're gonna throw your ass in the city joint.' Looked me in the eye and said, 'You get my point?' I said, 'Yeah! Oh, yeah!'

When I drive that slow, you know it's hard to steer. And I can't get my bike out of second gear. What used to take two hours now takes all day. It took me sixteen hours to get to L.A.

Go ahead and write me up for one twenty-five. Post my face wanted, Dead or Alive. Take my license, all that jive. I can't drive fifty-five!

Well, I feel like I'm running down a dead end road. I need someone to tell me which way I ought to go. Say goodbye to the morning. Down the road I am flying. If I look way beyond me, I'll be getting way behind.

I can't seem to catch up. Distance keeps pulling away. Makes no difference where I go. Dead end road every way. I feel like I'm running down a dead end road. I need someone to tell me which way I ought to go.

Well, goodbye world, it's sad but true. Got a date with the hangman, I have to leave you. I think I shot my Darlin' three times or more. The reason I'm going is the blood on the floor. The nights are so lonely; the days are so long. I'm headed for the jailhouse because they say I've done wrong. I don't say I'm sorry; I just say I'm sore. The reason I'm going is the blood on the floor.

Well, I visited her one night, and she was lying with her legs around another man's bod. She saw me, started laughing. But she cried when she saw my cold steel .44.

Heard it from another room. Eyes were waking up just to fall asleep. Love's like suicide. Dazed out in a garden bed. With a broken neck lays my broken gift. Just like suicide. And my last ditch was my last brick, lent to finish her.

Bit down on the bullet just now. I had a taste so sour. I had to think of something sweet. Love's like suicide. Safe outside my gilded cage with an ounce of pain, I wield a ton of rage. Just like suicide. With eyes of blood and bitter blue, how I feel for you, Linda Lou.

She lived like a murder. How she'd fly so sweetly. She lived like murder, but she died just like suicide.

Goodbye world, I guess we must part. They want to take my life because I shot my sweetheart. I don't say I'm sorry; I just say I'm sore. The reason I'm going is the blood on the floor.

My mind was half in a dream state again. When will these crazy thoughts ever end? I didn't shoot anyone, especially sweet Linda Lou. But, if you try to stop me now, I might shoot you.

I'm fading out of sight; my wheels are the only sound. Running at the speed of light, and I can't slow down now. Out on an open road, racing to beat the night. No matter where I'm going, I guess I'll be all right. So, why don't I understand what's tripping me up? It ought to be a simple thing. I can't hold on, and I can't return. It's time to let go and start to live and learn.

I took a one-way flight, too high to see the ground. Now, I know how long it takes a heart to come down. Alone on the highway now, taking it mile by mile. I'd rather be a lonely man than an imprisoned child. So, why do I feel the strain that keeps tripping me up? Will it ever be a simple thing?

Living easy, living free. Season ticket on a one-way ride. Asking nothing, leave me be. Taking everything in my stride. Don't need reason, don't need rhyme. Ain't nothing I would rather do, going down, party time. My friends are gonna be there, too. I'm on the highway to hell.

No stop signs, no speed limits. Nobody's gonna slow me down. Like a wheel, gonna spin it. Nobody's gonna mess me around. Hey, Satan. Paying my dues playing in a rock band. Hey, Momma, look at me. I'm on my way to the Promised Land. I'm on the highway to hell, Angus, my friend.

I can't hold on, and I can't return. Rivers will run and bridges will burn. I can't say just how, but there's no looking back now. It's time to let go and start to live and learn.

I had a match, but she had a lighter. I had a flame, but Linda Lou had a fire. I was bright, but she was much brighter. I was high, but Linda Lou was the sky. Oh, Baby, I am bound for Mexico. Oh, Baby, I was bound to let you go.

I don't know much about Cinco de Mayo; I'm never sure what it's all about. But, I said I want you, and you didn't believe me. You said you want me, but now I've got my doubts. Oh, Baby, I am bound for Mexico. Oh, Baby, I am bound to let you go.

You could see me reaching, so why couldn't you have met me half way? You could see me bleeding, but you could not put pressure on the wound. You only think about yourself. You'd better bend before I go on the first road to Mexico.

You could see me breathing, but you kept still. Your hand over my mouth, you could feel me seething. But you just turned your nose up in the air. You'd better bend before I go on the first road to Mexico.

This wasn't the first time I thought I was in Mexico. I remembered the real first time when I was just a lad of sixteen. There must have been a million stars in that desert sky, so high and lonesome that they drove my young blood wild. I should have learned my lesson from that first taste of Mescal and smell of sweet perfume. But, alas, I didn't. Instead, I was in that back room where I could see the burning glow of El Paso above that northern ridge. But now those memories seem so long ago.

It happened fast. It's over quick. A little dust and the engine kicks. Did your hands drift down off the wheel? Roll out, hit your windshield. An eyelash or a little lost sleep? Time stands still. Just call it now and you're on your way. All the ashtrays, cities, and the freeway drives. Broken casino and waterslides. Eighteen-wheeler, payback dice. Gravity flows on the power line.

Jet stream cuts the desert sky. This is a land that could eat a man alive. Say you'd leave it all behind.

There's a radio tower that's egging me on back to the place where you never belong. Where people thrive on their own contempt. Whatever meaning is long gone, spent. If you had to guess or make a bet, would you place yourself inside of it? The mountains yawn. The clouds let out a sigh. 'Tricked again'. Let's go, okay.

I remember what my old school friend Chuck told me. We were sitting on the back porch of his parent's house at the time, but it felt so real.

"Way down here you need a reason to move. Feel a fool running your stateside games. Lose your load, leave your mind behind, baby Joey.

"Oh, Mexico, It sounds so simple. I just got to go. The sun's so hot, I just forgot to go home. Guess I'll have to go now. Americano got the sleepy eye. But his body's still shaking like a live wire. Sleepy senorita with the eyes on fire.

"Oh, Mexico, it sounds so sweet with the sun sinking low. Moon's so bright like to light up the night. Make everything all right. Baby's hungry, and the money's all gone. The folks back home don't want to talk on the phone. You send a long letter, you get back a post card. Times are hard.

"Oh, down in Mexico, I never really been so I don't really know. I guess I'll have to go. I'm going down to Mexico where I can be free!

"If you're down in Acuna, and you ain't up for being alone, don't spend all your money on just any honey that's grown. Go find the Mexican blackbird and send all your troubles back home.

"They call her 'Puta' because no one really knows her name. She works the cantina, dancin' and a-lovin's her trade. Her momma was Mez'can, and her daddy was the ace of spades.

"Oh, let's drive that old Chysler down to Mexico, Boy. Said, keep your hands on the wheel there. Oh, it sure is fine, ain't it? Now ya got it! Hand me another one of them brews from back there. Oh, this is gonna be so good.

"Mmm, she's hot as a pepper but smooth as a Mexican brew. So, head for the border and put in an order or two. The wings of the blackbird will spread like an eagle for you.

"Oh, one more time, can you roll me another Bull Durham, please? Can't you do it with one hand, Joey?"

How I wished my friend Chuck were here with me now. He'd know what to do and how to make this situation fun. But my hopes and dreams never seem to come true.

Dust from the caked clay surface of the road swirled up and over the handlebars and windshield of my Harley making it almost impossible for me to see the curves that came at me at least every ten seconds. The dryness of the flying earth didn't prevent it from sticking to my old pair of goggles, which slid around on my face and bounced with every change in direction of the wind and crater encountered in the road, letting the grit slash across my tired eyes. I thought about plunging straight ahead with my eyes closed because the road itself was no better than the off-road that bordered it. What did I have to lose?

My head was growing heavy as my sight grew dim. Only the cool wind in my hair gave me much needed comfort. I definitely had to find a place to stop for the night. Shadows danced across the road from one side to the other. The dust in the air clouded my vision and made me want to smother. I was so weak. I was so scared. I was one of the meek in this crazy world. Where was my family? Where were my friends? Where was my one and only true love in this crazy world?

The answers were easy. The answers were clear. Neither my family nor my friends were anywhere near. All I had was the roar of my Harley and the strum of my Les Paul. They would have to be enough to let me stand tall and not fall.

But there was one comforting thought that kept coming back to me. Through all the bouncing and churning of my beloved Harley. I could feel my trusty guitar case banging lovingly against my back. Like my best friends, they were still here with me hanging on through thick and thin. Fortunately, I'd wrapped my guitar in several heavy towels inside the case so I had a faint hope that it was still in one piece.

I was living fast and running hard, that was for sure. But, it was no longer a joke. I was the prototypical man on the run. Accused of a crime I didn't commit, convicted by a jury that did not yet exist, and then busting out of a make-believe prison so I wouldn't face the gallows pole. It was all in my dreams, and I knew it.

I packed my bags in a hurry strapping on an old friend…not my gun. No, my guitar! Now I'm running down this road that never ends. I've never been to jail before, but one thing is clear. I'm never going back again!

I didn't dare look back for fear that he might be right on my tail. One slip and I could be dead as a doornail, either from a bullet shot from his gun or from the hangman's rope that my dreams said awaited me on the gallows pole. I didn't savor either possibility, but I was running low on gas and my body was ready to give out once and for all. Even though I'd never seen him in the flesh, I could see his face, the face of a cold-blooded killer, Sheriff John Brown, burned permanently into my brain. My fear and my hate battled to control my mind.

When I looked up through the haze, I saw something that sent a chill up my spine. It was an almost blood red moon…a bad moon rising into the sky to greet me. All the bad signs were here for me to see in my dream.

I see a bad moon rising. I see troubles on the way. I see earthquakes and lightning. I see bad times today. I shouldn't go around tonight. Well, it's bound to take my life. There's a bad moon on the rise.

I hear hurricanes a-blowing. I know the end is coming soon. I fear rivers overflowing. I hear the voice of rage and ruin. Hope I got my things together. Hope I'm quite prepared to die. Looks like I'm in for nasty weather. One eye is taken for an eye. There's a bad moon on the rise!

Oh, the devil is rising with the moon. He cries and my blood turns cold. Oh, no! Never was the darkness so black. No light and nowhere to go.

My spirit is crying for a love. So tired of being alone. I remember he came here to steal, and you, Linda Lou, are his stealer of souls. I see a black moon rising, and it's calling out my name. I've been blinded, lost and confused. Darkness will call me no more. Heaven is no friend of mine. No god ever knocked on my door.

I'm standing on the dark side reaching for the power of her hand. She's weaving an unholy light and calls from Lucifer's land. An angel of hell is rising. Heaven's no friend of mine.

I picked up a penny from the ground with tails pointing up. I walked without inspection under a ladder next to a truck. I had the numbers '666' tattooed on my wrist on Friday the 13th, a day of bad luck. The palm reader read the lines on my left palm, and without warning she ran and left me stuck. I was hit in the face by a horseshoe, and I turned blue when I gagged on a four-leaf clover leaf. My prize winning lottery ticket was purloined by an invisible thief. To top it off, all he left was a one-way ticket to hell and a book of matches as well to seal my grief.

I closed my eyes to try to erase the terrible images from my mind, and when I opened them again…that's when I first saw the sign. It was an old, battered billboard, but a few quick glances convinced me that it was an advertisement for a motel. It was the first piece of good news I'd had in a long time. On this godforsaken road somewhere near the border between California and Mexico, the existence of any civilization would surely be deemed a miracle. This dirty trail through a near desert could only be used to smuggle drugs and illegals into California from

Mexico. I wasn't even sure which side of the border I was on right now because there were no signs of any kind…except the billboard. But, I also knew Sheriff John Brown wouldn't let a mere change of lawful jurisdiction change his mind. After all, he had as much to gain or lose as I did.

I wanted so bad to stop and turn around…to go back and study the old sign. How far was it? Did it still exist, whatever it was? But I knew that was impossible. I had to be running low on fuel. My bike's broken fuel gauge didn't offer much solace with the arrow rigidly pointing at empty.

I watched the road rushing under the wheels of my bike. It was sad and funny at the same time. The rocks and dust and weeds shot past me like the years of my life. I remembered those many trips with my parents years ago up U.S. 1 when I knew exactly where I was and who I was. In my imagination, the chrome heart of my bike shone brightly in the sun as I whispered 'Long may you run' to the beast. And she ran and ran and ran into the darkness. But times were better then. My imaginary bike needed no gas.

Now, I don't know where I'm running to or just what road I'm running on. It's getting dark, yet, somehow, the sun is in my eyes. I'm running on empty, running blind, into a sun that wasn't there!

As I think back to those peaceful days of just a month or so ago, I'm confused. I was trying to survive and keep my love alive back there. I called the road my own, but I don't know exactly when or how that road turned into the road I'm on now. I remember my friends, the ones I turned to pull me through so often. When I looked into their eyes, were they running, too? I don't know how to tell you how crazy this life feels for me now. I'm surely running on empty.

After I don't know how long with my mind reeling and without thinking, I found myself slamming my mechanical beast to a dead stop. The cloud of dust caused me to gag and my eyes to burn like they were on fire. At least the rising moon in the distance will give me some light so that I can get down the road in the otherwise pitch-blackness that is closing in around me. There is so much dust on my one headlight that its feeble attempt to show me what lies ahead failed miserably.

But why did I stop? I shook my head and turned to continue my retreat. That's when I saw it out of the corner of my eye. Another sign!

I turned the Harley's engine off and as the sound slowly died away, I listened for the sound of the automobile that carried my adversary. I wondered if my luck would hold…had he taken the wrong fork in the road just outside of that last town? It was quiet, deadly quiet. I waited for what must have been two minutes, frozen on the seat of my bike. All that happened was that it became darker and darker and a deadly silence fell over me.

Suddenly I saw a tall dark figure waving in the gusts of wind. It seemed to be talking to me.

"See, I can't scare anybody. They come from miles around to laugh in my face and eat in my field." It was a scarecrow swinging on a pole. "Oh, the Lord gave me a soul, but forgot to give me common sense."

Then some blackbirds said, "What the thunder would you do with common sense?"

"Just to reason out the reason of the wishes and the whyness and the whence. I would while away the hours conferring with the flowers, consulting with the rain. And my head I'd be scratching while my thoughts were busy hatching, if I only had a brain.

"I'd unravel every riddle, for every individle, in trouble or in pain. With the thoughts I'd be thinking, I could be another Lincoln, if I only had a brain. I could tell you why the ocean's near the shore. I could think of things I never thought before. Then, I'd sit and think some more.

"I would not be just a nothing, my head all full of stuffing, my heart all full of pain. I would dance and be merry. Life would be a dingle derry, if I only had a brain. Yeah, it would be kind of pleasing to reason out the reason for the things I can't explain. Then, perhaps I'd deserve you and be even worthy of you, if I only had a brain."

I realized that the scarecrow was talking to me…about me. It was telling me that I didn't have a brain! When a blast of dust caused me to blink my eyes, the scarecrow disappeared. It was only in my brain all the time! So, I was wrong. I did have a brain.

Finally, my imagination and my fear released me, and I pushed the Harley off the dirt road, walking at first and listening for the telltale sounds of my pursuer. But they never came. I was safe, for now.

Then, just as I began to relax, another strange sense attacked my psyche. There was a smell in the air…a sweet smell. Not the smell of mescal and sweet perfume I enjoyed in El Paso. No, my mind instantly snapped back to that night in Lodi when I was playing a gig with some guys I met by accident. Their lead guitar player came down with a roaring case of the flu, and they happened by chance to spot my trusty guitar case strapped to the back of my Harley.

I stopped and inhaled deeply just to be sure. The pleasure bounced through my mind like an old friend. *Colitas!* The warm intoxicating smell of the tip of a marijuana branch, the pleasure spot defined by an abundance of sap…the most potent spot on the leaf. I remembered singing those intoxicating words up there in Lodi…*the warm smell of colitas*! I'd even sung the words in my dreams many times before, but for some reason I recall that gig in Lodi as something special probably because that was where I first saw her. But this was the first time I'd sensed that perfect aroma without having the precious weed in my hands.

It's the same kind of story that seems to come down from long ago. Two friends having coffee together when something flies by their window. It might be out on that lawn, which is wide, at least half of a playing field. Because there's no explaining what your imagination can make you see and feel.

Now, it's not a meaningless question to ask if they've been and gone. I remember a talk about North Carolina and a strange, strange pond. You see, the sides were like glass in the thick of a forest without a road. And if any man's ever made that land, then I think it would have showed.

The aroma and my imagination let loose together here in the desert and made me feel as if I were hypnotized. It seemed so much like a dream with me on the outside looking in. Somewhere, I had heard the story told of that special place down in Mexico. It is said that a man can fly over mountains and hills without needing an engine or an airplane.

I knew without reasoning that it's a meaningless question to ask whether those stories are right or wrong. What's important is not the truth but the feeling you get when you're hypnotized.

As wonderful as my thoughts were, this still wasn't the time or the place to mellow out. I made a beeline through the roadside sand for the signboard hoping that it would lead me to some kind of shelter. In the dust filled moonlight I gazed at the sign searching for some kind, any kind of information. Unfortunately, there was so much dirt on the board itself that I had to scrape it off as best I could before I could read the words.

After flaying at the surface for what must have been five minutes, I stepped back to view what I had uncovered. At first, I couldn't believe my eyes. There on the board was a two-story building, definitely an example of Spanish architecture, and an arrow pointing to my left. On the arrow in large letters were the words *Travelers Welcome.* They were in English. Below the arrow were the words *One Mile.*

I was in luck! It had to be a motel, a motel out here in the middle of nowhere. I immediately saw my mattress of sand and hard rock pillow transformed into a soft bed with clean sheets, and a feather pillow. I jumped up into the air like a cheerleader, then turned and ran as fast as my feet would carry me back to my bike. In seconds I was on my way to what I hoped and dreamed was a motel.

But suddenly I hesitated. *Would there be a vacancy?* As I gazed ahead through the ever-present dust, I realized that I might be their only customer on a night like this. No one else was on this road, coming or going. Then the real question hit me. *What would a motel be doing out here in the middle of nowhere?*

The mile flew by quickly and soon in the distance I saw a shimmering light. A lone building stood atop a hill just like a Spanish fort defending the vacant wilderness. Then I recalled the other words I saw on the old sign.

Welcome to the Hotel California. Such a lovely place!

16
Hotel California

Much to my surprise the parking lot in front of the building was almost full of older cars covered with the ever-present desert dust. At first glance it didn't appear as if any of them had been driven recently, but I just ascribed that to the swirling desert wind. I knew that in five minutes or less my Harley would be covered by a mound of dirt, too. But I had no choice. Besides, my motorcycle was built to endure the onslaught of the elements.

But a positive thought popped into my mind at the same time. With all these motor vehicles, there must be some gasoline somewhere nearby. So I parked my bike in a relatively sheltered spot under the only tree on the lot and headed for the front door. That's when I saw something that my mind couldn't believe.

There were no lights on the exterior of the building. The shimmering light I'd seen as I approached was the reflection of the moonlight off the Spanish tile that covered most of the structure. What startled me at first was the eerie tolling of a mission bell from the bell tower on the center of the roof. It had a hollow sound and a lower pitch than I would have expected. Again I realized that it must be covered with dust and grime from the surrounding desert.

Suddenly, I turned around, and she was standing there, with silver bracelets on her wrists, and flowers in her hair. There, ahead of me in the doorway, stood the shapely form of a young woman. At first I couldn't see her face, yet as I stared at her I knew she was a Mexican beauty. At the same time my mind was wondering how she knew I was coming.

She lit up a candle to show me the way inside. I smiled and nodded. Then, as I walked up the three stairs to the porch, I saw her face. My intuition was correct. She was one of the most beautiful women I had ever seen. She walked up to me so gracefully and took my crown of thorns.

It seemed as if I was in another lifetime, one of toil and blood. When blackness was a virtue and the road ahead was full of mud. I come in from the wilderness, a creature devoid of form.

"Come in," she said. "I'll give you shelter from the storm."

Before this moment, not a word was spoken between us, there was little risk involved. Everything up to this point had been left unresolved. Try imagining a place where it's always safe and warm. I was burned out from exhaustion, buried in the hail, poisoned in the bushes and blown out on the trail, hunted like a crocodile, ravaged in the corn.

"Come in," she said. "I'll give you shelter from the storm."

She looked over my shoulder directly at my Harley. Then she stopped me in my tracks and asked me about my motorcycle and the thrills it must have brought me. I couldn't resist. She wanted a story, and I needed to tell someone about my encounter with the police in the hills, or should I call them mountains, of California on my way west.

So, we sat down on the front porch of the Hotel California, and I began to spin my tale. There was excitement in her eyes.

"I was riding my Harley and playing my guitar. I was going down a mountain road doing 150 miles an hour. On one side of the mountain road there was a mountain. On the other side there was nothing. There was just a cliff in the air. But I wasn't paying attention, you know, I was just driving down the road playing my guitar.

"Now, when you're going down a mountain you've got to be very careful, especially if your guitar is an acoustic guitar. Because, if it's an acoustic guitar the wind pressure is greater on the box side than on the neck side because there's more guitar on the box side.

"All of a sudden, by accident, a string broke off my guitar. It broke, you know, right there, went flying across the road that way and wrapped itself around a yield sign. Well, the sign didn't break. It didn't come out of the ground, and the string stayed wrapped around it and stayed in the other end of my guitar. I held onto the bike with one hand and held on to the guitar with the other."

My beautiful companion stopped me for a moment as one of the servants brought us each a glass of cold Mexican beer. I was very grateful for that, believe me. With my thirst finally relieved, I continued.

"I made a sharp turn off the road. Luckily, I didn't go into the mountain. I went over the cliff. I was doing 150 miles an hour sideways and 500 feet down at the same time. Hey, I was looking for the cops because I knew that what I was doing was illegal.

"I knew that I didn't have long to live in this world. I realized that it was my obligation to write one last farewell song. I took out a piece of paper and a pen, but it didn't write. I put a new ink cartridge in my pen, and I sat back and thought for a while. It came to me like a flash.

"I don't want a pickle, just want to ride on my motor-cicle. And, I don't want a tickle, I'd rather ride on my motor-cicle. And I don't wanna die, I just want to ride on my motor-cy-cle.

"I knew it wasn't the best song I ever wrote, but I didn't have time to change it. But, you know, the most amazing thing was that I didn't die. I landed on top of a police car, and it died!"

"What happened then," she said enthusiastically as I sipped on my beer. I had to finish my story, if just for her.

"I came into town at a screaming 175 miles an hour singing my new motorcycle song. I stopped in front of Fred's Deli, and out front there was a man eating the most tremendous pickle, a pickle the size of four pregnant watermelons. He walked up to me, pushed the monster pickle into my face, and starting asking questions. I noticed a cord hanging from the long end of the pickle, going up his sleeve, down his shirt, into his pants and shoes, and finally out into a briefcase he had near his feet.

"Right then a four foot cop arrived with a five foot gun, a cop that at one time must have been six foot three. He walked up and with one tremendous hand he grabbed the pickle away from the other guy. He then threw it a hundred feet straight up in the air. And while the pickle was half way between going up and coming down, he took out his gun and put a three inch bullet hole right through the long end of the pickle.

"It started coming down so he stuck out his foot and caught the pickle on his big toe. And balancing the pickle on his toe, he reached his huge hand into his little pocket, pulled out a ten foot ticket, borrowed my pen, and wrote me up. Then he rolled it up and stuffed it into the bullet hole in the pickle. He then took the pickle with the ticket and shoved it down my throat! Right then I knew that I didn't want a pickle. I just wanted to ride my motor-cicle!"

My companion was laughing hysterically so I figured that it was a good time to stop. We both took a sip to finish our beers. I felt a lot better now.

As I started to speak again, she held up her hand and beckoned for me to enter through the doorway. I was a little tired and ready for a soft chair or comfy bed. In the distance I could hear music being played by a Mariachi band. Some food and more to drink would hit the spot right now. I assumed that this beautiful creature was taking me to the front desk to check in, but that was not to be. In a soft sweet voice she told me that my room was ready and that my dinner would be served in the master's chambers!

Now I began to become concerned. Had my pursuer gotten here first? Was this a trap? I had no weapon, no way to defend myself. Could this woman be trusted? But from the look on her face it was hard to believe that she was my enemy.

Soon, we came to a courtyard, the place where the band was playing. There was a bar and a group of small tables surrounding a rectangular dance floor. She seated me at a table and the Captain would soon be by to take my order. In moments a man dressed as a waiter approached my table. I tried to tell him that I had very little money, but that didn't seem to matter to him.

I asked for a glass of merlot, my favorite wine. The Captain merely shook his head and with a smile told me that they hadn't had that spirit at the Hotel California since 1969! Instead, he suggested a glass of sweet brandy that was the specialty of the house.

When he returned with my drink and some chips and salsa, I tried to ask him who the beautiful woman who had greeted me at the door was. I'll never forget exactly what he said to me. But first he sat down and whispered his answer in my ear.

"Her name is Camille, and she drives a brand new Mercedes Benz."

He had really bad breath and a voice I thought I'd heard before.

"No one told me about her, the way she lied. Well, no one told me about her, how many people cried. Well, it's too late to say you're sorry. How would I know? Why should I care? Please don't bother trying to find her. She's not there.

"Nobody told me about her. What could I do? Well, no one told me about her though they all knew. Well, let me tell you about the way she looked, the way she acted, the color of her hair. Her voice is soft and cool. Her eyes are clear and bright. But she's not there..."

Then he said something about Tiffanys that I couldn't understand. Finally, he told me that after I finished my drink she would accompany me to dinner. As I pondered that prospect, I pointed to the rather large preponderance of young men dancing nearby.

"Camille calls them her friends," the Captain responded. "These pretty boys dance in the courtyard every night, sweet summer sweat. Some dance to remember, some dance to forget."

That sounded ominous. Then he pointed to my glass.

"Strange brew. Killing what's inside of you. She's a witch of trouble in electric blue. In her own mad mind, she's in love with you. Now what you gonna do? Strange brew. She's some kind of demon dusting in the flue. If you don't watch out, it will stick to you. What kind of fool are you?

"On a boat in the middle of a raging sea, she would make a scene for it all to be ignored. And wouldn't you be bored? Strange brew."

At that moment I began to wonder whether this could be heaven or this could be hell. Some of the pretty boys dancing nearby were smiling while the rest seemed deep in despair. One of them came over and sat at my table. His name was Johnny. As we started to converse, I asked him how he came to be at the Hotel California. With a sad look on his face he told me his story.

"I went to the gypsy fortune teller to have my fortune read. I didn't know what to tell her; I had a dizzy feeling in my head.

"Tell me, gypsy, can you see me in your crystal ball? I'm asking you what I can do. My back's against the wall, and I can't hold on much longer. So I've come to you, my friend, for now my life seems at an end.

"I came to see you once before, one hundred years ago. You took my hand and broke the spell. That should have let me go. But my years have gone so slowly, so I'm here again my friend, for now my life is at an end.

"Cast your eyes into the crystal, deep inside the mystery. Is that a vision of a lonely man? I fear it looks a lot like me. Is that a man without a woman whose empty life is but a shell? Empty hearts will echo forever in the wishing well.

"Fortune Teller, you've got to help me find an end to the nightmare because I can't stand this pain and the curse of time. Somewhere in your eyes I'll find the answer. Give me the truth I've been looking for. Be my guiding light; I'll take my chances. Turn the card, seal my fate, close the door.

"Can you help me see, is there an end to the sorrow? Or was this slow ride to nowhere always meant to be? Some days come with a vengeance; some days I feel so bad. The mirror holds no secrets. I lost the best thing that I had."

He took a sip from his drink and then carried on.

"She said she'd take a look at my palm. She said, 'son, you feel kinda warm.' And she looked into her crystal ball and said, 'You're in love!'

"I said, 'It could not be so, I'm not passionate with the girls I know.' She said, 'When the next one arrives, look into her eyes.'

"I left there in a hurry looking forward to my big surprise. The next day I discovered that the Fortune Teller told me a lie. I hurried back down to that woman as mad as I could be. I told her I didn't see nobody; why'd she make a fool out of me?

"Then something struck me as if it came from up above. While looking at the Fortune Teller, I fell in love.

"Now, I'm a happy fellow; well, I'm married to the Fortune Teller. We're happy as we can be; now I get my fortune told for free. But I can never leave the Hotel California."

He pointed over into the corner where his spouse sat.

"I got a Black Magic Woman. Yes, I got a Black Magic Woman. She's got me so blind I can't see. But she's a Black Magic Woman, and she's trying to make a devil out of me. Don't turn your back on me,

Baby. Yes, don't turn your back on me, Baby. Don't mess around with your tricks. Because you might just wake up my magic sticks!

"You got your spell on me, Baby. Yes, you got your spell on me, Baby. Turning my heart into stone. Need you so bad, Magic Woman, I can't leave you alone.

"She lives here in the Hotel California. Like I said, I can never leave."

As I enjoyed my drink as best I could under the circumstances, I began to wonder whether I should split from this scene altogether. I probably would have, but I remembered my fuel problem and soon, there she was, standing before me in a beautiful evening gown ready to escort me to dinner.

I chose that moment to excuse myself to use the bathroom. Once inside I encountered an older man who walked with a limp. He wasn't smiling. Yet, he seemed to know that I had a problem.

"Where can a guy get some gasoline around here?" I said in a polite tone of voice.

The man grinned an almost toothless grin and shook his head.

"Yer gonna have to siphon it out of one of them cars outside…if there's any left."

I thanked the man as I realized that his advice was probably sound. Everyone here seemed trapped to me. As he reached the door to the men's room, the old man turned toward me one last time.

"You can checkout any time you like, but you can never leave."

With those words, the fear of my pursuer faded. I had to find my way back to the dirt road, back to the place I'd been before.

After finishing my business, I stopped to inspect my image in the bathroom mirror. For some reason I started talking to myself.

"Mirror in the bathroom, please talk free. The door is locked, just you and me. Can I take you to the restaurant, it's got glass tables. You can watch yourself while you are eating. I just can't stop it. Every Saturday you see me window shopping. I find no interest in the racks and shelves, just a thousand reflections of my own sweet self.

"Mirror in the bathroom, recompense, for all my crimes of self-defense. Cures you whisper make no sense. I drift gently into mental illness."

That's when I saw it. A phone number and name scrawled on the wall. I searched the pocket of my leather jacket and pulled out a scrap of paper. I looked at the name and number on the crumpled paper. I remembered the waitress bumping into me at Johann's in Wisconsin. Was it her phone number or Janie's number? It was the place where I met Janie. Could it have been her number? Jenny, the name is so close. I began to reminisce.

"Jenny, Jenny, who can I turn to? You give me something I can hold onto. I know you think I'm like the others before who saw your name and number on the wall. Jenny, I got your number. I need to make you mine. Jenny, don't change your number.

"Jenny, Jenny, you're the girl for me. You don't know me, but you make me so happy. I tried to call you before, but I lost my nerve. I tried my imagination, but I was disturbed. I got it! I got your number on the wall. For a good time call... For the price of a dime I can always turn to you. 8-6-7-5-3-0-9."

After gritting my teeth and resolving to find the first way out of the Hotel California, I left the relative safety of the restroom and followed my hostess to the main dining hall, which she referred to as the master's chamber. I didn't dare ask who this elusive master was. I had enough problems of my own.

The room was packed with guests. Before I could speak to any of them, my hostess grabbed me by the arm.

"They're living it up at the Hotel California! What a nice surprise. Bring all your alibis! We are all just prisoners here, of our own device."

There were mirrors on the ceiling. There was pink champagne on ice. And in the corner they gathered for the feast. I saw them stab their prey, which was still alive, with their steely knives, over and over. But the guests, the pretty boys, could not seem to kill the beast!

It was definitely time to go, and I was in luck. Camille reached over and began to offer an apology to me. Then she asked me where I was going and before I could speak she commenced to telling me.

"You're going around the world. You've got to find your girl. There is no time for spreading roots; the time has come to travel on. Got to find the queen of all your dreams. Yours is a tale that can't be told. Your freedom you hold dear. How days ago in times of old, when magic filled the air, t'was in the deepest depth of mordor, you met a girl so fair. But Gollum and the evil one crept up and slipped away with her. You think there's nothing you can do. Not so! You've got to ramble on!

"Take the highway to the end of the night. Take a journey to the bright midnight. Realms of bliss, realms of light. Some are born to sweet delight. Some are born to the endless night.

"Time to live. Time to lie. Time to laugh. Time to die. Take it easy, Joey. Take it as it comes. Don't move too fast if you want your love to last. You've been moving much too fast. Time to walk, time to run, time to aim your arrows at the sun. Go real slow, you'll like it more and more. Take it as it comes, specialize in having fun.

"Desperado, why don't you come to your senses? Been out riding fences for so long now. Oh, you're a hard one, but I know that you got your reasons. These things that are pleasing you can hurt you somehow.

"Don't you draw the queen of diamonds, Joe, she'll beat you if she's able. You know the queen of hearts is always your best bet. But it seems to me that some fine things have been laid upon your table. But you only want the ones you can't get.

"Desperado, oh, you ain't getting no younger. Your pain and your hunger, they're driving you home. And freedom, oh, freedom, well, that's just some people talking. Your prison is walking through this world all alone.

"Don't your feet get cold in the winter time? The sky won't snow, and the sun won't shine. It's hard to tell the nighttime from the day, and you're losing all your highs and lows. Ain't it funny how the feeling goes away?

"Desperado, why don't you come to your senses, come down from those fences. Open the gate. It may be raining, but there's a rainbow above you. You'd better let somebody love you before it's too late."

With those words, she kissed me gently and turned to walk away. She knew I wouldn't be staying even though I was sorely tempted. As she left, I heard her final words.

"Besides, I have another visitor coming to the Hotel California. Such a lovely place."

Something deep inside made me told her how I felt. I couldn't stay, but would she consider leaving?

"Come on, Baby, don't you wanna go? I could take you there. You could get what you want in the South; you could let down your hair." I said, "Do you? Don't you? Will you? Won't you? Baby, won't you please let me know? I ain't talking about Chicago; I'm talking about Mexico.

"I'm making a run for Mexico. Come on, Baby, because I gotta go; the law is after me. I killed a woman in a bar last night; there was no other way it could be. While the air in this joint could be cut with a knife as the jukebox got rocked into sections, bring a compass and some money for gas because I ain't gonna stop for directions.

"And every time the phone rings, it scares me to death. Saw my face in the paper today. I don't wanna hear the stories about your momma and poppa. No, I don't want to hear you cry. For me there's no second chance right now. It's the end for me; I can't lie. My life goes on in Mexico."

All she would do was shake her head 'no'. I could still see love in her eyes, but she told me she had to stay.

"You thought the leaden winter would bring you down forever, but you rode upon a steamer to the violence of the sun. And the colors of the sea bind your eyes with trembling mermaids, and you touch the distant beaches with tales of brave Ulysses. How his naked ears were tortured by the sirens sweetly singing, for the sparkling waves are calling you to kiss their white laced lips.

"And you see a girl's brown body dancing through the turquoise, and her footprints make you follow where the sky loves the sea. And when your fingers find her, she drowns you in her body, carving deep blue ripples in the tissues of your mind. The tiny purple fishes run laughing through your fingers, and you want to take her with you to the hard land of the winter.

"Her name is Aphrodite, and she rides a crimson shell, and you know you cannot leave her for you touched the distant sands with tales of brave Ulysses."

She smiled one last time as she turned to leave me.

I looked at the Captain who nodded knowingly as he motioned with his head toward a nearby door, which opened on a hallway leading to the parking lot. I put my last five spot on the table for him and headed for my bike in a hurry still wondering where I had seen him before. The patch over his eye and the scar on his face seemed familiar.

Once out on the front porch and down the stairs my eyes immediately caught the sight of a different car parked in the dusty parking lot. It was a 1969 Buick…hearse. It was Maggie's car…her farm car. The big questions loomed before me. How did it get here? Who was the driver?

It didn't take me long to answer my questions.

It was the sheriff! He probably shot and killed my girl, blamed me for the murder, and now he's stolen Maggie's car, and he's here to kill me! But I'll show him! I have the key right here in my pocket.

It was a lucky break that I still had the keys to the hearse, and it didn't take long to retrieve the hose and gas can from the trunk whereupon I siphoned enough gas out of the old hearse's tank to fill up the Harley. For once I had something to thank Maggie for. For some unexplained reason I didn't fear of the obvious fact that the sheriff might appear at any moment.

Another lucky break for me was the fact that I had parked the Harley in a spot behind the tree from which his view was completely obscured. I put the gas can and hose back and covered the trunk with a handful of dust so that my intrusion wouldn't be detected. Now I was ready to ramble on.

17
The Medicine Man

I walked the bike out to the road and nervously pondered my next move. I could go east into the desert or I could go west toward Baja and the ocean. I could go north back to the States or I could go south deeper into Mexico. With any luck, my adversary, the Sheriff John Brown and his henchmen had already checked in to the Hotel California, and would never leave! That would be revenge enough for me, but I knew I wasn't that lucky.

Just then an old man wearing tattered old clothes and carrying a dusty gray beard staggered up to me and asked me for a ride. I couldn't tell whether he came out of the hotel or not. He didn't say where he was going or how he came to be in the middle of nowhere without a means of transportation. But how could I refuse him? I had already been in that situation myself.

I must look like a good listener because as we started to leave, he began to whisper his story to me. I must admit that I was interested in how he got here.

"Just me and a friend roaming around. Him a magician, and I was a clown. Playing the streets for a dollar a day. Waiting for the right time and a sign to lead the way. Crossed over the border to a mystical land; sort of unexpected, didn't understand. On a razor's edge on a grain of sand, onward we wandered to the gates of oblivion."

When he mentioned the border I automatically assumed he meant the Mexican border. I wanted to ask him where his friend was, but I was sure he would get to that.

"On a roll of the dice we headed out west where the sage and the spice attracted us. Shadows fell down like a dark groping hand. Saw the teeth of the wolves and the blood of the lambs. On a turn of the cards I lightened my load, throwing off fear for the weakness it holds. On target and calm the vision was clear beyond the mirage I took for granted was here.

"On a flip of the coins we rode the coast trying to make the most of every situation that we witnessed near at hand on a drifters' crusade all over the land. Could it be in the stars, in the passing of cars, in a change in your mind, in the passing of time, in a ribbon of rhyme just down the line?"

He paused and pointed across the sand. I had asked myself those same questions so I listened carefully. Maybe he could shed some light on my problems.

"Very superstitious...writing on the wall. Very superstitious... ladder's about to fall. Thirteen-month old baby broke that looking glass. Seven years of bad luck. Good things in the past. Very superstitious... wash your face and hands. Rid me of the problem. Get all that you can. Keep me in a daydream. Keep me going strong. You don't want to save me. Sad is my song. Very superstitious...Nothing more to say. Very superstitious...Devil's on his way. When you believe in things you don't understand, you will suffer. Superstition ain't the way."

I couldn't agree more. The old man kept going.

"Follow me into the desert, as thirsty as you are. Crack a smile and cut your mouth and drown in alcohol. Because down below the truth is lying beneath the river bed. So quench yourself and drink the water that flows below her head. Oh, no, there she goes, out in the sunshine. The sun is mine!"

I had no idea whom he was referring to, but I decided to give him the benefit of the doubt and listen to his story. What else could I do?

"Close your eyes and bow your head, I need a little sympathy. 'Cause fear is strong, and love's for everyone who isn't me. So kill your health and kill yourself and kill everything you love. And if you live, you can fall to pieces and suffer with my ghost."

I was beginning to get a little freaked out by his focus on death, and his worn Black Sabbath T-shirt didn't lessen my fears. An old tattoo on his arm read 'Hell's Angels'.

"So, follow me into the desert, as desperate as you are, where the moon is glued to a picture of heaven and all the little pigs have God.

Just a burden in my hand, just an anchor on my heart, just a tumor in my head, and I'm in the dark.

"If I shot my love today, would you cry for me? If I lost my head again, would you lie for me? If I left her in the sand, would you die for me?"

He turned to look at me and must have seen the bewildered look on my face.

"Come, close your eyes to all you fear while the holy spirits gather, oh, so near. You need their help to send all evil away, and you require love to keep your senses at bay.

"My boy, you need to see the witchdoctor and the medicine man. I will show you the way. But we have to move fast because that cloud of dust back there could be the Sheriff John Brown and his henchmen."

I looked back at the approaching cloud. It was a speck in the desert floor, still maybe an important speck. Was it just dust in the wind?

I close my eyes only for a moment then the moment's gone. All my dreams pass before my eyes with curiosity. Same old song, just a drop of water in an endless sea. All we do crumbles to the ground though we refuse to see. Now don't hang on. Nothing lasts forever but the earth and sky. It slips away, and all your money won't another minute buy. Dust in the wind. All we are is dust in the wind.

I wondered how he knew about Sheriff John Brown? Had the sheriff planted this old man in my path to lead me to my capture? Was all this just a trick? But, then why didn't John Brown just grab me at the Hotel California? I immediately realized that I would have to be more careful in my dealings with strangers. But I did owe him an answer.

"Old man, look at my life. I'm a lot like you were. Twenty-four and there's so much more. Live alone in a paradise that makes me think of two. Love lost, such a cost. Give me things that don't get lost like a coin that won't get tossed rolling home to you. I need someone to love me the whole day through. Ah, one look in my eyes and you can tell that's true.

"Lullabies, look in your eyes, run around the same old town. Doesn't mean that much to me to mean that much to you. I've been first and last. Look at how the time goes past. But, I'm all alone at last, rolling home to where? If I only knew, I need someone to love the whole day through."

I looked back over my shoulder to see if anyone was following us. There was some smoke in the air, but it wasn't clear that a car or motorcycle rider was beneath it.

I guess I responded too slowly to his admonition because he pointed at the engine of my Harley.

"Revving up your engine, listen to her howling roar. Metal under tension, begging you to touch and go."

The old man pointed down the road in front of us.

"Highway to the danger zone, ride into the danger zone. Heading into twilight, spreading out her wings tonight. She's got you jumping off the deck and shoving into overdrive."

My Harley didn't have overdrive. But I knew it was just a metaphor.

"Highway to the danger zone. I'll take you right into the danger zone.

"You'll never say hello to yourself until you get it on the red line overload. You'll never know what you can do until you get it up as high as you can go. Out along the edges, always where I burn to be. The further on the edge, the hotter the intensity! Gonna take you right into the danger zone."

Before I could ask him what he meant by the danger zone, he signaled for me to pull to a stop at the next high ridge. From that spot he pointed to the east toward what appeared to be a slowly rising column of thick black smoke. Then he sat down cross-legged on the sand facing the east and motioned for me to do the same. At that moment I couldn't think of a good reason not to comply with his request especially since I could no longer see a cloud of dust behind us. As he again pointed eastward toward the smoke, he began to chant as he moved his hands slowly over his head.

"I got a coin in your palm. I can make it disappear. I got a card up my sleeve. Name it, and I'll pull it out of your ear. I got a rabbit in the hat. If you wanna come and see, this is what will be.

"I got shackles on my wrists. Soon I'll slip and I'll be gone. Chain me in a box in the river, and I'll be rising in the sun. Trust none of what you want and less of what you see. This is what will be.

"I got a shiny saw blade. All I need is a volunteer. I'll cut you in half while you're smiling from ear to ear. And the freedom that you sought is drifting like a ghost amongst the trees.

"Now, there's a fire down below, but it's coming up here. So, leave everything you know, carry only what you fear. On the road the sun is sinking low, bodies hanging in the trees. This is what will be."

I felt like the old man was talking to me, but I wasn't sure how to interpret what he said or how it applied to me. Still, he had more to say, and I was all ears.

"Many distant miles away, past the shores of ever dark, there stands a magic man, who bears an evil mark. He helps all concerned, those who come again return, injecting lies while fires burn, the devil's heart with angel's words. Have you wondered what heaven is like? He can show you in one night, overwhelming with euphoric lift, to lure you... to steal your gift.

"Intoxication seeping down to the bone, and there's no question where you have to go. Understand...just take his hand. He's the medicine man."

Don't ask me why, but something inside my rattled brain told me that this was the right way to go.

"Once proud and fearless men with desire in their eyes lost strong and fruitful lives to self-indulgent ties. Their souls were dipped in venom and put into a box, then placed upon a crowded shelf where countless souls now rot. Have you ever wondered what hell is like? He can take you there. Just one taste and you'll be back and by the high you will swear.

"Intoxication seeping down to the bone, and there's no question where you have to go. Understand...just take his hand. He's the medicine man."

As we walked toward the Medicine Man's teepee, the old man began staring into the sun and mumbling under his breath.

"Black witches sing their verses of charms, hexes, and curses. They tried to take out my eyes, but I don't have to hide. Black sunset's on its way down. I've got to go out on the town. I'm not afraid of the night. But I don't have to hide. Black moon dogs chasing at me way down to the sea. They want to steal my life, but I don't have to hide.

"It's the same kind of story that seems to come down from long ago. Two friends having coffee together when something flies by their window. It might be out on that lawn, which is wide, at least half of a playing field, because there's no explaining what your imagination can make you see and feel.

"Now it's not a meaningless question to ask if they've been and gone. I remember a talk about North Carolina and a strange, strange pond. You see, the sides were like glass in the thick of a forest without a road. And, if any man's hand ever made that land, then I think it would've showed."

Suddenly, the old man turned and looked me right in the eyes.

"They say there's a place down in Mexico where a man can fly over mountains and hills, and he don't need an airplane or some kind of engine, and he never will. Now you know it's a meaningless question to ask if those stories are right, because what matters most is the feeling you get when you're hypnotized. Seems like a dream; he's got me hypnotized."

Suddenly, there I was down on my knees in the sand in front of this yellow and brown teepee. The Medicine Man stood before me with a twinkle in his eyes. The old man was nowhere in sight, but I could still hear his voice. I began to wonder whether the old man and the Medicine Man were one and the same.

"There comes a time and it won't be the first, when the angels signal with a verse. And the lonely man for better or for worse, must seek his fate or forever be cursed.

"Two kinds of people in this world. Winners. Losers. You lost your power in this world, because you did not use it. Two kinds of trouble in this world. Living. Dying. You lost your power in this world, and the rumors are flying. So you go insane like you always do, and you call her name, she's a lot like Linda Lou."

I hadn't mentioned Linda Lou! How did he know about her? I was awash in uncertainty as he spoke.

"Lend me your ear while I call you a fool. You were kissed by a witch one night in the wood, and later insisted your feelings were true. The witch's promise was coming, believing she listened while laughing you flew.

"Leaves falling red, yellow, brown, all are the same, and the love you have found lay outside in the rain. Washed clean by the water, but nursing it's pain. The witch's promise was coming, and you're looking elsewhere for your own selfish gain. Keep looking, keep looking for somewhere to be. Meanwhile, leaves are still falling; you're too blind to see.

"You won't find it easy now, it's only fair. She was willing to give to you; you didn't care. You're waiting for more, but you've already had your share. The witch's promise is turning, so don't you wait up for her. She's going to be late."

He was speaking to me in rhymes and riddles, yet, I was beginning to see where he was going with these words. I had made bad assumptions and misread Linda Lou from the beginning. It was just the same as my misreading of Sally and Janie. I had to fix this problem before I would be able to find the right girl, that was certain. But I had bigger problems than my social life to deal with just now. Would I even survive long enough to find my own true love?

The Medicine Man studied the palms of my hands and had more to say. But this time he was speaking through me. I could feel the words flow from his mind into mine and then out of my mouth.

"Nobody's fault but mine. Trying to save my soul tonight. It's nobody's fault but mine. The Devil, he told me to roll. How to roll the log tonight. Brother, he showed me the gong. Brother, he showed me the ding dong, ding dong. Got a monkey on my back. Gonna change my ways tonight. I will get down rollin' tonight. Nobody's fault."

Next, the Medicine Man studied my face for a moment, then he issued a stern warning to me.

"You paint a picture so it's plain to see. Ain't no hiding, no security. He'll be watching every move you make. When you hear the rattle, better be awake.

"You leave a footprint for his eye to see, catch an echo from a lock and key, from a shadow, or behind a rock. He'll get you anywhere from the darkest shock.

"Hear a rustle from behind a tree, get you running home to sanctuary. Bolt the door and you think you're safe. The Sheriff is coming to get you if you're not awake. Got the snake eyes, they call him a snake in the bush. Just keep a look out for…snake eye!"

The Medicine Man laid his hand on my forehead. His hand was very cold. Then he began to speak in a deep tone as if he were reading my mind and calming me at the time.

"Oh, let the sun beat down upon your face, stars to fill your dreams. You are a traveler of both time and space, to be where you have been. To sit with elders of the gentle race, this world has seldom seen. They talk of days for which they sit and wait and all will be revealed. Talk and song from tongues of lilting grace whose sounds caress your ear.

"All you see turns to brown, as the sun burns the ground. And your eyes fill with sand, as you scan this wasted land, trying to find where you've been. Oh, pilot of the storm who leaves no trace, like thoughts inside a dream. Heed the path that led you to that place, yellow desert stream. Your Shangri-la beneath the summer moon, you will return again as sure as the dust that floats high and true when moving through Kashmir.

"Oh, father of the four winds, fill your sails across the sea of years, with no provision but an open face along the straits of fear."

Suddenly, he looked me right in the eyes.

"You were left as a child, dragged from the cradle. You were weaned in the wild, ran with the wolf pack, flesh torn to shreds. In the compensations, you were left there for dead.

"Read it in the paper; it ain't fair. You know who today don't seem to care. Living, loving, getting loose; masturbating with a noose. Now someone is kicking out the chair!"

He stopped right there for a moment. His chanting changed to a fatherly tone.

"My child, they mean to hang you!"

I already knew that Sheriff John Brown and his accomplices wanted to kill me. But with a noose in this day and age? I asked the Medicine Man why.

"Some kind of voodoo comes across this land. Some kind of voodoo...voodoo medicine man. Everyone is looking at the sky. Don't believe the cover-ups and lies they have been telling us since birth, pissing off old Mother Earth. My gones are bygones prophesied. Get ready!"

Again his cold hand pressed against my forehead. The serious expression on his face changed to a smile.

"Well, I'm a Voodoo Chile," his voice rang out. "Lord, I'm a Voodoo Chile.

"Well, the night I was born, Lord, I swear, the moon turned a fire red. Well, my poor mother cryin' out, 'Oh, Lord, the gypsy was right!' And I saw her fall down, right dead. Have mercy!

"Well, mountain lions found me there waiting and set me on an eagle's back. Well, mountain lions found me there and set me on the eagle's wing. It's the eagle's wing, baby, what can I say. He took me past the outskirts of infinity. And when he brought me back, he gave me the Venus witches' ring. Hey! And he said 'Fly on'. Fly on because I'm a Voodoo Chile, Baby."

The Medicine Man smiled again because he knew that I understood what he was saying. With a nod he went on.

"Wonder should you go or should you stay? Because what you got ain't working anyway. You did your best; God knows you tried. You feel like you've been crucified.

"Why did they take it all away? Tell me, please, oh voodoo, voodoo Medicine Man?"

Suddenly, almost as if in slow motion, the Medicine Man slumped to the ground seemingly unconscious. But as I reached over to see if he was okay, he began chanting in a strange accent. Yet, I could still understand his words.

"When the last eagle flies over the last crumbling mountain, and the last lion roars at the last dusty fountain, in the shadow of the forest, though she may be old and worn, they will stare unbelieving at the last unicorn.

"When the first breath of winter through the flowers is icing, and you look to the north and the pale moon is rising, and it seems like all else is dying and would leave the world to mourn, in the distance hear the laughter of the last unicorn.

"When the last moon is cast over the last star of morning, and the future has passed without even a last, desperate warning. Then, look into the sky where through the clouds a path is formed. Look and see her, how she sparkles. It's the last unicorn!"

Something made me look up, and I saw a flash of light crease the sky. Was it a falling star, or was it…the last unicorn. There was a rustling in a nearby hedgerow. I saw motion and sparks of light, but the source soon disappeared. I began to convince myself that I was just seeing things in the desert. This was all a giant mirage playing on my weak, tired mind. As I stared out across the plain, the Medicine Man rose up and grabbed me by the shoulders. His grip was firm but at the same time gentle.

It was truly strange. He looked at me as if this were the first moment of our meeting. He even smiled and asked me to tell him about my problems. I told him about Linda Lou and the Sheriff John Brown. He asked me to sit on the sand Indian style, and he placed his right hand on my forehead. All of a sudden, his hand was warm to the touch! He spoke softly to me.

"So twisted…under, sideways down. I know you're getting twisted, and you can't calm down. I see you under the midnight, love darts in your eyes. How far can you take it until you realize, there's magic in your eyes.

"Raven hair and ruby lips, sparks fly from her fingertips. Echoed voices in the night; she's a restless spirit on an endless flight. She held you spellbound in the night, dancing shadows and firelight. Crazy laughter in another room, and she drove herself to madness with a silver spoon.

"Well, I know you want to love her, let me tell you, brother, she's been sleeping in the devil's bed. And there's some rumors going around that someone's under ground. She can rock you in the nighttime until your skin turns red. See how high she flies. Woo, woo. Witchy woman. She's got the moon in her eyes."

Somehow I knew that his vision was of Linda Lou. He went on.

"You never leave her alone; I can see you never learn. When you are playing with fire, you get your fingers burned. There ain't no use in crying, Baby, don't delay. And here is what you say.

"You can call your doctor; I'll be here right away. I'm the medicine man, your doctor of love…your medicine man, your doctor of love. When there is a feeling inside that just can't be denied, I will be your medicine man.

"Now don't you ever worry, if you feel the fever rise. You will never fool nobody when there is fire in your eyes. There ain't no use denying when you need it deep inside. You've got your witch doctor to keep you satisfied. I am the medicine man, your doctor of love."

I looked into his eyes; there were tears in my eyes as I told him my thoughts.

"Marked for demolition, I'm just a time bomb ticking inside. No hope for the hopeless. I can see the pieces are laid out in front of me. No point in asking why. Couldn't help even if you try. Step inside and you might be the next contestant to feel the brutality. Devastation, obliteration are all in a part of exacerbation. There's no explaining my situation. Now why does this stuff keep happening to me?

"I've held on too long just to let it go now. Will my inner strength get me through it somehow? Defying the curse that has taken hold. Never surrender, I'll never be overcome. Too dark for forgiveness! I can't seem to do anything right. When I try to rebuild, I just see my humble shelter fall to the ground again.

"Object of an evil eye. No point to let anyone try. Take heed, my friend, lest you be torn asunder like all that's become of me."

I had more gloomy things to say.

"There's a tombstone in a snowy field close by an old ghost town. The epitaph's been weather-blown away. There's a bell tower where petitions peeled. It's been half torn down. But it must have softened every soul that came to pray.

"There's a schoolhouse full of broken glass and wounded walls. The rusty swings like derelicts sleeping in the weeds. There's a picture-graduation class staring down deserted halls. 'THE HOPE OF '44' is what it reads.

"It's just as if some restless wind blew their dreams away, far away. It's just as if those dreams had never been, but oh…I feel their ghosts around me now. I hear them say they've come back home to dream those dreams again.

"But for me a Tombstone Shadow is stretching across my path. Every time I get some good news, oh, there's a shadow on my back. I saw the gypsy man down in San Berdoo. Five dollars on the table, oh, keep me away from my tomb. He said I got thirteen months of bad luck, bound to be some pain. Don't you do no traveling, fly in no machines. Tombstone Shadow stretching across my path. Every time I get some good news, ooh, there's a shadow on my back.

"The man gave me a luck charm, cost five dollars more. He said, 'Put some on your pillow, and put some on your door.' He said, 'Take a long vacation, Ooh, for thirteen months or more.' Oh, Lord!

"Tombstone Shadow stretching across my path. Every time I get some good news, ooh, there's a shadow on my back. Oh, Lord."

The medicine man took my hands and stared deep into my soul.

"No matter what they may say, the truth is only one way. Man may be made of clay, yet your Linda Lou is still alive today.

"Eastern voices calling to you. Mystic magic oceans of blue. Timeless wonders cease to wonder when you know the spell you're under is mine. Many times you've seen the sunset only because you're trying to get all the love your mind is holding. Unseen pleasures are exploding for you.

"Secret sounds of giant sea birds singing songs of lonesome sailors. Golden cats in temples only knowing that the spell of time is yours."

He paused as my eyes opened wide, then he continued.

"In Mexico you seek a man named Jesus. You will find him and his associates in a town called San Miguel de Allende. Do what they ask, and you will have the money you require to fight for your freedom and clear your name. And may the spirits of the desert be with you."

18
San Miguel de Allende

As soon as the rooster crowed, I packed up my considerable load and pushed my Harley onto the road in order to get out of Tijuana before it snowed. The roar of the engine soothed my brain despite the fact that it had begun to rain. And a glance over my shoulder helped me relax because the Sheriff John Brown was not on my tracks or at least he didn't appear to be.

In a gesture of kindness the Medicine man gave me an envelope full of pesos. He said that I could repay him by finding and helping Jesus. I thanked him for his help and understanding. Streams of memories of Linda Lou ran through my mind as my Harley strained to cover a long incline, yet she still seemed to be the girl of my dreams.

Southbound again. I don't know if I'm going or leaving home. Boy, I got to be moving. Seems like the boy is bound to roam. Southbound again, got a little money, but I've got no place of my own to go. That woman's dead or with her lover boy, but the Medicine Man did say she was still alive. Never want to see her face no more.

Every single time I roll across the rolling River Tyne, I get the same old feeling every time I'm moving down the line. Southbound again, last night I felt like crying. Right now I'm sick of living, but I'm going to keep on trying.

I prayed that Mexico would open the light that would brighten my dismal life, which was shadowed by night no matter how difficult to me that seems. I began to imagine a beautiful Mexican girl waiting for me down south.

But dreaming about beautiful women has only brought me trouble. No matter how hard I try they always seem to burst my bubble. I try to relax and not get too tense. Then, in time I realize that it's all just nonsense.

Well, I'm southbound, Lord, I'm coming home to you. I've got that old lonesome feeling that's sometimes called the blues. Well, I've been working every night, traveling every day. You can tell the other man that sweet daddy's on his way.

Got your hands full now, baby, as soon as I hit that door. You'll have your hands full now, woman, just as soon as I hit that floor. Well, even though we don't know each other I'm gonna make it on up to you for all the things you should have had before.

As I rolled along the southbound road I remembered more details of what the Medicine Man told me out in the desert. His instructions were very explicit, but he gave me a history lesson, too.

"He came dancing across the water with his galleons and his guns looking for the new world and the palace in the sun. On the shore lay Montezuma with his coca leaves and pearls. In his halls he often wandered with the secrets of the worlds. And his subjects gathered around him like the leaves around a tree in their clothes of many colors for the angry gods to see. And the women were all beautiful, and the men stood straight and strong. They offered life in sacrifice so that others could go on.

"Hate was just a legend. War was never known. People worked together, and they lifted many stones. Then they carried them to the flatlands, but they died along the way. Then they built up with their bare hands what we still can't do today. And I know she's living there, and she loves me to this day. I still can't remember where or how I lost my way. He came dancing across the water. Cortez, what a killer!"

But I had to focus on my immediate problem, and where the Medicine Man told me where to go.

"Down in Mexicali there's a crazy little place that I know called Hoja Seca. It's the Dry Leaf in English, where the drinks are hotter than the chili sauce and the boss is a cat named Jose. He wears a red bandana, plays a blues pianna in a honky-tonk down in Mexico. He wears a purple sash and a black moustache that turns gray in a flash. And Jesus is his best friend.

"Well, the first time that I saw him in my imagination, or maybe it was a dream, he was sitting on a piano stool. I said "Tell me, Dad, when does the fun begin?' He just winked his eye and said, 'Man, be cool!'

"All of a sudden in walks this chick named Claudia; Jose starts playing on a Latin kick. Around her waist she wore three fishnets. She started dancing with the castanets. I didn't know just what to expect. She threw her arms around my neck. We started dancing all around the floor. And then she did a dance I never saw before!

"So, if you're south of the border, I mean down in Mexico, and you wanna get straight, Man, don't hesitate. Just look up a cat name Jose at the Dry Leaf, and you'll be great."

A dusty road made of cobblestone. The sun goes down, I'm here alone. The day is hot. The night gets hotter. Whatever you do, don't you quench your thirst on the local water. Oh, no!

Yeah, the music's sweet like cool Santana. I wring the sweat from my red bandana. Like a flash from the past through the pale green glow. A smoky room, senorita spinning round on straight Tequila. It's all too fast when you're moving slow. This ain't Hollywood. This is Mexico.

Soon, I was in San Miguel de Allende sitting at a small table outside a bar called the Dry Leaf. I had a clear view of the center of town from where I sat. It was a cozy place. Jose was nowhere around, but it was also the place where I was supposed to meet a man named Jesus. This was exactly what the Medicine Man told me to do.

Staring out into the wild blue yonder, so many thoughts to sit and ponder, about life and love and lack of...and this emptiness in my heart. I felt too old to be wild and free, yet, still too young to be over the hill. Should I try to grow up? But who knows where to start?

So I just...sit right here and have another beer in Mexico. I do my best to waste another day. Sit right here and have another beer in Mexico. Let the warm air melt these blues away. Sun comes up and sun sinks down, and I've seen them both in this tourist town. Up for days in a rage just trying to search my soul for the answers and the reasons why I'm at these crossroads.

I really don't know which way to go. So I just sit right here and have another beer in Mexico. Do my best to waste another day and let the warm air melt these blues away.

Maybe I'll settle down, get married, or stay single and stay free. Which road I travel is still a mystery to me. To pass the time, I ordered another beer, and asked the bartender to tell me more about Jose. He was glad to oblige.

"There was a man who owned a part of this town. He approached Jose in this very saloon and said, 'Hey, boy, sit yourself down. Are you employed? Would you like a job?' He said he owned the stage line, and there were men who liked to rob. He offered Jose his daughter's hand, advance of salary, a fancy gun, a pair of boots, and a share in the company.

"Jose rode shotgun on his stage line. He rode shotgun on his life. He rode shotgun on his money. He rode shotgun on his wife.

"There were outlaws who waited on the trail for the stagecoach daily run with payrolls and the mail. They spied the dust and saddled up to ride. They saw the worried driver with Jose sitting at his side. They circled around the stagecoach, it was their daily fun, until they saw the driver smile and spied Jose's trusty gun.

"They caught the outlaws and took them back to jail, sent for the county marshal and would not post a bail. They were sent up the river; that sure cleaned up the town. Jose was elected sheriff, and the mayor asked him down. Now, Jose owns half the stage line and half the rest of town. He goes to church on Sunday; I think he's settled down. He's gonna shoot 'em out ..don't get in his way!"

How I wished I could meet and talk with Jose because he was obviously a man with connections, and he might be willing to provide me with some protection against the sheriff. Instead, I had another beer. I had noticed a girl dancing in the corner. She was thin and beautiful so I asked the bartender if he knew her name. His name was Fred, and he was American. He just shook his head and smiled. 'Lolita is her name…I believe.' Then he began to tell me a story about how he met her in a little town down south of here under interesting circumstances.

"They're picking up the prisoners and putting 'em in a pen, and all she wants to do is dance. Rebels been rebels since I don't know when, and all she wants to do is dance. Molotov cocktail is the local drink; they mix'em up right in the kitchen sink. Crazy people walking around with blood in their eyes, wild-eyed pistol-wavers who ain't afraid to die.

"And all she wants to do is dance and make romance. She can't feel the heat coming off the street. She wants to party; she wants to get down."

I was getting more interested in this little lady. But there was more.

"Well, the government bugged the men's room in the local disco lounge to keep the boys from selling all the weapons they could scrounge. But that don't keep the boys from making a buck or two. They still can sell the army all the drugs that they can do.

"Well, we barely made the airport for the last plane out. As we taxied down the runway, I could hear the people shout. They said, 'Don't come back here, Yankee.' But, it I ever do, I'll bring more money, because all she wants to do is dance."

I took another look at her, and decided to leave well enough alone. Fred poured me another drink. He knew exactly what my thoughts were.

"Her real love was a dude named Pancho. Pancho was a bandit boy. His horse was as fast as polished steel. He wore his gun outside his pants for all the honest world to feel. Pancho met his match, you know, on the deserts down here in Mexico. Nobody heard his dying words, ah, but that's the way it goes.

"Pancho had a friend named Lefty. He can't sing the blues all night like he used to. The dust that Pancho bit down south ended up in Lefty's mouth. The day they laid poor Pancho low, Lefty split for Ohio. Where he got the bread to go, there ain't nobody knows.

"Poets tell how Pancho fell, and Lefty's living in a cheap hotel. The desert's quiet, and Cleveland's cold. And so the story ends we're told. Pancho needs your prayers it's true, but save a few for Lefty, too. He only did what he had to do, and now he's growing old.

"All the Federales say they could have had Lefty any day. They only let him slip away out of kindness, I suppose."

Fred smiled as he poured me another drink on the house. Right at high noon an American-looking fellow walked up and without introducing himself asked me a question.

"Are you looking for Jesus?"

I was a bit surprised by the question especially with his pronunciation…'Hey-sus'. I hesitated so he went on.

"Jesus just left Chicago, and he's bound for New Orleans. Working from one end to the other and all points in between. Took a jump through Mississippi. Well, muddy water changed to wine. Then, out to California though the forests and the pines. You might not see him in person, but he'll see you just the same. You don't have to worry, because taking care of business is his name."

The Jesus I was supposed to meet here was a Mexican drug smuggler, but up to now I had no way of knowing for certain which Jesus this man was referring to. But then I realized that he must be talking about the man I was looking for. He found me here at the bar with no trouble.

"My name is Elvis…really," he said and extended his right hand with a smile on his face. I had no choice, but to offer him a seat. He was tall with wavy black hair and wore a weather-beaten cowboy hat.

"You're Joe, right?"

I nodded emphatically.

"You're the one taking the opals to Brownsville, right? We're supposed to leave tonight. I've got a brand new truck. With luck, we should reach the U.S. in two days."

"Elvis," I said quietly, "I know I'm supposed to carry something into the U.S. in exchange for some cash…you should know that I'm broke."

"Hey, don't worry, Joe. Jesus pays very well. Otherwise Jose wouldn't deal with him. He saved my ass on quite a few occasions. You're the kid that sheriff from California is chasing, aren't you? Jose wanted me to tell you about the big man with the scar and a glass eye. He came through here several days ago looking for you. He said he was a friend of yours. Do you know who he is?"

I didn't really answer him because all I could think of was the Monkey Man, and to change the subject I ordered a beer for Elvis. Now that I think of it, I could swear that I saw the Monkey Man at the Hotel California. He even waited on me!

"Elvis, I must admit that I have my problems, but out of curiosity, how did you get here?"

Elvis was more than happy to tell me his story first. A waiter named Emerson brought the beer. It seems that he and Elvis were on a first name basis so Elvis invited him to sit down and listen to his story. Soon, we were joined by the beautiful Claudia.

"I've heard his stories many times before," whispered Emerson to me, "but they become more beautiful each time he tells them. Claudia will agree."

Claudia smiled as Elvis raised his hands as if requesting silence and began the tale. Before he spoke, he looked around to be sure that we were the only ones listening.

"Come gather around me, people, here's a story you've never heard, about me and my friends and some things that occurred. We thought we'd get some money; we thought that we might go spend a weekend pleasant down in Mexico."

He explained that he and his friends lived in Brownsville, Texas, which is right on the border.

"I was working at McDonalds doing the late night run, when a car pulled up the drive thru and someone pointed a gun. They said 'Give us all your money and three Big Macs to go!' I stuffed them all in a bag, and I ducked down below.

"Well, the boss got very angry when he found out I didn't call the police. I guess I was kind'a nervous; there was a warrant out on me concerning some jay-walking tickets I couldn't afford to pay. Needless to say, I got the axe that same day.

"Well, me being out of work just then, I didn't want to go home. My Mom said if I lost this job, I'd have to go out on my own.

"I was so mad, all I could think of was heading south. Greedy people take what's mine. I can leave them all behind, and they can never cross that line when I get to the border.

"Saw-bones standing at the door, waiting until I hit the floor. He won't find me anymore when I get to the border. If you see a box of pine with a name that looks like mine, say I drowned in a barrel of wine when I got to the border.

"A one way ticket's in my hand headed for the chosen land. My troubles will all turn to sand when I get to the border. A soft girl with yellow hair waiting in that rocking chair, and if I'm weary, I won't care when I get to then border.

"A dusty road that smells so sweet paved with gold beneath my feet, and I'll be dancing down the street when I get to the border.

"So, I went over to Dave's house and got really stoned, called up some girls, but none of them were home.

"Steve came over, and he brought some alcohol. We were all getting real depressed just staring at the wall. Then, we thought we'd get some money; we thought that we might go spend a weekend pleasant down in Mexico.

"Steve's Dad had a hunting rifle, and we went and picked it up. And we stopped into a 7-11 just to try our luck. We raised up that hunting rifle, but the counter guy just laughed. As he pulled out an Uzi, we turned and hauled ass.

"We were running so fast until we came to the McDonalds where I used to work. We walked up to the drive thru and gave my boss a jerk. Said 'Give us all your money and three Big Macs to go! And suck on this you weasel, we're goin' to Mexico!'

"Down South we all got wasted, Dave got a case of the runs. We're all really hung over and getting low on funds. Dave and Steve called their parents and took the bus back home. I went down to the crossroads, fell down on my knees. Asked the Lord above for mercy, 'Save me, if you please'.

"I went down to the crossroads, tried to flag a ride. Nobody seemed to know me. Everybody passed me by. And, I was standing at the crossroads. I believe I'm sinking down.

"Then like a flash it hit me. I should do what I can do. So…me, I got a job at McDonalds down in Mexico."

And with a flourish of his arms, Elvis pointed across the street at the McDonald's restaurant where he worked. Its signs were all in Spanish, and it was where Elvis worked as a clerk.

After some small talk, Claudia wanted to know my story. It seems that in Mexico everyone has a story and everyone else is willing to listen and compare.

"The hand of fate is on me now," I began. "It picks me up and knocks me down. I'm on the run; I'm prison bound. The hand of fate is heavy now. Supposedly, I killed someone; I'm highway bound. The wheel of fortune keeps turning 'round. I should have known it was a one-horse town.

"He said, 'My sweet girl was once his wife.' He lied. He had papers that a phony judge had signed. The wind blew hard. It was a stormy night. He shot at me once, but I shot at him twice. The hand of fate is on me now. It picked me up and kicked me right down.

"I had to save her life. He shot first. Yeah, I gunned him twice. Yeah, and I thought I watched him die. Watch out, boy, he didn't die.

"He was a sheriff of ill repute and a barroom man, the violent kind. He had no love for that gal of mine. Then, that day in a drinking bout, he swore from the town he'd throw me right out. The hand of fate is on me now. I shot at that wicked man; I wanted to put him underground. Yes, I did.

"I'm on the run; I hear the hounds. My luck is up; my chips are down. I said goodbye to my love, so long now. Wish me luck, Linda Lou, I'm going to need it, child. The hand of fate is on me now. Yeah, it's too late. Too late, baby, too late now.

"He said I missed him by a thread, and my second bullet hit her instead. And as her blood flowed thick and red, he swore he'd see a rope around my head.

"The hand of fate is heavy now. It picks you up and knocks you down."

Claudia kissed my cheek and expressed her grief. She had words of encouragement for me.

"We got something, we both know it. We don't talk too much about it. Yeah, it ain't no real big secret, but somehow, we get around it. It don't really matter to me, Baby, you believe what you want to believe. You don't have to live like a refugee.

"Somewhere, somehow, somebody must have kicked you around some. Who knows why you want to lay there and revel in your abandon. It don't make no difference to me, Baby, everybody's had to fight to be free. You see, you don't have to live like a refugee.

"Baby, we ain't the first. I'm sure a lot of others have been burned. Right now, this seems real to you, but it's one of those things you gotta feel to be true."

As I was thanking her for her concern, Emerson came to my relief by bringing another drink. The happy moments in life are soon gone like a thief. I'll never forget my friends down there at the Dry Leaf.

"This is really good, Emerson," I said after a few sips. "What is this excellent brew?"

"Mescalero! Es lo que quiero combinacion peligroso. Y estaba especial este cosas bueno mmm. I know you know so… Mescalero turn your head like a red sombrero. Mescalero!

"Que es esto? No se mi companero. Mescalero! Que es esto? Pero este es yo que quiero. Mescalero light me up like a flaming arrow."

Just then, the owner, Jose, ran up to our table. He was out of breath. He had a warning for Elvis and for me. Before I could ask him, he told me that I would meet Jesus in Brownsville and that Elvis would drive me there. Emerson quickly supplied Jose with his favorite drink and after catching his breath, he sat down next to me and began to whisper.

"There's trouble on the streets tonight, I can feel it in my bones. I had a premonition that Jesus should not go alone. I knew the gun was loaded, but I didn't think he'd kill. Everything exploded, and the blood began to spill. So, Joe, here's your ticket. Put the suitcase in your hand. Here's a little money now. Do it just the way we planned. You be cool for twenty hours, and I'll pay you twenty grand. I'm sorry it went down like this and someone had to lose. It's the nature of the business; it's the smugglers' blues.

"The sailors and pilots, the soldiers and the law, the payoffs and the rip offs and the things nobody saw. No matter if it's heroin, cocaine, or hash, you've got to carry weapons because you always carry cash. There are lots of shady characters, lots of dirty deals. Every name's an alias in case somebody squeals. It's the lure of easy money. It's got a very strong appeal.

"Perhaps you'd understand it better standing in my shoes. It's the ultimate enticement. It's the smugglers' blues.

"See it in the headlines. You hear it every day. They say they're gonna stop it, but it doesn't go away. They move it through Miami, sell it in L.A. They hide it up in Telluride; I mean it's here to stay. It's propping up the governments in Columbia and Peru. It's a losing proposition, but one you can't refuse. It's the politics of contraband. It's the smugglers' blues."

Jose handed me a burlap bag.

"Put the opals in here. Take them to Jesus in Brownville. And... don't get caught!"

I was already in so much trouble that the idea of getting caught wasn't anything new. Now I was a suspected killer and a smuggler. As I walked to the truck with Elvis, I asked about the opals.

"There's an opal...mine on the outskirts of town. We have to go get some for this bag. If we get caught, the opals are what we are smuggling...not the heroin and hash hidden in the trunk. Don't worry, even the sniffer dogs at the border won't suspect. If they do find the opals, we just play dumb and they let us proceed with a slap on the wrist...they keep the opals. It's a fair trade and keeps them diverted from the real game that's afoot."

We had a little time so we sat in Elvis' truck talking, mostly about the girls we've known. He loved my story about Janie because he had once been to Black Diamond Bay on vacation. I guess that's when I first realized that Janie's misfortune wasn't just a dream. I recalled the TV commentator mentioning a Panama hat. That had to be Janie's hat.

Elvis lit up a joint and offered me one. I thanked him, but declined the offer. I was with a stranger in a strange land. The Medicine Man had warned me to stay straight and alert. That wasn't always easy for me to do.

19
Back to the U.S.A.

We threw my Harley in the back of Elvis' truck and went to the opal pit to collect a bunch of shiny rocks. Elvis was humming a verse to himself in a happy voice so I listened to every word.

"Almost cut my hair! Happened just the other day. It's getting kind of long. I could have said it was in my way. But I didn't and I wonder why? I feel like letting my freak flag fly. And I feel like I owe it to someone.

"Well, must be because I had the flu this Christmas. Oh, yeah, and I'm not feeling up to par. Oh, I tell you, Joey, this increases my paranoia. Yeah, like looking in my mirror and seeing a police car.

"Well, I'm not giving in an inch to fear. Well, you know I've promised myself this year, when I get myself together, you can find me in this sunny southern weather. I'm gonna find a space inside a laugh. Separate the wheat from the chaff. Oh, and I feel like I owe it to someone."

Elvis patted me on the shoulder as he went on, but he never said whom he was referring to.

"Smugglers drink of the Frenchmen's wine, and the darkest night is the smuggler's time. Away we run from the taxman's grasp. It's a smuggler's life for me!

"Must I use old homely goods while there's foreign goods so fine? Must I drink at the waterside when France is so full of wine? My heart is now with a gallant crew that plough's through a wayward life. It's an angry sea. For me it's the bigger gale or the tightest sail and the sheltered bay or goal. It's the wayward life. It's the smuggler's strife. It's the joy of the smuggler's soul.

"And when at last the dawn comes up, and the cargo's safely stored, away like sinless saints to church we go, God's mercy to afford. And it's

Champagne fine for communion wine, and the parson drinks it, too. With a sly wink, he prays 'Forgive these men for they know not what they do'."

We laughed and grabbed the small burlap bag. Elvis spoke with a man at the gate, and it was obvious that they knew each other quite well. The man was asking something about a stereo and a big screen television set which Elvis apparently promised he would bring back from the states. Later he told me that TVs available locally were substandard and way too expensive. This gave Elvis something to trade for access to the opal mine. It was obvious that these trades were the key to Elvis' success as a smuggler.

After thrashing around in the dirt for an hour, we had a nice cache of rocks that fit the bill. Elvis was happy so I was, too. We stashed the opals in the back of the truck so they could easily be found by someone searching for contraband. Our work here was done.

Then we set out for the border and Brownsville. Elvis told me to drive first and said he'd coach me on the route. He said we would meet his uncle, Arthur McBride, near the border and that he would get us across in style. That made me feel a whole lot better. For the first half hour all went well, but Elvis was smoking reefer and soon started to get paranoid.

"You can follow the road to the mountain or the track leading down to the beach. You can go where your life goes, go left or go right. It's you in the driver's seat. But if the rain starts swamping your windshield and the lights don't piss through the night, and the trucks coming at you just going to splash you, the highway's blinding bright. You're going out of your brain, out of your mind. You're so deranged; you're going blind.

"You're driving too fast. You went straight past the curve, and you can never go back. Driving too fast. The road was a blur, and it all turned to black. Driving too fast! Hang on to the wheel; I think you're going to crash.

"You can see the freeway dividing. It's a pity you can't take'em both. One leads to the valley or down some blind alley, the other runs down to the coast. Too many roads lead to nowhere, but how they twist and they turn and they dead end in a dusty old strip mall where your tires are all shredded and burned.

"You're going out of your brain, out of your mind, going insane, you're going blind… Yeah!

"You're driving too fast. You slip through the curve and you slam through the flat. Driving too fast; now you never go back. It's all time to pass. Hang on for your life; I think you're gonna crash."

Elvis reached into his pocket for another joint. He continued his rant as he almost fell out of the passenger side window.

"Jump back! What's that sound? Here she comes, full blastin' and top down. Hot shoe, burning down the avenue. Model citizen. Zero discipline. Don't ya know she's comin' home with me. You'll lose her in that turn. I'll get her! Panama!

"Ain't nothin' like it. It's a shiny machine. Got the feel for the wheel. Keep the movin' parts clean. Hot shoe, burnin' down the avenue. Got an on-ramp comin' through my bedroom.

"Yeah. We're runnin' a little hot tonight. I can barely see the road from the heat comin' off. Know what I'm sayin'? Uh, I reach down between my legs and ease the seat back. She's runnin'. I'm flyin'. Right behind in the rearview mirror now. Got the fearin', power steerin'. Pisons poppin'. Ain't no stoppin'…now. Panama!"

I must admit that he had a pretty good singing voice. But he wanted me to stop at an upcoming intersection for some food. The joints must have made him hungry. He pointed toward a small shack. We parked and went inside.

The lady who ran the place gave us some burritos and warm beer. It was obvious that she knew Elvis quite well. She held a mock telephone in her hands, and she seemed to be speaking to me.

"Calling Elvis, is anybody home? Calling Elvis, I'm here all alone. Did he leave the building, or can he come to the phone? Calling Elvis, I'm here all alone. Well, tell him I was calling just to wish him well. Let me leave my number…Heartbreak Hotel. Oh, love me tender. Baby, don't be cruel. Return to sender. Treat me like a fool.

"Why don't you go get him? I'm his biggest fan! You gotta tell him he's still the man. Long distance, baby, so far from home. Don't you think maybe you could put him on?"

Then she came over and literally sat on my lap. She ran her hands over my face and began purring.

'If your life ain't been all it should be now, this girl will put you right. I'll show you what you can be now, just give me one night. Give us a room, close the door. Leave us for a while. You won't be a boy no more. Young, but not a child.

"Gather your wits and hold them fast. Your mind must learn to roam. Just as the Gypsy Queen must do, you're gonna hit the road. When my work is done, just look at yourself. You've never been more alive. Your head shakes, your fingers clutch, watch your body writhe.

"I'm the Gypsy, the Acid Queen. Pay me before I start. I'm the Gypsy, I'm guaranteed to tear your soul apart.

"So I'm back to the velvet underground, back to the floor that I love, to a room with some lace and paper flowers. Back to the gypsy that I was. And it all comes down to you, well, you know that it does. Well, lightning strikes, maybe once, maybe twice. And it lights up the night, and you see your gypsy."

From the empty parking lot, and her enthusiasm over an unknown like me, it appeared that I was her first potential customer in some time. I smiled and she continued.

"To the gypsy that remains, faces freedom with a little fear. I have no fear. I have only love. And if I was a child and the child was enough, enough for me to love, she is dancing away from me now. She was just a wish, and a memory is all that is left for me now. I still see your bright eyes, and it all comes down to you."

She kissed me gently. I was moved, but I told the lovely lady that I didn't have enough money on me, but that I would definitely stop on the way back. She had more to say as we walked toward the door.

"I am the crazy person who lives inside your head. But I think I'm breaking through the wall. You are the innocent convicted of the crime. No one was ever there to catch you when you fall. I see the diamonds, but you only see the rock. I need to run, but you only crawl.

"It's time to open up all the doors that you keep locked. Nobody gives without a take. Let's take it all. One more crucifixion. One more cross to bear. You're a hole in a photograph. Go on, lose it in the city. The city can feel no shame. See the world with an electric eye.

"They call it mystery, but any fool can see. You thought she walked on the water, but when the pain was gone, you were free to run away and get out. Did you get out of there or did you really care? It's not safe and easy, and maybe now that you're gone, you just won't belong, at all.

"You've been twisted into pieces by the hands of your emotions. You're the only witness to the murder of an angel. How much longer are you going to pay for yesterday? Sins of the father!

"It's just another crucifixion. One more cross to bear. Go on, lose it in the city. Take a look at the world. You've got electric eyes.

"Just because in a moment of madness, she took advantage of your sweet love, don't just hand yourself a lifetime of sadness because there's so little beauty. Oh, Joey, one chain don't a prison make. Two wrongs don't make a right. One rain don't make no river. One punch don't make no fight.

"Can't you spare me a little affection? Would that be asking too much of you? Don't point love in another direction. I swear I'll make it all up to you. There's a bed I'm keeping room in for you. There's a lot I know I gotta do. Don't let a simple misunderstanding be a mountain that we can't move.

"One chain don't make no prison. Two wrongs don't make no right. One rain don't make no river. One punch don't make no fight."

She closed her eyes and continued.

"In my eyes, indisposed. In disguise as no one knows hides the face, lies the snake, the sun. In my disgrace, boiling heat, summer stench. Beneath the black, the sky looks dead. Call my name through the cream, and I'll hear you scream again.

"Black hole sun, won't you come and wash away the rain. Black hole sun, won't you come? Cold and damp steal the warm mind. Tired friend, times are gone for honest men. And sometimes far too long for snakes. In my shoes, a walking sleep and my youth I pray to keep. Heaven, send hell away. No one sings like you anymore.

"Hang my head, drown my fear, until you all just disappear."

She opened her eyes and smiled. She seemed satisfied, so I grabbed Elvis by the neck and pulled him outside. We got back in the truck, and as we drove off, Elvis resumed his singing as he kissed and lit another joint.

"She grew up in an Indiana town. Had a good-looking momma who never was around. But she grew up tall, and she grew up right with them Indiana boys on an Indiana night. Well, she moved down here at the age of eighteen. She blew the boys away; it was more than they'd ever seen. I was introduced, and we both started grooving. She said, 'I dig you, baby, but I've got to keep moving.'

"Well, I don't know what I've been told. If you never slow down, you never grow old. I'm tired of screwing up. I'm tired of going down. I'm tired of myself. I'm tired of this town. Oh, my, my. Oh, hell, yes! Honey, put on that party dress. Buy me a drink. Sing me a song. Take me as I come because I can't stay long.

"There's pigeons down in the market square. She's standing in her underwear. Looking down from a hotel room. Nightfall will be coming soon. I hit the last number. I walked to the road. Last dance with Mary Jane. One more time to kill the pain. I feel summer creeping in, and I'm tired of this town again."

Elvis gently kissed the side of the joint he was smoking.

"Mary Jane! Mary Jane! Please don't leave me, baby, I'll just find you again.

"I asked my uncle, if I could go. Yes, yes, go out and take Mary Jane to the picture show. But, Uncle Bob sighed, he could not answer. He died one second before in the arms of a go-go dancer.

"I wanna roll you way down in the fields where you were born. I wanna roll you when I'm ragged and forlorn. You have no friend. You have no pet. If there's anything better than you, you know they haven't found it yet. Mary Jane. Please don't leave me, baby, I'll just find you again."

I was beginning to get in the mood so I took up Elvis on his offer of a joint. I figured that just one wouldn't hurt me. Meanwhile, Elvis kept singing.

"Living easy! Loving free! Season ticket on a one way ride. Asking nothing, leave me be. Taking everything in my stride. Don't need reason. Don't need rhyme. Ain't nothing that I'd rather do going down…party time! My friends are gonna be there, too. I'm on the highway to hell!"

Elvis started to reach for the steering wheel, but I shoved him back to his side.

"No stop signs, speed limit. Nobody's gonna slow us down. Like a wheel, gonna spin it. Nobody's gonna mess me around. Hey, Satan, paying my dues playing in a rocking band. Hey, momma, look at me, I'm on the way to the promised land."

And then Elvis passed out. I was relieved and alarmed at the same time. I was relieved that his jabbering had ceased. I was driving very conservatively. Still, I'd have to find my way to Brownsville on my own. I guess that was the lesser of two evils. But then I remembered what he said about his uncle, Albert McBride. When we reached the border, I'd have to straighten Elvis out so we could find Uncle Albert.

To pass the time I decided to play a mind game with myself. I harkened back to New York and the night we took a cab ride. It was a ride I would never forget.

Another New York waltz at four A.M., in the canyons lost at night. The city's just a jail for me, full of high-rise prison walls. And I'm riding through this darkness because I know there's life within. And I'm searching through the shadows, just to find that light again. Keep driving. Let the meter run. Oh, the night's not really done.

And I'm hanging on a memory, and I feel it in the air. I'm a prisoner of these lonely streets, but I know I'll find you there. And, oh, Lord, you look so pretty, but you can see it in my eyes. And just before my tear will fall, you smile and get inside.

It seems so real until the light turns green. Don't wake me up. Don't ruin this dream. Don't take me from my scene. Keep driving. I can't go home. Don't take me home! I can't go home alone.

They don't tell you when the music stops or how the movie ends. Is it too late once the feeling's gone, to back it up and start it all again? Oh, the night's still young. I've got to find someone.

I hit a big pothole in the road, and it snapped me out of my reverie. Good thing because I was driving much too fast on this strange road. Back in the city I often fancied myself as a fearless cabbie. I never understood why.

Hours later we arrived at the spot Elvis had described before he passed out. There in front of us stood a man fitting the description of

Albert McBride. Soon the two of us were walking down by the seaside on a road followed by our truck with Elvis inside driving. Mark now what followed and what did betide, for it being Christmas morning.

Now, to get to our destination we went on a tramp, and at the border we met Mexican Sergeant Napper and Corporal Vamp and a little wee drummer intending to camp for the day being pleasant and charming.

"Good morning, good morning," the Sergeant he cried. "And the same to you, gentlemen," we did reply intending no harm but meant to pass by for it being on Christmas morning. From the look on Albert's face, these were not the Mexican soldiers he expected. He turned to me and whispered, "We stall 'till Carlos and Juan appear on the scene to give us safe passage."

So, Elvis went over to the border guards with a smile on his face.

"Bless on the border guard," he said reverently, "so cold and alone. Bless on the child so far from his home. Pity on the border guard who feels like a woman to cry. Pity on the border guard whose life guards the line. A light is a funny thing, a border sometime. A light is a hurting thing, use only to divine. I pity the refugee whose home lies behind; I pity the border guard and his border line. He keeps his machine gun nose pointed to the sky. The nighttime is his master, and you know the dawn light brings his captor.

"And, I pity the border guard as he walks, well as he walks his own. The echo of his footsteps is all a friend would know. A home is a funny thing; you get tied to the earth. Like a love is a crazy thing in the eye of a child.

"I pity the border guard whose soul was taken captive at birth. May the sweet brace of his grief show him how to be so wild. He who made the open plains and the world one and all could not have conceived them with a barbed wire brain."

"Sergeant," said Uncle Albert before the Sergeant could respond, "forgive my young friend for he has often pondered becoming a border guard and his enthusiasm often gets the best of him." Elvis nodded.

"But," says the Sergeant smiling as he spoke, "my fine fellows, if you will enlist, ten pesos in gold I'll stick in your fist, and a crown in the bargain for to kick up the dust and drink to the president's health in the morning.

"For a soldier he leads a very fine life, and he always is blessed with a charming young wife. And he pays all his debts without sorrow or strife, and he always lives pleasant and charming. And, a soldier he is always descent and clean; in the finest clothing he's constantly seen, while other poor fellows go dirty and mean, and sup on thin gruel in the morning."

"But," said Arthur, "I wouldn't be proud of your clothes, for you have only the lend of them, I suppose. But you dare not change them one night, for you know, if you do, you'll be flogged in the morning. And although that we're single and free, we take great delight in our own company. We have no desire, strange places to see, although that your offers are charming.

"And we have no desire to take your advance; all hazards and dangers we barter on chance. For you'd have no scruples for to send us to France, where we would get shot without warning."

"Oh, no," said the Sergeant. "I'll have no such chat, and neither will I take it from snappy young brats. For if you insult me with one other word, I'll cut off your heads in the morning."

And Albert and I, we soon drew our hogs, and we scarce gave them time to draw their own blades when a trusty shillelagh came over their heads and bid them take that as fair warning. And their old rusty rapiers that hung by their sides, we flung them as far as we could in the tide.

"Now, take them up, devils!" cried Arthur McBride, "and temper their edge in the morning."

And the little wee drummer, we flattened his bow, and we made a football of his rowdy-dow-dow, threw it in the tide for to rock and to roll, and bade it a tedious returning. And we having no money paid them off in cracks. We paid no respect to their two bloody backs, and we lathered them there like a pair of wet sacks and left them for dead in the morning.

And so, to conclude and to finish disputes, we obligingly asked if they wanted recruits. For we were the lads who would give them hard clouts and bid them look sharp in the morning. For Juan and Carlos had finally appeared to give the Sergeant and his men their relief and to give us safe passage over the border with the cargo our truck was carrying.

Mark now what followed and what did betide for it being on Christmas morning. Carlos was very sorry that he and Juan were late to their posts.

"We're so sorry, Uncle Albert; we're so sorry if we caused you any pain. We're so sorry, Uncle Albert, but there's no one left at home, and I believe it's gonna rain. We're so sorry, but we haven't heard a thing all day, but if anything should happen, we'll be sure to give a ring.

"We're so sorry, Uncle Albert, but we haven't done a bloody thing all day. We're so sorry, Uncle Albert, but the kettle's on the boil, and we're so easily called away.

"Hand across the water, heads across the sky. Admiral Halsey notified me; he had to have a berth, or he couldn't get to sea. I had another look and I had a cup of tea and butter pie. The butter wouldn't melt so I put it in the pie."

Then Juan chimed in. "Live a little, be a gypsy, get around. Get your feet up off the ground."

Albert just shrugged his shoulders, and we jumped in the truck and started across the border. It was obvious that Elvis had his mind on something else.

"You must be lost in a faraway land; I searched forever for your footsteps in the sand. I feel you need me; I have to answer that desperate call that I do not understand.

"A burning bridge, a lonely highway, another dark night of thinking alone. What could have happened? Am I just dreaming? It doesn't matter, but there's one thing that I know. If I could make it to the border; if I could make it to the coast; I'd be in the arms of the girl I love most.

"So, on and on I keep driving to make the border before the light. Just one more river, then I can make it. Again, you'll be in my arms tonight.

"Well, since she put me down, I've been out doin' in my head. Come in late at night and in the morning I just lay in bed. Well, Rhonda, you look so fine, and I know it wouldn't take much time for you to hold me, Rhonda, help me get her out of my heart.

"She was gonna be my girl, and I was gonna be her man. But she let another guy come between us, and it shattered all our plans. Well, Rhonda, you caught my eye, and I can give you lots of reasons why you gotta help me, Rhonda, help me get her out of my heart."

Now all we had to do is get across the border to Brownsville without the Americans spotting us. We had the truck, my bike and the payload intact. Uncle Albert knew of a little side road that would get us across without hitting the big inspection stations. Still, I wondered whether I should just turn around and stay in Mexico, safe from Sheriff John Brown. Elvis could see that look in my eyes.

"You're a rich man, but a poor man with your pockets lined with gold. Always in the middle, neither hot nor cold. And you think you've found your freedom, but it always slips away. Nothing ever satisfies; you always have to pay.

"So much indecision leaves you hanging in the air. You can't remain forever because there's nothing there. With one foot in the ocean and the other on the shore, you'll be going nowhere until you step on through the door.

"Now I know your wheels are spinning, but you never seem to move. I can see right through you so what are you trying to prove? And it's not coincidental that you're always on the run. No more second chances now, the day is almost done."

We were on our way into the U.S.A. Uncle Albert was listening to the radio and had a few words of advice.

"If the storm doesn't kill me, the government will. I've got to get that out of my head. It's a new day today, and the coffee is strong. I've finally got some rest.

"So a man's put to task and challenges. I was taught to hold my head high, collect what is mine, and make the best of what today has. Houston is filled with promise. Laredo is a beautiful place. Galveston sings like that song that I loved. Its meaning has not been erased. And so there are claims forgiven. And so there are things that are gone. And some things, they fall to the wayside. Their memory is yet to be, still belief has not filled me. And, so, I am put to the test.

"The lights in my eyes, they are stating to hurt me. I no longer need them to see where to go. You're showing me signs in too many directions. I'll find my own way home. 'I've got something fantastic I know you can use,' said the five and dime prophet on the ten-dollar news. He's asking me to share his vision while looking down at his shoes. How can I work out what he's saying? How will I know if he's telling the truth?

"For the secret to romance turn to page 94. Then count all the boxes and add up your score. Radio heartbreak can save any marriage, and that's what "AM" is for. Opinions of numbers don't add up to nothing. I've already done it. I've been there before.

"Leave me alone. I'll find my own way home!"

I was more than a little baffled by the words, but I knew better than to ask. Elvis and his family seemed to have more personal problems than I had, if that's possible? Our future in Texas would undoubtedly unlock the secrets they were talking of if there really were any there to be unlocked.

20
Brownsville Girl

In spite of all our difficulties, Elvis, Uncle Albert and I managed to get the truck across the border into Texas and soon we were inside the city limits of Brownsville. We had to wait until midnight to exchange the contraband for cash, so we decided to find a restaurant and bar to pass the time. We would take turns watching the truck. My Harley was still in the back, and I was anxious to get back on it the following day.

The first restaurant we found was near the water so we got an outside table from which we could watch the truck. Elvis didn't particularly like this neighborhood although Albert didn't seem to care much either way.

Uncle Albert got up to make the phone call to his people here in Brownsville. When he returned he pointed at the pay phone near the bar. "Wait for the Sidewinder to call!" Then he handed a card to Elvis.

"This here is the place I will be staying. There isn't a number. You can call this pay phone. Let it ring a long, long, long, long time. If I don't pick up, hang up, call back, let it ring some more. If I don't pick up, the Sidewinder sleeps in a coil.

"There are scratches all around the coin slot. Like a heartbeat, baby trying to wake up, but this machine can only swallow money. You can't lay a patch by computer design; it's just a lot of stupid, stupid signs.

"Tell Jesus he can kiss my ass, then laugh and say you were only kidding. That way he'll know it's really, really, really, really us.

"Boys, instant soup doesn't really grab me. Today, I need something more sub-sub-sub-substantial. A can of beans or black-eyed peas, some Nescafe and ice, a candy bar, a falling star, or a reading from Doctor Seuss.

"The Cat in the Hat came back, wrecked a lot of havoc on the way. Always had a smile and a reason to pretend. But their world has flat backgrounds and little need to sleep but to dream. The sidewinder sleeps on his back. I can always sleep standing up. Call me when Jesus wakes you up.

"We've got to moogie, moogie, move on this one!"

Elvis' somehow understood what his uncle was saying. But his attention had shifted to several members of the fairer sex sitting at the bar. He had a story to tell about his last trip here.

"I was down at the New Amsterdam staring at this yellow-haired girl. Uncle Albert strikes up a conversation with a black-haired flamenco dancer. You know, she dances while the band plays. And so, she's suddenly beautiful. And we all want something beautiful. Joey, I wish I was beautiful."

Uncle Albert cast a hard stare at Elvis. He sat straight up and pointed to Albert.

"Sorry, Joey. Let me introduce you to Mr. Jones."

Uncle Albert relaxed. What I didn't know until then was that Albert went by the fictitious name 'Mr. Jones' when they were in public in Brownsville. It was just a safety precaution.

"Cut up, Maria, Show me some of that Spanish dancing. And, pass me a bottle, Mr. Jones. Believe in me. Help me believe in anything because I want to be someone who believes. Mr. Jones and I used to tell each other fairy tales, and we stared at the beautiful women. 'She's looking at you. Ah, no, she's looking at me!' Smilin in the bright lights, coming through in stereo. When everybody loves you, you can never be lonely."

It was pretty obvious that the alcohol had induced a state of loneliness in Elvis. I began to feel sorry for him despite the fact that I was lonely, too.

"Well, Joey, I'm gonna paint my picture, paint myself in blue and red and black and gray. All of the beautiful colors are very, very meaningful. Yeah, well you know, gray is my favorite color. I felt so symbolic yesterday. If I knew Picasso, I would buy myself a gray guitar and play.

"I wanna be a lion. Everybody wants to pass as cats. We all want to be big, big stars. But, we've got different reasons for that. Believe in me because I don't believe in anything. And I want to be someone who believes.

"Mr. Jones and I go stumbling through the barrio. We stare at the beautiful women. 'She's perfect for you. Man, there's got to be somebody for me!' I wanna be Bob Dylan. Mr. Jones wishes he was someone just a little more funky. When everybody loves you, ah, Joey, that's just about as funky as you can be.

"Mr. Jones and I stare at the video. When I look at the television I want to see me staring right back at me. We all want to be big stars, but we don't know why, and we don't know how. When everybody loves me, I will never be lonely!"

From the look on Uncle Albert's face, I could tell that he was beginning to worry about Elvis' state of mind. Meanwhile Elvis and I each sipped on our beers. Uncle Albert's face turned more sour when Elvis began to express his misgivings.

"When the red light shines on the streets of hate, where the devil dines, who knows what he ate. It's a simple thing trying to stay afloat, the captain said without his boat. Some things are getting better, other things a little worse. It's a situation much like a curse.

"It's the devil's sidewalk, Brownsville. It's the devil's door, Brownsville. There's a garden growing and a million weeds with no way of knowing who has done which deed.

"Big wheel's still rolling down on me, one thing I can tell you is you got to be free. John Lennon said that and I believe in love. I believe in action when push comes to shove."

"Who cares what you believe?" said Uncle Albert fully amazed and in obvious frustration. "If you stood in my shoes, your eyes would be glazed!"

Elvis had more to say.

"The sweet pretty things are in bed now, of course. The city fathers, they're trying to endorse the reincarnation of Paul Revere's horse. But the town has no need to be nervous. The ghost of Belle Starr, she hands down her wits to Jezebel, the nun. She violently knits a bald wig for Jack the Ripper, who sits at the head of the Chamber of Commerce.

"The hysterical bride in the penny arcade screaming, she moans, 'I've just been made.' Then sends out the doctor who pulls down the shade. Says, 'My advice is not to let the boys in.' Now the medicine man comes, and he shuffles inside. He walks with a swagger and he says to the bride, 'Stop all this weeping, swallow your pride. You will not die; it's not poison.'

"Well, John the Baptist, after torturing a thief, looks up at his hero, the Commander-in-Chief, saying 'Tell me, great hero, but please make it brief. Is there a hole for me to get sick in?'

"The Commander-in-Chief answers him while chasing a fly saying, 'Death to all those who would whimper and cry.' And dropping a barbell he points to the sky saying, 'The sun's not yellow; it's chicken.'

"The king of the Philistines, his soldiers to save, put jawbones on their tombstones and flatters their graves, puts the pied pipers in prison and fattens the slaves, then sends them out into the jungle.

"Gypsy Davey with a blowtorch, he burns out their camps. With his faithful slave Pedro behind him, he tramps, with a fantastic collection of stamps to win friends and influence his uncle.

"The geometry of innocence, flesh on the bone, causes Galileo's math book to get thrown at Delilah, who's sitting worthlessly alone. But the tears on her cheeks are from laughter. Now I wish I could give Brother Bill his great thrill. I would set him in chains at the top of the hill. Then send out for some pillars and Cecil B. DeMille. He could die happily ever after.

"Where Ma Raney and Beethoven once unwrapped their bed roll, tuba players now rehearse around the flag pole. And the National Bank for a profit sells roadmaps for the soul to the old folks home and the college. Now I wish I could write you a melody so plain that could hold you, dear friends, from going insane. That could ease you and cool you and cease the pain of your useless and pointless knowledge."

Elvis fell to his knees.

"As I walked out in Laredo one day, I spied a poor cowboy wrapped up in white linen as cold as the clay. 'I see by your outfit that you are a cowboy,' he whispered as I proudly stepped by. 'Come, sit down beside me and hear my sad story. I'm shot in the breast, and I know I must die. T'was once in the saddle I used to go riding. Once in the saddle I used to go gay. First led to drinking and then to card-playing. I'm shot in the breast, and I'm dying today.

"'Let six jolly cowboys come carry my coffin. Let six pretty gals come carry my pall. Throw bunches of roses all over my coffin. Throw roses to deaden the clods as they fall. Oh, beat the drum slowly, and play the fife lowly and play the Dead March as you carry me along. Take me to the green valley, and lay the earth over me. For I'm a poor cowboy, and I know I've done wrong.'

"We beat the drum slowly and played the fife lowly and bitterly wept as we carried him along. For we all loved our comrade, so brave, so young and handsome. We all loved our comrade although he'd done wrong."

I could see a tear in Elvis' eye. Then his eyes started to flutter and his body began to sway and crumble to the floor.

"Mama's in the factory; she ain't got no shoes! Daddy's in the alley; he's looking for food. I'm in the kitchen with the Brownsville blues."

Uncle Alert just made a face and shook his head. It was obvious that the constant consumption of drugs and alcohol were finally having their effect on Elvis.

"So, my fair-minded Joey, won't you take your leave? Are you headed for the country where you wear the green sleeve, and the children laugh, and the old folks sing, and the church bells toll for a miraculous thing, where the big red furnace just glows and glows, where the big heart beats, where the big wheel rolls?"

I didn't get a chance to answer because Albert grabbed me with a smile on his face.

"No, Joe. Let's go get the money we've earned instead! I wanna live with a cinnamon girl. I could be happy the rest of my life with a cinnamon girl. A dreamer of pictures, I run in the night. You see us together chasing the moonlight. My cinnamon girl.

"Ten silver saxes, a bass with a bow. The drummer relaxes and waits between shows for his cinnamon girl. All I need is my cinnamon girl."

I was all for it. I would never have suspected that such romantic thoughts were racing around Albert's mind. But, why not.

We revived Elvis and followed Uncle Albert to our meeting with Jesus. The contraband was intact so we assumed that Jesus would be happy. We were correct.

Jesus reached into the container and cautiously pulled out a small rectangular package. Slowly and carefully he unwrapped the solid black substance and placed the hashish on the table in front of him. He tasted a small sample, and a smile broke out on his face.

"Whoa, Black Betty!"

He reached out and shook Elvis' hand vigorously. He looked at me and nodded his head. I saw a look of trust in his eyes. His big worry was always whether Elvis would drop the ball before he could get the cargo to Uncle Albert. I could tell that he credited me with stabilizing his mule on the journey. I smiled in acceptance, but deep down inside I knew I was lucky.

"Black Betty had a child," chanted Elvis. "The Damn thing gone wild. She said, 'I'm worryin' outta mind. The damn thing gone blind.' I said, 'Oh, Black Betty. Whoa, Black Betty'."

"She really gets me high," Jesus chimed in. "You know that's no lie. She's so rock steady, and she's always ready. She's from Bogota way down in Columbia Well, she's shakin' that thing. Boy, she makes me sing. Whoa, Black Betty. Bam-A-Lam!"

Jesus was obviously pleased with the product delivery. But he grabbed Elvis by the collar and offered him some advice.

"Some say the State of Texas could accommodate the entire human population. Five point six billion versions of the truth under one roof. Some revelation! Take a bit of this. Give a bit of that. Put it in a blender. Pull it out of a hat. There's no going back. It's a lie; it's a fact. Has the cat got your tongue? Been too long in the sun? There's dust on your tracks. There's no going back.

"If you wanna hang out, you've got to take her out…cocaine. If you wanna get down, get down on the ground…cocaine. If you got bad news, you wanna kick them blues…cocaine. When your day is done, and you wanna run…cocaine. If your thing is gone, and you wanna ride on…cocaine. She don't lie; she don't lie; she don't lie… cocaine."

Then he sent us on our way, but knowing Elvis, he realized that we wouldn't leave until Sunday morning. He handed Elvis a little package intended for the two of us. I wondered what was in it, but Jesus immediately answered my question. But he directed his comments directly to Elvis.

"Saturday night, and you're still hanging around. Tired of living in your one-horse town. You'd like to find a little hole in the ground for a while. So you go to the village in your tie-dyed jeans, and you stare at the junkies and the closet queens. It's like some pornographic magazine. And you smile.

"Your sister's gone out, she's on a date. You just sit at home and masterbate. Your phone is gonna ring soon, but you just can't wait for that call."

I didn't think Elvis had a sister? Then I realized it was just Jesus' sense of humor in play.

"So you stand on the corner in your new English clothes. And you look so polished from your hair down to your toes. Ah, but still, your finger's gonna pick your nose after all.

"So, you decide to take a holiday. You got your tape-deck and your brand new Chevrolet. Ah, there ain't no place to go anyway. What for? So, you got everything, awe, but nothing's cool. They just found your father in the swimming pool. And you guess you won't be going back to school any more.

"So, you play your albums, and you smoke your pot. And you meet your girlfriend in the parking lot. Oh, but still you're aching for the things you haven't got. What went wrong?

"And, if you can't understand why your world is so dead, why you have to keep in style and feed your head. Well, you're 26 and still your mother makes your bed. And that's too long!"

Elvis was getting mad, but I nudged him and he calmed down for the moment. Jesus kept going. He pointed at the package.

"But Captain Jack will get you high tonight and take you to your special island. Well, now, Captain Jack will get you by tonight. Just a little push, and you'll be smiling. Well, now, Captain Jack could make you die tonight."

That last line was obviously a warning. I could tell that Jesus wanted me to keep an eye on Elvis. We still had one more delivery to make for Jesus. After a fuzzy but successful night, we set out for our delivery destination. I hadn't been there before so I had to rely on a fairly wobbly Elvis.

"When the sun comes up on a sleepy little town down around San Antone, and the folks are rising for another day 'round about their homes. The people of the town are strange, and they're proud of from where they came. Well, you're talking about China Grove.

"Well, the preacher and the teacher, Lord, they're a caution. They are the talk of the town. When the gossip gets to flyin', and they ain't lyin' when the sun goes fallin' down. They say that the father's insane, and there's Missus Perkins again. But every day there's a new thing coming in praise of an oriental view. The sheriff and his buddies carry their samurai swords. You can even hear the music at night. And though it's a part of the Lone Star State, people don't seem to care. They just keep on looking to the East talking about China Grove."

We got back in the truck, but something was wrong. It wouldn't move. Elvis told me that we should get my bike down and that we should part ways. There was something wrong with the transmission. The way Elvis expressed his plan was a little weird.

"I met a man who bought up land wherever his feet would tread. He asked me to El Paso, said I could stay on his spread. He has horses and cows and tractors and plows and all kinds of money to burn. But how can I get to El Paso when my wheels won't turn. They just won't move.

"There was a lady from Spain who had a fine frame. Then she moved to Hollywood. She said, 'Come and stay for a week and a day.' I said that I didn't think I could. She said, 'The sunshine's fine; I could spend some time. There are lessons I could learn.' But how can I get to L.A. when my wheels won't turn? Mmmm. They just won't move and my fuel won't turn.

"At a college of knowledge I tried to learn all the tricks to beat the system. I'd hide in nooks and memorize my books until I knew I'd never, never miss them. Eventually, I got my degree. But the real thing I did learn was that you just can't hit your home run if your wheels won't turn.

"There was a man in white who did things right. Now he watches from above. He said, 'Here is the way I want you to pray and the way to live and love.' So, I saw the light and did things right. But, the candle would not burn. Tell me, how can I get to heaven if my wheels won't turn?

"How can I get to Texas? How can I get to L.A.? How can I hit my home run? How can I get to heaven? My wheels won't turn. I'm spinning!"

I knew it was Elvis' way of saying that we should separate now. There would be less danger of being apprehended by the law. I knew he wanted to get back to his new home in Mexico from the way he sang as he prepared to leave. Now that I had some cash I felt much more secure.

"Riding into town alone by the light of the moon. I'm looking for old Carmalita Chacon at the Crazy Horse Saloon. Barkeep he gave me a drink. That's when she caught my eye. She turned to give me a wink that makes a grown man cry. Come easy, go easy. All right until the rising sun. I'm calling all the shots tonight. I'm like a loaded gun. Peeling off my boots and chaps, I'm saddle sore. Four bits gets you time in the racks. I scream for more.

"Fools' gold out of their mines. The girls are soaking wet. No tongue is drier than mine. I'll come when I get back. I'm back in the saddle again. I'm riding. I'm loading up my pistol. I'm riding. I really got a fist full. I'm riding. I'm shining up my saddle. I'm riding. This snake is gonna rattle.

"I'm back in the saddle again!"

He took a bottle of whiskey out of his jacket and downed a considerable belt of the fluid. Then he spoke very softly.

"The lunatic is on the grass. The lunatic is on the grass. Remembering games and daisy chains and laughs. Got to keep the loonies on the path.

"The lunatic is in the hall. The lunatics are in my hall. The paper holds their folded faces to the floor. And every day the paperboy brings more.

"And if the dam breaks open many years too soon. And, if there is no room upon the hill. And if your head explodes with dark forebodings, too, I'll see you on the dark side of the moon.

"The lunatic is in my head. You raise the blade. You make the change. You rearrange me until I'm sane. You lock the door and throw away the key. There's someone in my head, but it's not me.

"And, if the cloudbursts thunder in your ear. You shout, and no one seems to hear. And if the band you're in starts playing different tunes, I'll see you on the dark side of the moon."

Elvis took another drink as he prepared to take his leave. But, he had one more thought to purge from his soul.

"I am an outlaw. I was born an outlaw's son. The highway is my legacy. On the highway I will run. In one hand I've got a Bible. In the other I've got a gun. Well, don't you know me? I'm the man who won. Women! Don't try to love me, don't try to understand. A life upon the road is the life of an outlaw man.

"First left my woman, it was down Houston way. Headed for Mexico, I was riding night and day. All my friends are strangers. They quickly come and go. And all my love's in danger, because I steal hearts and souls.

"Some men call me Abel. Some men call me Cain. Some men call me sinner, Lord. Some men call me saint. Some say there's a Jesus. Some men say there ain't. When you got no life to lose, then there's nothing left to gain. Outlaw man!"

That was the last I saw of Elvis. I could only hope that the best of his dreams eventually came true. He was a good soul.

21
Smokey Joe's Cafe

After wandering alone for a day, I came across some fellow travellers. We were out in the desert near Houston sitting around the campfire, singing songs and drinking beer. This was a friendly bunch, and they seemed quite adept at camping out in the wilderness. The biggest one of them all was called Bugsy, and he was definitely the friendliest toward me from the start. His clothes were a little worn with bib-overalls over a flannel shirt being his preference. But his reddish beard and moustache were neatly trimmed. Unfortunately, as our conversation developed, he had a sad tale to tell.

"In life I never meant for things to be this way. But when I was a child with toy guns I used to play. And my father was a dedicated member of the N.R.A. And finally, hunting poor defenseless little animals just for the thrill of the kill pushed me into the fray.

"Who would have thought that a sweet young boy would be herded into the slammer by a plastic toy. But, alas, as fate would have it, my future wouldn't be worth a...the powder to blow it to hell."

I wanted to console Bugsy, but he moved on.

"Not so long ago, just a few years back, we used to hang out by the railroad track. The guitars, they played, and the singers made rhyme. It was a good time for being free. With a bouquet of flowers on her kitchen windowsill, we listened to Bob Dylan's new stuff he'd just done in Jacksonville. We would lie down on the hillside and look up at the sky. We had it all, her and I.

"And the lives we were living started to feel like yesterday. People started drifting and going their separate ways. The wind started blowing, and the sky began to cry. Her and I, we didn't make it. I wish we'd never said goodbye!

"I hope I never see those eyes again, eyes that used to be my best friends. And we gave it all away for the diamonds in the dust with a hungry voice still howling in the wind. A heart of stone no longer lasts. Her eyes no longer cry. I know I'll never see those tombstone eyes again.

"No more religious message, just a story to tell. I keep on track on Sunday, peace and love, heaven and hell. I'm a mean, beat street drifter with the sun shining from a face. Ah, but that was long ago, another time, another place."

There was no stopping Bugsy now. He was on a roll.

"Down every road there's one more city. I'm on the run; the highway is my home. I raised a lot of cane back in my younger days. While mama used to pray, my crops would fail. I'm a hunted fugitive with just two ways, outrun the law or spend my life in jail.

"I'd like to settle down, but they won't let me. A fugitive must be a rolling stone. I'm lonely, but I can't afford the luxury of having one I love to come along. She'd only slow me down, and they'd catch up with me. For he who travels fastest goes alone. I'm on the run; the highway is my home."

Still I didn't know my new friends very well, so at what seemed to be the right moment I asked them where they were headed. I had been told that they were former members of a rock group called A Bad Company. I was curious whether they still played their music. I was also really interested in learning more about exactly who Jesus was because all the old man had told me was that he was a Mexican educated in the United States and that he had connections almost everywhere. And these guys seemed to know him.

Roberto was a Mexican lawyer who played the flute. He knew Jesus best of all.

"He's a perfect stranger, like a cross of himself and a fox. He's a feeling arranger and a changer of the way he talks. He's the unforeseen danger, the keeper of the key to the locks. Know when you see him, nothing can free him. Step aside, open wide. It's the Loner.

"If you see him in the subway, he'll be down at the end of the car, watching you move until he knows he knows who you are. When you get off at your station alone, he'll know that you are. Know when you see him, nothing can free him. Step aside, open wide.

"South of the border and busted, caught by a woman he trusted. Now don't you call him a fool! It could have happened to you. It's just his luck, it happened to be him.

"Sweet Carmelita betrayed him. She said, 'Take me home, serenade me'. He figured a song could do him no harm. He didn't know how wrong he could be. Easy money for just one run to Peru. It'll be so easy. We'll have no trouble getting through. Well, he almost made it except for that one border guard. He opened up Jesus' guitar. Hello prison yard. Just to make him mad the border guard smashed Jesus' guitar. Goodbye easy money.

"The chiquita must have told them his story. Because when his eyes finally focused the next morning, Carmelita had spoken about guitars and some coke. And she laughed as they slapped him in chains.

"He was thrown in a cell with a killer, a convict who coughed through the night while he laid awake with the chills and shakes, hoping for a file in a cake. Easy money for just one run to Peru.

Well, when it comes to freedom, Jesus is not known to be lazy. For their acts of cowardice the border guard and Carmelita are pushing up daisies. Now the pipeline from Peru runs cool and very smooth, and now we all make easy money because of Jesus.

"So there is a lesson to be learned here, my friend. When you touch a man's guitar without his permission, you'd better not make it bend. So when Jesus comes back from his vacations in Peru, Mister Border Guard, you'd just better let him through!"

Roberto smiled a crafty smile as he shook my hand. I think he realized that I was someone he and Jesus could trust.

"That's not all," he said. Then he told me Jesus' favorite story in the first person.

"Forty thousand headmen couldn't make me change my mind. If I had to take the choice between the deaf man and the blind. I know just where my feet should go, and that's enough for me. I turned around and knocked them down and walked across the sea.

"Hadn't traveled very far when suddenly I saw three small ships a-sailing out towards a distant shore. So, lighting up a cigarette

I followed in pursuit and found a secret cave where they obviously stashed their loot. Filling up my pockets, even stuffed it up my nose. I must have weighed a hundred tons between my head and my toes. I ventured forth before the dawn had time to change its mind, and soaring high above the clouds I found a golden shrine.

"Laying down my treasure before the iron gate. Quickly, I rang the bell hoping I hadn't come too late. But someone came along and told me not to waste my time. And when I asked him who he was, he said, 'Just look behind'.

"So, I turned around, and forty thousand headmen bit the dirt, firing twenty shotguns each. And, man, it really hurt. But, luckily for me they had to stop and reload. And, by the time they'd done that, I was heading down the road."

Roberto and his friends were rolling on the ground laughing. They told me it was Jesus' favorite story, one he told inmates and the law when he was incarcerated. In the smuggling community, Jesus was known as 'The Gagster'.

The one they called Shifty Henry turned to Bugsy and asked him to explain their situation to me. Bugsy, whose hair seemed to grow in all directions, reminded me a lot of Tommy Chong. To be honest, Henry had facial features similar to Cheech Marin. In my mind they were already 'Cheech and Chong'. Shifty started to explain his situation.

"Got out of prison back in '86, and I found me a wife. Walked the clean and narrow just trying to stay out and stay alive. Got a job at a rendering factory, it ain't gonna make me rich. In the darkness before dinner comes sometimes I can feel the itch. I got a cold mind to go tripping across that thin line. I'm sick of doing straight time.

"My uncle's at the evening table; makes his living running hot cars. Slips me a hundred dollar bill, says, 'Shifty, you best remember who your friends are.' Eight years in you feel like you're gonna die. But you get used to everything. Sooner or later it becomes your life.

"Kitchen floor in the evening, tossing my little babies high. Mary's smiling, but she watches out of the corner of her eye. Seems you can't get any more than half free. I step out onto the porch and suck the cold air deep inside of me.

"In the basement, hunting gun and a hacksaw. Sip a beer and thirteen inches of barrel drop to the floor. Come home in the evening, can't get the smell from my hands. Lay my head down on the pillow and go drifting off to a foreign land. I'm sick of doing straight time."

Soon Bugsy started into their mutual story.

"We are as bad as a band can be. To hit the highest note, we often must steal from the highest mountain to the deepest sea. All of our movements we must conceal.

"We are A Bad Company, always on the run. We play our music when we can, but for us, destiny is the rising sun. Oh, I was born six-gun in my hand, as were these other fellas in the band. So, behind a gun or a guitar, we'll make our final stand. That's why they call me… call us, A Bad Company. And if you can play that guitar of yours like Eddie Van Halen and play your cards right, you can be part of A Bad Company, too.

"Rebel souls, deserters we are called. Chose a gun and threw away the sun. Now these towns, they all know our name. The six-gun sound, not the wail of our guitars, is now our claim to fame. I can hear them say…A Bad Company! And we won't deny we are Bad Company until the day we die. We could say we are not thieves…oh, but we are. It's the way we play. Dirty for dirty. If someone double-crossed us, yeah, we're A Bad Company. We would kill in cold blood."

After talking with the boys for a while and assessing our fugitive situations, it dawned on me that a more ordinary life wasn't really that bad. Then, when Shifty Henry asked me what I was pondering, I had to let it out, and he seemed like the perfect person to listen.

"Shifty, I'm going to rent myself a house in the shade of the freeway. I'm going to pack my lunch each morning and go to work each day. And when the evening rolls around, I'll go on home and lay my body down. And when the morning light comes streaming in, I'll get up and do it again."

Shifty said he wasn't sure he agreed, but he wanted to hear more about my idea.

"I want to know what became of the changes," I said, "we waited for love to bring. Were they only the fitful dreams of some greater awakening? I've been aware of the time going by; they say in the end it's the wink of an eye. And when the morning light comes streaming in, you'll get up and do it again, Amen!"

Just then Bugsy sat down next to Shifty. He had overhead our conversation and was interested in the subject.

"Caught between the longing for love and the struggle for the legal tender, where the sirens sing and the church bells ring and the junk man pounds his fender. Where the veterans dream of the fight fast asleep at the traffic light, and the children solemnly wait for the ice cream vendor. Out into the cool of the evening strolls the pretender. He knows that all his hopes and dreams begin and end there."

Shifty looked up and nodded his head acknowledging that once he himself had been The Pretender.

"Ah, the laughter of the lovers," Bugsy whispered, "as they run through the night, leaving nothing for the others but to choose off and fight and tear at the world with all their might while the ships bearing their dreams sail out of sight."

Shifty jumped up and pointed a finger at the sky.

"I'm going to find myself a girl who can show me what laughter means. And we'll fill in the missing colors in each other's paint-by-number dreams. And then we'll put our dark glasses on, and we'll make love until our strength is gone. And when the morning light comes streaming in, we'll get up and do it again!"

Shifty kept looking at the sky almost as if he were praying to an unseen force that controlled his life.

"I'm going to be a happy idiot and struggle for the legal tender where the ads take aim and lay their claim to the heart and the soul of the spender and believe in whatever may lie in those things that money can buy...though true love could have been a contender.

"Are you there? Say a prayer for The Pretender who started out so young and strong only to surrender."

But then trouble struck Shifty.

"I come in that night about a half-past ten. That baby of mine wouldn't let me in. So move it on over. Rock it on over. Move over, little dog, a mean old dog is moving in.

"She told me not to mess around. But I done let the deal go down. She changed the lock on my back door. Now my key won't fit no more. She threw me out just as pretty as she pleased. Pretty soon I was scratching fleas."

He turned to talk to an imaginary dog sitting next to him.

"Yeah, listen to me dog before you start to whine. That side's yours and this side's mine. Move over cool dog. A hot dog's moving in."

Then he petted the imaginary dog.

"I need a drink," said Shifty after a few moments. "Now if you wanna hear some boogie like I'm gonna play, it's just an old piano and a knocked out bass. The drummer man's a cat called Charlie McCoy. You know, Bugsy, remember that rubber legged boy? Mama cookin' chicken fried in bacon grease. Come on along, boys, it's just down the road apiece.

"Well, there's a place where you really get your kicks. It's open every night about twelve to six. Now, if you wanna hear some boogie you can get your fill and shove and sting like an old steam drill. Come on along, you can lose your head, down the road, down the road, down the road apiece.

"We can walk to Smokey Joe's Café for a thrill and our fill right from here."

"Well, show me the way to the next whiskey bar," shouted the bass player whose name was Rapid Jack. He supported his singing by plucking the strings of his bass. "Oh, don't ask why. For if we don't find the next whiskey bar, I tell you we must die. Oh, moon of Alabama, we now must say goodbye. We've lost our good old momma and must have whiskey. Oh, you know why.

"Well, show me the way to the next little girl. Oh, don't ask why. For if we don't find the next little girl, I tell you we must die. Oh, don't ask why."

The keyboard player was named Fast Eddie. As we walked toward town, we got to talking about our situation. He also seemed to have had problems with a female so his tale made me feel I wasn't alone.

"I used to smoke my face out right through the sky. I used to love to freak out, do you wonder why? I'd hear the Stones rollin', and I'd roll, too. I didn't care what I was doing, as long as I was with her.

"I was blown, and that's what she was, too. I was blown; I didn't care why or how. Rant, jump, and scream, right inside a dream. I used to tell my story right out loud. I was sure in my glory; I was sure proud. But, then one day I fell down. I couldn't get up. People were crowding all around. That's when they locked me up!"

But Eddie told me that things all worked out when he met Shifty in jail.

So we all applauded the concept of getting a few drinks in civilization and got up to make our way into town. When we arrived, I must admit that Smokey Joe's wasn't much to look at. The building was in a state of total disrepair. Even the sign was tilted at a 45 degree angle.

We all took seats at the bar and ordered some food and drink. Then a chicken walked in through the door that I had never seen before, and it scared me when she sat down right next to me.

Her knees were almost touching mine at Smokey Joe's Café. A chill was runnin' down my spine at Smokey Joe's Café. I could smell her sweet perfume; she smiled and made my heart go boom! I don't know what came over me, but I wanted her so bad. But, not here.

"In this dirty old part of the city, where the sun refuses to shine, people tell me there ain't no use in trying. Now, my girl, you're so young and pretty, and one thing I know is true. You'll be dead before your time is due. I know. You watched your daddy in bed dying. You watched his hair turning gray. He's been working and slaving his life away."

I had no idea where these thoughts of mine were coming from, but she was listening and nodding.

"We gotta get out of this place if it's the last thing we ever do. We've got to get out of this place, because girl there's a better life for me and you. Somewhere, baby, somehow I know it's true!"

Everybody else in the room at Smokey Joe's Café was listening to what I was saying. Finally, they said, "Be careful, that chick belongs to Smokey Joe!"

The cowboy next to me at the bar added some thoughts.

"Danger is out into the night. Danger, she's such a pretty sight. She was treated so badly it seems. Now, she's looking for a dream. Danger is out into the night. Danger, she walks the streets alone. Danger, all the bars she has known. All the men that look her way could be hers today.

"Locked into a love affair that didn't seem to go nowhere. With no choice, she thought she might throw caution to the wind, right into the night. How long will she take to find someone new? She goes nowhere I've been. She's gone out to the night."

The cowboy turned and looked right at me.

"Danger, she's out into the night. Danger, she's such a pretty sight. Danger, she's out with you tonight!"

And from behind the counter I saw a man, a chef's hat on his head and a knife in his hand. He grabbed me by the collar and began to shout, "You better eat up your beans, Boy, and clean right on out!" He was angry. He put the kitchen knife down and pulled something out of his pocket.

"My six blade knife! It'll do anything for me. Anything I want it to. One blade for breaking my heart. One blade for tearing you apart! My six blade knife do anything for me.

"I can take away your mind like I take away the top of a tin when I come up from behind and lay it down cold on your skin. I took a stone from your soul when you were lame just so I could make you tame. I'll take away your mind like I take away the top of this tin.

"Everybody got a knife, it can be just what they want it to be. A needle, a wife, or something that you just can't see. You know it keeps me strong. Yes, and it'll do you wrong. My six blade knife...do anything for me."

Smokey Joe flashed the knife in my face again, but then he put it back in his pocket. But I was still the focus of his attention.

"Your butt is mine. Gonna take you right. Just show your face in broad daylight. I'm telling you on how I feel. Gonna hurt your mind. Don't shoot to kill. Come on. Lay it on me all right.

"I'm giving you on the count of three to show your stuff or let it be. I'm telling you just watch your mouth. I know your game, what you're about. Well, they say the sky's the limit, and to me that's really true. But, my friend, you have seen nothing, just wait until I get through. Because I'm bad!"

Then he turned his attention to the woman who'd been quietly listening all this time.

"Now, you're a whiskey-headed woman, and you stay drunk all the time. If you don't stop drinkin', I believe you're gonna lose your mind.

"Well now, every time I see you, you're at some whiskey joint, standing at the back door asking for a half-pint. If you don't stop drinking, I believe you're gonna go stone blind. Well, now, I took you off the street, Baby, when you didn't have no place to stay. You ain't acting nothing but a fool dogging me around this way.

"Well now, every time I meet you, Baby, you're walking up and down the street, grinning, laughing, and talking with every man you meet, because you're a whiskey-headed woman, and you stay drunk all the time.

"The word is out. You're doing wrong. Gonna lock you up before too long. Your lying eyes gonna take you right. So listen up. Don't make a fight. You're throwing stones to hide your hands. We can change the world tomorrow. This could be a better place. If you don't like what I'm saying, why don't you slap my face."

Big Ernie, one of the drummers came to my side and stood between me and Smokey Joe. He grabbed Smokey by the shoulder and offered up some advice.

"It's getting late. Have you seen my mates? Smokey, tell me when the boys get here. It's seven o'clock, and I want to rock. Want to get a belly full of beer!

"My old man's drunker than a barrel full of monkeys. And my old lady she don't care. My sister looks cute in her braces and boots. A hand full of grease in her hair.

"Don't give us none of your aggravation, Smokey. We've had it with your discipline. Saturday night's all right for fighting. Get a little action in.

"Get about as oiled as a diesel train. Gonna set this dance alight. Because Saturday night's the night I like. Saturday night's all right.

"Well, they're packed pretty tight in here tonight. I'm looking for a dolly who'll see me right. I may use a little muscle to get what I need. I may sink a little drink and shout out, 'She's with me!'

"A couple of the sounds I really like are the sounds of a switchblade and a motorbike. I'm a juvenile product of the working class whose best friend floats in the bottom of a glass."

Well, I know I'll never eat again at Smokey Joe's Café. Smokey Joe wasn't kidding. Then Ernie popped Smokey in the chops and the brawl was on. The boys came to our aid and started throwing punches around and soon the local police had us all in handcuffs. Lucky for me, they assumed I was just one of the band, A Bad Company, and never figured out that Sheriff John Brown was on my tail. However, everyone else was wanted for something or other.

One of the officers asked me for my version of the fight.

"I was cutting a rug down at a place called Smokey Joe's Café with a girl named Linda Lou."

Since I never did get the girl's name, Linda Lou seemed appropriate.

"When in walked a man with a knife in his hand, and he was looking for you know who. He said, 'Hey there, fellow, with the hair colored yellow, what are you trying to prove? Because that's my woman there, and I'm a man who cares, and this might be all for you!'

"I was scared and fearing for my life. I was shaking like a leaf on a tree. Because he was lean and mean, big and bad, Lord, pointing that knife at me. I said, 'Wait a minute, mister, I didn't even kiss her. Don't want no trouble with you. And I know you don't owe me, but I wish you'd let me ask one favor from you. Won't you give me three steps toward the door, gimme three steps, mister, and you'll never see me no more.'

"Well, the crowd cleared away, and I began to pray as the water fell on the floor. And, I'm telling you, son, well it ain't no fun staring straight down a six-blade knife. Well, he turned and screamed at Linda Lou, and that's the break I was looking for. And you could hear me screaming a mile away as I was headed out towards the door!"

So, into the paddy wagon we were loaded for a trip downtown to the local jail. For some reason to my surprise we were allowed to keep our musical instruments with us. I figured that the local sheriff must be a retired musician. The deputy asked me to strum a few tunes to keep the prisoners quiet during the trip. I was glad to accommodate him.

What was immediately apparent to me was the fact that the other prisoners seemed so calm and resigned to their fate. When I mentioned my observation, the deputy told me that, except for me, he already knew each prisoner's name and probably what instrument he played. That's how many times they'd been arrested before in this town. I breathed a sigh of relief as I realized that the band members were a perfect cover for me. When the deputy asked for my name and address, I gave him my Cousin Dupree's name and address and told him my nickname was Joe. It worked. I struck up a little tune for the deputy and his prisoners they thought was pretty funny.

"Fame makes a man take things over. Fame lets him loose, makes him hard to swallow. Fame puts you there where things are hollow. Fame, it's not your brain. It's just the flame that burns your change to keep you insane.

"Fame, what you like is in this limo. Fame, what you get is no tomorrow. Fame, what you need you have to borrow. Fame, nein! 'It's mine' is just his line. To bind your time, it drives you to crime!

"Could it be the best, could it be? Really be, really, babe? Is it any wonder I reject you first? Is it any wonder you are too cool to fool? Fame, bully for you, chilly for me. Got to get a rain check on pain. Fame, what's your name?"

22
30 Days in the Hole

If you're ever in Houston, well, you better do right. You better not gamble, there; you better not fight, at all, or the sheriff will grab you and the boys will bring you down. The next thing you know, boy…Oh! You're prison bound.

I was a little surprised by my first real experience with a jail. The jailhouse in the city was full so they sent us out to a Federal prison camp for storage. It was a minimum security facility for most of the inmates although we found ourselves locked up with the high security bunch at first. The cell block was in the center of the prison grounds, and through the barred windows we could see the trustee inmates walking around and playing basketball. I must admit that it was a little disconcerting.

Well, inside you wake up in the morning; you hear the work bell ring. And they march you to the table to see the same old thing. A'int no food upon the table and no pork up in the pan. But you better not complain, boy, you get in trouble with the man.

I asked myself what it was that I did to deserve such a fate? If you add up all of my worldly possessions and my cash, the total isn't that great. And although I have thought many bad thoughts about them from time to time, I never called any of our politicians a louse. So, why in the world are they treating me worse than they'd treat a mouse?

Stuck inside these four walls, sent inside forever, never seeing no one nice again like you Mama, you Mama. Deep inside I hoped that my poor mother was alive and well. If I ever get out of here, I thought about giving everything I had, as little as it was, away to a registered charity. All I need is a pint a day. But here I am, thirty days in the hole. Shifty Henry came over to where I stood and began telling me more about his life. But first he pointed to a cell in a dark corner where he said his old friend, Freddie the Gun, was chained. We went over and listened to his story.

"I saw her standing on her front lawn just twirling her baton. Me and her went for a ride, Sir, and ten innocent people died. From the town of Lincoln, Nebraska, with a sawed off .410 on my lap, through the badlands of Wyoming, I killed everything in my path.

"I can't say that I'm sorry for the things that we done. At least for a while, Sir, me and her, we had us some fun.

"The jury brought in a guilty verdict, and the judge, he sentenced me to death. Midnight in a prison storeroom with leather straps across my chest. Sheriff, when the man pulls that switch, Sir, and snaps my poor head back, you make sure my pretty baby is sitting right there on my lap.

"They declared me unfit to live, said into that great void my soul would be hurled. They wanted to know why I did what I did. Well, Sir, I guess there's just a meanness in this world. But it's not all my fault and my way. 'Be a man,' my teachers would call. 'Make your mark and stand tall', they would say. So I pushed that old man up against that concrete wall. And blasted away until he did fall. For its purpose my gun was properly used. If it had stayed in a rack on the wall, its existence would have been abused.

"What else are guns for? They shoot bullets and buckshot to make a score. And that score can only be to make a kill. And when you make a kill, it's such a thrill! Why is it that no one understands? How else do you become a man in this land?"

Shifty Henry was almost crying as he chimed in so Freddie could hear.

"Breaking rocks in the hot sun. I needed money because I had none. I left my baby, and it feels so bad. Guess my race is run. She's the best girl that I ever had.

"Robbing people with a six-gun. I lost my girl, and I lost my fun. I fought the law and the law won.

"Like a bluebird with his heart removed, lonely as a train, I've run just as far as I can. If I never see the good old days shining in the sun, I'll be doing fine and then some.

"Well, I'll be doing time in a lonesome prison where the sun doesn't shine. Just outside, the freedom river runs. Out there in that shiny night with the bloodhounds on your mind, don't you know it's the same sad situation.

"Everybody feels all right, you know, I heard some poor fool say. Somebody. oooh, everyone is out there on the loose.

"Well, I wish I lived in the land of fools, no one knew my name. But what you get is not quite what you choose.

"But, I lie like a tiger in wait, in the shadows near the front gate. Waiting for the man with the keys to take leave. Then, I'll grab him by his right sleeve. He won't have a chance to resist. I'll just give his hand a little twist, write my number on his shirt for all to see, and give him a little kiss. Then the tiger will slip unseen through the gate, and the man who had the keys will have to wait…for the parole board."

Freddy's friend Al chimed in.

"I've been caught stealing once when I was five. I enjoy stealing. It's just as simple as that. Well, it's just a simple fact. When I want something, I don't want to pay for it. I walk right through the door. Hey, all right! If I get by, it's mine! Mine all mine!

"My girl, she's one, too. She'll go and get her a shirt. Stick it under her skirt. She grabbed a razor for me. And she did it just like that. When she wants something, she don't want to pay for it. We sat around the pile. We sat and laughed. Waved it into the air. And we did it just like that.

"For a while we did pretty damn good. Empty shelves were there where products for sale once stood. We laughed and we sang all the way to the front door. And soon we were back inside shopping some more. Alas, our luck couldn't hold forever. A man behind the counter pulled some kind of lever. And soon we were inside a police car driven by a man wearing a star.

"I haven't seen my girl again, except for that one day in court. They put the cuffs on me while she walked away with a snort. To this day I can't believe she pointed that finger at me. She was just as guilty as anyone could see. But here I am doing time in the local slammer, while she's somewhere in the south getting tanner. It's just not fair."

After we said goodbye to Freddie and Al, Shifty reached into his pocket and pulled out a cigarette. He offered me one, but I told him I didn't smoke…cigarettes. Then, he went on with his story.

"Chicago Green, talking about Black Lebanese, a dirty room and a silver coke spoon give me my release…come on. Black Napalese, it's got you weak in your knees. Sneeze some dust that you got buzzed on; you know it's hard to believe…thirty days in the hole. That's what they give you, thirty days in the hole…I know!

"Newcastle Brown, I'm telling you, it can sure smack you down. Take a greasy whore and a rolling dance floor, it's got your head spinning round."

Then Henry grabbed me by the shoulders and looked me straight in the eyes.

"My brother went to prison. He's in Kingston doing time. He got seven years for selling what I've been smoking all my life. Time off for good behavior. But the boy don't feel too good locked behind those steel bars. I don't know if he should.

"Yeah, a few years ago they called me back home to get a big award. They also called my brother, but they made him say 'My Lord'. They locked me up in the Hall of Fame and threw away the keys. But when they put my brother away, it really did something to me.

"Now I'm guilty as hell for saying, 'Boy, you better go back home.' You know you'll get a fair shake there. We're running all alone. When he called me up from the border with the Mounties on his tail, I said, 'Go back to Canada. We can raise the bail.'

"Now I get these letters from a cell with no TV. He says he's outside one hour and inside twenty-three. He got seven years for selling what I've been smoking all my life. Time off for good behavior.":

Henry was almost crying, but he went on.

"If you live on the road, well, there's a new highway code. You take the urban noise with some Durban Poison; it's gonna lessen your load.

"What are you doing, Boy? You're here for thirty days. Get… get…get your long hair cut and cut out your ways…thirty days in the hole…"

Right there, Shifty Henry passed out. Bugsy came over and dragged his friend into a dark corner of the cell. He held his index finger up to his lips.

"Tonight there's gonna be a jailbreak somewhere in this town. See me and the boys we don't like it, so we're getting up and going down. Hiding low, looking right to left, if you see us coming, I think it's best to move away. Do you hear what I say from under my breath?

"Tonight there's gonna be trouble; some of us won't survive. See, the boys and me mean business, busting out dead or alive. I can hear the hound dogs on our trail. All hell breaks loose; alarms and sirens wail. Like the game, if you lose, go to jail!

"Tonight there's gonna be a breakout into the city zones. They'd better not try and stop us; no one could for long. Searchlights are on our trail. Tonight's the night all systems fail."

I had to ask Shifty just what chance we had of making it out alive. I had never done this sort of thing before from inside a real prison. Shifty smiled and commenced to tell me about a friend of his.

"There was a friend of mine accused of murder, and the judge's gavel fell. Jury found him guilty and gave him sixteen years in hell. He said, 'I ain't spending my life here; I ain't living alone. Ain't breaking no rocks on the chain gang, I'm breaking out and heading home. Gonna make a jailbreak, and I'm looking towards the sky. I'm gonna make a jailbreak, oh, how I wish I could fly. All in the name of liberty, got to be free. Jailbreak, let me out of here, sixteen years, had more than I can take. Jailbreak, yeah!'

"He said he'd seen his lady being fooled with by another man. She was down, and he was up. He had a gun in his hand. Bullets started flying everywhere, and people started to scream. Big man lying on the ground with a hole in his body where his life had been. But it was all in the name of liberty.

"He had to be free; he had to break out. Heartbeats, they were racing. Freedom he was chasing. Spotlight, sirens, rifles firing. But, he made it out…with a bullet in his back. Jailbreak!"

Needless to say, I wasn't inspired by Shifty's story, but I wasn't going to stay behind. I had to hope my luck would hold. It was time to work on the detailed plan. Everyone was excited and ready to go.

But before we could fix the details of our escape plan, the warden threw a party in the county jail. We had the prison band there and soon A Bad Company began to wail. The band was jumping and the band began to wing. You should have heard those knocked out jailbirds sing. Let's rock, everybody, let's rock. Everybody in the whole cell block was dancing to the jailhouse rock.

Spider Murphy played the tenor saxophone. Little Joe was blowing on the slide trombone. The drummer boy from Illinois went crash, boom, bang. The whole rhythm section was the purple gag. Number forty-seven said to number three: You're the cutest jailbird I ever did see. I sure would be delighted with your company. Come on and do the jailhouse rock with me.

I asked Spider Murphy how he got here. He smiled sheepishly.

"I had a friend named Rambling Bob who used to steal, gamble and rob. He thought he was the smartest guy in town. But I found out last Monday that Bob got locked up Sunday. They've got him in the jailhouse way down town. I told him once or twice to quit playing cards and shooting dice. He's in the jailhouse now. Thank, God, he's not a member of our band.

"He played a game called poker pinoccle with Dan Yoker, but shooting dice was his greatest game. Now, he's downtown in jail; no one to go his bail. The judge done said that he refused a fine.

"I went out last Tuesday. Met a gal named Susie. Told her I was the swellest guy around. We started to spend my money. Then she started to call me honey. We took in every cabaret in town. I told the judge right to his face that we didn't like to see this place."

He pointed across the room where Susie sat in the female block.

"We're in the jailhouse now."

Just then I noticed a prisoner dressed in a tattered wedding dress. It was one of the strangest sights I'd ever seen. And being from New York, that's saying a lot. I almost freaked out when he came over to me with his story. As it turned out, his name was Jesse but the inmates called him Jesse Jane.

"I'm in jail in a Texas town in my sister's wedding gown. I drive a truck all night long listening to Judy Garland songs. Now I'm locked behind bars of steel. I was just looking for a happy meal. I parked my rig, and I went inside. They've never seen such a pretty bride. I paid my bill, and I turned around facing every red neck in that one-horse town. His face was red. His fist was clenched. He threw his Coke, and he got me drenched.

"Well, I guess that was the final straw. I pulled a pistol from my Wonder-bra. I killed him dead. I killed them all. And they finally caught me in the bathroom stall. And now I'm doing ten to life. But I'll tell you one thing, Joey, someday I'm gonna make someone in here a hell of a wife."

Spider Murphy grabbed Jesse and pointed to his cell. He wanted him to leave us.

"Jesse Jane, are you insane? Or are you a normal guy who dresses like a butterfly? Or are you just an average Joe looking for a fashion show? Or are you just a Peter Pan looking for his Neverland?"

Jesse Jane just smiled and walked away. Every eye in the cellblock was on her…him. I think everyone felt sorry for him.

Little Joe stopped playing after a short while. A sad look covered his face. It seems that his girl had come to see him and to beg for his release. This is what she told the local sheriff.

"Please Mister Jailer, won't you let my man go free? He don't belong in prison though he's guilty as can be. But the only thing he's guilty of is simply loving me. Please, Mister Jailer, won't you let my man go free?

"Well, I know it won't be long now 'till they cut his hair off, too. Still, I'm hoping there's one favor that I could beg of you. So, please, Mister Jailer, won't you let my man go free? Just look into his eyes, open up that door. Just listen to his slide trombone, you'll know the score."

While we were talking, I asked Spider Murphy what he was in for before this incident. He responded with a big smile on his face.

"When you're driving down the highway at night, and you're feelin' that wild turkey's bite, don't give Johnny Walker a ride 'cause Jack Black is right by your side. You might get taken to the jailhouse and find you've been arrested for driving while blind.

"Now just the other night with nothin' to do, we broke a case of proof 102 and started itchin' for that wonderful feel of rollin' in an automobile. You could say we was out of our minds, and let me tell you, we were flyin' while blind.

"Then they had us up against the wall. Hey, it's only blood grain alcohol! And there ain't no cause for alarm. We ain't out to do nobody no harm. How could anyone be so unkind to arrest a man for drivin' while blind?"

Spider went back to his saxophone. Almost immediately, Charlie Bill walked up with his story. He was a Missouri boy, and was very polite. Seems he had experience as a pilot.

"As I was going over the Cork and Kerry mountains, I saw Captain Harry Hill and his money he was counting. I first produced my pistol and then produced my rapier and said, 'Stand over and deliver or the devil might take ya.'

"I took all of his money, and it was a pretty penny. I took all his money, and I brought it home to Molly. She swore that she loved me, never would she leave me. The devil take that woman for you know she tricked me easy.

"Being drunk and weary, I went to Molly's chamber taking my money with me, and I never knew the danger. For in about six or seven seconds in walked Captain Hill. I leapt up, fired off my pistols, and I shot him with both barrels.

"Now, some men like the fishing and some men like the fowling. And some men like to hear a cannon ball a roaring. Me, I like sleeping, especially in my Molly's chamber. But here I am in prison, here I am with a ball and chain, yeah!"

"But, Molly, when she saw me, she had no sympathy. I felt sorry for her because all she was left with was all of Harry Hill's money. Now Harry, though deceased, had another girlfriend named Sally. And as fate would have it, Sally met Molly and her money in the alley. Molly was self-righteous. It was money she had earned. Sally, however, was the one with a gun as Molly too late did learn.

"So, I don't feel too bad about the whole thing," said Charlie Bill with a smile. "Sally is my sister, and as soon as I get out of here, I'll be living in style."

With a smirk on my face, I told Charlie Bill that he had all my sympathy and wished him good luck on an early release. I think he knew that release would be sooner than I could imagine.

The sad sack was sitting on a block of stone, way over in the corner weeping all alone. The warden said, 'Hey, Buddy, don't you be no square. If you can't find a partner, use a wooden chair.' In response the sad sack stood up and began to complain.

"A man stands up before God and country, raises his right hand and takes an oath, swears he has acted in the line of duty, and he more than anyone wants to tell the truth.

"But there is a need to keep some things a secret…some weapons shipments…some private wars. In the future democracy will be defended behind closed doors.

"Now the men of Congress who convene to determine if covert war is a business or a crime are the same men who routinely give their permission for the shedding of blood in security's name.

"And there is a need to keep some things secret…the names of some countries…the terms of some deals. And, above all the sounds of the screams of the innocent beneath our wheels. Does the word 'Justice' mean anything to you? Are the features of a lie beginning to come through?

"In the streets of America the children are buried, caught in an avalanche of weapons and drugs. They lie and they die in the bowels of a business that's disguised as a war between The Crips and The Bloods.

"And there is a need to keep some things secret. The C.I.A. deals protecting the source and the government policies directly connecting the drugs and our wars. Does the word 'Justice' mean anything to you?

"As the battlefield comes home and democracy falls through, I am waiting for the time to come when the word will be real for everyone. And not just a word, but a thing that can be done. But 'Justice' must be won!"

Several other prisoners who were listening began nodding their heads. Shifty tapped me on the shoulder to get my attention.

"It's not like we did something wrong. We just burned down the church while the choir within sang religious songs. And it's not like we thought we was right. We just played with the wheels of a passenger train that cracked on the tracks one night. It's not like we ain't on the ball. We just talk to our shrinks. Huh? They talk to their shrinks. No wonder we're up the wall. We're not stupid or dumb. We're the lunatic fringe that rusted the hinge on Uncle Sam's daughters and sons.

"With roller coaster brains, imagine playing with trains! Lizzie Borden took an axe and gave her mother forty whacks. And don't think we're trying to be bad. All the innocent crime seemed all right at the time. Not necessarily mad, we watch every day for the bus. And the driver would say, 'That's were the lunatics stay'. I wonder if he's talking about us?

"It's not like we're vicious or gone. We just dug up the graves where your relatives lay in old Forest Lawn. And it's not like we don't know the score. We're the fragile elite they dragged off the street. I guess they just couldn't take us no more.

"Good old boys and girls, congregating, waiting in some other world. We're all crazy!"

Shifty Henry said to Bugsy, 'For heaven's sake; no one's looking, now's our chance to make a break'. Bugsy turned to Shifty and he said, 'Nix, nix. I wanna stick around a while and get my kicks!'

Anyway, the party lasted into the night, but Bugsy and Shifty along with Spider Murphy and Little Joe finally put their plan into action.

Well, the rain exploded with a mighty crash as we fell into the sun. And the first one said to the second one there, I hope you're having fun. Band on the run! And the jailer man and sailor Sam were searching everyone for the band on the run. Well, the undertaker drew a heavy sigh seeing no one else had come, and a bell was ringing in the village square, for the rabbit's on the run.

"Ain't the weather fine," said Henry, "ain't a cloud in sight. It's a lovely day to be out of jail. How that sun do shine like a golden light. I've been in the shade, if you know what I mean. No thanks to legal aide, I'm back on the scene.

"If the sky turns gray, that'll be okay. I don't care if there be thunder and hail. Because the fact remains, even if it rains, it's a lovely day to be outta jail. Even winter ain't no thing. No, I don't give a damn. Every day is spring when you're sprung from the slam!

"This morning I could hardly wait until it was time to journey through that iron gate. I threw my head back, looked up at the sky and said, 'Ain't the weather fine. Ain't a cloud in sight. It's a lovely day to be outta jail!"

As we trudged through the woods, our weary band became wary so we stopped to rest. One of the prisoners I hadn't met before was named Willie. He was certainly happy to be out again although his freedom was unexpected. He had escaped once before, and was scheduled to be returned to his original digs at Raiford just the next day. Prison life had made its impression on his psyche.

"Well, them four walls of Raiford, closing in on me, doing three to five hard labor for armed robbery. I had two years behind, but I could not wait the time. Every time I thought about it, well I died some more inside.

"And I had stripes on my back, memories that hurt. For the only time I seen sunshine was when I hit the dirt, digging ditches for the chain gang, sleeping in the cold. Oh, Lord, please forgive me for I could not wait no more.

"And I'm coming home to see you, Jesus. Well, it feels so close this time. Please take mercy on this soldier from the Florida-Georgia line. When they find me, they must kill me. Oh, Jesus, save my soul. I can't go back down to Raiford. I can't take that anymore.

"Well, these last few years behind me, Oh, lord, have been so sad. I fought proudly for my country when the times were bad. Now they say I'm guilty. When they find me, I must die. Only me and Jesus know that I never stole a dime.

"Well, when Vietnam was over, there was no work here for me. I had a petty wife a-waiting and two kids I had to feed. Well, I'm one of America's heroes, and when they shoot me down, won't you fly Old Glory proudly, put my medals in the ground."

Well, soon the night was falling as the desert world began to settle down. In the town they're searching for us everywhere, 'cause we never will be found. And the county judge who held a grudge will search forever more, for the band on the run.

23
Free at Last

I ran as fast as my legs could carry me back to the place in town where I left my Harley before the incident at Smokey Joe's Café. Through some sort of miracle, it was still there in the alley chained to the same old lamppost whose light was still out. I unlocked her and after checking things I jumped aboard. Just sitting on the bike gave me confidence. Without the lights on I roared out of the back end of town. Well, it was more of a creep than a roar. The last thing I needed was attention. Feeling better about things, I started humming to myself.

"Diamonds in the sunset, now your time has come. Pretty yellow bird fly away into the sun. Spread your broken wings and learn how to fly. Take the diamonds from the sun. Wipe the tear from your eye.

"When the candles are all burned down and the world has turned to stone, that's when you've got to fly, fly your way home. Don't look down. Follow the sound. Get out of town. Don't look down!

"And I've got to run to keep from hiding. And I'm bound to keep on riding. And I've got one more silver dollar, but, I'm not gonna let them catch me, no. I'm not gonna let them catch the midnight rider.

"And I don't own the clothes I'm wearing, and the road goes on forever. And I've gone past the point of caring, whose old bed I'll soon be sharing. No, I'm not gonna let them catch the midnight rider."

I was finally on my way, alone. The great jailbreak was successful, at least for me. I wanted to celebrate, and the time was right. Somehow I had to shake this feeling of depression that was overhanging me. I began to convince myself it could be done.

I asked myself what my Uncle Jim would do under these circumstances. I haven't mentioned him because I haven't seen him in quite a while. But I do remember what he told me at my high school graduation.

"Getting bombed out on booze, got nothing to lose. Run out of money, disposable blues. Sleazy hotels, like living in hell. The girls on the hustle with nothing to sell want something for nothing. It's always the same. Keep pushing and shoving, and I'm down on the game. Always in trouble; forever detained. Goodbye, goodbye, goodbye, and good riddance to bad luck.

"Well, spread out the news. There's a free man loose, back out of jail and chasing some flooze. Bad luck has changed, broken the chains. Lay down a claim for monetary gains. Wonder what's coming out for the take. Freedom for loving and lust for the taste. Eyes are wide open, wild to the game. Goodbye, goodbye, goodbye, and good riddance to bad luck. I'll never again be stuck because I threw down the gates of bad luck."

Getting that off my chest made me feel so much better. I pressed on for quite a while. After I crossed the Texas state line, I began to relax. After a while I was headed north toward Memphis. I walked down the main street of a small town in Mississippi looking for something to eat. Actually, what I wanted was a drink so I kept my eyes open for a bar. I'd been up for twenty-four hours.

Wet wind on the sidewalk, I'm staring at the rain. Walking up the street, yeah, and walking down again. And my feet are tired, and my brain is numb. See that broken neon sign saying, 'Hey, in you come'. Got the scent of stale beer hanging around my head. Old dog in the corner sleeping like he could be dead. A book of matches and a full ashtray. Cigarette left smoking its life away.

An old guy pulled up a stool next to me, and before I could speak, he welcomed me to Harry's. He said his name was Alvin, and he had his own pint of whiskey. There was no bartender in sight, so when he offered me a drink, I accepted. This was no time to refuse some much-needed libation.

"Well, yes, Joey, I am a poor, drunken-hearted boy."

He stopped and smiled. "I like to think of myself as a boy instead of an old fart. I hope you don't mind?"

I patted Alvin on the back, and he went on with his story.

"Well, yes, Joey, I am a drunken-hearted boy. I have a whole ocean of trouble and just a little half-pint of joy. I drink because I'm worried.

I don't drink because I'm dry. I know that if I keep on drinking, I'm liable to drink away my life. But that's all right."

Then Alvin had a little advice for me. I don't think he really meant what he said because he was quite talkative.

"Don't tell me hard luck stories and I won't tell you mine. Every time you're feeling fine, got another good one on the line, it slips away. You feel it slip away. I don't want no more from you. Won't do what you want me to. Come on, turn me loose."

Alvin was obviously bombed, but he meant no harm so I stayed.

"Every time I'm feeling good, the phone rings, and I knock on wood. Hoping that it won't be you calling like you always do. All you ever seem to say is how much bad luck came your way."

I reminded Alvin that I'd never called him, but that didn't stop him.

"You won't try to start again. You just count on your old friends. Now you call up every day. Got no money, no place to stay. That girl made a mess of you. You got what was coming, too. Build her up and let her down. Tasting everything in town. Treat her right; you never treat her right. Now she's gone and you're alone. Bite your fingers to the bone.

"You don't know what's going on. How you lost it, what went wrong? Whatever happened to the love that you once knew? Don't tell me hard luck stories, and I won't tell you mine."

I was speechless. How could he know about me and Linda Lou? Or was he just guessing from my appearance? Alvin started humming as he spoke.

"Bartender, bring me another half-a-pint. I'm trying to drown these blues. Yes, I am. Joey, if you had my trouble, I know you'd be drinking, too. All right, Bartender, bring me some Old Grand Dad's one hundred proof. If I keep on drinking, I know I can't last too long. That's all right, because when I'm dead and buried, please think about me when you hear this song."

I was sipping my drink and somehow it began to taste better with each of Alvin's words. He had a special way of describing his surroundings.

"God's tears on the sidewalk," he whispered. "It's the mother of all rain. But in the thick blue haze of Harry's, you will feel no pain. And you will feel no soft hand slipping on your knee. You don't have to pay for memories; they will all come free. Another Harry's Bar, or that's the tale they tell. But, Harry's long gone now, and the customers as well. Me and the dog and the ghost of Harry will make this world turn right. It'll all turn right.

"Now, when Harry was a young man, Harry was so debonair. He walked a bouncy step in his shiny shoes. And, when Harry was a young man, well, Harry could walk on air. He mixed a mean cocktail, and he talked you through the late news. You want to hear some great news? Harry's still here!

"He fell victim to the gypsy woman's passion. As he walked all alone in a dead end down the block, the gypsy woman spotted him and on him put a lock. She bought his bills saying it would cure his ills, but the debt to her turned hot. His daddy told him neither a debtor nor a creditor be. But under the gypsy's spell he could not see.

"Down by the old sweet mountain, there's a psychic woman under the old North Star. She could read old Harry's mind from near or from far. The gypsy woman's passion tied up his heart, so when she told him what to do, he only asked when to start.

"We never saw old Harry again. There was only a faint glow in the sky. But over in yonder cemetery his remains do lie."

Alvin raised his glass as he prepared to sing what he called Harry's anthem. But after a few lines, I really believe it was his story.

"Wanna tell you a story about the house-man blues. I come home one Friday, had to tell the landlady I'd lost my job. She said that don't comfort me, as long as I get my money next Friday. Now, next Friday came, and I didn't get the rent. And out the door I went.

"So I go to the landlady and I said, 'Will you let me slide? I'll have the rent for you in a month.'

"I noticed that when I came home in the evening, she ain't got nothing nice to say to me. But for five years she was so nice. Oh, she was lovey-dovey. I came home one particular evening and the landlady said, 'You got the rent money yet?' I said, 'No, I can't find a job, therefore, I ain't got no money to pay the rent' She said, 'I don't believe you're trying to find no job! I saw you yesterday. You was standing on a corner, leaning up against a post.' I said, 'But, I'm tired. I've been walking all day'. She said, 'That don't comfort me. As long as I get my money next Friday'. Now, next Friday come, and I didn't have the rent. And out the door I went.

"So, I go down the street, down to my good friend's house. I said, 'Look man, I'm outdoors you know. Can I stay with you maybe a couple of days?' He said, 'Let me go and ask my wife.' He came out of the house. I could see it in his face. I knew the answer was 'no'. He said, 'I don't know, man, she's kind of funny, you know. I said, 'I know. Everybody's funny. Now you're funny, too'.

"So, I go back home. I tell the landlady that I've got a job. I'm gonna pay the rent. She said, 'Yeah?' I said, 'Oh,Yeah!' And then she was so nice. She was lovey-dovey.

"So, I go in my room, pack up my things, and I go. I slip out the back door and down the street I go. She was howling about the front rent. She'll be lucky to get any back rent. She ain't gonna get none of it.

"So, I stop in a local bar...this place. I go to the bar, I hang my coat, then I call the bartender. I said, 'Look, man, come down here.' He got down here and asked me, 'So, what do you want?'

"I said, 'One bourbon, one scotch, one beer! Well, I ain't seen my baby since I don't know when? I've been drinking bourbon, whiskey, scotch, and gin. Gonna get high, man. Gonna get loose. Need me a triple shot of that juice. Gonna get drunk. Don't you have no fear. I want one bourbon, one scotch, one beer.'

"But, I'm sitting now at the bar. I'm getting drunk. I'm feeling mellow. I'm drinking bourbon. I'm drinking scotch. I'm drinking beer. Gotta get a drink man. I'm gonna get gassed. Gonna get high, man. I ain't had enough.

"Now, by this time I'm pretty high. You know that when your mouth gets dry, you're pretty high. I said, 'Look, man, what time is it?' He said, 'The clock on the wall says three o'clock. Last call for alcohol. So what do you need?'

"I said, 'One bourbon, one scotch, one beer. No, I ain't seen my baby since a night and a week. Gotta get drunk, man, until I can't even speak. Gonna get high, man, listen to me. One drink ain't enough, Jack, you'd better make it three. I wanna get drunk. I wanna make it real clear. One bourbon, one scotch, one beer.'

"And then I passed out."

Alvin took a dive into his drink, which gave me a chance to look around. But all I saw was another man in shabby clothes walking toward us in the otherwise deserted bar. He stopped next to Alvin and had a few words.

"Well, there's a devil in the bottle, staring straight at me. Daring me to reach out, but I know he's testing me. If I take just one sip, I become that devil's son. Act a fool, sell my soul before God and everyone. Oh, Lord, I know I only hurt the ones I love.

"I'm walking down this dead end road, all alone and by myself. Wish I could blame the whisky, but I can only blame myself. Running out of chances, and Lord, that's such a crime. I've got to find the answer before I lose my mind. Oh, Lord, it's a crying shame. Oh, Lord, I've caused so much pain. I only hurt the ones I love.

"There's a devil in the bottle that just won't let me be. So many times I've been hurting my soul and family. But I got free on the day I fought the devil in the bottle.

"The next time that old devil tries to get the best of me, I'll smash this bottle against the wall and know I'm finally free. There's a devil in this bottle that just won't let me be. There's so many times I let him hurt me. I got free the day I fought the devil in the bottle."

Then, without hesitation, he stuffed his half-filled bottle of Scotch whisky into his coat and stumbled for the door.

"There goes another one of those traveling wilburys," my new friend Alvin said. "They keep coming back for more."

I wasn't sure what or who a traveling wilbury was. He could see that written all over my face.

"The wilburys were not always known as the traveling wilburys. They were originally anti-nomadic. They were stationary. But after one courageous wilbury survived a trip to the end of the block, they started walking short distances. Soon, the trips got longer and longer.

"When they would return from an adventure, the travelers developed a unique system of rhythmic forms to describe their adventures to their other fellow wilburys. Each ditty became more complex and yet more pleasing to the ear. As this new musical form evolved, the elders of the tribe urged its adoption, claiming it had the power to stave off madness, turn natural brunettes into blondes, and increase the size of their ears.

"According to my research, as the wilburys developed their musical inspiration, less developed species like night club owners, tour operators, and recording executives were drawn into their influence. It was a blow that many wilburys never recovered from since they had just learned how to deal with wives, roadies, and drummers. Many of them became hairdressers or TV rental salespersons.

"But a tiny fraction of the tribe survived, and gave us the magnificent music we have today. For all I know you might be one of their number."

I'd heard some Traveling Wilbury's songs, but I never imagined they had such an interesting and dynamic history. But me, a traveling wilbury?

Soon, my cohort started scanning the bar as if he were looking for someone. I asked him if he was looking for one of his friends.

"Whiskey Man's my friend; he's with me nearly all the time. He always joins me when I drink, and we get on just fine. Nobody has ever seen him; I'm the only one. Seemingly, I must be mad. Insanity is fun if that's the way it's done.

"Doctors say that he's just a figment of my twisted mind. If they can't see my Whiskey Man, they must be going blind. Two men in white collected me two days ago. They said, 'There's only room for one, and Whiskey Man can't go'.

"Whiskey Man will waste away if he's left on his own. I can't even ring him because he isn't on the phone, hasn't got a home. Life is very gloomy in my little padded cell. It's a shame there wasn't room for Whiskey Man as well.

"Whiskey Man's my friend. He's with me nearly all the time. He always joins me when I drink, and we get along just fine."

Alvin hesitated for a moment and went on.

"But, memories and drinks don't mix too well. And jukebox records don't play those wedding bells. Staring at the world through the bottom of a glass. All I see is a man who's fading fast.

"Tonight I need that woman again. What I'd give for my baby just to walk in, sit down beside me and say it's all right. Then, take me home and make love to me tonight. But here I am again, mixing misery and gin, sitting with all my friends and talking to myself. I look like I'm having a good time, but any fool can tell that this honky-tonk heaven really makes me feel like hell.

"I light a lonely woman's cigarette. We both start talking about what we want to forget. Her life story and mine are the same. We both lost someone and only have ourselves to blame.

"Well, I met this old woman. She was as hard as nails. I think she just come out of the county jail. Would I loan her some money just to pay her rent? If I would, she would put me in her Last Will and Testament. Well, I've got lots of children, an ex-wife or two. I never hear from them until the bills are due. The money I gave them they already spent. If I could just help them out, they would put me in their Last Will and Testament.

"You know I'm going over sixty. I'm older than most. It won't be long now; I'll be nothing but a ghost. It's my intention to leave all of them people out of my Last Will and Testament. And when it's all over and they put me in the ground, send my belongings to the Lost and Found."

Despite the gloom in his voice I was enjoying this conversation with Alvin. He pulled another bottle from his coat and refilled my glass. He asked me how life was treating me, and I guess I trusted him because I told him about the Sheriff John Brown and my loss of Linda Lou. In response his eyes popped open, and he had another story to tell.

"In Cumberland, Kentucky, on a cool hot evening, Billy lay in love with Marianne. She was a rich judge's daughter. He was the son of a coal miner. But that night their love was more than they could stand.

"The judge said to his daughter that the son of that coal miner is someone you'd better leave alone. She knew her dad so well, and she knew she couldn't tell, but the truth was bound to show before too long. Their love had started growing on its own.

"Billy placed his hand on Marianne, and he felt the baby's moving. He kissed her, and said I'll see you when I can. The judge had made a promise that when he caught up with Billy, he'd send him far away from Marianne. The whole town knew it, too. Many times he'd proved it to at least a hundred men behind the wall.

"He smiled behind that frown, and when he brought that gavel down, he called himself the long arm of the law. And, he'd set his mind on seeing Billy fall.

"In a hot, humid mine shack, a mid-wife pulled the sheet back and placed a cool, damp towel on Marianne. Billy's eyes were wide with wonder from the spell he was under, when she placed the newborn baby in his hands. He didn't hear the siren, just a baby's crying. That miracle of love was all he saw.

"When the door came smashing down and Billy turned around, he felt the heart and soul inside him fall. He stood face to face with the long arm of the law.

"You can't outrun the long arm of the law. No, you can't outrun the long arm of the law. You can hide out for a while, he says with a smile. But you can't outrun the long arm of the law.

"Seemed like everyone down in Cumberland, Kentucky came out that day to see poor Billy's trial. The court was called to order. There sat the judge's daughter. She looked so proud holding Billy's child. When they brought Billy into the court, the judge just looked right through him as he held that Holy Bible in his hand, and he smiled at his grandson.

"Then, his eyes cut back to Billy, and he said 'I think this time the law will understand. Son, I sentence you to live with Marianne!'

"Then the judge said, 'You know you can hide out for a while. Ah, but you can't outrun the long arm of the law!'

"With those words the gavel came down in the hand of the long arm of the law."

Alvin poured one last drink for each of us and began speaking to an imaginary bartender.

"I'm sick and tired of your excuses. Can't deal with living anymore. I'll give you reasons to continue while you lie writhing on the floor. I'll wash away your eyes, and have you hypnotized. There'll be no compromise today. I'll share your life of shame. I think you know my name. I'll introduce you today. You're the demon alcohol.

"If you could deal with your reflection, I'm sure you'll see into my eyes. There'll be no need for resurrection. Let's drink to people of the lies. Although that one's too much, you know ten's not enough. There'll be no compromise today. I'll watch you lose control, consume your very soul.

"I'm sick and tired of resolutions. You've quit me time and time again. Don't speak of suicide solutions. I took your hand. You're here to stay. This time it's you or me. You'll never set me free. There'll be no compromise today. So satisfy my lust. Too much can't be enough. You'll introduce yourself today. You're the demon alcohol. Let's party!"

Alvin raised his glass and almost fell off of the barstool. I caught him just in time. He caught his breath and carried on humming his song.

"Last time I was sober, man I felt bad. Worst hangover that I ever had. It took six hamburgers and Scotch all night. Nicotine for breakfast just to put me right. Because if you wanna run cool, you've gotta run on heavy, heavy fuel.

"My life makes perfect sense, lust and food and violence. Sex and money are my major kicks. Get me in a fight, I like dirty tricks. My chick loves a man who's strong. The things she'll do to turn me on. I love the babes, don't get me wrong. Hey, that's why I wrote this song.

"I don't care if my liver is hanging by a thread. I don't care if my doctor says I ought to be dead. When my ugly big car won't climb this hill, I'll write a suicide note on a one hundred dollar bill. Yes, if you want to run cool, you got to run on heavy, heavy fuel.

"If I go before I'm old, oh, brother of mine, please don't forget me if I go. Bartender, please fill my glass for me with the wine you gave Jesus that set him free after three days in the ground. I'm on bended knees. I pray, Bartender, please.

"Bartender, you see, the wine that's drinking me came from the vine that strung Judas from the devil's tree, it's roots deep, deep in the ground. When I was young, I didn't dream about it. Now I think about it all the time."

With those words, Alvin finished his drink with one gulp, shook my hand, and headed toward the back door of Harry's Bar. Suddenly, he stopped short and turned around.

"Your name is Joe, right?"

I nodded.

"I just thought I'd mention that there was a man here yesterday looking for a fella named Joe. He was pretty big and had a glass eye and a scar running across his face. The other man with him called him the Monkey Man or at least that's what it sounded like to me."

Then Alvin turned and left.

24
Memphis Blues

I'm shufflin' thru the Texas sand, but my head's in Mississippi. The blues has got a hold on me. I believe I'm getting' dizzy. Help me now!

Linda Lou was on my mind again. I started talking to her imaginary spirit.

"She came without a farthing, a babe without a name. So much ado about nothing is what she'd try to say. So much ado, my lover. So many games we played. Through every fleeted summer we missed. Through every precious day not there.

"All dead. All dead. All the dreams we had. And I wonder why I still live on. All dead. All dead. And alone I'm spared. My sweeter half instead, all dead and gone. All dead.

"All dead. All dead at the rainbow's end, and still I hear her own sweet song. Take me back again. You know my little friend's all dead and gone. Her ways are always with me. I wander all the while. But, please, you must forgive me. I am old but still a child.

"All dead. All dead but I should not grieve. In time it comes to everyone. All dead, but in hope I breathe. Of course, I don't believe you're dead and gone. All dead and gone."

I shook my head. I needed some rest, but my situation still bothered me as I rolled toward Memphis.

Lights out tonight. Trouble in the heartland. got a head-on collision smashing in my guts, man. I'm caught in a crossfire that I don't understand. But there's one thing that I know for sure. I don't give a damn for the same old played out scenes. I don't give a damn for just the in betweens. I want the heart. I want the soul. I want control right now. Talk about a dream and try to make it real. I wake up in the night with a fear so real. I spend my life waiting for a moment that just won't come.

Badlands, I gotta live it every day. Let the broken hearts stand as the price I've gotta pay. I'll keep pushing until it's understood, and these badlands start treating me good!

Working in the fields until I get my back burned. Working beneath the wheels until I get my facts learned. I got my facts learned real good now. Poor man wanna be rich. Rich man wanna be king. And a king ain't satisfied until he rules everything. I wanna go out tonight. I wanna find out what I got.

I believed in the love Linda Lou gave me. I believed that my faith in Janie could save me. I believed in the hope that Sally would some day raise me above these…Badlands!

For the ones who had a notion, a notion deep inside, that it ain't no sin to be glad you're alive. I wanna find one face that ain't looking through me. I wanna find one place. I wanna spit in the face of these… Badlands!

I woke up this morning with the sundown shining in. I found my mind in a brown paper bag within. I tripped on a cloud and fell-a eight miles high. I tore my mind on a jagged sky. I just dropped in to see what condition my condition was in.

I pushed my soul in a deep dark hole and then I followed it in. I watched myself crawling out as I was crawling in. I got up so tight I couldn't unwind. I saw so much I broke my mind. I just dropped in to see what condition my condition was in.

Someone painted *April Fool* in big black letters on a *Dead End* sign. I had my foot on the gas as I left the road and blew out my mind. Eight miles outta Memphis and I got no spare. Eight miles straight up downtown somewhere. I just stopped in to see what condition my condition was in.

I keep thinking about that night in Memphis, Lord, I thought I was in heaven. But in the end, I was just stumbling through the parking lot of an invisible Seven-Eleven. What was I doing out there?

I've seen the bright lights of Memphis and the Commodore Hotel. And underneath a street lamp I met a southern belle. Well, Marie took me to the river where she cast a spell. At first I saw a cowgirl. She was floating across the ceiling. That's when I saw a naked cowgirl; she was mumbling to some howling wolf about some voodoo healing. And in that southern moonlight she sang this song so well.

"If you'll be my Dixie chicken, I'll be your Tennessee lamb, and we can walk together down in Dixieland.

"Take that night train to Memphis and when you arrive at the station, I'll be right there to meet you. So, don't turn down my invitation. Oh, we'll have a jubilee down in Memphis, Tennessee.

Tell that engineer to pull the throttle open. Keep that engine stack a smokin'. I'm not kiddin'. I'm not jokin'. And soon you'll be with your girl, I'm hopin'"

Yeah, well, we made all the hot spots; my money flowed like wine. And then that low-down southern whiskey began to fog my mind. And I don't remember church bells or the money I put down on the white picket fence and boardwalk of the house at the edge of town. Oh, but boy do I remember the strain of her refrain and the nights we spent together and the way she called my name.

But then she ran away; I guess that other guitar player sure could play. She always liked to sing along. She's always handy with a song.

Then I'm walking in Memphis, walking with my feet ten feet off of Beale. Walking in Memphis but do I really feel the way I feel? Saw the ghost of Elvis on Union Avenue. Followed him up to the gates of Graceland, then I watched him walk right through. Now security, they did not see him. They just hovered 'round his tomb. But, there's a pretty little thing waiting for the King down in the Jungle Room.

Then, one night in the lobby of the Commodore Hotel, I chanced to meet a bartender who said he knew her well. And as he handed me a drink, he began to hum a song. And all the boys there at the bar began to sing along.

If you'll be my Dixie chicken, I'll be your Tennessee lamb, and we can walk together down in Dixieland.

"They've got catfish on the table; they've got gospel in the air. And Reverend Green be glad to see you when you haven't got a prayer. But boy you've got a prayer in Memphis!

Now Muriel plays piano every Friday at the Hollywood, and they brought me down to see her and they asked me if I would -- do a little number and I sang with all my might. And she said -- "Tell me, are you a Christian child?" And I said "Ma'am, I am tonight."

Where's my head, baby? Somewhere in Mississippi! So I grabbed the nearest phone.

Long distance information, give me Memphis Tennessee.

Help me find the party trying to get in touch with me. She could not leave her number, but I know who placed the call 'cause my friend took the message and he wrote it on the wall.

Help me, information, get in touch with my Marie. She's the only one who'd phone me here from Memphis Tennessee. Her home is on the south side, high up on a ridge just a half a mile from the Mississippi bridge. Help me, information, more than that I cannot add. Only that I miss her and all the fun we had. But, we were pulled apart because her mom did not agree and tore apart our happy home in Memphis Tennessee.

Last time I saw Marie, she's waving me good-bye with hurry home drops on her cheek that trickled from her eye. Marie is only twenty years old, information please try to put me through to her in Memphis Tennessee.

Put on my blue suede shoes and I boarded the plane, waiting to lift off in the land of the Delta Blues in the middle of the pouring rain. W.C. Handy -- won't you look down over me? Yeah, I got a first class ticket, but I'm as blue as a boy can be. So, I got back off and went to get back on my Harley.

I was really getting hungry so when I finally reached Nashville, I began looking for a place to eat. I saw a bunch of people standing on the corner, and I thought it would be a good idea to ask them because they appeared to be locals. I was really surprised and amazed when they responded in unison and pointed down a side street.

"You can get anything you want at Alice's Restaurant!"

The name sounded familiar. I could swear there was an Alice's Restaurant in New York City, but my memory was a little fuzzy. One of the fellows walked up to me with more specific directions.

"Walk right in, it's around the back. Just a half a mile from the railroad track."

The railroad track was right in front of me so I thanked them for their courtesy, and I rumbled down the street toward Alice's. As I rolled forward, I thought I heard someone say that the name actually wasn't Alice's Restaurant, but that Alice, whoever she was, owned it.

I found the building with a restaurant in it, which was across the street from an abandoned church. I went around back, parked my bike, and walked in. The word Restaurant was engraved on the wall, but I didn't see any other name. The place was pretty busy, so I took a seat at the counter next to two young men. They were very friendly and said hello right off.

After we talked for a while, I asked about the name of the place. All they could tell me was that it was owned by a woman named Alice. They glanced around, but apparently Alice wasn't anywhere in sight so they just shrugged their shoulders and smiled at each other. It was obvious that they had a story to tell about the place so I encouraged them to proceed.

"Now it all started two Thanksgivings ago when my friend and I went up to visit Alice at the restaurant. But Alice doesn't live in the restaurant. At that time she lived in that church across the street, in the bell tower with her husband Ray and their dog Fasha. And living in the bell tower like that, they had a lot of room downstairs where the pews used to be. Having all that room, seeing as how they took out all the pews, they decided that they didn't have to take out their garbage for a long time.

"We got up there and we found all that garbage there. So we decided that it would be a friendly gesture for us to take the garbage down to the city dump. So we took a half a ton of garbage, put it in the back of a red VW microbus, took shovels and rakes and implements of destruction and headed on toward the city dump.

"Well, we got there and there was a big sign and a chain across the dump saying, "Closed on Thanksgiving." And we had never heard of a dump closed on Thanksgiving before, and with tears in our eyes we drove off into the sunset looking for another place to put the garbage."

I was really enjoying this weird tale so I ordered a beer for each of my two new friends, Richard and Jordan. Richard thanked me and continued.

"We didn't find one until we came to a side road, and off the side of the side road there was another fifteen foot cliff and at the bottom of the cliff there was another pile of garbage. And we decided that one big pile was better than two little piles, and rather than bring that one up, we decided to throw ours down.

"That's what we did and drove back to the church, had a Thanksgiving dinner that couldn't be beat, went to sleep and didn't get up until the next morning, when we got a phone call from Officer Obie. He said, "Kid, we found your name on an envelope at the bottom of a half a ton of garbage, and I just wanted to know if you had any information about it." And I said, "Yes, Sir, Officer Obie, I cannot tell a lie. I put that envelope under that garbage."

"After speaking with Obie on the telephone for about forty-five minutes, we finally arrived at the truth of the matter and said that we had to go down and pick up the garbage. And we also had to go down and speak to him at the police officers' station. So, we got in the red VW microbus with the shovels and rakes and implements of destruction and headed on toward the police officers' station.

"Now Joe, there were only one or two things that Obie could'a done at the police station, and the first was he could have given us a medal for being so brave and honest on the telephone, which wasn't very likely, and we didn't expect it. And the other thing was he could have bawled us out and told us never to be seen driving garbage around the vicinity again, which is what we expected. But, when we got to the police officers' station, there was a third possibility that we hadn't even counted upon. We was both immediately arrested and handcuffed! And I said, 'Obie, I don't think I can pick up the garbage with these handcuffs on.' He said, 'Shut up, kid. Get in the back of the patrol car.'

"And that's what we did, sat in the back of the patrol car and drove to the quote Scene of the Crime unquote. I want to tell you about the little suburb of Nashville where this happened. They've got three stop signs, two police officers, and one police car. But, when we got to the Scene of the Crime, there were five police officers and three police cars, being the biggest crime of the last fifty years. Everybody wanted to get into the newspaper story about it. And they were using all kinds of COP equipment that they had hanging around the police officers' station. They were taking plaster tire tracks, foot prints, dog smelling prints, and they took twenty-seven eight-by-ten color glossy photographs with circles and arrows and a paragraph on the back of each one explaining what each one was to be used as evidence against us. They took pictures of the approach, the getaway, the northwest corner, the southwest corner, and that's not to mention the aerial photography."

It was time for another beer, and I had just enough money to treat them so I waved to the bartender for more.

"After the ordeal, we went back to the jail. Obie said he was going to put us in the cell. He said, "Kid, I'm going to put you in the cell. I want your wallet and your belt." And I said, "Obie, I can understand you wanting my wallet so I don't have any money to spend in the cell. But, what do you want my belt for?" And he said, "Kid, we don't want any hangings." I said, "Obie, did you think I was going to hang myself for littering?" Obie said he was making sure, and friends Obie was, because he took out the toilet seat so I couldn't hit myself over the head and drown. And he took out the toilet paper so I couldn't bend the bars, roll the toilet paper out the window, slide down the roll and have an escape.

"It was about four or five hours later that Alice came by and with a few nasty words to Obie on the side, bailed us out of jail. And we went back to the church, had another Thanksgiving dinner that couldn't be beat and didn't get up until the next morning, when we all had to go to court.

"We walked in and sat down. Obie came in with the twenty-seven eight-by-ten color glossy pictures with circles and arrows and a paragraph on the back of each one, sat down. A man came in and said, "All rise." We all stood up and Obie stood up with the twenty-seven eight-by-ten color glossy pictures. Then the judge walked in and sat down with a seeing-eye dog. He sat down, and we sat down. Obie looked at the seeing-eye dog and then at the twenty-seven eight-by-ten color glossy pictures with circles and arrows and a paragraph on the back of each one, and looked at the seeing-eye dog again. He began to cry because Obie came to the realization that it was a typical case of American blind justice, and there wasn't nothing he could do about it. And the judge wasn't going to look at the twenty-seven eight-by-ten color glossy pictures with the circles and arrows and a paragraph on the back of each one explaining what each one was to be used as evidence against us. And yet we were fined fifty dollars and had to pick up the garbage in the snow, but that's just the beginning of our story about Alice's Restaurant."

Before we could get started on the second part of the story, I asked the boys how they liked it here in Tennessee. The response surprised me.

"I've been real stressed, down and out, losing ground. Brothers and sisters keep messing up. Why does it have to be so damn tough? I don't know where I can go to let these ghosts out of my skull. Where the ghosts of childhood haunt me walked the roads my forefathers walked. Climbed the trees my forefathers hung from, ask those trees for all their wisdom. They tell me my ears are so young. Go back from whence you came. For some strange reason it had to be. He guided me to Tennessee."

All of a sudden they seemed really depressed. I asked why as best I could.

"There's colors on the street, red, white and blue. People shuffling their feet. People sleeping in their shoes. But there's a warning sign on the road ahead. There's a lot of people saying we'd be better off dead. Don't feel like Satan, but I am to them. So I try to forget it, any way I can.

"I see a woman in the night with a baby in her hand under an old street light near a garbage can. Now she puts the kid away, and she's gone to get a hit. She hates her life and what she's done to it. There's one more kid that will never go to school, never get to fall in love, never get to be cool.

"We've got a thousand points of light for the homeless man. We've got a kinder, gentler machine gun hand. We've got department stores and toilet paper. Got styrofoam boxes for the ozone layer. Got a man of the people who says 'Keep hope alive'. Got fuel to burn. Got roads to drive.

"Keep on rocking in the free world."

I was out of cash, the balance of which was locked in my Harley, and it was getting to be time to leave. As I got up, the boys began to sing me a little tune in honor of the occasion.

"You can get anything you want at Alice's Restaurant…excepting Alice. Walk right in, it's around the back, just a half a mile from the railroad track."

Don't ask me why, but after listening to the story of Alice's Restaurant I decided to do something I thought was impossible. I thought about returning to New York! You might very well ask why. Well, I missed my mother, and I wanted to see her again. Not my father. Just my mother. I didn't want to call the house directly for two reasons. First, Sheriff John Brown might have the phone tapped. Second, my father might answer the phone. So, I decided to dial up my Cousin Dupree. He always had his ear to the ground and might be able to tell me if the coast was clear.

I got some change off the bike, found a nearby pay phone, and got Dupree's number out of my wallet. I dialed the number and listened as the ring tones sounded. Five, six,…then on the seventh ring a male voice answered. I was in luck because it was Dupree!

"Joe, good thing you called," said my cousin. "This sheriff fellow was here yesterday looking for you. I have no idea how he knew we were cousins."

"Was his name Brown, Sheriff John Brown?"

"That's it," Dupree replied. "And he left a letter for you."

A letter? That was weird.

"What does it say?" I asked.

After about thirty seconds of searching, Dupree returned and began reading it.

"Well, I'm the new sheriff. My name is John Brown. Come up and see me, dead or alive."

"He even sent you your own picture…of yourself," Dupree disclosed.

"How do I look, cousin, dead or alive?"

That comment generated a laugh from Dupree who continued reading.

"Well, he said he would pay expenses, and he said he would feed you, too. Just come dead or alive."

"Dupree, do me a favor. Give me his return address and I'll send him a reply. I'm sorry, but I can't come, Sheriff John Brown. I don't like your hard rock hotel. And I've got a date to see my sweet little thing instead."

We talked about my Mom and Dad, and he promised not to tell anyone that I might be coming for a brief visit. We wished each other good luck but before I hung up I had an idea. I told Dupree that I might have something for him to tell Sheriff John Brown should he call again.

"Oh, God said to Abraham, 'Kill me a son'. Abe says, 'Man, you must be puttin' me on?' God said, 'No!' Abe said, 'What?' God said, 'You can do what you want, Abe, but the next time you see me coming, you'd better run!' Well, Abe said, 'Where do you want this killing done?' God says, 'Out on Highway 61.'

"Well, Georgia Sam, he had a bloody nose. Welfare Department wouldn't give him no clothes. He asked poor Howard, 'Where can I go?' Howard said, 'There's only one place I know.' Sam said, 'Tell me quick, man, I gotta run.' Old Howard just pointed with his gun and said, 'That way down on Highway 61.'

"Well, Mack the Finger said to Louie the King, 'I got forty red, white and blue shoe strings and a thousand telephones that don't ring. Do you know where I can get rid of these things?' And Louie the King said, 'Let me think for a minute, son.' And he said, 'Yes, I think it can be easily done. Just take everything down to Highway 61.'

"Now the fifth daughter on the twelfth night told the first father that things weren't right. 'My complexion,' she said, 'is much too white.' He said, 'Come here and step into the light.' He says, 'Hmmm, you're right. Let me tell the second mother this has been done.' Awe, but the second mother was with the seventh son, and they were both out on Highway 61.

"Now, the roving gambler, he was very bored. He was trying to create a next world war. He found a promoter who nearly fell off the floor. He said, 'I never engaged in this kind of thing before. But, yes, I think it can very easily be done. We'll just put some bleachers out in the sun and have it on Highway 61.'

"If he calls again, tell Sheriff John Brown that I'm meet him out on Highway 61!"

25
The End of the World

I decided not to go back to New York. Sheriff John Brown and the Monkey Man were looking for me there. Mexico would be safe and warm. My first real stop would be El Paso. I wanted to find Jesus and make some more money. I made it there without incident, but I was exhausted from the road.

I was lying on my back in the grass down by the river playing my guitar and singing. Don't ask me why.

"Be on my side, I'll be on your side, baby. There is no reason for you to hide. It's so hard for me staying here all alone when you could be taking me for a ride. Yeah, she could drag me over the rainbow, send me away. I shot my baby down by the river. Dead!

"You take my hand. I'll take your hand. Together we may get away. This much madness is too much sorrow. It's impossible to make it today. I shot my baby down by the river..."

I tried to leap up, but my legs were too wobbly for me to stand. I didn't shoot anyone down by any river? Where were these strange thoughts coming from? Slowly, things were coming back to me. Very slowly.

Out in the West Texas own of El Paso, I fell in love with a Mexican girl. Nighttime would find me at Rose's Cantina. Music would play and Felina would whirl. Black as the night were the eyes of Felina. Wicked and evil while casting a spell. My love was strong for this Mexican maiden. I was in love, but in vain I could tell.

One night a wild young cowboy came in, wild as the West Texas wind. Dashing and daring, a drink he was sharing with wicked Felina, the girl that I loved. So, in anger I challenged his right for the love of this maiden. Down went his hand for the gun that he wore. My challenge was answered in less than a heartbeat. The handsome young stranger lay dead on the floor.

Just for a moment I stood there in silence, shocked by the foul evil deed I had done. Many thoughts ran through my mind as I stood there. I had but one chance and that was to run. If Sheriff John Brown learned about this, I'd be a dead man. Out through the back door of Rose's I ran to where my Harley stood tied. I jumped on the back of Detroit Demolition and away I did ride.

I rode as fast as I could from the West Texas town of El Paso out through the badlands of New Mexico. Back in El Paso my life would be worthless. Everything is gone in life. Nothing is left.

But it's been so long since I've seen the young maiden. Unlike with Linda Lou, my love was stronger than my fear of death. I saddled up my Harley, and away I did go, riding alone in the dark. Maybe tomorrow a bullet may find me. That night nothing was worse than the pain in my heart.

And at last there I was on the hill overlooking El Paso. I could see Rose's Cantina below. My love was strong and it pushed me onward, down off the hill to Felina I go. Off to my right I see five mounted cowboys. Off to my left ride a dozen or more. Shouting and shooting! I can't let them catch me. I've got to make it to Rose's back door.

Something is dreadfully wrong for I feel a deep burning pain in my side. It's getting harder to stay on my bike. I'm getting weary, unable to ride. But my love for Felina is strong, and I rise where I've fallen. Though I'm weary I can't stop to rest. I see the white puff of smoke from the rifle. I feel the bullet go deep in my chest.

From out of nowhere Felina has found me, kissing my cheek as she kneels by my side. Cradled by two loving arms that I'd die for, one little kiss and Felina goodbye.

Suddenly, I found myself gaining consciousness. It was all a dream, except that I was in jail! I was drinking and feeling sorry for myself as I prepared to journey back into Mexico when I passed out at the bar at Rose's Cantina. Then the worst luck in my life kicked in. Just before my head fell to the bar, I saw a large man with a glass eye and a mean scar on his face coming toward me.

I couldn't see straight from all the gin I'd consumed. All I knew was that this large man whose face I couldn't see had dragged me into a small room in the city jail. How did I know this was the city jail? I saw the sign on the wall as they dragged me through the front door. 'El Paso City Jail'!

El Paso? How in the world did I get to El Paso? I knew I would never forgive myself for letting down my guard and allowing myself to be captured. What scared me the most was that I heard the man referred to as the deputy sheriff say the name 'Sheriff John Brown'.

Then he came to see me, and took the mask off of my face. He offered me a drink of water, then asked me to tell him about the trial.

"There was no trial, no real judge or jury. Just the Sheriff John Brown and his brother, Big, Bad Leroy Brown. From the little I could see, Leroy Brown walked with a terrible limp and was missing a few teeth. I tried to speak, but they wouldn't let me. At first all I could hear was Leroy Brown saying, 'That's not the man!'

"Then other people came into the room and sat in two rows. A funny-looking man sat higher than the rest and was addressed by the Sheriff John Brown."

"Good morning Worm your honor. The prosecution will plainly show that the prisoner who stands before you was caught red-handed showing feelings…showing feelings of almost a human nature. This will not do! They called the Sheriff John Brown. That would be me.

"I always said he'd come to no good in the end, your honor. If they'd let me have my way, I could have easily flayed him into shape. But, my hands were tied. The bleeding hearts and artists let him get away with murder. Let me hammer him, today!

"Crazy toys in the attic. I am crazy. Truly gone fishing. Crazy toys in the attic. He is crazy. They must have taken his marbles way. You little shit, you're in it now. I hope that they hang you or throw away the key. You should have talked to me more often than you did. But, no, you had to go your own way. Have you broken any homes up lately? Just five minutes Worm your honor, him and me alone!"

The judge responded to the sheriff in a voice I'd heard before.

"The evidence before the court is incontrovertible. There's no need for the jury to retire. In all my years of judging I have never heard of someone more deserving the full penalty of the law. The way you made them suffer, Big Bad Leroy Brown, Linda Lou and Sheriff John Brown, fills me with an urge to defecate. But my friend you have revealed your deepest fear. I sentence you to be exposed before your peers and hung from the gallows pole."

As the judge pounded his gavel, his glass eye fell from his face and bounced directly toward me. A hand, that of Sheriff John Brown, snatched it out of mid-air. I'd seen a glass eye before but I wondered where?

What kind of trial was this? I didn't even get to plead my case to the hangman jury! And to tell the truth I never heard the foreman of the jury read its verdict. It was all the Sheriff John Brown. I didn't even get to cross-examine Bad Leroy Brown. He would have told them all that it wasn't me!

But a lot of the blame falls on me. I was drinking too much for starters.

Drank so much hooch, it made my eyes get blurry. They say I nailed her to the wall. A stitch in time don't mean a thing. No hangman jury could make me crawl because I'm just a poor boy.

What do you, Sheriff John Brown, do with a gun that's loaded? You shot her dead, and her heart exploded. Tell me, baby, now don't you worry, like lying to a hangman jury.

I swear I didn't know that cold steel .44 was loaded. In fact, my memory ain't so clear. That's not to say she didn't get what she deserved. At least, that's the way it looks from here.

If I could, I surely would stand on the rock upon which Moses stood. I'm a poor boy sweating in the hot summer night. The hangman is out there waiting for the early morning light.

Must be getting early, clocks are running late. Paint by number morning sky looks so phony. Dawn is breaking everywhere. I should light a candle, curse the glare. Draw the curtains. I don't care because it's all right.

I see you got your fist out. Say your piece and get out. Yes, I get the gist of it, but it's all right. Sorry that you feel that way. The only thing there is to say is 'Every silver lining's got a touch of gray.' It's a lesson to me; the Ables and the Beggars and the C's. The ABC's we all must face to try to keep a little grace.

It's a lesson to me; the Deltas and the East and the Freeze. The ABC's we all think of to try to play a little love. I know my rent is in arrears, and the dog has not been fed in years. It's even worse than it appears. But it's all right. The cows are giving kerosene. Kids can't read at seventeen. The words they know are all obscene.

The shoe is on the hand it fits. There's really nothing much to it. Whistle through your teeth and spit. Oh, well, a touch of gray kind of suits me anyway. That was all I had to say. I will get by. I will survive.

I was trapped. I had to face it. Only a miracle could save me now. I remembered back to New York and the night I heard the story of Captain Ahab. My imagination created an image of the swarthy captain and his sailing ship. I called out for help.

"Help, I need somebody! When I was younger, so much younger than today. I never needed anybody's help in any way. But now those days are gone. I'm not so self-assured. Now I find I've changed my mind and opened up the doors. And now my life has changed in, oh, so many ways. My independence seems to vanish in the haze. But every now and then I feel so insecure. I know that I just need you like I've never done before.

"Help me if you can; I'm feeling down. I do appreciate your being around. Help me get my feet back on the ground. Won't you please, please help me?"

It seemed to work. I'm sailing away! Set an open course for the virgin sea, 'cause I've got to be free! Free to face the life that's ahead of me. On board, I'm the captain, so climb aboard. We'll search for tomorrow on every shore. And I'll try, oh, Lord, I'll try, to carry on.

I look to the sea. Reflections in the waves spark my memory. Some happy. Some sad. I think of childhood friends and the dreams we had. We lived happily forever, so the story goes. But somehow we missed out on the pot of gold. But I'll try best that I can to carry on.

A gathering of angels appeared above my head. They sang to me this song of hope and this is what they said. They said come sail away, come sail away with me, lad. I thought that they were angels, but much to my surprise, we climbed aboard their starship. We headed for the skies.

But suddenly it became dark as if a massive black cloud covered the sky in all directions. A figure whose face I couldn't see approached me. His eyes began to glow in the dark. Somehow my lips began moving and strange words came forth.

"There's a pale horse coming. I'm gonna ride it. I'll rise in the morning, my fate decided. I'm a dead man walking!

"In New York City, I was born and christened. Now I've got my story. No need for you to listen. It's just a dead man talking. Once I had a job; I had a girl. But between our dreams and actions lies this world. In the deep forest their blood and tears rushed over me. All I could feel were the drugs and the cold steel .44, and my fear inside of me. Like a dead man talking.

"Beneath a summer sky my eyes went black. I won't ask for forgiveness, my sins are all I have. Now the clouds above my prison move slowly across the sky. There's a new day coming, and my dreams are full tonight."

That's when I woke up! I was dreaming again. The cell walls were still there trapping my body and soul.

26
The Gallows Pole

"Ein! Zwei! Drei! Hammer! Oh, they cannot reach you now. Oh, no matter how hard they try. Goodbye, cruel world, it's over. Walk on by."

It was a voice out here singing. I couldn't open my eyes no matter how hard I tried. I also got the impression that he was talking to me. He had a mock German accent. All I could do was listen.

"Sitting in a bunker here behind your wall waiting for the worms to come. In perfect isolation here behind your wall, waiting for the worms to come."

Worms? Why was he talking about worms?

"Waiting to cut out the deadwood. Waiting to clean up the city. Waiting to put on a black shirt. Waiting to weed out the weaklings. Waiting to smash in their windows and kick in their doors. Waiting to follow the worms."

I suddenly realized that I recognized the voice. I'd heard it before, several times. Now he was definitely talking to me.

"Hello, is there anybody in there? Just nod if you can hear me. Is there anyone at home? Come on now. I hear you're feeling down. I can ease your pain and get you on your feet again. Relax. I'll need some information first. Just the basic facts. Can you show me where it hurts?"

Someone was talking to me, all right, but who was he? And, where was I? I tried to respond. My voice was weak.

"There is no pain. You are receding. A distant ship, smoke on the horizon. You are coming through in waves. Your lips move, but I can't hear what you're saying. When I was a child I had a fever. My hands felt just like two balloons. Now I've got that feeling once again.

I cannot explain. You would not understand. This is not how I am. I have become comfortably numb."

The voice came back.

"O.K. Just a little pin prick. There'll be no more aaaaaaah! But you may feel a little sick. Can you stand up? I do believe it's working. Good. That'll keep you going through the show. Come on, it's time to go."

I was being helped up some stairs. My hands were bound behind me. There was a burlap bag with eye holes over my head. I started to faint.

"When I was a child, I caught a fleeting glimpse out of the corner of my eye. I turned to look, but it was gone. I cannot put my finger on it now. The child is grown. The dream is gone. And I have become comfortably numb."

A man dressed in black who claimed to be a minister from the local church gave me some advice.

"Go to the wind, though the wind won't help you fly at all. Your back's to the wall. Then, chase the sun, and it tears away, and it breaks as you run. You run! Behind the smile, there's danger and a promise to be told. You will never get old. Life's fantasy. To be locked away and still to think you're free. You're free! So, live for today. Tomorrow never comes."

I tried to tell him that his advice was a little late. Yet, he went on.

"Well, they'll stone you when you're trying to be so good. They'll stone you just like they said they would. They'll stone you when you're trying to go home. Then they'll stone you when you're there all alone. But I would not feel so all alone. Everybody must get stoned.

"Well, they'll stone you when you're walking along the street. They'll stone you when you're trying to keep your seat. They'll stone you when you're walking on the floor. They'll stone you when you're walking to the door.

"They'll stone you when you're at the breakfast table. They'll stone you when you are young and able. They'll stone you when you're trying to make a buck. They'll stone you and then they'll say 'Good luck!'

"They'll stone you and say that it's the end. Then they'll stone you and then they'll come back again. They'll stone you when you're riding in your car. They'll stone you when you're playing your guitar.

"They'll stone you when you walk all alone. They'll stone you when you are walking home. They'll stone you and then say you are brave. They'll stone you when you are set down in your grave. But I would not feel so all alone. Everybody must get stoned!"

I couldn't agree more under the circumstances. But there was still more.

"Die young! Die young! Can't you see the writing in the air? Gonna die young. Someone stopped the pain. So, live for today. Tomorrow never comes."

I was relieved to see him turn and walk away. He joined the crowd of observers, and kept his head down so our eyes wouldn't meet. I was back in my own thoughts.

My life began as a dream, and now I'm there again. I made a wrong turn, somewhere along the line, but I don't remember exactly when. The sky was still above me, and my feet were on the ground. Still, no matter how hard I listen, I cannot hear a sound.

Now I find that I've been lifted off this Mother Earth. My hands have been bound and ropes restrain my girth. They blinded me with a sack-cloth over my eyes. And it's clear that they mean to put an end to my sighs.

I am smelling like a rose that somebody gave me on my birthday death bed. I am trampled under the soles of another man's shoes. Guess I walked too softly. I ran through the world thinking about tomorrow. I feel I've come of age. You can't swallow what I'm thinking.

Finally, the bag over my head was gone. I could see much better. I was on a stage…a scaffold. A crowd of people surrounded me. They all had curious, yet serious, looks on their faces.

"My name is Joe, you see; I stand before you all on this scaffold made of wood. I was adjudged by Sheriff John Brown as a murderer, and the hangman's knot must fall. I will die upon the gallows pole when the moon is shining clear. And these are my final words that you will ever hear."

I was pretty much mumbling to myself.

I left my home in New York when I was very young. I landed in the old Northwest, California and Washington. Although I traveled many miles, I never made a friend, for I could never get along in life with people that I met.

I have not been home since I left long ago. I'm thumbing my way back to heaven, counting steps, walking backwards on the road. I'm counting my way back to heaven. I can't be free with what's locked inside of me. Linda Lou, if there was a key, you took it in your hand. There's no wrong or right, but I'm sure there's good and bad. The questions linger overhead. No matter how cold the winter, there's a spring time up ahead. I wish that I could hold you, Linda Lou; I wish that I had.

I let go of a rope, thinking that's what held me back, and in time I've realized, it's now wrapped around my neck!

There I was completely wasting, out of work and down. All inside it's so frustrating as I drifted from town to town. I feel as if nobody cares if I live or die. So, I thought I might as well begin to put some action in my life. Breaking the law!

So much for the golden future I can't even start. I've had every promise broken; there's anger in my heart. You don't know what its like; you don't have a clue. If you did you'd find yourselves doing the same thing, too. You don't know what it's like breaking the law.

If I had some education to give me a descent start, I might have been a doctor or a master in the arts. But I used my hands for toiling when I was very young, and they locked me down in jailhouse cells, that's how my life's begun.

Oh, the inmates and the prisoners, I found they were my kind, and it was there inside the bars I found my peace of mind. But the jails they were too crowded, institutions overflowed, so we turned ourselves loose to walk upon life's hurried tangled road.

And there's danger on the ocean where the salt sea waves split high, and there's danger on the battlefield where the shells of bullets fly, and there's danger in this open world where men strive to be free, and for me the greatest danger was in society.

And I'm glad I've had no parents nearby to care for me or cry, for now they will never know the horrible death that I shall die. And I'm also glad I've had no friends to see me in disgrace, for they'll never see that hangman's hood wrap around my face.

Farewell unto the old north woods in which I used to roam; farewell unto the crowded bars, which have been my home. Farewell to all you people who think the worst of me. I guess you'll feel much better when I'm on this hanging tree.

But there's just one question before they kill me dead. I'm wondering just how much to you I really said, concerning all the boys that come down a road like me. Are they enemies or victims of your society?

I still don't know what I was waiting for, and my time was running wild. A million dead-end streets, and every time I thought I'd got it made, it seemed the taste was not so sweet. So, I turned myself to face me, but I've never caught a glimpse of how the others must see the faker. I'm much too fast to take that test.

I watch the ripples change their size, but never leave the stream of warm impermanence. So, the days float through my eyes, but still the days seem the same. And these children that you spit on as they try to change their worlds are immune to your consultations. They're quite aware of what they're going through.

Strange fascinations are fascinating me. Ah, changes are taking the place I'm going through. Changes…turn and face the strain. Changes… don't want to be a richer man. Pretty soon now you're gonna get a little older, but I won't. Time may change me, but I can't change time.

I can feel the rope pulled snuggly around my neck. From where I am standing on the scaffold I can see the winding dirt road that leads out of town. I can also see the deputy staring through the sheriff's office window, his big sympathetic eyes focused right on me. Then there is the presence of a somber preacher and an ominous looking undertaker.

No one knows what it's like to be the bad man, to be the sad man behind blue eyes. No one knows what it's like to be hated, to be fated, to telling only lies. But my dreams they aren't as empty as my conscience seems to be. I have hours, only lonely. My love is vengeance that's never free.

No one knows what it's like to feel these feelings like I do, and I blame you. No one bites back as hard on their anger; none of my pain and woe can show through. When my fist clenches, crack it open, before I use it and lose my cool. When I smile, tell me some bad news before I laugh and act like a fool.

If I swallow anything evil, put your finger down my throat. If I shiver, please give me a blanket. Keep me warm; let me wear your coat. No one knows what it's like to be the bad man, to be the sad man behind blue eyes.

Body…touched by the toil and plunged into my arm. Cursed through the night through eyes of alarm. A melody black flowed out of my breath. Searching for death, but bodies need rest. Black Juju.

Under the soil now waiting for worms. All that I feared is all that I've earned. All that I know is all that I think. Dead feelings are cool. Down lower I sink. Clutching and biting, my soul has caught fire. My evil is now, and I'm caught up in desire. Everything I'm living for is all that I am. Liking it and loving it, that's all in the plan. Black Juju!

But it was too late for me, too late to complain. I made a final assessment of exactly where I was on this earth. It seemed as if an angel was looking down over me. I heard its soft voice that sounded so much like my dear mother.

"Oh, what'll you do now, my blue-eyed son? Oh, what'll you do now, my darling young one?"

Without thinking, I had an answer.

"I'm a-goin' back out before the rain starts a-fallin'. I'll walk to the depths of the deepest dark forest, where the people are many and their hands are all empty, where the pellets of poison are flooding their waters, where the home in the valley meets the damp dirty prison, where the executioner's face is always well hidden, where hunger is ugly, where souls are forgotten, where black is the color, where none is the number, and I'll tell it and think it and speak it and breathe it, and reflect it from the mountain so all souls can see it. Then, I'll stand on the ocean until I start sinking. But I'll know my song well before I start singing. And it's a hard rain's a-gonna fall!

"It's too late, my time has come. Sends shivers down my spine, body's aching all the time. Goodbye everybody, I've got to go. Got to leave you all behind and face the truth. Mama, ooooh, anyway the wind blows, I don't want to die. I sometimes wish I'd never been born at all.

"Mama, life had just begun, but now I've gone and thrown it all away. Mama, oooh, didn't mean to make you cry. If I'm not back again this time tomorrow, carry on, carry on, as if nothing really matters."

Next to me wearing a cloth sack with eye holes over his head stood the Hangman, a large man over six foot four inches tall. Even with all the distraction attending my certain death, as the Hangman stood there near me, there was something very familiar about him. His heavy breathing was almost a snoring noise that I'd heard before.

Well, the deputy walks on hard nails and the preacher rides a mount, but nothing really matters much, it's doom alone that counts. And the one-eyed undertaker, he blows a futile horn. I've heard newborn babies wailing like a mourning dove and old men with broken teeth stranded without love. Do I understand your question, man, is it hopeless and forlorn?

In this little hilltop village, they gamble for my clothes; I bargained for salvation, and they give me a lethal dose. I offered up my innocence and got repaid with scorn.

Then I looked up at the bell tower that rode atop the nearby church. The church bells had begun to ring. In tune with the bells, the Hangman seemed to be celebrating my detention. He knew that I could hear him.

"I'm a rolling thunder, pouring rain. I'm coming on like a hurricane. My lightning's flashing across the sky. You're only young, but you're gonna die. I won't take no prisoners, won't spare no lives. Nobody's putting up a fight. I got my bell. I'm gonna take you to hell.

"I'll give you black sensations up and down your spine. If you're into evil, you're a friend of mine. See my white light flashing as I split the night. Because if Good's on the left, then I'm sticking to the right. You got me ringing Hell's Bells.

"Satan's coming to you. He's ringing them now. The temperature's high across the sky. They're taking you down. They're dragging you under. Gonna split the night. There's no way to fight. Hell's Bells!"

There between the church and my scaffold stood a group of townspeople dressed in black. They were carrying books, which seemed to be Bibles. Some appeared to be offering up prayers. For a moment

I thought I recognized one of their faces, but the glimpse was so short that I couldn't connect the image to anyone I know.

"Help me!" I cried out to them. "I am not guilty! I have had no trial! I am being lynched by the evil Sheriff John Brown! Where is your forgiveness? Where is justice?"

The crowd just stared at me. Anger rose inside my being. I shouted at them.

"Where were you when I was burned and broken while the days slipped by from my window watching? Where were you when I was hurt and helpless because the things you say and the things you do surround me? While you were hanging yourself on someone else's words, dying to believe in what you heard, I was staring straight into the shining sun!

"Lost in thought and lost in time while the seeds of life and the seeds of change were planted. Outside the rain falls dark and slow while I pondered on this dangerous but irresistible pastime. I took a heavenly ride through our silence. I knew the moment had arrived for killing the past and coming back to life.

"I took a heavenly ride through our silence. I knew the waiting had begun. And headed straight into the shining sun!"

Members of the crowd began searching their Bibles for verses. Others in the mob merely pursed their lips and issued curses. While they searched for a cross on which to nail me, I looked in vain for a friendly face to bail me! Again, for a moment, I thought I had a glance at a profile that might give me a chance. But. alas, the photons were playing tricks, and where I thought there stood trees there were only sticks.

Just then a shadowy figure floated in front of me. Immediately, I sensed who it was and began to beg for my life.

"Oh, Death, won't you spare me over until another year. Well, what is this that I can't see, with ice cold hands taking hold of me?"

The shadowy figure spoke softly.

"Well, I am Death, none can excel. I'll open the door to heaven or hell."

"Whoa, Death," I cried, "someone would pray. Could you wait to call me another day?"

"The children prayed, the preacher preached, time and mercy is out of your reach. I'll fix your feet until you can't walk. I'll lock your jaw until you can't talk. I'll close your eyes so you can't see. This very air, come and go with me. I'm Death, I come to take your soul, leave the body and leave it cold. To draw up the flesh off of the frame, dirt and worm both have a claim."

I was getting angry with Death. He didn't deserve my respect.

"Death, I would rather see you sleeping in the ground than to stay around here if you're gonna pull me down. Well, I give you all my money, everything I own. And some day I'm gonna get lucky, and down the road you know I'm going! Well, I'd rather see you sleeping in the ground than to stay around here when you're gonna pull me down. Well, today I'm gonna get lucky, and down the road I'm going!"

It was a hollow threat I my part. At least I thought so. But something made me keep going.

"You suck my blood like a leech. You break the law and you preach and screw my brain until it hurts. You've taken all my money, and you want more. Misguided old mule with your pig-headed rules. With your narrow-minded cronies who are fools of the first division. Death on two legs, you're tearing me apart. Death on two legs, you've never had a heart of your own. Kill joy, bad guy, big talking small fry. You're just an old barrow boy. Have you found a new toy to replace me? Can you face me? But now you can kiss my ass goodbye. Feel good? Are you satisfied? Do you feel like suicide? I think you should! Is your conscience all right? Does it plague you at night? Do you feel good?

"You talk like a big business tychoon. You're just a hot air balloon. So no one gives you a damn. You're just an overgrown schoolboy. Let me tan your hide. A dog with disease, you're the king of the sleaze. Put your money where your mouth is, Mister Know-it-all. Was the fin on your back part of the deal? Shark! Death on two legs you're tearing me apart. Death on two legs, you've never had a heart. Insane, you should be put inside. You're a sewer rat decaying in a cesspool of pride. Should be made unemployed. Then make yourself null and void. Make me feel good…I feel good!"

I could sense that Death wasn't the answer to my prayers. He had no sympathy whatsoever for my situation. Despite my direct insults, he stayed right near me. I wasn't a religious man, but I had to drive him off before I could get help.

"I can feel it coming in the air tonight, oh Lord. I've been waiting for this moment, all my life, oh Lord. Can you feel it coming in the air tonight, oh Lord?

"Well, Death, if you told me you were drowning, I would not lend a hand! I've seen your face before, my friend, but I don't know if you know who I am. Well, I was there, and I saw what you did. I saw it with my own two eyes. So, you can wipe off that grin. I know where you've been. It's all been a pack of lies.

"Well, I remember, don't worry. How could I ever forget? It's the first time, the last time we ever met. But I know the reason you keep your silence up. No, you don't fool me. The hurt doesn't show, but the pain still grows. It's no stranger to you or to me. And I can feel it coming in the air tonight, oh Lord."

And then, without another word, Death disappeared. I turned my attention back to the people standing near the scaffold. I repeated my cries for justice.

My pleas for help fell on deaf ears. No one else in the crowd had seen his form or heard his words. I became convinced that these people were here to watch me die, not to appeal for my soul or forgiveness. I fell back to listening to the tolling bells. What else could I do?

Then the strangest thing happened. The deputy came up to where I stood and waved the Hangman away. Then he whispered in my ear as he checked my hands and the rope around my neck. I assumed he was reading the charges against me, but I was wrong.

"You've got nothing to fear but fear itself. Not pain, not failure, not fatal tragedy. Not the faulty units in this mad machinery. Not the broken contacts in emotional chemistry. With an iron fist in a velvet glove, we are sheltered under the gun. In the glory game on the power train, thy kingdom's will be done.

"The sheriff's not afraid of your judgment. He knows of horrors worse than your hell. He's a little bit afraid of dying. But he's a lot more afraid of your living. And the things that he fears are weapons to be held against him.

"Can any part of life be larger than life? Even love must be limited by time and those that push us down that they might climb. Is any killer worth more than his crime? Like a steely blade in a silken sheath, we don't see what they're made of. They shout about love, but when push comes to shove, they live for the things they're afraid of. And the knowledge that they fear is the weapon to be used against them."

The deputy looked around to assure himself that the coast was clear. Then he continued.

"When you're sad and when you're lonely and you haven't got a friend, and all that you've held sacred, falls down and does not mend, just remember that death is not the end. When you're standing at the crossroads that you cannot comprehend, and all your dreams have vanished, and you don't know what's up the bend, just remember that death is not the end.

"When the storm clouds gather around you, and heavy rains descend, and there's no one there to comfort you, with a helping hand to lend, just remember that death is not the end. When the cities are on fire with the burning flesh of men, and you search in vain to find just one law abiding citizen, oh, the tree of life is growing where the spirit never dies, and the bright light of salvation shines in dark and empty skies.

"Energy is contagious. Enthusiasm spreads. Tides respond to lunar gravitation. Everything turns in synchronous relation. Laughter is infectious. Excitement goes to your head. Winds are stirred by planets in rotation. Sparks ignite and spread new information. Respond, vibrate, feedback, resonate.

"Sun dogs fire on the horizon. Meteor stars rain across the night. This moment may be brief, but it can be so bright. Hope is epidemic. Optimism spreads. Bitterness breeds irritation. Ignorance breeds imitation. Reflected in another source of light, when the moment dies, the spark still flies reflected in another pair of eyes. Love responds to your invitation. Love responds to your imagination.

"Dreams are sometimes catching. Desire goes to your head. Don't give up hope!"

He closed the book and returned to his office. Was he just trying to cheer me up or did he know something? Soon, my attention was back on the bell tower.

Ring them bells, ye heathen from the city that dreams. Ring them bells from the sanctuaries cross the valleys and streams, for they're deep and they're wide and the world's on its side. And time is running backwards.

Ring them bells St. Peter where the four winds blow. Ring them bells with an iron hand so the people will know. Oh, it's rush hour now on the wheel and the plow. And the sun is going down upon the sacred cow. Ring them bells sweet Martha for the poor man's son. Ring them bells so the world will know that God is one. Oh, the shepherd is asleep where the willows weep, and the mountains are filled with lost sheep.

Ring them bells for the blind and the deaf. Ring them bells for all of us who are left. Ring them bells for the chosen few who will judge the many when the game is through. Ring them bells for the time that flies, for the child that cries when innocence dies.

Ring them bells Saint Catherine from the top of the room. Ring them from the fortress for the lilies that bloom. Oh, the lines are long and the fighting gets strong, and they're breaking down the distance between right and wrong.

Then I recalled what the old man in the desert told me.

"What you gonna do? Time's caught up with you. Now you wait your turn. You know there's no return. Take your written rules. You join the other fools. Turn to something new. Now it's killing you. First, it was the bomb. Vietnam napalm. Disillusioned, you push the needle in. From life you escape. Reality's that way. Colors in your mind satisfy your time.

"Oh, you know you must be blind to do such things like this, to take the sleep that you don't know. You're giving Death a kiss now, you fool. Your mind is full of pleasure. Your body's looking ill. To you it's shallow leisure. So drop the acid pill. Don't stop to think now.

"You're having a good time, Joey, but that won't last. Your mind's all full of things. You're living far too fast. Go out and enjoy yourself. Don't bottle it in. You need someone to help you, to stick the needle in.

"Now you know the scene. Your skin starts turning green. Your eyes are no longer seeing life's reality. Push the needle in. Face Death's sickly grin. Holes are in your skin caused by a deadly pin.

"Head starts spinning around. You fall down to the ground. Feel your body heave. Death's hands start to weave. It's too late to turn. You don't want to learn. 'It's the price of life,' you cry. Now, you're gonna die!

"Read it in the paper, it ain't fair. You know who today don't seem to care. Living, loving, getting loose, masturbating with a noose. Now, someone is kicking out the chair!"

But there were wise and comforting words the Medicine Man whispered to me out on the desert floor. 'Just about the time you've given up on life, that's when you should expect more. The forces of evil have their weak spots, and over-confidence is their flaw. Your Monkey Man will be there, and that's when his blood you'll draw!'

How the Medicine Man knew about the Monkey Man I'll never know. He must surely have a friend in the cosmos with a big eye watching this whole show. I decided not to give up. What choice did I have?

27
Thought I Heard a Shot

Well, now the stars are falling while I'm drawing a card of death. It is torn from above the curtains of our loving, and it shows nevertheless. Something made of spiny hair has crept into this room. Made of silk, satin and coal, it leads to the freedom of the tomb. Silent eyes are staring with voices calling me to be free.

If I look at my reflection in the bottom of a well, what I see is only on the surface. When I try to see the meaning hidden underneath, the measure of the depth can be deceiving. The bottom has a rocky reputation. I can feel it in the distance the deeper down I stare. From up above it's hard to see, but you know when you're there. On the bottom words are shallow. On the surface talk is cheap. You can only judge the distance by the company you keep in the eyes of the Confessor.

In the eyes of the Confessor there's no place I can hide. I can't hide from the eyes of the Confessor so I won't even try. In the eyes of the Confessor I can't tell a lie. I cannot tell a lie to the Confessor. He'll strip me down to size as naked as the day I was born. Take all the trauma, drama, comments, the guilt and doubt and shame, the what if's and only if's, the shackles and the chains, the violence and aggression, the pettiness and scorn, the jealousy and hatred, the tempest and discord, and give it up! Give it up!

I turned to the Hangman to argue my feeble case. What did I have to lose?

"Hangman, Hangman, I'm not an evil man. I even pay my taxes as best that I can. I pet stray dogs, and absolutely never molest any sheep. So why would you want to send me into the dark, so deep?

"You somehow seem familiar. Maybe we could have been good friends? I find it hard to understand why you would want to see my life end.

"Some people stay far away from the door if there's a chance of it opening up. They hear a voice in the hall outside and hope that it just passes by. Some people live with the fear of a touch and the anger of having been a fool. They will not listen to anyone so nobody tells them a lie.

"Hangman, I know you're only protecting yourself; I know your thinking of someone else, someone who hurt you. But I'm not above making up for the love you've been denying you could ever feel. I'm not above doing anything to restore your faith if I can. Some people see through the eyes of the old before they ever get a look at the young. I'm only willing to hear you cry because I am an innocent man."

The Hangman stopped what he was doing, and he seemed to be listening to what I had to say.

"Some people say they will never believe another promise they hear in the dark, because they only remember too well, they heard someone tell them before. Some people sleep all alone every night instead of taking a lover to bed. Some people find that it's easier to hate than to wait anymore.

"I know you don't want to hear what I say. I know you're gonna keep turning away. But, I've been there, and if I can survive, I can keep you alive. I'm not above going through it again. I'm not above being cool for a while. If you're cruel to me, I'll understand.

"Some people run from a possible fight. Some people figure they can never win. And, although this is a fight I can lose, the accused is an innocent man.

"You know you only hurt yourself out of spite. I guess you'd rather be a martyr tonight. That's your decision, but I'm not below anybody I know if there's a chance of resurrecting a life. I'm not above going back to the start to find out where the hatred began.

"Some people hope for a miracle cure. Some people just accept the world as it is. But, I'm not willing to lay down and die because I am an innocent man!"

Yet, I was remarkably calm considering the circumstances. I guess I was just resigned to my fate. Then, out of the corner of my eye I saw a cloud of dust approaching on the road. My hopes were rekindled. Could it be the help I needed?

"Hangman, Hangman, hold it a little while! I think I see my friends coming, riding many a mile. They could be bringing silver. They could be bringing gold…all to keep me from this terrible gallows pole."

For his part the Hangman merely shook his head.

"It's Sheriff John Brown, my son, coming to see you swing from the gallows pole. He told me to wait for him. Besides, your friends came over an hour ago. They had no silver. They had no gold. They had nothing to keep you from the gallows pole."

My friends were here? Where are they now? Why would they leave me without saying goodbye? Did the deputy scare them off? He's looking at me through the window…I can see him.

Then I realized something else that sent a chill up my spine. It was his voice…the Hangman's voice. I had heard it before. But as familiar as it was, I couldn't place it because of the fear beating a tattoo on my brain.

I looked up again into the distance. The cloud of dust was drawing nearer. But there was no way to tell if it was Sheriff John Brown coming to town.

"Hold on, Hangman!" I cried. "I think I see my brother coming, riding many a mile. My brother will bring some silver. My brother will bring some gold. All to keep me from the gallows pole."

I could almost see the Hangman smile under his mask as he spoke. He must have known that I didn't have a brother.

"Your brother came, and he brought some silver and gold, all to get you off the gallows pole. But, sad to say, it wasn't enough."

My brother is here somewhere? Did one of my few friends show up and try to help. If that's the case maybe he'll get help to rescue me.

"But, fortunately, your sister was here, too," whispered the Hangman.

"Hangman, Hangman, below that mask upon your face I detect a smile. Pray tell me that I am free to ride, ride for many a mile."

"Oh, yes," said the Hangman. "You got a fine sister. She took me to a shady place and warmed my blood from the cold and brought my blood to boiling hot, all to keep you from the gallows pole. Your brother brought me some silver, your sister warmed my soul. But now I laugh and will pull so hard when the sheriff comes to see you swinging on the gallows pole.

"That's because I'm a flea-bit peanut monkey and all my friends are junkies. I'm a cold Italian pizza, and I could use a lemon squeezer. I've been bitten by a boar, and I was gouged and I was gored. But I pulled through. Yes, I'm a sack of broken eggs; I always have an unmade bed... don't you? I hope I'm not too messianic or a trifle too satanic. But I'm The Monkey Man!"

The Hangman pulled off his shroud. There was the scar and the glass eye I had feared. I almost passed out. No wonder the Hangman's voice seemed so familiar. Because of the mask he wore, I couldn't see the scar or his one glass eye. The Monkey Man was here, and with the help of the sheriff he was going to kill me dead! He kept rubbing it in.

"I love the dead before they're cold. They're bluing flesh for me to hold. Cadaver eyes upon me see nothing. I love the dead before they rise. No farewells. No goodbyes. I never knew your rotting face while friends and lovers mourn your silly grave. I have no other uses for you, Joey. I love the dead, Yeah!

When I looked up, there was Sheriff John Brown getting off his dark horse with a big grin on his face. He waved for the deputy to join him, but the deputy declined. Then he stared a hateful stare at me as he walked up to the scaffold and then mounted the stairs.

"The end is near, Joe. Take a last deep breath and enjoy it." The sarcasm in John Brown's voice was obvious.

"I'll use a lock that has no key. Bind you with chains that no one else can see. Let the water creep over your face. I'll send it in waves just to watch you perform the great escape. How long can you hold your breath while you hold mine and wait? I'll pull your arms tight behind your back. Use myself as weight and wonder while you fade. How long can you hold your breath?

"This is the end, beautiful friend. This is the end, my only friend, the end of our elaborate plans. The end of everything that stands, the end. No safety or surprise, the end. Linda Lou will never look into your eyes again.

"Can you picture what will be, so limitless and free, desperately in need of some stranger's hand in a desperate land lost in a Roman wilderness of pain, and all the children are insane waiting for the summer rain.

"There's danger on the edge of town. Ride the king's highway. Ride the snake to the lake, the ancient lake. The snake is seven miles long. Ride the snake, he is old and his skin is cold.

"The killer awoke before dawn. He put his boots on. He took a face from the ancient gallery, and he walked on down the hall, and he came to a door and he looked inside. 'Joe?' I whispered. 'Yes, Sheriff?' you replied. 'I want to kill you!' I said.

"This is the end, beautiful friend. This is the end, my only friend, the end. It hurts to set you free, but you'll never follow me. The end of the laughter and soft lies, the end of night we tried to die. This is the end.

"So glad you see yourself well. Overcome and completely silent now. With heaven's help, you cast your demons out. And not to pull your halo down around your neck and tug you off your cloud, but I'm more than just a little bit curious how you're planning to go about making your amends to the dead?

"Recall the deeds as if they're all someone else's. Atrocious stories. Now you stand reborn before all of us. So glad to see you well with your halo slipping down, your halo slipping down to choke you now.".

I wanted to grab him by the throat and strangle him. I struggled with the ropes holding my hands. The deputy had tied them loosely. My hands were coming loose, but I knew I would be too late as the Hangman reached for the rope that would snap my neck. I closed my eyes, maybe for the last time. But just as I did, I heard a familiar voice. I opened my eyes again. It was Linda Lou. She was alive! Tears were running down her cheeks.

"I'm sorry, Joey. It wasn't my idea. In California the sheriff told them I was dead. He threatened me with death if I said a word. Can you forgive me, Joey?"

Then I responded as best I could.

"Black hearted woman, can't you see your poor man dying? Can't count on both hands all the lonely nights I've been crying. Well, I'm tired of all your slippery ways. I can't take your evil lying. Black hearted woman, cheap trouble and pain is all you play. Yesterday I was your man. Now you don't know my name. Soon, I'll be moving on down the road to start all over again.

"I remember the burning I felt inside as you touched my frozen heart. I remember the screams and the pain within as my soul was torn apart. I recall being hungry and for years I stood my ground. Even though you were never around, God, how I needed you.

"I remember they warned me, and oh, how they told me yours was a kiss of shame. I remember the devil coming to steal my soul again and again. I remember the dawn was breaking in cathedrals of unholy light. I was searching for answers where singers and dancers will travel on through the night. I've been hurt by evil games. First you're here and then you ain't. Cloak and dagger.

"Oh, there's something about you that doesn't seem real. You said if I don't sell my soul, you will steal a promise that should stand. I know the command. And me like a fool took it in. In the Valley of Death, do I stand in the shadow or fight for the right to be free? A kiss on the wind whispers 'die', die for the glory. No, no.

"Cloak and dagger, you've been playing those evil games. Set me free, I don't need this pain. Something about you just doesn't seem real. You said if I don't sell my soul, you will steal. Your kiss of shame has been hunting me. Cloak and dagger, God, how I needed you.

"I hate myself for loving you and the weakness that it showed. You were just a painted face on a trip down Suicide Road. The stage was set, the lights went out all around the old hotel. I hate myself for loving you, and I'm glad the curtain fell.

"I hate that foolish game we played, and the need that was expressed, and the mercy that you showed me, whoever would have guessed? I went out on Lower Broadway, and I felt that place within, that hollow place where martyrs weep and angels play with sin.

"Heard your songs of freedom and man forever stripped, acting out his folly while his back is being whipped. Like a slave in orbit, he's beaten until he's tame, all for a moment's glory, and it's a dirty rotten shame.

"There are those who worship loneliness, I'm not one of them. In this age of fiberglass I'm searching for a gem. The crystal ball up on the wall hasn't shown me nothing yet. I've paid the price of solitude, but at least I'm out of debt.

"Can't recall a useful thing you ever did for me except pat me on the back one time when I was on my knees. We stared into each other's eyes until one of us would break. No use to apologize, what difference would it make?

"So, sing your praise of progress and of the Doom Machine. The naked truth is still taboo wherever it can be seen. Lady Luck, who shines on me, will tell you where I'm at. I hate myself for loving you, but I should get over that!

"Do you still say your prayers, little darlin'? Do you go to bed at night praying that tomorrow, everything will be all right? But tomorrows fall in number, in number one by one. You wake up and you're dying. You don't even know what from.

"Well, they shot you point blank. You've been shot in the back, Baby, point blank. You've been fooled this time, little girl, that's a fact. Right between the eyes, Baby, point blank. Right between the pretty lies that they tell, little girl, you fell.

"You grew up where young girls they grow up fast. You took what you were handed and left behind what was asked. But, what they asked, Baby, wasn't right. You didn't have to live that life. I was gonna be your Romeo. You were gonna be my Juliet. These days you don't wait on Romeos, you wait on that welfare check and on all the pretty things you can't ever have and on all the promises that always end up point blank. Right between the eyes!

"Point blank like little white lies you tell to ease the pain. You're walking in the sights of point blank, and it's one false move and the lights go out. Once I dreamed we were together again, back home in those old clubs the way we used to be. We were standing at the bar. It was hard to hear. The band was playing loud, and you were shouting something in my ear. You pulled my jacket off and as the drummer counted four, you grabbed my hand and pulled me out on the floor. You just stood there and held me. Then, you started dancing slow. And as I pulled you tighter, I swore I'd never let you go.

"Well, I saw you in this mob tonight. Your face was in the shadows, but I knew that it was you. You were standing in the doorway out of the rain. At first you didn't answer when I called out your name. You just turned, and then you looked away like just another stranger waiting for me to get blown away. You've been twisted up until you've become just another part of it."

It seemed ironic that I was now considering the concept of forgiveness.

"I don't mind just what you say. I never heard you, baby, never heard you anyway. I don't care what you do just so long as it ain't me and you. Sly, sly, sly like a demon's eye!

"Everything's good. I said, 'Everything's fine'. You don't know, don't know that it's the end of your time. How does it feel to be turned away? I've known it, baby, almost every day. I don't need you any more. I don't want you, baby, hanging around my door. You slip and slide around my brain. You think you're so clever, yeah, but you know you're insane.

"I don't mind just what you say. I never heard you, baby, I never heard you anyway. No, I didn't. Everything's good. Everything's fine. You don't know it's the end of your time. Sly, sly, sly like a demon's eye."

But, that's when it happened. As I stared at her face, my mind began screaming for me to wake up. Something was happening. Was the trap door on the scaffold about to open? I took a deep breath, probably my last.

Well, our souls are all mistaken in the same misguided way. We all end up forsaken, we're just choosing our own way. The future now incinerates before my eyes, and leaves me with the emptiness of no more tries.

Well, my visions of glory have spiraled down the drain. The best of my intentions come crashing down in flames. The depths of my despair I am unable to contain. It's shallow living.

The noose is falling and all my friends are crawling. The noose is falling and enemies are rising. A truth appalling, our Maker comes calling.

Well, the tracers from yesteryear are burning in the dust. My bruises are reminders of naivety and trust. I'm only feeling stronger because my body's getting numb. Now they lay me down, put coins in my eyes and blow the candles out.

I closed my eyes again for what would be the last time. Then it happened!

I thought I heard a shot!

It was at that moment when I realized that I heard not one, but two sharp cracking and pinging noises in rapid succession. Was it my neck snapping? Then, there was a third sharp noise followed by an eerie silence as I felt the tension release on the rope around my neck.

My eyes snapped open. My heart skipped a beat.

There, before me almost as if they were frozen in time, stood the Hangman and Sheriff John Brown. Their knees were buckling as they began to fall to the scaffold. Each had a fresh bullet hole in his forehead and a look of total surprise on his face. Sheriff John Brown uttered some final words as he fell.

"Mama, take this badge off of me. I can't use it any more. It's getting' dark, too dark for me to see. I feel like I'm knockin' on heaven's door.

"Mama, put my guns in the ground. I can't shoot them any more. That long black cloud is comin' down. I feel like I'm knocking on heaven's door."

An object was falling from the Hangman's head as a hiss issued from his lips. It was his glass eye! It hit the wood of the scaffold with a sharp ping and then bounced off onto the ground and began to roll out of sight.

Suddenly, a dark form shot through the air and captured The Monkey Man's glass eye. As the Monkey Man's knees hit the scaffold, he began to mumble his last words.

"My mother came to my bed. Placed a cold towel upon my head. My head is warm, my feet are cold, Death is a-moving upon my soul. Oh, Death, how you're treating me. You've closed my eyes so I can't see. Well, you're hurting my body; you make me cold. You run my life right out of my soul.

"Oh, Death, please consider my age. Please don't take me at this stage. My wealth is all at your command, if you will move your icy hand. Oh, the young, the rich or poor, hunger like me, you know. No wealth, no ruin, no silver, no gold. Nothing satisfies you but my soul."

With those words The Monkey Man keeled over…dead. I thought I felt a smile start to form on my face. I was still alive, and Death had disappeared!

I ripped the rope from my hands, threw off the noose, and turned to see who had fired the shots. There, near the back of the scaffold stood my friend Don with a huge smile of satisfaction on his face. He was dressed in black. Now it made sense. He disguised himself as a churchgoer in order to get close to the scaffold. Maybe God was on my side? I was so excited that I could hardly speak to express my gratitude.

Then, I saw another familiar face in the crowd. It was Floyd, the truck driver who gave me a ride to Detroit. He was smiling from one ear to the other. Somehow Don and Floyd got together and came to my rescue.

"Joe, I didn't bring any silver to save you from the gallows pole, because I had none" said Don. "And I didn't bring any gold either. I am poor and forlorn just as you are. But,…we are both traveling wilburys, one helping another."

At least now I knew what a traveling wilbury was, and I was one!

Don paused as he held his weapon up in the air for me to see.

"I did remember to bring your cold steel .44!"

Then he turned to the church people who were gathering around us and began to lecture them.

"So you were just going to stand there and watch Joe die! You weren't going to do a thing to help. What good are you?

"And I don't want you, and I don't need you. Don't bother to resist, or I'll beat you. It's not your fault that you're always wrong. The weak ones are there to justify the strong.

"The beautiful people, the beautiful people, it's all relative to the size of your steeple. You can't see the forest for the trees. You can't smell your own shit on your knees. There's no time to discriminate, hate every mother-fucker that's in your way."

Suddenly, Don turned to the leader of the group with a pointed finger.

"Hey, you, what do you see? Something beautiful, something free? Hey, you, are you trying to be mean? If you live with apes, man, it's hard to be clean. The worms will live in every host. It's hard to pick which one they eat most. The horrible people, the horrible people, it's as anatomic as the size of your steeple."

He then pointed to the surprised face of the stunned deputy who was now outside of his office surveying the situation.

"I shot the sheriff," said my friend matter-of-factly. "But I didn't shoot no deputy!

"We're not gonna take it any more. We've got the right to choose, and there ain't no way we'll lose it. This is our life. This is our song. We'll fight the powers that be just don't pick our destiny because you don't know us. You don't belong!

"You're so condescending. Your gall is never ending. We don't want nothing, not a thing from you. Your life is trite and jaded, boring and confiscated. If that's your best, your best won't do.

"We're right. We're free. We'll fight! We're not gonna take it any more!"

The dream was over. I looked for Linda Lou, but she was gone. That was okay. She taught me a lot about life and love. And despite the close calls I had faced, I was better for the whole journey. Granted, the rest of my life might seem a little boring, but I believe I've used up most of my bad luck.

"Don and Floyd, for all you've done for me and others of my kind, you're the best friends one could ever find. Please take my Les Paul and my cold steel .44. I really don't believe that I'll need them any more. I'm going to go somewhere that I've never been, and begin a simple life where I can win. Fate has dealt me some nasty cards. And some of the people I've met are real retards. Still, I think that if I lead a simple life, I will find a pretty girl to call my wife. Even if I don't, all is not lost. Peace is never achieved without some cost."

They both gave me a hug, but when it came to my Les Paul guitar, Don insisted that I keep it and follow my dream to be a musician. Then he told me that his band had a gig in Chicago in two days, and that I was to be the lead guitar player! Floyd was our drummer!

I asked how they managed to track me down, but Floyd said that was a story for another day. But Don whispered that a Monkey's tracks were easy to follow. I was still in a state of euphoria over the sudden turn of events. Don grabbed the guitar and began a song.

"I just want to celebrate another day of living! I just want to celebrate another day of life."

Soon the crowd gathered around us, and we all were singing along.

"Put my faith in the people, but the people let me down. So I turned the other way, and I carry on anyhow. Had my hand on the dollar bill, and the dollar bill flew away. But the sun is shining down on me, and it's here to stay.

"Don't let it all get you down. No, no! Don't let it turn you around and around. That's why I'm telling you that I want to celebrate another day of living. I just want to celebrate another day of life!"

Oh, well, here I go again! I jumped on my Harley with Don and Floyd in hot pursuit in Floyd's truck. Chicago, here we come! I started singing.

"It's a beautiful day, the sun beat down. I had the radio on. I was driving. Trees flew by, Don and Floyd were singing Little Runaway, I was flyin'. I feel so good, like anything is possible. I hit cruise control and rubbed my eyes. The last three days the rain was unstoppable. It was always cold, no sunshine.

"I rolled on as the sky grew dark. I put the pedal down to make some time. There's something good waiting down this road. I'm picking up whatever's mine.

"Yeah, runnin' down a dream that would never come to me. Working on a mystery, going wherever it leads. Runnin' down a dream!"

Appendix

Title[chapter]	**Band/Artist**
1 Bourbon, 1 Scotch, 1 Beer[23]	George Thorogood
7 Deadly Sins[11]	Traveling Wilburys
8675309 Jenny[16]	Tommy Tutone
#9 Dream[3]	John Lennon
30 Days in the Hole[22]	Humble Pie
41 Shots[3]	Bruce Springsteen
99 Year Blues[12]	Hot Tuna
115th Dream[2]	Bob Dylan
A Glimpse of Home[8,9]	Kansas
A Hard Rain's A-Gonna Fall[26]	Bob Dylan
A Heart in New York[3]	Simon and Garfunkel
A Life of Illusion[6]	Joe Walsh
A Lovely Day to be out of Jail[22]	The Life
A Town Called Paradise[7]	Van Morrison
Acid Queen[19]	Tina Turner
Against the Wind[9]	Bob Seger
Alabama Song [21]	The Doors
Albert McBride[19]	Bob Dylan
Alice's Restaurant[24]	Arlo Guthrie
All Dead All Dead[24]	Brian May/Queen
All the Way to Reno[9]	R.E.M.
All She Wants to do is Dance[18]	Don Henley
Almost Cut My Hair[19]	David Crosby
Alone Together[11]	Richie Havens
Angry Young Man[6]	Billy Joel
An Innocent Man[27]	Billy Joel
Another Harry's Bar[23]	Jethro Tull
Another Lonely Night in New York[5]	Bee Gees

Another One Rides the Bus[4]	Weird Al Yankovic
Arrested for Driving While Blind[22]	ZZ Top
At the Station[4]	Joe Walsh
Away from Home[4]	Bachman Turner Overdrive
Back in the Saddle[20]	Aerosmith
Bad[21]	Michael Jackson
Bad, Bad Leroy Brown[13]	Jim Croce
Bad Company[21]	Bad Company
Bad Moon Rising[15]	Creedence Clearwater Revival
Bad to the Bone[13]	George Thorogood
Badlands[24]	Bruce Springsteen
Band on the Run[22]	Paul McCartney
Barrel of Pain[4]	Crosby, Stills and Nash
Barstool Blues[7]	Neil Young
Bartender[23]	Dave Matthews Band
Beast of Burden[14]	Rolling Stones
Been Caught Stealing[22]	Jane's Addiction
Beer in Mexico[18]	Kenny Chesney
Before They Make Me Run[11]	Rolling Stones
Beggar's Farm [11]	Jethro Tull
Behind Blue Eyes[26]	The Who
Berkshire Poppies[2]	Traffic
Big Gun[14]	AC/DC
Black Betty[20]	Ram Jam
Black Days[1]	Soundgarden
Black Diamond Bay[9]	Bob Dylan
Black Hearted Woman[27]	Allman Brothers
Black Juju[26]	Alice Cooper
Black Magic Woman[16]	Santana
Black Moon[15]	Deep Purple
Blood on the Floor[15]	Fleetwood Mac
Blow by Blow[3]	Fleetwood Mac
Blown[21]	Bachman Turner Overdrive
Bohemian Rhapsody[3,26]	Queen

Border Guard[19]	Bruce Springsteen
Borderline[19]	Kansas
Born to Run[8]	Bruce Springsteen
Born to be Wild[8]	Steppenwolf
Born Under a Bad Sign[2]	Cream
Boulevard[3]	Jackson Browne
Bound for Colorado[4]	Jackson Browne
Boys of Summer[4]	Don Henley
Breaking the Law[26]	Judas Priest
Breathe[3]	Pink Floyd
Brain Damage[20]	Pink Floyd
Buffalo Gals[5]	Bruce Springsteen
Bullet with Butterfly Wings[2]	Smashing Pumpkins
Burden in my Hand[17]	Soundgarden
California[10]	Joni Mitchell
California[10]	Metro Station
California Dreaming[3]	Mamas and Papas
California Girls[9]	Beach Boys
Calling Elvis[19]	Dire Straits
Can't Live Here[5]	J. J. Cale
Can't You See[6]	Marshall Tucker Band
Can't You Hear Me Knocking?[4]	Rolling Stones
Captain Jack[20]	BillyJoel
Chain Lightning[26]	Rush
Changes[26]	David Bowie
China Grove[20]	Doobie Brothers
China White[8]	Little Feat
Christmas at Ground Zero[2]	Weird Al Yankovic
Cigarettes and Alcohol[5]	Counting Crows
Cinnamon Girl[20]	Crosby, Stills, Nash&Young
Cloak and Dagger[27]	Black Sabbath
Cocaine[20]	Eric Clapton
Columbus[2]	David Crosby
Come Sail Away[25]	Styx
Comes a Time[7]	Neil Young
Comfortably Numb[26]	Pink Floyd

Coming Back to Life[26]	Pink Floyd
Cortez the Killer[18]	Neil Young
County Jail Blues[5]	Eric Clapton
Country Girl[10]	Neil Young
Cousin Dupree[5]	Steely Dan
Coward of the County[12]	Kenny Rogers
Crazy Train[6]	Ozzie Osbourne
Crime in the City[3]	Neil Young
Crime of Passion[14]	Bee Gees
Crime Pays[14]	Hall and Oates
Crossroads[18]	Robert Johnson
Cute Kid[3]	Bob Dylan
Daddy Don't Live in that New York City[5]	Steely Dan
Dancing in the Dark[4]	Bruce Springsteen
Danger [10]	Bee Gees
Danger[21]	J.J. Cale
Danger Zone[17]	Kenny Loggins
Dazed and Confused[4]	Led Zeppelin
Dead and Bloated[26]	Stone Temple Pilots
Dead at Last[27]	REO Speedwagon
Dead End Road[15]	J. J. Cale
Dead Man Walking[25]	Bruce Springsteen
Dead or Alive[24]	Deep Purple
Death is Not the End[26]	Bob Dylan
Death on Two Legs[26]	Freddie Mercury
Deep Elem Blues[5]	Grateful Dead
Demon Alcohol[23]	Ozzy Osbourne
Demon's Eye[27]	Deep Purple
Detroit Breakdown[7]	The Bellrays
Detroit City[7]	Alice Cooper
Detroit Rock City[7]	Kiss
Desert Mountain Showdown[10]	Hootie and the Blowfish
Desperado[16]	Eagles
Devil in the Bottle[23]	Lynyrd Skynyrd
Devil's Sidewalk[20]	Neil Young
Die Young[26]	Black Sabbath

Dirge[26]	Bob Dylan
Dirty Deeds Done Dirt Cheap[13]	AC/DC
Dixie Chicken[24]	Little Feat
Does This Bus Stop at 82nd Street? [4]	Bruce Springsteen
Dogs[13]	Pink Floyd
Donald White[27]	Bob Dylan
Don't Get Me Wrong[8]	The Pretenders
Don't Look Down[23]	Lindsey Buckingham
Down by the River[25]	Neil Young
Down-bound Train[2]	Bruce Springsteen
Down in Mexico[18]	The Coasters
Down on the Farm[11]	Little Feat-Lowell George
Down on the Farm[11]	Joe Walsh
Down the Road Apiece[21]	Foghat
Downtown[7]	Jackson Browne
Dream Within a Dream[1]	The Yardbirds
Drifter[15]	Deep Purple
Drifter's Escape[2]	Bob Dylan
Drive All Night[9]	Bruce Springsteen
Driving Too Fast[19]	Rolling Stones
Drunken Hearted Boy[23]	Allman Brothers Band
Dust in the Wind[17]	Kansas
Eastern Spell[17]	Marc Bolan and T. Rex
Easy Money[21]	REO Speedwagon
El Paso[25]	Grateful Dead
End of the Night[17]	The Doors
Erie Canal[6]	Bruce Springsteen
Everybody Has a Dream[1]	Billy Joel
Evil Louie[20]	Deep Purple
Evil Ways[8]	Santana
Fairytale of New York[3]	Shane MacGowan-Jem Finer
Falling Down[13]	Joe Walsh
Fame[21]	David Bowie
Fast Train[6]	Van Morrison
Father to Son[5]	Brian May

First Girl I Loved[4]	Jackson Browne
Five Long Years[7]	Eric Clapton
Flatbush Avenue[2]	Weird Al Yankovic
Follow That Dream[1]	Bruce Springsteen
Forty Thousand Headmen[21]	Traffic
Fortune Teller[16]	Hollies
Fortuneteller[16]	Deep Purple
Four Walls of Raiford[22]	Lynyrd Skynyrd
Fourth and Main[5]	Jackson Browne
Free Bird[8]	Lynyrd Skynyrd
Freeways[9]	Bachman Turner Overdrive
Further On Up the Road[8]	Eric Clapton
Gallows Pole[27]	Led Zeppelin
Garden Party[5]	Ricky Nelson
Get It On[4]	Marc Bolan and T. Rex
Ghosts[17]	Kansas
Gimme a Bullet[13]	AC/DC
Gimme Three Steps[21]	Lynyrd Skynyrd
Gimme Your Money Please[2]	Bachman Turner Over-drive
Go Insane[17]	Lindsay Buckingham
Go Your Own Way[9]	Fleetwood Mac
Going Down to New York Town[2]	Counting Crows
Going to California[9]	Led Zeppelin
Gold Dust Woman[8]	Fleetwood Mac
Goodbye and Good Riddance to Bad Luck[23]	AC/DC
Goodbye Girl[9]	Rolling Stones
Got My Mind Set On You[10]	George Harrison
Gotta Get Away[4]	Rolling Stones
Gun[12]	Soundgarden
Gunface[14]	Rolling Stones
Guns for Hire[14]	AC/DC
Gypsy[19]	Stevie Nicks
Gypsy Biker[5]	Bruce Springsteen
Gypsy Woman's Passion[23]	REO Speedwagon

Hand of Doom[26]	Black Sabbath
Hand of Fate[19]	Rolling Stones
Hanging Tree[1]	Counting Crows
Hangman Jury[25]	Aerosmith
Hard Luck Stories[23]	Neil Young
Heavy Fuel[23]	Dire Straits
Hello Again[12]	The Cars
Hell's Bells[26]	AC/DC
Help[25]	Beatles
Help Me Rhonda[19]	Beach Boys
Hey, Joe[1,12]	Jimi Hendrix
Highway[10]	Moody Blues
Highway 61 Revisited[24]	Bob Dylan
Highway to Hell[15,19]	AC/DC
Hometown Blues[8]	Tom Petty
Homeward Bound[3]	Simon and Garfunkel
Hotel California[15, 16]	Eagles
House of Cards[9]	Radiohead
House Of the Rising Sun[13]	The Animals
Houston[19]	R.E.M.
How Long[21,22]	Eagles
Hypnotized[15,17]	Bob Welch
I Can't Drive 55[15]	Sammy Hagar
I Don't Have to Hide[17]	Bachman Turner Overdrive
I Drink Alone[8]	George Thorogood
I Fought the Law[22]	John Mellencamp
I Just Want to Celebrate[27]	Rare Earth
I love the Dead[27]	Alice Cooper
I Shot the Sheriff[27]	Bob Marley
I Think I Heard a Shot[27]	Rage Against the Machine
I want to be King[12]	Soundgarden
If I only had a Brain[15]	Jackson Browne
If You Don't Start Drinking[9]	George Thorogood
I'm a Free Man Now[5]	Kenny Loggins
I'm a Lonesome Fugitive[21]	Merle Haggard

In the Air Tonight[26]	Phil Collins
In the City[2]	Joe Walsh
In the Jailhouse Now[22]	Soggy Bottom Boys
Industrial Disease[2]	Dire Straits
Inmates[22]	Alice Cooper
Interstate Love Song[5]	Stone Temple Pilots
Into the Mystic[5]	Van Morrison
It's My Life[7]	The Animals
Jailbreak[22]	AC/DC
Jailbreak[22]	Thin Lizzy
Jailhouse Rock[22]	Elvis Presley
Jane[9]	Jefferson Starship
Jane Says[8]	Jane's Addiction
Janie, Don't You Lose Heart[8]	Bruce Springsteen
Janie Needs a Shooter[8]	Bruce Springsteen
Janie Runaway[8]	Steely Dan
Janie's Got a Gun[8]	Aerosmith
Jersey Girl[4]	Bruce Springsteen
Jesus Just Left Chicago[18]	ZZ Top
Kashmir[17]	Led Zeppelin
Keep Driving[19]	Meatloaf
Keep on Smilin'[12]	Wet Willie
King of El Paso[15]	Boz Scaggs
Kiss Me on the Bus[4]	The Replacements
Knocking on Heaven's Door[27]	Bob Dylan
L.A. [12]	Neil Young
Last Will and Testament[23]	J. J. Cale
Laundry Mat Blues[7]	Joe Walsh
Law Man[14]	Jefferson Airplane
Lawless Avenues[3]	Jackson Browne
Lay Down Sally[4]	Eric Clapton
Layla[5]	Duane Allman/Eric Clapton
Leaving New York[4]	REM
Let's Roll Another One[8]	Pink Floyd
Like Suicide[15]	Soundgarden
Little Joe[3]	Soundgarden

Losing End[11]	Neil Young
Low Desert[15]	R.E.M.
Low Rider[13]	Jim Capaldi
Low Rider[9]	J. J. Cale
Magic[17]	Bruce Springsteen
Magic[17]	The Cars
Magic Bus[4]	The Who
Maggie's Farm[11]	Bob Dylan
Man on Your Mind[14]	Little River Band
Manhattan[2]	Bob Seger
Manhattan[13]	R.E.M.
Mary Jane[19]	Spin Doctors
Mary Jane's Last Dance[19]	Tom Petty
Me and Julio Down by the School Yard[2]	Paul Simon
Medicine Man[17]	Pantera
Medicine Man[17]	Whitesnake
Memphis[24]	Chuck Berry
Mescalero[18]	ZZ Top
Mexico[18]	Beck
Mexico[15]	Cake
Mexico[15]	Incubus
Mexico[18]	Sammy Hagar
Mexico[15]	James Taylor
Mexican Blackbird[15]	ZZ Top
Midnight Rider[23]	Allman Brothers Band
Mirror in the Bathroom[16]	The English Beat
Misery and Gin[23]	Merle Haggard
Misty Mountain Hop[10]	Led Zeppelin
Money[12]	Beatles
Money[12]	Pink Floyd
Money for Nothing[2]	Dire Straits
Monkey Man[27]	Rolling Stones
Mother[3]	Pink Floyd
Motherless Child[4]	Eric Clapton
Move It On Over[21]	George Thorogood
Movin' Out[2]	Billy Joel
Mr. Jones[20]	Counting Crows

My Generation[8]	The Who
My Head's in Mississippi[24]	ZZ-Top
My Own Way Home[19]	Little River Band
My Wheels Won't Turn[20]	Bachman Turner Overdrive
Mystic Journey[17]	James Rider
Nebraska[22]	Bruce Springsteen
New York City[3]	John Lennon
New York City Blues[2]	Yardbirds
New York City Serenade[3]	Bruce Springsteen
New York Minute[3]	Eagles
New York, New York[5]	Frank Sinatra
New York State of Mind[2]	Billy Joel
Night Train to Memphis[24]	Ricky Nelson
Nineteenth Nervous Breakdown[8]	Rolling Stones
No Excess Baggage[5]	Yardbirds
No Looking Back[15]	Kenny Loggins
No Son of Mine[3]	Genesis
Nobody's Fault But Mine[17]	Led Zeppelin
Oh, Death[26]	Ralph Stanley
Old Man[17]	Neil Young
On the Bus[4]	Evan and Jaron
On the Road Again[8]	Canned Heat
On the Road Again[10]	Willie Nelson
Once Bitten, Twice Shy[11]	Guns 'n Roses
Once Upon a Time in the West[12]	Dire Straits
One Chain Don't Make No Prison[19]	Santana
One More Cup of Coffee[9]	Bob Dylan
One Way Road to Hell[2]	Guess Who
Only the Good Die Young [2]	Billy Joel
Out of the Cradle[3]	Rush
Outlaw Man[20]	Eagles
Panama[19]	Van Halen
Pancho and Lefty[18]	Merle Haggard
Part Man, Part Monkey [13]	Bruce Springsteen
Pawn Shop[12]	Sublime
Pawnshop wedding rings[12]	Derailers

Peaceful Easy Feeling[10]	Eagles
Piano Man[7]	Billy Joel
Please Come to Boston[7]	Dave Loggins
Please Mister Jailer[22]	Rachel Sweet
Point Blank[27]	Bruce Springsteen
Porcelain[1]	Moby
Post-Toastee[14]	Tommy Bolin
Pressed Rat and Warthog[13]	Crea
Private Investigations[13]	Dire Straits
Questions of my Childhood[9]	Kansas
Rainy Day Women #12 & 35 [26]	Bob Dylan
Ramblin' Man[6]	Allman Brothers Band
Refugee[19]	Tom Petty-Mike Campbell
Ridin' the Storm Out[9]	REO Speedwagon
Ring Them Bells[26]	Bob Dylan
Rockin' in the Free World[24]	Neil Young
Rocky Mountain Way[8]	Joe Walsh
Roll Me Away[8,9]	Bob Seger
Run Away[3]	Great White
Running Down a Dream[27]	Petty/Lynne/Campbell
Running on Empty[15]	Jackson Browne
Run to Mexico[16]	John Waite
Safe in New York[2]	AC/DC
San Francisco[10]	Scott McKenzie
Saturday Night's All Right[21]	Elton John
Second-Hand Store[13]	Joe Walsh
Shaky Town[6]	Jackson Browne
Sheep[1]	Pink Floyd
She's Not There[16]	Zombies
She's So Cold[9]	Rolling Stones
Shelter from the Storm[16]	Bob Dylan
Shelter from the Storm[27]	Bob Dylan
Shock the Monkey[13]	Peter Gabriel
Shoot to Thrill[13]	AC/DC

Shotgun Rider[18]	Bachman Turner Overdrive
Should I Stay or Should I Go[2]	The Clash
Signed, Sealed and Delivered[9]	Peter Frampton
Sins of the Father[19]	Black Sabbath
Six Blade Knife[21]	Dire Straits
Sleeping in the Ground[26]	Traffic
Smoke on the Water[9]	Deep Purple
Smokey Joe's Café[21]	The Coasters
Smugglers' Blues[18]	Glenn Frey
Snake Eye[17]	AC/DC
Somebody Stole My Guitar[12]	Deep Purple
Southbound[18]	Allman Brothers
Southbound Again[18]	Mark Knopfler
Stairway to Heaven[11]	Led Zeppelin
Start All Over Again[4]	Van Morrison
Station Man[5]	Fleetwood Mac
Statute of Liberty[3]	Little River Band
Staying Alive[10]	Bee Gees
Stepping Stone[8]	Monkees
Story of Reuben Clamzo…[2]	Arlo Guthrie
Straight Time[21]	Bruce Springsteen
Strange Brew[16]	Eric Clapton
Stuck In Lodi[11]	Credence Clearwater Revival
Sunshine of Your Love[10]	Eric Clapton
Superstition[17]	Stevie Ray Vaughn
Sweet Jane[8]	Lou Reed
Sweet Janie[4]	Van Morrison
Take It As It Comes[16]	The Doors
Taking Care of Business[12]	Bachman Turner Overdrive
Tales of Brave Ulysses[16]	Cream
Teenage Wasteland[8]	The Who
Tell Me[11]	The Beatles
Tempted[11]	Squeeze
Tennessee[24]	Arrested Development

That's When I Reach for my Revolver[1]	Moby
The Beautiful People[27]	Marilyn Manson
The Border[19]	America
The Boxer[3]	Simon and Garfunkel
The Confessor[27]	Joe Walsh
The Curse[17]	Disturbed
The End[27]	The Doors
The Farm[3]	Aerosmith
The Farm[10]	Jefferson Airplane
The Gambler[6]	Kenny Rogers
The Great Escape[27]	Moby
The Gypsy[16]	Deep Purple
The Hitman[14]	Queen
The Lamb Lies Down on Broadway[3]	Genesis
The Last Unicorn[17]	Kenny Loggins
The Loner[21]	Neil Young
The Long Arm of the Law[23]	Kenny Rogers
The Midnight Special[21]	Creedence Clearwater Revival
The Motorcycle Song[16]	Arlo Guthrie
The Noose[27]	Offspring
The Noose[27]	A Perfect Circle
The Passenger[4]	Iggy Pop
The Pretender[21]	Jackson Browne
The Real Me[3]	The Who
The Road[6]	Jackson Browne
The Saga of Jesse Jane[22]	Alice Cooper
The Sheriff[1,14]	Emerson, Lake and Palmer
The Sidewinder Sleeps Tonight[20]	REM
The Smuggler[19]	Plumber Boys
The Stranger[14]	Billy Joel
The Streets of Laredo[20]	Arlo Guthrie
The Trial[25]	Pink Floyd
The Weapon[26]	Rush
The Word Justice[22]	Jackson Browne
Things I Miss the Most[7]	Steely Dan

Thumbing My Way[26]	Pearl Jam
Time Off for Good Behavior[22]	Neil Young
Times in New York Town[2]	Bob Dylan
Tombstone Blues[20]	Bob Dylan
Tombstone Eyes[21]	Dickey Betts
Tombstone Shadow[17]	Creedence Clearwater Revival
Too Much Time on My Hands[8]	Styx
Touch of Gray[25]	Grateful Dead
Train Time[4]	Cream
Tramp[2]	Bachman Turner Overdrive
Traveling Band[12]	CreedenceClearwater Revival
Travelin' Man [6]	Ricky Nelson
Traveling Wilbury's Tribal History[23]	Hugh Jampton
Truck Driving Man[6]	Ricky Nelson
Trucking[6]	Grateful Dead
Truckstop Blues[6]	NoFX
Truckstop Salvation[6]	Jimmy Buffett
Tumbling Dice[9]	Rolling Stones
Turn the Page[6]	Bob Seger
Tweeter and the Monkey Man[12]	The Traveling Wilburys
Uncle Albert/Admiral Halsey[19]	Paul McCartney
Uncle Jeff[6]	Arlo Guthrie
Under Pressure[5]	David Bowie/Queen
Us and Them[6]	Pink Floyd
Volcano[9]	Jimmy Buffet
Voodoo Chile[4,17]	Jimi Hendrix
Voodoo Medicine Man[17,27]	Aerosmith
Waitin' for the Bus[4]	ZZ Top
Waiting for the Worms[26]	Pink Floyd
Waitress[6]	Hopesfall
Walkin' in Memphis[24]	Marc Cohen
Wanted Dead or Alive[15]	Bon Jovi
We Gotta Get Out of This Place[21]	The Animals

Welcome to the Machine[2]	Pink Floyd
We're Not Gonna Take It[27]	Twisted Sister
What condition my Condition was in[24]	Kenny Rogers
What is Life? [11]	George Harrison
When I get to the border[18]	Arlo Guthrie
Whipping Post [7]	Allman Brothers Band
Whiskey-Headed Woman[21]	Tommy Bolin
Whiskey in the Jar[21]	Thin Lizzy
Whiskey Man[23]	The Who
Whiskey on the Rocks[5]	AC/DC
White Rabbit[9]	Jefferson Airplane
White Room[4]	Jack Bruce/Pete Brown
White Wedding[3]	Billy Idol
Who Are You[8]	The Who
Wild Thing[10]	The Troggs
Willin'[6]	Little Feat
Wish You Were Here[5]	Pink Floyd
Witch's Promise[17]	Jethro Tull
Witchy Woman[16]	Eagles
You Ain't Seen Nothing Yet[10]	Bachman Turner Overdrive
You May Be Right[4]	Billy Joel

About the Author

James Wollrab is currently working on several projects for future publication.

The first is a science fiction thriller entitled **Perturbation Theory**. American scientists release an unexpected terror when they develop a biological computer that is capable of predicting the future.

The second is a mystery entitled **Death by Bingo**. An old lady in a nursing home helps her son solve a convoluted string of murders.

My Uncle Frank is a collection of approximately one hundred original cartoons drawn by a soldier in the Pacific theatre during World War II. Yes, he really was my uncle.

The fourth project is entitled **Leaving Reality** and chronicles the life of a boy from Alaska destined to play in the National Hockey League. This is a joint project with my good friend and fellow hockey fan, Rob Collett.

Way on the horizon is **China White**. Heroin smugglers and the government run afoul of a devious defense attorney.